LifeGAMES
Corporation
—Your Future ◆ In Our Hands—

Michael Smorenburg

First published in the United States of America by *CreateSpace* in 2016.
Copyright © Michael Smorenburg, 2015
The moral right of Michal Smorenburg to be identified as the author of this work has been asserted
by him in accordance with the Copyright, Designs and Patents Act of 1998.

Some of the concepts and quotations expressed in this fictional tale first appeared, some in a
different form, in various print or electronic expressions by the originators, authors or presenters so
named.

5 7 9 8 6 4

www.MichaelSmorenburg.com/LifeGames
FaceBook.com/MichaelSmorenburg
MichaelStheWriter@gmail.com

House of Qunard Publishing

ISBN Print: 978-0-620-62734-4

ISBN eBook: 978-0-620-62735-1

DEDICATION

This novel explores the games people play; games with one another, games with their own minds, games with society, and the games that become our collective future.

LIFEGAMES

In this work of fiction: Names, characters, places and events are products of the author's imagination or are used fictitiously. Any resemblance to actual events or locales or persons, living or dead, is entirely coincidental.

Author's statement about this work:

This fictional story is based on some facts, probabilities and plausible scenarios. Its aim is to entertain by blending fact with fiction.

Also by Michael Smorenburg:

- Ragnarok—*Qunard Publishing—2016*
- The Praying Nun—*Qunard Publishing—2016*
- A Trojan Affair—*Qunard Publishing—2016*
- The Everything Sailing Book Part 2—*Adams Media 1999*
- The Everything Sailing Book Part 1—*Adams Media 1998*
- Business Buyer's Kit—*Career Press 1997*

ACKNOWLEDGMENTS

In 1995, while sitting on a beach near the village of Nerja in southern Spain, a story jumped into my head; I picked up a pencil and began to write furiously. Nobody was more amazed than I was when—two weeks later—I put the pencil aside. The holiday was over, but there it lay, a complete and quite complex novel with all kinds of interesting plot twists.

What to do with it?

I typed it out and then went and did other things, business mostly. Indeed, for twenty more years, I did other things.

Then, after publishing a second novel I'd written, *A TROJAN AFFAIR – The S.K.A. at Carnarvon*, I started thinking about that first novel. I gave it a read and thought, "Hey, this is not bad at all."

So… here it is.

My blanket gratitude to the thousands of people in life and on social media who have helped me to grasp new ways of looking at the world.

A special "thank you" to my darling, Kirstin Engelbrecht, for once again putting up with me in all ways and for so much hard work, and for prompting me to resurrect this. Most particularly, thank you for working like, dare I say it—a *demon*—to get this done.

To the many, many beta readers who gave feedback, thank you: Colleen Balfour, Anneke Bright, Luzelle Poppie Davids, Peter J. Earle, Caity Farley, Barbara George, Tanja Kirkham, Jill Goldschmidt, Glenn Goldswain, Sian Lilford. There are so many others I have heard snippets from, but I'm in a rush to get this out before the festive season takes hold, and I'll certainly include you in the next reprint. Special thanks to Carel Hauptfleisch, whose enthusiasm for the story and edits were invaluable. I'm most grateful to Roy Herold for your excellent input.

A huge special thank you, Alastair Crewe, for your conception and design of the cover—I think it looks absolutely fantastic. As the book gains traction, the reward will flow back to you.

Chapter 1

"Ready?" Catherine asked. Ken nodded.
She tapped the play button.

*****

"I'm God..."
The man's voice sounds soulless and matter of fact, the green murk of night vision before him a meandering network of tracks through scrubland. Telemetry data and a compass ticker scroll with leisurely precision.
"...all-seeing, I'm Jehovah hovering above with lightning bolts to touch the wicked."

The camera tracking the night below drifts onto a deserted rural village. Half a dozen phantoms busy themselves around a pickup as it falls squarely into the crosshairs. The scurrying figures are ethereal, pale-green spooks on a hurried mission hefting loads into the vehicle.

"Their bad choices make my choices easier."
The Almighty sounds a bit Southern.
"Being God," he pauses unhurriedly, "has consequences. First rule: don't think too much. Let them make the decisions, let them be responsible for my actions."

Threadbare lightning bolts streak away, fairy lights of death diving toward the green unfortunates. The vehicle has swallowed four of them; six have become two and then the two evaporate into the vehicle just as the tracers stitch the ground toward it.

BOOOOM!

The night vision is blown-out for a silent instant to white light.

"Go with God." His intonation is matter of fact. "*Allahu Akbar*... straight to hell."

It's eerily silent as the burning flotsam of the explosion rains to stillness.

Moments later, startled greens come pouring out of the houses, scattering or running toward their dead.

"A peculiar Top Gun *I* am... my justice delivered half a world away. I hang up the headphones and grab milk on the way home."

The view widens, retracting, pulling back from the action.

God's a bald guy.

The screen with the dead ghosts is still alive beyond his silhouette.

"The right choices take training," he rambles.

The camera pulls back further still, now revealing a man topped by a virtual-reality helmet.

"You can relax now. *Sleep!*"

The man obeys the hypnotic instruction and slumps to unconsciousness.

The movie pixilates to blackness and white writing fades in. The tinny voice of an android female reads the words, "The Raw Power of LifeGames Corporation."

She sounds hollow and timeless.

"Your Future... Safe… in our hands."

*****

Lights in the boardroom rise warmly to life, the curtains roll back and daylight streams in.

The android's words remain frozen across the wall monitor.

"That's the cripple's work?" Ken sounded unimpressed.

A shard of ice plunged through Catherine, the man's provocation twisting her gut.

"Yes Ken, Mark led the team." She parried his antagonistic question with all the restraint she could muster.

This relentless game of taunts with smiles was never-ending. Kenneth Torrington controlled his environment with contempt and charm.

"I'd really appreciate keeping with the review," Catherine urged. It was all the rebuke she dared venture.

"I'm not saying it's bad, Cath, I just don't see how you can work with such a freak show. Frankly, they sicken me. If they're not faggots, they're rolling obese or wrapped in tattoos. Don't you creative types come in any flavour but weird? It's depressing..." He huffed, "Somehow you're alright, though."

As always, this session of creative review was deteriorating into another grueling ordeal; a grinding tribulation played out at the whim and tempo of the boss-man. She pressed her hands to the desk till the colour drained from the tips, physically restraining her shudder of fury. She would not rise to the bait. There were good reasons for taking on the ones who nobody else would employ; they repaid her belief in them with results that no competitor could match.

"I'm glad you at least approve of the work," she said, with as steady a voice and gaze as she could manage. "Shall we move on to the next?"

Ken eyed her with an engaging smile, one crafted to melt an unaccustomed stranger.

And *it* happened again—this time less subtle. His eyes dropped for just an instant to her lips, caressing them.

It was so fleeting and quick that she second-guessed whether she'd seen it at all. Only that *something* that stirred in her loins confirmed that the animal feeling, the buzz between them, beyond perception, was real.

He gripped her in another stare down, but now his face had softened and a smirk crept in.

Without breaking eye contact, he dabbed the intercom button on the conference table. "Nance, before you leave, a coffee for me and one for Catherine; she's got a long evening ahead."

He cut the connection halfway through the confirmation.

Catherine tried but couldn't hold his gaze. "Thanks," she offered and looked down. When she looked back, he was poking away at his iPad as if she didn't exist.

She waited patiently, the uncomfortable noise of silence stretching time. Determined to roll with Ken's punches, she pushed the awkwardness aside, silently repeating her drilled pledge to avoid snapping at the goading lures he tossed her way, laced as they were with devilish charm.

Catherine Kaplan's presentation represented her team's best efforts; these video clips along with her team at Kaplan Advertising & PR, were world-class. Nothing he could say would diminish that fact. It wasn't her first choice, but he'd insisted on shock and gore and she'd delivered.

Months of exposure to his manipulation had taught her to stay a step ahead of Ken's maneuvering. *A greedy man,* she thought, *so competent at humiliation.*

Just then, a knock at the door interrupted her daydream and it opened without Ken's permission. Ken, with the desk phone to his ear, glared a lightning bolt at Nancy, his personal assistant.

"Sorry to interrupt," she fawned and groveled suitably. "It's an *emergency* on hold."

She mimicked a phone held to her own ear and then slunk backward out of Ken's line of view, her eyes round and the tendons of her neck standing out with a big-trouble-brewing face dragging the corners of her mouth down.

Ken cut his call and the phone immediately rang again. "What?!" he bit into it.

A high-pitched treble of explanation came pouring out of the earpiece; audible but incomprehensible from where Catherine sat.

"Oh Jesus *fucking* Christ," Ken stood with menace, "where's Leon?"

Catherine had met Leon on several previous occasions. A wizened little man with an internationally acclaimed string of books on psychology and regressive hypnosis to his name, he was a Director at LifeGames and in charge of the critical hypnosis sequence that Catherine knew was a cornerstone of the company's operation.

The earpiece prickled with response, "...paramedics..." Catherine heard, then "...security dealing..."

"What have you clowns done!" He punched the phone down onto its cradle. "Wait here," he ordered Catherine and stormed out the door, leaving it open.

A few minutes later Nancy's head appeared nervously around the door.

"Big shit," she said.

"No kidding. What's up?"

"Shew... you saw the mood. Can't say too much. One of our subjects... you know."

"I figured as much."

"Heads gonna roll."

"I'm keeping mine very low."

"Yeah," Nancy rolled her eyes. She hadn't advanced into the room and hung onto the door with both hands, her stance suggesting she'd beat a retreat at the smallest noise from down the corridor.

"Going on *here*? In this facility?" Catherine asked.

"Yep. Special Forces General, Pentagon boy. Poop's hitting the fan *BIG* time. Gone full retard, breaking the place up down there."

"Wow!" Catherine gulped, estimating whether it was going to make a public mess she'd have to clean up. "He mad at someone?"

"Worse. Much worse." Nancy looked behind her in a conspiratorial manner, dropping her voice and leaning in with apparent concern for being overheard. "Sounds like something wrong in our systems, Cath. He's having a reaction to the virtual reality or hypnosis sequence. I didn't want to cut in on your meeting here, it's been going on an hour. Guy's a loon, like... ranting about the Spanish Inquisition or something... Bipolar, Leon said. Had a complete personality collapse. Thinks it's the 1500s and on abo... *shit*."

She straightened as Ken came striding silently through the door behind her, his eyes fixed ahead.

Without any greeting to the women, he went directly into his private restroom and the door slammed behind him. Nancy pulled the round-eyed facial expression again and evaporated without another word, closing the office door with only a click.

Catherine sat fearfully in silence, wondering what new hell she'd inherit from all this drama. Just then, with no sounds to announce that the toilet had been flushed or faucets used, Ken appeared through the restroom doorway.

"Idiots." It was all he said.

He slumped into his seat and began to poke again at the iPad. Only the occasional sniff and dab at his nose betrayed why he seemed suddenly so calm.

Catherine twisted within. The uncomfortable, unmentioned elephant of his recent explosive reaction to the phone call was still looming in the room. Ken seemed genuinely oblivious to it. *Talk about bipolar*, she thought, to lighten her mood of foreboding.

Finally, Ken placed the pad aside then slowly reclined his chair, deliberately making a show of gently touching thumbs and fingers together in front of his face. Head tilted slightly and jaw jutting out aggressively, his index fingertips tapped out the rhythm from a cat's tail before the cat pounces. It was his standard pose that always preceded a monologue.

Was this the moment he'd tell her about the crisis? She was unsure if she wanted to know or be part of it.

"From what we've covered, I give you points for effort. It's reasonable stuff..."

Clearly, he was going nowhere near the crisis elephant. It was business as usual, back to the matter of review. He paused and nodded—evidently agreeing with a thought in his own head— and then smiled ingratiatingly in a most unsettling way.

"...You see, I'm always right in the long run. Always... But I give you a little credit, you take criticism well. It spurs you, you need it—kids always do." He paused a long moment then unexpectedly declared, "Good thing I didn't drop you last quarter."

Again, he initiated an uncomfortable and challenging stare-down, appearing to contemplate his own wisdom as he tapped at his pouting lips with his index fingers, the other fingers now laced together.

"I was on the chopping block last quarter?" Catherine attempted a polite smile and suppressed shuffling her feet, but the smile hung at the awkward angle of an unloved painting.

Ken didn't acknowledge the question, rendering it rhetoric. He just sat, comfortable and powerful in the charged silence. "Run it again or move on?" she offered again, hoping to propel the conversation out of the quicksand of Ken's mind-games.

Ignoring the question, Ken studied her intently. His fingers began tapping together once more to the same predatory rhythm, and then they stopped and he looked hard at her, square in the face.

"I know exactly what you're thinking, honey." His forefinger and thumb began to smooth a non-existent moustache. "I'm a difficult son-of-a-bitch. But put yourself in my shoes." A moment of dramatic pause. "I'm only interested in dealing with adults, you see, with..." he searched for the word, "...*professionals*. But here," he indicated the screen, frozen in place, "we can see the results. I eventually get acceptable work."

Catherine was silent, waiting for him to finish.

Ken remained silent too, allowing for the thought to resonate. "People don't understand me, Cath," he suggested in contemplation, suddenly bipolar in his warmth. "I don't intend to be a tyrant, I'm pushed to it." He huffed the sigh of a tired man, then suddenly snatched up iPad and began poking at it as he spoke. "You stick with me young Catherine... Stick with me and I'll make something out of you and your little company."

"Just glad you approve, Ken." Catherine gagged on the involuntary response that spilled from her mouth.

He said the same thing during the last three reviews, she silently consoled herself as the lava of the "little company" insult boiled within. She hesitated a moment, collected her composure like tattered rags, and when she felt she'd given him enough of her expensive time, volunteered once more to press the meeting ahead. "Run the spot again or move on?"

Ken declined to acknowledge Catherine's question as he persisted with the distraction in his hands. She sat silently, waiting.

While she waited, Catherine's thoughts detached and a frigid trickle of memories seeped within, Ken's snide abuses triggering emotions that cartwheeled her back through time. For long moments, she slid deep into the morass of nearly forgotten territory—an archive of pain suffered at the hands of an estranged father, a charmer who'd so closely resembled this arrogant man.

Ken flicked leisurely back and forth across his screen, occasionally poking at it while conducting two brief monosyllabic personal calls when his mobile buzzed.

As the moments labored by, an agonizing procession of submission to the whim of this anchor client, Catherine reeled her thoughts back to the present. She began to contemplate the months of grind that had transported her to this moment. Bruised by Ken's affront, she took refuge in assessing how professionally she'd overridden so many urges to turn the contract down time and again. But this was undoubtedly her desperately needed break into the industry's big-time.

Despite her instincts, she'd stuck it out and miraculously held her ground against the biggest competitors around the globe. It had been a coup that bore testimony to work that was fast becoming legendary for its creativity and attention to detail. Half a year of groveling had brought her from that day of signing the contract to this—a review of the finished product and twenty-three weeks of endless re-edits. *But worth it?* she mulled for the umpteenth time. *No question! Contracts like this seed empires.*

"Run it again," Ken ordered, in answer to Catherine's question asked many minutes before, and it tugged her from the daydream.

The monitor responded immediately to the click of Catherine's finger and the sequence replayed and ended.

"Again?" Catherine queried.

"Again," Ken insisted.

For forty minutes, Ken demanded that the same thirty-second slot be relentlessly repeated, occasionally querying something, taking a note or making a call. Catherine knew all too well that Kenneth Torrington was a stickler for perfection, the obsession driving the man on his maniacal quest to uncover criticisms. But, try as he might, during the rest of the session he could find little room to gripe at any of Catherine's several commercial masterpieces that all screamed the same message: "Benefits to humankind through the best training technology can offer."

The review was endless, but the view out the board room window was magnificent. Having weathered Ken's initial thrusts and having shown him her firm but accommodating stance, Ken had moderated his attitude. He dropped the sparring and was now focusing entirely on results and outcomes. Catherine was having an easier time of it.

He broke from review to take more calls, one or two of them clearly about the earlier incident, raising his hackles.

She entertained herself, soaking in the vista of meadows draped around the private lake on the outskirts of the city where Ken had erected the headquarter of his empire. Though the meeting had been set for midday, she'd canceled all appointments into the evening, fully anticipating that the constant and endless interruptions that always swarmed around the man would stretch the review till the black of night. This was proving to be the case.

Catherine maintained a resigned temperament until the sun pulled its final rays over the lip of the horizon and twilight set in. At this point, even her Job-like patience could endure no more. "Satisfied?" she ventured at the conclusion of another run-through of the last video-slot. Even after so many hours of grind, she maintained a flat tone that divulged no hint of the irritation seething within.

"A few more runs before we call it a day." Predictably, Ken had found it necessary to entrench his authority, prolonging the moment.

Ten minutes later, his appetite satiated, Ken closed proceedings. "Not bad, Cath. Overall, a pretty good effort."

Catherine was astonished. For Kenneth Torrington, "pretty good effort" meant giving a piece of himself, and she reckoned he must have heard his own voice speak the words before he could bite them back. Her eyes glinted with triumph and she cocked a brow. "High praise indeed," she crooned with practiced effort, her expression stoic, her tone betraying only a hint of sarcasm.

As the hours had tumbled by, Catherine had noted how Ken's personality would alter. *Now he's calm and complementary,* then *ranting on the intercom or into the phone like a maniac. Now, rational and calculating,* then *passionate and fixating on some apparently immaterial detail.*

During the multiple interruptions of conference calls and intrusions, she'd had ample time to consider the turbulent eddies of Ken's character as he careened through a jungle of confrontations. She'd noted how his frequent sorties to the restroom had invariably brought on a mood swing.

It's a nasty habit, she'd privately thought. Catherine was sufficiently streetwise to have a reasonable idea of Ken's vice. It was an old story she'd seen many times before—designer narcotics fueled so many in the highest executive echelons.

It was clear he could barely cope otherwise. Ken piled his plate impossibly high with commitments and stress. That fact stirred an uneasy empathy within her for his interminably objectionable character, a primitive and irresistible admiration for the hunter who brings in the kill. Try as she might, the enigma Ken presented choked her ability to reject this master of men.

No matter how much she felt she should hate this man, she could do little but admire his legacy and hate herself for what he somehow stirred in her.

In less than a decade, Kenneth Torrington had grown the LifeGames Corporation from concept to knocking on the door of becoming a trillion-dollar gargantuan. Even now, surrounded by a team of executives with the keenest minds money could buy, Ken remained distrustful of delegation, stubbornly clinging by only the most slender of autocratic threads and dominating every facet of management.

How to sum the man up? Catherine had often pondered. *Obsessive...? Sure. Megalomaniac...? Psychopath? Definitely! Like he's possessed.*

While Catherine shuffled her belongings into her bag, Ken launched into another round of ferocious phone discussions with someone buried somewhere in the depths of the monolithic building. She waited patiently for him to finish before making obvious gestures to leave.

His questions answered by the voice on the other end of the line, Ken truncated the conversation with a grunt as he turned his attentions back to Catherine. "Let's call it a day," he instructed, then offered a consolation to a tedious afternoon. "Stick around and I'll buy you dinner?" He was suddenly charm and roses.

"Thanks... I've got plans."

"They just changed..." he assured her.

She checked her watch.

"I've made a booking already," he disclosed, inclining his head, leaving her no doubt that they'd be dining together.

There was no real way to refuse the man, besides, getting any hint of what was going down had been eating at her.

She did the best she could to make a show of resisting, "Hmmm... not sure. I'd make a call but my battery's dead."

Ken held the door open, "Use Nancy's line."

As they moved out of the boardroom, Catherine wrestled with the prospect of spending more time in Ken's company than duty required. Better instincts urged her to refuse the offer, yet, there were many questions she desperately wanted answers for and dinner seemed the ideal forum to conduct an excavation of truth.

Since Ken ran LifeGames on a strictly *need-to-know* basis, details of the company were acutely opaque. The door to understanding its operations and technologies had only been opened a sliver. A barely sufficient overview of intricacies had forced Catherine to interpret much of what she'd produced, and then weather Ken's abuse and castigation for errors she'd inevitably make. With scarcely adequate grounding to get her job done through the months, she'd become intrigued, fueled by her curiosity to understand what truly lay at the heart of this tightly guarded, private empire.

As they walked, as if to goad her interest, from several floors deep below their feet came the vibrations of life and the tremble of heavy machinery. Catherine knew she could not resist; silently she had already accepted the date regardless of the sham telephone call she would make.

They entered Ken's private wing and Catherine stopped at Nancy's desk where she slid one cheek of her pencil-skirted rump onto the corner, leant over and scooped up Nancy's receiver. Ken walked on alone into his office. Out of sight, he stepped back close enough to the doorway to eavesdrop on the first part of Catherine's conversation before he backed up and moved on into his adjoining office.

"Hi Jacks, I'm going to be in late, hope the flight went well. Love ya, sweetie."

The resonating quality in Catherine's voice piqued Ken's curiosity but he drove the thought away as he swung in behind the mahogany desk, braced and ready for action.

Back at Nancy's desk, Catherine replaced the handset but delayed making her way into Ken's office. He sounded demented, tearing through three abrupt telephone conversations in quick succession. Something was up and it sounded big, it sounded big and bad. She tried to tune in but her mind kept drifting and sifting through the events of the afternoon: She recalled with inward embarrassment the unfamiliar feelings of lust that had knotted in the base of her gut as she had watched the sun's shadows creeping across the floor bringing on inevitable dusk. She remembered, now knowing—as only a woman can with a man like this—that this dinner invitation tonight was inevitable. And, strangely, she'd decided that perhaps the interruptions that had drawn the meeting out were fated.

As Ken's voice ebbed and flowed in the other office, she had time to delve deeper. Catherine found her feelings of sexuality toward this man both repulsive and titillating. But, try as she might to divorce herself from a lust she could not fathom, it remained there, ugly and lurking in the shadows of her mind, attached by a primitive umbilical cord to a past she'd never managed to uncover. Intellectually, she grasped well enough how her father—a man so similar, yet only a shadow of this monster—had snared her with his noxious charm, and opened the floodgates of her emotions to a string of lovers who'd possessed that same ability to manipulate. Psychologically, she remained powerless to resist the fierce who prowl, seeking willing participants in their game of persecutor-and-victim.

Catherine turned her thoughts about Ken over in her mind, trying to uncover the foundations of electricity that sparked and danced between them. With this knowledge, she hoped she might free herself of his unwanted spell. Though brusque and rude, she could not deny that Ken could be afire with rare charm when the mood took him. But, admitting what next creeped into her mind felt like a personal heresy to the point of revulsion—it horrified her that it was Ken who continually crashed into her fantasy world at night as she slept. The dreams of him, potent and real, had begun the moment they had first met and the specter of all he represented had gripped her.

For so many years, no male had spontaneously appeared on the stage of her mind, yet somehow, this one had slipped through and it plagued her.

As though someone had just walked over her grave, Catherine felt a cold shudder rack her body. Alone in the deserted office wing she began to feel vulnerable, as if unseen eyes were leering and prying into her soul and gloating at every lurid thought. It suddenly felt cold and foreboding in the room.

She slipped off the desk and made her way toward the ranting that emanated from Ken's lair.

Catherine settled onto a sofa arranged around the low-slung coffee table off to one side of the expansive office. With her back to the corner, tranquility returned and she resumed mulling the events of the day and her thoughts of Ken.

Just then Ken hung up. "I'll be another while," he warned. "Problems here and strife in the Korea division." He grimaced theatrically. "Grab yourself more coffee or a drink and pour me a Chivas on the rocks."

He instructed Catherine with such an ease of authority that she was halfway to the liquor cabinet before she realised the impertinence in his order. She poured two whiskeys and turned to see a wildfire blazing in Ken's eyes as he began a harangue on the phone in a language that sounded like bad Italian.

After receiving no response to her efforts, Catherine swished across the room and sprawled out across the leather lounge suite. Mirroring Ken's lack of acknowledgement of her presence, she began leafing through the coffee-table books as she sipped the astringent honey-colored spirit.

She worked carefully to cultivate an air of disinterest in Ken's presence and conversation, yet in truth, she remained finely tuned to his every nuance, gleaning whatever she could from the stream of visual cues that punctuated the flow of communication.

Call after call involved business matters; surveys, pricing structures, marketing concerns and detailed technical jargon far beyond her knowledge or interest. All churned out with commanding eloquence, often while switching among an impressive range of foreign languages.

Then came a call in English. Ken's demeanor became guarded, his tone hushed, his answers truncated. Chemicals seemed to be featured heavily—technical terms and talk of polymer strings, peptides and the like. *No, more like pharmaceuticals,* Catherine thought. *His dependence?*

She listened more carefully; the context seemed to *definitely* relate to the LifeGames operation. She could swear it hinted of the earlier crisis. Nothing tangible to solidly link to, just a woman's instinct.

Catherine reclined deeper into the luxurious embrace of the leather and let out an audible sigh of boredom, magnifying her sham disinterest in the hopes that Ken might be lulled into speaking more freely. Her ploy proved wholly unsuccessful. Ken remained guarded to her presence, allowing her to snag only a few shards of seemingly unrelated details from the conversation. None of it made sense in isolation.

Catherine focused her attention on Ken's jerky hand-movements as they fidgeted. He seemed uncharacteristically rattled. The downlights glinted off his forehead, sprinkled as it was with a fine mist of adrenaline sweat. Before she could gather more information, Ken abruptly ended his conversation.

"Ready?" He shot Catherine a smile that could not have been more dissonant from his mood an instant earlier. His disposition flipped to charm. A boyish mischief twinkled in his eye.

On instinct, Catherine beamed Ken a wide smile. "Guess so," then cursed herself for so readily snapping at every scrap he tossed her way.

Chapter 2

The dimly lit *trattoria* serving hearty peasant food and plum red wine came as a surprise—she'd not have guessed it to be his style, imagining he'd lean more toward the ostentatious.

As they settled in, she realized it was ideal; the perfect atmosphere of anonymity she needed to angle him toward her objectives.

Nobody gave Ken a second glance. Wealthy as he was, he'd successfully avoided the public limelight of celebrity, an ongoing task that Catherine was charged with maintaining.

Catherine had her objectives clearly in mind; she intended for this evening to liberate a hearty dollop of LifeGames' back-story from Ken's habitually guarded tongue. She certainly hoped for details on the mysterious crisis that he'd stormed off to confront earlier in the day.

Until this evening, all that Catherine had learned of the company and its genesis were the *need-to-know* details of LifeGames' marketing strategy. Since during all of their previous meetings they'd been accompanied by a group of colleagues from their respective companies, she was determined that this evening alone with him would yield answers.

The idea to hold the review through most of the day, alone with Ken, had been at his instruction. When Catherine had called to confirm that the campaign was ready for the review, Ken had insisted on a private meeting without respective teams. His copious note-taking suggested that when the full review was conducted, he'd have insight to run circles around his executives who'd be seeing it for the first time—a shrewd move to give him the edge in the meeting.

Catherine knew all too well how he would grill them, seeming to do so from instinct rather than effort. *Keeping them off balance and subordinate,* she thought. Ken was a gifted general and tactician and there was no doubt in her mind that this evening would require a great deal of finesse to lure this devil of a man out of his craftily defended den.

As they settled into the meal, the conversation relaxed and Catherine probed until she saw her moment. "What's a hedge trader doing running a technology company?" she asked. She spotted what looked like a flash of suspicion and danger move behind Ken's eyes and she hesitated momentarily. "Uhhm... you were a fund trader I believe?" she stammered, to dodge the landmine so nearly trodden on.

Ken eyed her carefully, weighing her question with suspicion. He hated probes in any part of his business anatomy, but he especially loathed any discussion of his *pre*-LifeGames dealings.

"*Yes,* and the eleemosynary thing," Ken replied, his answer deliberately and cryptically weighted with the definite article 'the' to buy him time to think and to gauge if she already knew details he'd rather remain cloaked.

"What?" Catherine frowned with bemusement.

"*Yes*—my foundation was in the hedge business, and of course, *eleemosynary...* which you'd know about from your own due diligence... it was covered in the Fortune interview. No doubt you picked it up in the original briefing documents?"

Eleemosynary—the word was a challenge and Catherine had tripped over it. It was obscure enough that she'd betrayed her confusion for a nanosecond.

An instant later, her mind flipped up the answer—Ken had been shredded before a senate inquiry into his dealings with one of the rarest forms of financial trust. He'd been accused of routing vast fortunes of questionable funds, laundering them out beyond the grasp of any tax authority in the world.

Eleemosynary Trusts were the hidey-holes for the super wealthy. Safely sequestered behind legal barriers put in place before the Magna Carta and modern fiscal entities, the happy beneficiaries of vast wealth could enjoy tax-free status.

A Fortune magazine article had concluded that this trust was the foundation for LifeGames' murky beginnings.

She scrambled to cover and detour around Ken's change of topic.

"Of course—I'm sorry. Long day," she tried to deflect weakly, knowing he'd bumped her off balance, cursing herself for allowing the conversation—moving so precisely in the direction she intended—to need rescuing.

By his expression, she knew it was a tipping point, a watershed moment to get the momentum back without him realizing that she had an agenda.

"It's just... to a layperson like me, all this high-tech wizardry is a far leap from running a hedge fund. Nobody wakes up and decides one morning, 'Reckon I'll become a computer wizard'." Catherine suggested.

"Strangely," Ken looked a little surprised, "You got that right... You're somehow in my head or just making a lucky guess."

"Really?"

"Yeah... waking part... that's true." He stopped talking to top off their wine glasses, and she thought he might slip out of the noose, but she got lucky. "I do find it strange that you put it like that; I literally opened my eyes one morning with the concept of LifeGames fully installed in my head. I say 'installed', because I didn't have to think about it any further than that." He took a sip, clearly weighing something on his mind. "All I needed to make the idea work was the computer wizard you mentioned—the computer wizard and a billion or six."

His demeanor and pauses told Catherine he was mulling over the tack the conversation was on. "This level of VR... virtual reality... it doesn't come cheap. Remember—nothing remotely like it existed when we got our start." He pushed away his half-finished plate of food.

Catherine studied him intently from behind a pointedly engaging smile. All the while, with every fiber of her being, she hoped her devoted attention would keep the information flowing.

Though Ken saw her eagerness, he'd begun to feel comfortable and in total control of the subject, so he rode onward on her cue and reciprocated the attention. "I already had a bundle, but *OPM*... 'other people's money'... is how you really get big, quick. Leverage. I had a track record, but convincing investors that their money is safe in high-tech with a technophobe takes a certain degree of..."

"Persuasion...?" her mouth ventured without first checking in with her brain.

"You get it," he smiled slyly. "You're learning to think like me," and it didn't seem like a compliment. But he nodded to himself, making a note, and then went on. "Then the surprise; financing infrastructure and software was the smallest piece of the problem. You can't scale this business with manpower, with one-on-one hypnotists; we needed to make that automated, managed by the computer."

"I'm not surprised."

"Why would you say that?" Ken's question sounded surprised.

"I've got an inkling that there's a huge feedback loop going on during the hypnosis that a human hypnotist wouldn't even notice... I don't know how a computer can have that sort of empathy."

"I'd say you're psychic... or have been sneaking info out of our IP."

"Your IP?"

"Our Intellectual Property, our ops manuals. They're supposed to be classified."

Catherine looked surprised, and Ken studied her; her surprise appeared honest.

"I swear—It must be instinct on my part, because your operation's tight-lipped."

"Good." He relaxed a smidgen. "But you're an insider now, and we have momentum that competitors won't easily emulate. I can confirm it without giving away state secrets: we hit our biggest problems with automating the computer-generated hypnosis.... And patching it to each subject's personal psyche... Creates situations you wouldn't believe."

"Situations?" Catherine challenged.

"The details could take hours," he assured her and ordered another bottle.

"I'm in no hurry." It was music to his ears.

Catherine waited patiently for him to continue, coaxing with cues and feminine wiles. "The third subject we hooked up... Oh, I must caution, Cath, this is strictly, and I mean *strictly* off of the record." His voice was laced with unmistakable menace.

"What happens in Vegas," she gestured, zipping her lips. Her eyes were sparkling, as she willed them to be.

Ken grinned, seeming to relax a little. It was then, in that moment, that he seized on his opportunity to aim the conversation down a path he was edging toward; cementing his advantage in the power play run. By using jargon she certainly would not comprehend, he knew he could force her into subordination to his superior knowledge. His mouth began to run, relating all manner of trials and tests in the early days.

"Our first two runs were short and sweet with no hint of trouble, but the third attempt was a little unfortunate. We'd run the full ritual on the subject, and he was already neural-linked when he went meltdown." He paused for dramatic effect.

"As we swung him out over a precipice, he went into cardiac. Without medical on hand, he was a goner. But the worst of it was, we weren't yet using the bags and he soiled himself pretty good."

He left the statement hanging.

Catherine deliberately showed no response, just a lopsided grin of assumed bewilderment hanging across her face.

Ken spotted the pantomime he'd angled to achieve. "What?" he asked, faking ignorance of his own over-complicated account.

"*The full-ritual? Melt down...?* What else...? *Bags?* I think I'm missing something here." She maintained the pose—she actually knew or could guess the meaning of the terms, but she also knew it was a game that he wanted her to play.

"Yeah, company jargon. This is actually fortuitous... we need you up to speed on everything for the next rollout phase."

"Sure," Catherine invited by leaning her elbows on the table.

Unaccustomed as he was to more than a sip or two of wine, it now had control of his tongue.

They each felt they'd won a victory; felt they were directing the conversation.

"You're, of course, familiar with what we do? The virtual reality, the technicalities of VR I mean? The economics of it?" Ken quizzed.

"Reasonably, but run it by me anyway, treat me like I know nothing," Catherine suggested.

Ken's vanity overflowed in his tone as he laid before her the foundations of the LifeGames operation. "We're way more cost-effective than any field assessment, so it's only in the backwaters that serious training and benchmarking for almost any human endeavor is still conducted the old-fashioned way. The airlines, of course, have simulated flight training forever, but we take it just so much further. Our first contracts were military special forces and tacticians; these are all obvious angles. But then the courts began assessing judges and we uncovered huge incompetence. It was a coup. Law firms started pushing their people through, then politicians got into it coming into the election. Now, even school teachers need our certification before they're hired on."

He paused for a swig from his glass. "Okay so far?"

Catherine nodded, "Standard stuff; VR is common enough. I think I get what you're introducing that's different..." It was more of a leading question.

"Sure, virtual reality's now pretty much off-shelf technology," he agreed. "Drop enough cash and you have a facility. But what does it deliver? A simulation. And what's a simulation when there are no consequences for the candidate? The plane's tumbling in a death spiral, all the alarms and lights flashing exactly as they would in reality. But a VR pilot knows it's a trumped-up game. He knows his balls aren't on the line. If the bird goes down, they just set up the scenario again, and off he goes into the next module. As you know, I bring in a new angle—give him consequences, or, at least, take away his knowledge that there aren't consequences in a simulation."

"You hypnotize him," Catherine encouraged.

"We hypnotize him before the simulation—yep. Persuade him to believe that what he's experiencing is the real thing. And, of course, these days we don't have to put a helmet on him with tiny screens to give him an eyeball view or stick him in a pressure suit and rock him around in a gyroscope. We found that subjects weren't buying into the illusion of it. No... that was our other big innovation... to establish a neural link with subjects. Hijack the central nervous system with electrodes and provide a four-dimensional experience; immersed totally into a three-dimensional world with an authentic fourth-dimensional time component."

"Time component?" Catherine was afraid to overplay her hand—she knew what it was. "I mean, yeah, I know about the time dilation; but it's very superficial."

"I'll dig into that in a moment. It's heady stuff," he looked for her agreement.

"I don't doubt it."

"Like I said, we started out with trained psychologists conducting hypnosis, but that's not scalable—there are only so many of those nutcases available that you'd want to employ. We needed to be scalable to go global, so we encoded the sequence to software; now computers can take upper-ninety percent of clients from full consciousness to the fourth level comatose state in under fifteen seconds. Psychologists differ in their abilities, but even the best will take a minute or more—and time is money. It was our first real triumph."

Catherine made a show of wide-eyed wonder as if hearing it for the first time, feeding Ken's super-ego, willing him not to pause.

"We swept the board clean; without a LifeGames training certificate, no one has a prayer to get above middle management. We dominate global powers through our facilities—Legislators in parliaments, senates in States, the judiciary in every country that counts, military strategists. Friends or foes—we hold the strings, and train and review them all."

"God—WOW!" Catherine knew they were powerful, but the impact from the implications was a genuine shock that she didn't need to fake. He was on a roll now, needing no more encouragement.

"The computer's got an integrated fMRI scanner, logging vast data fields, instantly compiling on-the-fly critical appraisals, re-training sequencing, retesting—all in one run. Months and years of real-world performance all in a single session, all under one roof and at the touch of a button."

He was striding, rambling, unable to halt his mouth. "Ritual... you're a smart cookie, you'll have guessed... it means hypnotizing the subject, fitting bags. The hypnosis suspends the knowledge that it's a simulation. The action kicks off and the subject's lost in a world that's deadly real to him," he hesitated a moment, "or her. See—no gender bias," he assured. "He... she... they're really, truly there, immersed in the selected world. We deliver the goods—every time. Nobody can touch us."

He was unnerving. For all he was saying, something was carefully *not* said, and it drew her in like a fish to a lure. There was fire here—something warm, reassuring and appealing about this discussion, this technology, this character, but something deeply sinister too.

Ken had already finished his glass and was pouring another. Catherine hadn't remembered to sip yet. "You see, Cath, that's the valid reaction, the real one, the true one, that'll happen when a trainee confronts the real-life situation. Using other training methods, other VR without hypnosis—certainly, failing to get the subject down to level four, something only our software can do—you just don't see our kind of results."

The alcohol was working its magic; Ken's tongue was as slick as greased Teflon, information flowing over without any friction. Catherine kept the taps open with "oohs" and "ahhs" at judiciously chosen moments. So, as Ken swallowed the last in his glass, Catherine signaled for a new bottle of liquid truth.

"And it was that number-three subject that taught us to use bags. What a mess... These days, the bags are standard operating procedure; catheter and rectal."

It wasn't an angle she cared to pursue. Below the veneer of his billions, she reminded herself, Ken displayed a vulgar and ill-bred origin.

"And melt-down," she offered, "must be jargon for an operating problem—right?"

"Right," he confirmed. "And the next phase for expansion will be the use of nutrition plasters."

He paused a moment—a moment that seemed terminal to the momentum—and Catherine feared that the spell was gone, but he then tantalized her with a promise.

"I need to brief you on this. Guess now's as good a time as any. First, I need to take a leak." He stood up.

Catherine watched Ken make his way through the dimly lit tables. In an obvious attempt to stave off the onset of advanced inebriation, he was forcing a stiffly disciplined control into his stride.

Three minutes later Ken returned and, predictably, he had assumed the different personality his vice lent him.

"Where was I?" he asked rhetorically, gliding back to where he'd left off in his account. "Ah, yes. The next phase of our PR campaign will be way bigger, Cath. Our primary test-market results in operations have been staggering."

Catherine's eyes widened with genuine dismay. This first phase of the campaign was paying beyond her wildest imaginings; a bigger payday would be obscene. She was sorely tempted to suggest a sliding commission on increased revenues, estimating he might just agree; but it would derail the drift of the conversation so she let the strategic idea pass in favor of details.

"Now that I've given the world the idea, there isn't anything too mystical about our cocktail of hypnosis and virtual reality. Eventually, there'll be corporate espionage, a breach. The competition's plenty far behind, but I need them out of the game, and we do that through innovation they can't figure out." He said it smugly. "I've got insiders on retainer, and I know the Chinese, Koreans, and Israelis are all chasing hard—they hate depending on us."

It was all "I"—unadulterated vanity—and Catherine forced a smile to mask her aversion to the self-gratifying indulgence.

"As you know, all the stuff you've been working on is our next phase but not yet ready to go to press, so this is all strictly off the record. Only executive level clearance for now... you're in the inner circle. Do I have your commitment?" Ken urged.

"Absolutely," Catherine crossed her fingers, "hope to die!"

He chuckled and seized the interlude to slide his hand across the table, cupping her crossed fingers in his palm. It was a shock—something she hadn't expected, and it caught her off guard. The candle flickered from his movement, and the room's temperature seemed to rise a degree.

Catherine let his hand linger a moment before covering his hand with her other hand, squeezing it, and withdrawing to fold her napkin.

Ken left his hand there, waiting in vain for a return touch. It did not come.

Her inner-circle status was hanging in the balance, evidently consummated if she returned his touch. But she gambled—more power in a promise than an action—and deliberately let her eyes caress his lips as she wet her own. "You were saying..? This next phase?"

"Time dilation..." he said, with reverence, almost mesmerised.

It was show-time. Catherine cocked her head to one side. It was a deadly game, but she was in it and needed to break the impasse, so she did it with flattery, giving Ken the power by playing the student hanging on her master's every word. "Einstein? Relativity? Speeding time up?" she reminded him.

"Yeah, Einstein..." he nodded, "also a genius, yes." Ken included himself in an exclusive club. "He used the term first, this we must grant him." He touched the wine to his lips. "But my breakthrough's right up there, equally monumental, and of course, genius. But, no... time dilation isn't about speeding time *up*, it's slowing it *down*."

"Sorry, that's what I meant." He'd bought it, and she knew she'd played the ruse expertly. "But how? How can you slow time down?" The concept appeared unlikely, and Catherine's puzzlement at the possible mechanics of achieving the feat was absolute.

"With our original combination of hypnosis and software—but we've got a new module that puts the brain into a... a sort of hyper-drive. When you go through the new sequence, everything seems normal enough to you, but the data is supercharged, pumping in and out of the neural connection at up to ten times—sometimes twenty times—the throughput. The effect is more training in a fraction of the time. What happens is, it seems normal to you, because you're time dilated. But in our testing—and that means our billing cycle—it's more training in less time, very *very* profitable for me. We are through trials and are test marketing to a limited group of premium clients."

There was a sudden, minute flutter at the corner of Ken's eye, a nervous twitch that brought his hand up to worry at it. It was a lie, and Catherine saw it. The twitch had betrayed him and she pretended not to notice.

"Decode that for me, please," she prompted, knowing *something* was a lie, but whatever that something was, it wasn't clear.

"I'm vastly simplifying this. Using an upgraded hypnosis sequence, we suggest to the subject that images will be coming at them a little quicker than in real life. They respond. It's been very successful in trials, and… uhmmm… some limited rollout."

The nervous twitch flicked again, she was closing in.

"The computer then sends the images at the correspondingly faster rate suggested in the cue, and with the subject's brain stimulated and their adrenaline going, they're able to rise to the occasion." There was a moment of sobriety and she saw caution in him.

"You've done this? It works?"

"That's what I'm telling you. Yes, it's already in operation to our top clients. We bill on the outcome, on how much assessment and training has been achieved, so that they don't need to know how we achieve those results, as long as we produce. The improvement in efficiency has exceeded predictions by three hundred percent—and that's multiplied over our estimations that were already a four hundred percent increase in productivity."

Catherine whistled, giving Ken a sense that she was counting his money, and he appeared to like that.

"I'm, of course, a wealthy man already. This is going to, well, I'll be in a league of my own."

"Undoubtedly." She moistened her lips again. "But the function of it; I'm imagining it's like being in a car accident? That feeling of time going by in slo-mo?"

"You've got it!" Ken agreed enthusiastically.

"Can the mind take it?"

"The body has proven to be the bigger problem. Most of our subjects on the physical routines are athletes of one sort or another. But we're herding fat politicians and lawyers through and we're not yet certain of the implications. We've still got it notched down; one slip and it's, well..."

She found herself chuckling with him, the mood between them becoming ever more familiar.

"So, there is a level of fatigue?" Catherine prompted, with the instinct to further propel the conversation. "The extra load—the subjects must surely experience some degree of physical cost or exhaustion?" She squinted. "Even I understand physics enough to know that for a given amount of work there has to be a given amount of energy spent. Athletes aren't immune, nobody goes on indefinitely."

"Smart cookie," Ken grinned, the compliment seeming for once valid. "Another huge breakthrough. We're using patches. You see, in our modern era, the human body is physically underutilized. Actually, we're all a bunch of hypochondriacs."

Catherine looked skeptical and she let it show. "Hypochondriacs." A thought nagged at her; something amiss.

"I'll give you an example of how underutilized our bodies are below their capacity," Ken continued, running with the doubt she'd conveyed. "You ever seen a hypnosis session, Cath, an ordinary stage show?"

She shook her head. "Nope."

"Worth a laugh. Subjects do some pretty amusing things."

The conversation was drifting off track, and she needed to coax it back but the timing was off, so she waited and listened.

"I've seen needles stuck into people fairly deep," he rambled, "and they don't feel a thing, even if they're awake and looking at it. There's no real explanation for it—the wounds don't bleed. What can I say? It's the power of the mind when it chooses to ignore something."

"Can't imagine..." Catherine displayed a small show of puzzlement, then thought she saw a way to get back to her subtle interrogation. "But fatigue is different, Ken; fatigue's like a car without gas, when the tank's empty it's done. Surely?"

"A little patience," Ken assured, swallowing one of the several Jägermeister shots he'd lined up. Catherine's didn't match him. "We needed to give our investors something tangible, so we took a street kid, maybe nine or ten, skinny as a rail. Our hypno-sequence did its thing, convincing him he was a steel rod that couldn't flex." He held up his middle finger, provocatively gesturing at more than extreme skinny stiffness. "We stuck his heels on one chair and just his head resting on another, no support in between. It was astonishing to behold; no flex in his body and stiff as a plank. I got one of the porkier bankers, maybe two-forty-plus pounds of lard, and sat him squarely on the middle of the kid. And you know what? Nothing—he didn't budge, not an inch, like a park bench."

"A bit irresponsible!" Catherine blurted, unimpressed.

"Not at all, Cath," Ken offhandedly brushed her concerns aside. "Forget the kiddie sentiments, my point is that there's no way a kid like that—malnourished into the bargain—no way he could've done it awake—not a chance. But with self-doubt removed and replaced by affirmation—no problem."

As Ken mused at the strange power lurking within even the lowliest human cur, Catherine once again felt irked by Ken's brash disregard. An experiment like this was outrageous yet he seemed unable to grasp that. The strains of hypocrisy accused her again. Ken's attitude belied all the warm and fuzzy PR spin her company was trying to weave for LifeGames as a benevolent caregiver of humanity's needs.

Everything about him caused her agony from wrestling with her own hypocrisy; she was attracted to him and repulsed at the same time. It wasn't because of the money or power—those would be things she could still justify to herself—no, it was worse than that; it was the danger he represented, and she was a dreadful risk-taker.

Ken was entirely oblivious to her expression of distaste for him, and just laughed at her in condescension, as he would to a child.

"That's just history, my girl. You're too funny with your concerns for the great unwashed. You can't save them all, you know. What's important is what I need to discuss with you—

something that has an impact on our next PR phase. I did brief you about our new innovation? Well, this is it, it's time I disclosed it: nutrition patches. They're performing great in trials."

There wasn't time to mull the awkward sentiments of moments before, as it was go-time and Catherine needed to be up to the task.

"You're saying, it's the answer to fatigue?"

"You got it! Pretty trusted technology, borrowed from NASA but amended for our needs. We're almost ready for commercial applications."

"Ahhhh, I remember some noise about the NASA breakthrough..."

"Not really rocket science, just a high-yield enzyme-catalyzing *monomer* held on a transdermal patch. It facilitates *gluconeogenesis*... it's a whole mouthful of *polysaccharide* jargon that I'm too battle-weary tonight to recount, but it's a dynamite little innovation! In layman-speak, it supplements energy—a real kicker for the metabolism, directly through the skin."

"It's a *sucrose* plaster? You've added more sucrose?" Catherine quizzed, intending to gain Ken's confidence. She pretended to know less science than she feigned through her question; she'd read up on the NASA innovation when *Newsweek* had covered it years before.

"A bit more than that; you're a girl, it may be a bit much for you." Ken winked as if it was a joke, but there was too much truth in his attitude for it to be funny. He was contemplating a thought and smoothing a non-existent moustache, weighing how far he'd open up. "I'm going to disclose some facts, strictly off the record—above top-secret, understand?"

He lifted another shot glass, examining it closely. It was a ruse; using his peripheral vision, he scanned past it, looking at Catherine for any flinch that might suggest she was not worthy of the Top-Secret confidentiality rating on her file.

"You want the lay-speak or you want it raw...?"

He was confident she'd overestimate her own smarts and opt for the detail. He intended to lay it on thick, to bury her in so much information that she'd retain none of it; exaggerating some aspects, inventing others. But he'd be faithful to the details that she needed in order to do her job.

"Pretend I'm smart," she challenged.

"Fine... Do you know why we never patented the process?" he posed, then continued without waiting for an answer. "It's the *Cola* strategy. When you patent, you've gotta reveal the details of the process, and that's the worst tactical move, so we buried what's a fairly simple concept behind a firewall of physical security and complex jargon. Once we had it configured, the truth is that there wasn't much to it. By reverse engineering our breakthroughs, our two or three competitors are actually closer on our heels than we'll publicly admit. We know how close they are, we know what they're not yet seeing... fortunately *they* have no clue how close they are. I've got the inside scoop on them; they're right there with our processes, probably a month or two from cracking them. They even have innovations of their own that are, well... worrying. We can no longer rely on first-move advantage. Off the record, we desperately need this breakthrough to put real distance between us and them."

Catherine felt her pulse quicken. He was telling her that the company was in a crisis—desperate—and they were facing strong competition from government agencies that were their key clients. She'd heard murmurs that something fundamental was shifting in the organization, something groundbreaking; she'd been stonewalled on details, and now she realized why.

"Do you understand epilepsy?" he asked unexpectedly.

"A neurological disease," Catherine replied without hesitation, a sudden shift in her mood and trepidation in her voice.

"No, not a disease, a neurological state—there's a difference."

"That's what I meant—a genetic... uhmm... disorder."

"No, again—in this case it's a state... and not a genetic one. You're correct to call it *genetic* and *disorder* when it occurs naturally, but we've mastered the process of inducing it at will, so it's just a state. We can switch it on and off as we need to." He looked at her closely. "You look like you're in shock."

"I... I'm sorry, I'm taken aback," she stammered. "My... my family..." searching for the words. "We have a, uhhmm... a history." Ghosts moved behind her eyes. "...When I was a toddler I lost my older sister to it, to epilepsy. She had a, uhhmm... an event... in the pool. I thought it was just a game. I still remember the funeral like yesterday, it was raining."

"Jeepers..." Ken said, sounding hollow. "Sorry.'

Clearly he was no good with emotional sentiments. He hesitated looking for words.

"Sure..." Catherine filled the uncomfortable moment.

"Thirty years ago treatments were crude," he deferred from emotion back to firmer ground, "A cure's much closer to reality now."

Even he saw how awkwardly it came out, so he added, "I'm... sorry Cath. Sorry about your sister... if it was today..." then ran out of small talk.

It was an uncomfortable moment, Ken and Catherine both wanting the sidetrack behind them so that the conversation could move on. Each with their own objectives for it to do so.

"Crap happens. As you say, it was long ago; just got me off balance."

She gave him a smile to acknowledge the gaffe as unintentional and meaningless.

"Anyway...." she brightened, "interesting stuff you're up to. I had no idea about the medical... the pharmaceutical angle within LifeGames."

The diversion aside, this was gold for Catherine; a new thread to unpick that might run all the way to snippets of conversation she'd picked up earlier in his office.

"Good... it's good you had no idea, because it means we're getting it right, keeping the news under the radar. Now it's time for disclosure, and you need to have a grasp of what we're doing to do your job properly."

"Great. But if you're messing with... with epilepsy and inducing it, that's pretty heavy. That's *proper* medicine, genetics? Where are you hiding the white coats?"

"Not on the admin floors."

"Fair enough. But if you're employing specialists, with those skill sets, surely a flag would pop up somewhere? The press would've been on it in a second."

"Keep going," he encouraged, "it's why we're still talking now, off the record. You need to be briefed as we've had, well... a few... problems recently and the press is starting to sniff. You might have heard a few of my calls earlier. I wasn't happy."

She allowed that she had.

"I don't want anyone getting hurt, but we have had to—how shall I put it delicately?—*persuade* a few of the more persistent editors that there isn't a story here. You're going to have to run interference, I'm afraid."

He looked at her intently now and she responded on cue.

"That's what I do."

"Good. What *I* don't do," Ken responded, "is the details of all the science; so don't quiz me. I've got a fair working knowledge, enough to be dangerous, and I'll give you access to some of the operations people if you need to get confirmations," he offered. "Our team is off-site, the one working on the pharmaceuticals. It's rather, well, *clandestine* at the moment. We anonymously and openly support certain charities who, in turn, make large donations to universities. Sometimes the money goes halfway around the world through various gateways before it lands in the, uhhmm, *right* hands."

"And the right hands are university research labs?" she ventured.

"Sure."

"Cardiff? San Diego? Nagasaki? Petersburg?"

"You *have* been doing homework." There was suspicion in his voice.

"No—I read it in Newsweek, I've got a good memory for detail. There was speculation as to why and how unrelated universities had all come into the money at once. As you say, ears prick up when teams of neural specialists come into unaccounted money for research. My ears pricked up because you *don't* have facilities in these centers. It struck me as... significant."

Ken had hoped that the press articles wouldn't make the associations so obvious, but he consoled himself that it was only because she now had privileged information that it became possible for a smart person with a good memory to make the connections.

"Okay—so you provide finance, and the results of key research finds its way back to you?"

"A little more complicated than that, but it'll do." He sipped and continued, "The early pharmaceuticals for epilepsy were called anticonvulsants. Now, there's a wide range of new and exotic cocktails: gabapentin, topiramate, levetiracetam, lamotrigine, pregabalin, tiagabine. The pronunciation's a bitch, don't quote me."

"Like I could," Catherine quipped.

"Collectively, they're called anti-epileptic drugs, AEDs. What I'm painting for you is a picture of our extreme vigilance, our meticulous attention to detail. It's an insurance policy when things go wrong. You may need this info if we ever need to defend ourselves to the press."

"Is something wrong?"

"Nothing important, but the potential is always there. It's important we know how to turn off what we trigger. The cocktails to turn off the epilepsy that we induce work by blocking sodium channels and modulating calcium channels. The effect is that we inhibit neuron firing and interrupt neurotransmitters; more details than that aren't important right now. What *is* important for this conversation is that we've developed *anti-AEDs*. It's a delicate push-pull to control the condition; we prompt it and we turn it off very precisely."

Catherine suppressed her shock this time. An inkling of something sinister stirred within her that went beyond her personal attachment to the malady; they *were* playing with fire. She knew it instinctively and it terrified her.

"So, anti-AEDs have a similar effect to strobe lights? Like in the TV news warnings about flash photography?"

"Clever girl, yes. But flashing lights only trigger epileptic events in epileptics."

"By events, you mean fits?"

"Fits are a symptom, don't get confused and hung up on fits. We're not triggering fits, we're triggering a special class of epilepsy. Epilepsy only describes the brain activity, not the reaction, understand?"

She nodded.

"Fits are out of control; we control everything, absolutely *everything*."

"Are you currently administering the anti-AEDs...? Or the AEDs for that matter?"

"I was wondering when you'd twig to that. The software needs to do the magic with the AEDs and for the Anti, it needs to dole them out according to the second-by-second telemetry data returning from our monitor. Now, all that detail stays within these four walls. The patch's main function used to be as a carrier for the nutritional side—we'll just keep that idea rolling along in the public's perception, so the patch is front of mind from here on out—that's all we feed to the press when the time comes, got it?"

"It's great for my professional ethics," she grimaced.

"If you're having problems with ethics, tell me now and…"

"You'll have me eliminated?" She said it as a joke but he nodded just perceptibly. She hated herself all over again for being attracted to danger.

"You're on the inside now, Cath. I'm serious, so take this seriously."

She looked down into her lap, chastened.

"I'm not threatening, not trying to scare you. You'll be well paid. Trust me, it's very controlled."

She nodded agreement.

"The patch proved to be perfect for a dual role. We paste it strategically where the blood supply is close to the surface. The NASA patch was *dumb*—it was passive, simple. It was slow-bleed, slow-release. If we used anti-AEDs on a passive patch, we'd definitely induce a fit that could run out of control. So, we made it active, releasing the active chemicals to match our need. The patch is RF active, Wi-Fi radio linked to the computer, and the computer is monitoring metabolic rate and neural activity, releasing dosage on demand. The whole system's now run by AI."

"A I...?"

"Artificial intelligence..."

"The patch has artificial intelligence?"

"Yes. It's integral to the entire system. It's like another neuron bundle in the brain. It has circuitry and some autonomy. But the whole process—our back-end with the patch—it morphs together to collectively act as the AI. This coalition learns on the fly, it teaches itself, it spawns new sub-routines. We're at the point where we can create a new routine by giving the system specific URLs, bona fide web addresses where details are available."

Catherine was puzzled and wore the scowl that said as much.

"I can see you're confused… stay with me and you'll get it…. Our AI system interrogates the sites in order to build its program from it, just as a human operator would…"

"You mean…" Catherine cut in.

"No. Just listen," Ken cut her off. "Let's say we need to assess a Emergency Response Manager to oversee civil response teams…. We could test him on the largest disaster of all, say, the 9/11 Twin Towers. To build that simulation, all we need do is point the AI to 9/11 websites that detail the facts, findings, and footage of that disaster. For an illustration, let's say we point it to Wiki, and the AI takes it from there. It creates the whole program from what it finds. A bit of tweaking to ensure it's right, and its done."

"Your AI can really do that?"

"Sure—that's what artificial intelligence is. It's intelligent. It's autonomous. It's a neural network like a brain. It comprehends, compares and makes decisions. In many respects, we're now just handlers. Jockeys steering it. And *that*—the fact that our AI is this advanced—is off the record. It doesn't leave this table."

"You gotta be kidding. Amazing," she mumbled dreamily, captivated by what she was hearing, back under Ken's spell, lost again in her detestable lust for danger. "I want to make sure I'm following this." Her mind tumbled with the revelations. "What exactly are you getting out of all this?"

Ken sipped again, smacking his lips at the sting of the liquor, deliberately letting her stew, considering how much more to impart. He'd opened a Pandora's box and taken out enough of its toys to manipulate her for his purposes, but he was mindful to keep the rest of the skeletons sequestered safely inside.

Catherine observed his cageyness so she angled as best she could to get him back to details. "Come on Mr. Torrington; you've got my attention, you have my word," she demanded with her most girlish charm.

"Are you religious?" he suddenly asked.

Again, it wasn't a question she'd anticipated and her mind raced to formulate her best response. "If I was, what would it matter?"

"Oh, it wouldn't matter a great deal. Just that, with a religious disposition you may have a specific view on what I'm about to tell you. The downside is that your barriers will go up—you'll have the urge to deny what I'm going to say."

"Okay... no, I'm not, for what it's worth... not at all religious. I'm a bit spiritual, I guess you could say, but not religious."

"Spiritual's same as religious in this regard, only less... uhhmm," he searched for a word, "less... *feral*, perhaps. People who label themselves religious tend to be hostile to facts they fear might explain their mindset. It's in their outlook to remain ignorant of some facts as a goal." He sipped again. "Epilepsy has several dozen manifestations. You heard of temporal lobe epilepsy, or TLE?"

"No."

"'Temporal' tells you where it's located in the brain, just above the ears. Now when this sector malfunctions, it causes hallucinations, visions and voices that aren't really there. A lot of research has been conducted on this branch of medicine. Several decades ago, a researcher—Geschwind, a neurologist—first noted hyper-religious symptoms that stemmed from TLE. It's called the Geschwind syndrome. There's a whole branch of study called neurotheology that investigates the symptoms. It's fascinating and answers a lot of questions about our superstitious minds."

"Really?" Catherine was riveted.

"They speculate that individuals with temporal lobe epilepsy tend to experience states of consciousness called euphoria or *samdhi*. These characters often find their place in traditional cultures as religious figures, as shamans and witch doctors. It explains a lot about our cultures."

Ken was relaxed now, on firm territory and egged on by her enthusiasm for the topic.

"We use a technique called transcranial magnetic stimulation. By electromagnetically stimulating the temporal lobe just above the ear, we can trigger these hallucinations—make ghosts or UFOs appear or have God's voice boom inside the subject's head. We're reverse-engineering biology. We initiate and control what has spontaneously been happening to some people for all of history."

"You don't think it's dangerous messing with the brain?"

"Not at all," Ken assured her. "We're riding on an evolutionary adaptation. You want a side lesson? It'll help you grasp the scope and context of what we do."

"Of course I do."

"We, as humans, obviously have something that makes us very different from our ape cousins. They need to watch thousands of repetitions of an action before they grasp it. We grasp it in one or two viewings. The question is…"

"Why?" she finished.

"Mirror neurons. You experience them when you see someone, say, twist their ankle, and you physically cringe, sort of feeling your own ankle twist along with their pain. Psychopaths don't have this response."

"Oh, good… I'm not a psychopath." She almost asked if he felt others' pain, but she already knew the answer.

"The evolutionary scientists tell is it's why we developed so fast. Our mirror neurons, in our temporal lobes, run a sort of virtual reality software. They recreate a simulation so that in my brain I can actually get a solid understanding of what someone else is thinking or feeling, and really feel it inside of myself. This helps me understand that someone has intentions and predicts what they're going to do; it helps me come to someone's rescue or neutralize something negative they're going to do before they do it. It's obviously a very advantageous faculty to have. It means we can watch an action once and then imitate it. No other animals have the same density of these neurons, and none of them can do this."

"And this is established fact?"

"Sure," he insisted. "For example, accident victims, people who've had their corpus callosum cut—the connection between the two halves of the brain. You wind up with two separate people in one head; one half of the brain might believe in a god, the other half's an atheist."

"Why don't they teach this? Maybe in schools?"

"They'll probably receive too much resistance. The explanation for why humans are honest or kind and why we had a huge leap in cooperation that led to the world we've built, flows directly from mirror neurons—the implications from such a simple explanation is not popular with people who want a good mystery."

"But still…" Catherine was frowning, thinking of those implications. "So, you're saying you're not doing anything more than what the brain is already doing?"

"Sort of… yeah… that's not a bad way of putting it. The brain's already running virtual reality software, we're just amplifying it. Very good, Cath."

"It's how I earn the big bucks."

Catherine's mind somersaulted; the scope of LifeGames' new dabbling suddenly crystalized for her. Chemically open up pathways within any healthy mind and then electrically stimulate the brain to control it. Together with the autosuggestion of hypnosis already gripping a subject, LifeGames would have total control over the mind, thoughts and actions of the subject.

With a shock, she realized she was at risk of being hypnotized by Ken's carefully modulated voice, and she silently reminded herself that she was with a man of unfathomable capacity and unknown motives. For certain, he was intelligent and manipulative, and his grasp of psychology was obvious.

"Whoa! Whoa, Whoa!" She rubbed her own temples as if what she was hearing was an illusion. "I'm going numb here."

She'd said it loudly, in an outburst, and some of the other patrons looked across at them.

"My mind is tumbling, Mr. Torrington. What precisely are you doing to me?" She was only half joking; the information was overwhelming, but something in his manner had her captivated, under his spell.

"You're right, I should stop."

"You dare!" Catherine threatened with impish radiance. Again, it worked and he smiled the grin of realizing another small victory before continuing.

"In the early days, our operation—the infrastructure—was quite crude. Great big sets to accommodate clients' training needs. They'd don helmets that were feeding them visuals with integrated audio and pneumatic pressurized suits for haptic feedback… it was a mess. What we have now makes that look laughable by comparison. We used to deck-out entire airline cockpits to train pilots and we'd hang Special Ops military personnel in giant gyroscopes, like the one in your advert. That's all passé, pretty shortly it'll be redundant."

"What was I hearing then in the corridors?"

"The last of the old tech. It's not our future, not as profitable, not as... sexy."

"You had me fooled, I thought infrastructure was your competitive edge, and I'm supposed to be an insider."

"You're *becoming* an insider."

It was a promise of a great deal more information dangled close enough so that she could smell it. He implied that she could taste it too if she played her cards just right.

"It's not prudent just *yet* for the general public, non-personnel or key clients to think we're moving as fast as we have been to the new process. It suits us for the public to think our trainees are physically hurling themselves around in 3D virtual-reality suits, dangling in gyros; but the change is coming fast. All our top clients are already on the new systems. And," he dropped his voice so only she could hear it, "my darling, love you as I do, if you breathe a word of this before I'm ready, I will personally bury you."

It felt like he'd wrapped a crowbar around her head. In that instant, she knew he meant it and it gave her a buzz to be riding this wave so close to its deadly curl.

"Ken," Catherine said just as quietly, almost huskily, "I can keep a secret."

"You will."

"It's the people I tell that can't." She shrugged, with a smile.

He laughed, and that was something she'd never seen him do. "Well...?"

"Well what?" Catherine responded.

"What do you want to talk about now? Now that you've admitted you're untrustworthy and I'm going to have to kill you...?"

"More of the, uhhmm..." she said, and then blurted something she wasn't thinking and it shocked her "...something sexy."

"Something sexy?" he repeated slowly, and there was a glint in his eye that made her wonder how deep into her head he had gotten during his manipulation. He clinked her glass for her to drink.

"We've also got a 'God Helmet'."

"A God Helmet?"

"The name's a bit off—it's not a helmet at all, just a webbing band with electrodes. The name comes from the early days of TLE, it's jargon. The electrodes generate specific magnetic pulses that the computer controls, interacting directly with their biological neurons. It's full-immersion virtual reality from within the nervous system. We can shut down the signals coming from the real senses and replace them with the signals that the brain would be receiving if it were in the virtual environment. The result is that it feels totally real. The 'God' part comes from the early days when scientists first proved they could create religious experiences on demand, under laboratory conditions. Of course, we're farther along the track on that now, and working on having a subject go there interactively with other people and share any kind of experience with anyone involving all of the senses—we call it 'beaming'. Impressed?"

She nodded, too stunned to talk.

"We'll eventually be able to route an entire flow of sensory emotions out via the Internet. You'll be able to plug in and experience what it's like to be someone else. Can you imagine the boon for human intelligence when individuals can merge with our technology? Factor in our R&D on nanotechnology to push life expectancy and you'll be talking centuries. And imagine, just imagine..."

"And you can also do this? Already?"

"Oooh, no. We're not beaming yet, but it's in the cards. Right now, we have nodes that neuro-lock with the central nervous system—it's a two-way bridge. Like I said, we use it to bypass the sensory organs when we stimulate our programs directly inside the brain. We retrieve the experience our subject is having via fiber optic cables that display on our monitors. In effect, we're looking through their eyes, we see what they see, we sense and feel what they feel. It's where that footage we reviewed today in your campaign came from—directly from a typical feedback loop."

"What? I thought that was a set, a CGI mock-up. A computer graphic interface simulation..." She was dumbfounded. "You're telling me that was someone's thoughts we were viewing? Actual recorded thoughts?"

"Yes."

"I... I... well. Ken, I'm..."

"It's quite something, isn't it?" He let the silence hover—he hadn't lost track of his objectives. Adjacent diners had come and gone, and the evening had tumbled by precisely as he'd planned.

There was something about this woman that bewitched him. He'd had this feeling before for a woman, but those occasions had been fleeting and rare. He knew that the only way to exorcise the uncomfortable crush from within would be to have her, to *know her* according to the biblical euphemism.

"You still got an appetite for details?" he posed.

Her mind reeling, stunned by revelations she'd not begun to guess at, Catherine nodded and murmured something encouraging; an agreement that emerged from her mouth, bypassing her mind.

"We need the public to continue believing that the operation is mechanical. We keep the decoy alive, and use our equipment to run a few subjects, to show it's business as usual. We maintain a full complement of staff and maintenance division. Nothing seems to have changed from the outside. Meanwhile, we're ratcheting down the old program, only putting the less important subjects through it. The VIPs, world leaders in their field, high rollers, big bankers, politicians, military strategists... we've started pushing them through the latest programs. They don't know it because we take them down, hypnotize them in a green room and only usher them into operations when they're under. They're of course coded to remember it differently. So, when I tell you there's a lock-down on who knows these functions, I'm talking life and death. Just about nobody outside of a closed ring. That's how I'll know if you ever leak it."

"Fine—got that." She was now truly terrified and deeply aroused. "Keeping pretenses is my job. I sense there's something you're working toward; you have a problem that needs my attention?"

"Let's call it a teething problem."

"You need it sanitized—kept from the press?"

"Precisely."

"Then why did you tell me all this, burden me with the convoluted mess? Why make it possible that I slip up?"

"Because I trust you, and I want you to experience it, to run a session—awake and in the flesh. No hypnosis sequence."

"What? No, Ken. No, I don't think so," Catherine denied vigorously, but the fear factor was screaming within her for a yes. "There is absolutely no way..."

"Don't be so nervous. I'll arrange it—no patch and you won't go through the whole ritual; it'll be light, very vanilla. We'll do a mechanical, not a TLE, and won't use the new electrodes. You'll be totally awake, lucid and cognizant."

"There's for sure no way I'd do the hypnosis..."

"But you'll do it without?"

She shook her head, pretending to not like the idea but tumbling inexorably toward a yes. "Ken... no... I just can't, I won't."

He smiled and tilted his head, nodding.

"Okay... all right." She began to relent. "I'm not agreeing to this at all... but I'm *definitely* not doing the hypnosis."

"I agree—no hypnosis. We can do it that way, just a very mild ride, the helmet and the feeds. I want you to really understand. In your position as spokesperson for our company, you absolutely have to."

It was nonsense and posturing, they both knew it. In spite of herself, Catherine knew she had capitulated and was buying it. "I'm absolutely not agreeing," she affirmed, "but... I'm intrigued. Let's just leave any thought of my participation out of the conversation and tell me more. Give me a picture; what exactly goes on behind that smoke screen, Mr. Torrington?"

She tried to employ the girlish grin for a third time, but it was unconvincing. Ken gave himself to it willingly.

"We bring the subject in from the green room. With the need for heavy machinery now eliminated, we need surprisingly few staff—just one or two. In fact, just a single member can run the whole show—it's all software and automated."

"Good for integrity and confidentiality," she observed.

"Precisely. We bed them down, it's all very clinical. There is some question about the, uhhmm, bodily functions—the bags and catheters--that's handled by medics."

49

"I'm not having any of those." Catherine smiled, making it a joke.

"But you're not doing it—remember?" He winked. "We fit the God Helmet and the patches, and let the secondary hypnosis sequence begin. It takes them through another stage, or several stages, as deep as we need them to be for our purposes. The software begins to run—there's some twitching, there's a grunt, a grimace, sometimes mumbling, and then it's over. We debrief, we de-hypnotize, remove the hardware, return to the green room, and begin the process over again with the next subject. The results are all recorded. Recordings are analyzed and graded, and results are posted to whoever is footing the bill."

"And you're cramming in more training like this?"

"Depending on the sequence and application, severalfold, actually, dozens of times the normal pace that can be achieved with other advanced methods. That's hundreds, possibly thousands of times quicker than in real life. A year's worth of piloting or courtroom dramas or political electioneering—trained, practiced, assessed, repeated—over and over again in a single session. You come out of it a different person."

"And that returns us to my earlier question about expending energy and replenishing it. I'd imagined the subject actually *doing* whatever it is they're signed in to learn—fighting a war, running, tumbling, firing, whatever—like we had in the board room. God..." she looked awed. "I feel so dumb, so... so silly."

"Don't—it's a natural assumption to make."

"But the physical routine; surely they'd thrash themselves to pieces?" she posed.

"A good observation. But you don't when you sleep, right?"

"What?"

"When you sleep, you can have all kinds of outlandish dreams; falling, running, fighting, driving, whatever. And you don't actually run or fight in your bed—it happens in the theatre of your mind. That's what we're doing and all we're concerned with is your mind. The physical health of your body is not our concern—we are only interested in getting information into you and reactions to those stimuli back out of you. That's a cognitive exercise. What we really do is control sleep, control dreams."

"Aahhhhh....!"

"You're getting it. When you sleep, your body is paralyzed, it has to be; it's an evolutionary reality. If you weren't paralyzed, you'd beat yourself and any sleeping partners to a pulp. We have a sequence in the hypnosis sequence, the secondary sequence, when we add the God Helmet that takes care of that. It paralyzes the body, just like sleep."

"Oh-kaaay....!" Catherine exclaimed. "You know," she added, digging into the recesses of her mind, "I read about something like this somewhere. One of the dog breeds, Rottweilers, have a mutation and those affected don't experience dream paralysis. I remember now because I had one; fortunately not one of the mutants. It was mentioned in the training book. They don't have the suppression and it makes them act out their dreams, and can cause them to tear a house to pieces in their sleep."

"Not the best breed to act out," Ken observed.

"No kidding!"

"You want to know something else about temporal lobe epilepsy? It heightens religiosity. When someone's in this state, their responses to words associated with religious thought are hyper-stimulated, their reactions to neutral words are unchanged, and their response to sexual words diminishes."

"Which means?"

"Which means you're safe." He said it as a joke, but they both caught the moment and knew it wasn't.

"And you want to bring up sex because....?" Again, she'd spoken the words as if a ventriloquist had control of her voice; the ventriloquist in the wine glass.

Ken was momentarily knocked off balance by her forthrightness and she perceived that fact.

Now it was *his* mouth that spoke before checking his words. "Just me wondering what gets you turned on when the power suit comes off. What really turns you on?"

She'd exposed her weakness to the angle he'd been aiming for. Instinctively, she knew that this sudden swing in conversation had placed her on a ledge; a pivotal moment. She could pursue one of several directions; she decided to drive the conversation to where she'd prefer it to go.

There was something wicked in her tonight and it wasn't just the wine; she was in a reckless mood, of a mind to be blunt, frank, and shocking. It was a tactic she'd often used to instantly neutralize a man's advances.

Nothing had been said between them for several seconds and she weighed how far she dared push her next statement. It was a moment of conflict—half in deliberate control, and half under his hypnotic spell that had been building throughout the night.

She rolled the dice.

"What turns me on?" Catherine repeated Ken's question with deliberately slow cadence, looking him directly in the eye. She spiced the words with her voice and pronounced them emphatically with her lips, lobbing the dangerous subject like a grenade.

She continued confidently, "I'm thirty-six. Never married; doubt I ever will. I've had six heterosexual relationships, two serious. Anything else?"

She was now confident, treading firmly on certain ground. This was her terrain, the social environment, toying with the unspoken.

"Six *heterosexual* relationships? That suggests an alternative." Ken was uncharacteristically bashful.

"Lesbian?" she countered, and smiled, folding her napkin very deliberately. "It's an ugly word. I have a female lover, if that's what you're asking."

The concept gripped him. Catherine was a breathtaking woman of poise. She'd never hinted at this aspect of her life, and Ken felt a stir within that he couldn't explain. It was a peculiar challenge to him as a man—that he should dine with her, but find her suddenly so unavailable. By the sound of his voice—when he found it—it appeared that this was an entirely new concept to him. "Why a woman?"

He made the word "woman" sound like the description of a disease and Catherine retorted with a well-rehearsed answer, "Wait till you see her."

"Which one's the man?" Ken rebutted, feeling cheated.

"We're lesbians, Ken, we're not confused!" She smirked.

"Well now, isn't that just interesting. And you know what..."
A new trajectory veering off the flight path Ken had been
navigating toward suddenly loomed into sight, so he took the
initiative. "You ever thought about cyber-sex? Ever wondered
what our systems could do... to boldly go where no man has
gone before?"

It made her laugh and he joined her.

"I'm serious Cath. Imagine, just imagine where you could go."

"Hmmm," Catherine made a show of considering it. This was
still dangerous ground, flirting with this man, but there was a
devil on her shoulder. "Let me guess—you've got a range of sex-
game software?"

"It can be arranged. I have influence you know..."

"You drive a hard bargain, Mr. Torrington. Can you do
spectacular things? Things I can't imagine?"

"I sure can," he bragged, "and our system certainly can. You
brave enough? A small try?"

"I must be nuts, but I'll try anything once."

Her voice seemed to echo down a tunnel in both their minds.

"It'll take a bit to set it up."

The company hadn't previously had a need for this class of
training or software before.

"So, who would I get? What image? How does it work? Do I
get to choose a... uhhmm... partner?"

"I'll arrange a surprise."

"And you?" Catherine quizzed. "You'll probably expect to
watch my, uhhmm... game?"

"Naturally, there's got to be something in it for me. Call it a
rental of my very expensive equipment!"

"All right, okay. I'm up for it. But—no other spectators! Just
you, me, and the machine."

Outwardly, Catherine was as cool as ice; inwardly, she quaked
and quivered.

The deal had truly been struck and their respective spoils
agreed upon.

Ken rarely drank and never suffered hangovers, but next
morning was slow death.

Anton Lim, one of his brightest from software was summoned to Ken's office, where the boss-man ventured a cautious approach. "It's a Saudi Prince," he asserted. "Discretion is essential, you understand?"

And all the software necessary for Catherine's sequence was quickly and surreptitiously put into motion.

Chapter 3

"Fuck-sake, Ken. You knew there were risks. This is experimental and we've pushed it into operations too fast."

Craig Angelis was, with good reason, a *very* worried man; the stakes were greater than just his career.

It seemed ages since Ken had first put his nomination to the board, a nomination that was unanimously rejected.

Passions had been ignited when Ken refused to back down, insisting that the nomination be carried. To emphasize this, he'd walked over and locked the door, pocketing the keys. A Mexican wave of nervous looks had traveled around the boardroom table.

The board meeting had ran on for three hours with that single issue remaining relentlessly on the table. Craig's fourth tabling for nomination had been grudgingly accepted, and Craig's name had duly been added to the stationery. From that moment forth, LifeGames had consumed Craig, becoming the focus of his existence.

With a PhD in pharmaceutical sciences, Craig's responsibilities as Chief Operating Officer included peculiar language: "The ongoing development of nutritional supplements, procurement of raw materials, and maintenance of supplies."

"What does he bring, Ken?" Henry Fowler had stood firm, deeply opposing the nomination. As the largest shareholder following Ken, Henry had a sizable vested interest in the company and he—in theory at least—carried persuasive clout. But Ken did not defer to democracy in business matters beyond lip service.

"Cash injection to start with, Henry," Ken had insisted. "The dilation project has pushed us far into the red, and our cash flow could use the injection." Ken had then shot a glare at Chief Financial Officer, Grant Poole, the one man who could and should have disagreed strongly; which was nonsense. Ken was gambling on Henry's sketchy comprehension of accounting matters to confound his ability to see through the lie.

Grant had dutifully nodded in agreement. If he *had* planned to correct Ken's statement, the idea had been withered by Ken's glare and the carefully canted position of his head that only Grant could see.

"If you ask me, the only money he can offer us is black market," Henry had grumbled, irate at being dragooned into accepting a "zonked-out ex-hippie type" as he'd labeled Craig, onto the board.

"Black market money's as green as anybody's, Henry," Ken had pointed out in off-handed fashion, uncluttered by ethics as he was.

To the silent board members, the most curious aspect of the election saga had been the reason for Ken's obsession with Craig's inclusion.

Financial considerations aside, LifeGames already had better qualified employees more suitable for pressing needs than any skills that Craig might have brought to the table. In short, from the perspective of the board, there would no tasks to occupy Craig.

Yet, even more curious, was a fact that only Ken had known; Craig didn't possess a penny to invest.

Ken had secretly taken out a life policy on Craig, assigning the beneficiary for any payout as a spaghetti of trusts that eventually led back to him. On the strength of that surety, he'd seeded Craig the millions he'd needed in order to purchase his shares. Had *that* truth ever leaked, the well-founded suspicions of fraud, corruption and gross nepotism would certainly have ripped a hole in the company.

Equally hidden, was the murky history of Ken and Craig's skullduggery half a lifetime ago. The two had met twenty-five years previously while backpacking around the world. At the time, both had been experimenting with dangerous street narcotics.

Craig was several years Ken's senior, a university grad with a genius ability to concoct hallucinogenic potions.

Having nearly killed the pair of them twice with his brews, a third mistake had proven less fortunate for an acquaintance that had been with them. On that occasion, the victim had been another drifter whom they had befriended. Ken had been in the frequent habit of befriending others and magnanimously letting them take the first hit whenever Craig brewed up a new batch.

After it had gone wrong, they'd left the unfortunate man comatose on the roach-infested floor of a cheap brothel hotel in the back streets of Athens.

Soon after that incident, they'd gone their separate ways, only to re-establish contact many years later. By that time, Craig's career had progressed slowly and he was pigeonholed. He'd settled into a neat nine-to-five, two-and-a-half-dog, suburban lifestyle. With his career having stagnated well short of his ambitions, his most precious assets were his wife and toddler son. Ken, in contrast, had been high-rolling in the hedge-fund business; fast cars and faster women. Their divergence had posted them on opposite sides of the financial spectrum; Craig was drowning in debt but devoted to his family.

Ken had subsequently launched LifeGames with a grand dream that he would bring Craig in. But, in order to capitalize on the idea, he knew that he would have to remain patient and wait until the company had built a proven track record.

Then, as soon as the track record had been established, he'd gone to Craig with the teaser, inviting him out for a social evening of discussion and "a few laughs about the old days".

As the evening had worn on, Ken had cast the lure across Craig's bow. "You're pretty familiar with our virtual reality business. What would happen if someone was tripping? Let's say, if he was on one of those hallucinogens from the bad old days?"

"Whoa!" Craig had blurted, with more than a little bit of shock and terror at the thought. "From the little I know about your operations, if you coupled hypnotic hallucinations with chemical hallucinogens... Jeez, brother... you'd probably overload and fry a brain."

Craig's own words had instantly plucked images of Athens from his long-hidden vault of suppressed memories and he'd shuddered with guilt.

Ken had known full well that Craig had gone cold turkey immediately after the Athens incident and never touched the dope again.

Ken had also known that Craig had done it alone and in a strange foreign land; an experience that had nearly killed the man. Though Ken had spotted the agony and guilt from the triggered flashback on his face, he wasn't about to let sentiment derail his critical goal. "Ok, something other than a main-line, Craig. What about something more sophisticated, more current? Something kinder, gentler, softer; maybe electronically monitored and controlled?"

"What's soft about drugs? Everything's got side effects, it all does damage," Craig had shrugged, quickly sobered from his initial reaction and trying to distance himself from the proposal.

"Granted. But what I meant was tailoring something. A natural amphetamine to boost the central nervous system." Ken had pressed ahead, deliberately keeping their conversation informal, but calculated to pique Craig's natural curiosity for experimentation. "It's just something I'm toying with. If we don't do it, our competitors will; and it's big—I mean BIG, BIG dollars. I'm contemplating it, but it's still *strictly* off the record, you understand?"

He had waited till Craig committed. Craig had known Ken's propensity for a violent reaction to broken promises, and had enthusiastically agreed.

"Good. What I'm imagining, Craig, is that we hook a subject up for an hour of training, but instead of experiencing only one hour, we get the mind racing and introduce the computer-generated data stream into the subject at an elevated rate. I'm estimating we could condense a full working day of training into less than an hour. What do you reckon?"

Craig had fallen hypnotically for Ken's nodding affirmations. Earlier in the evening, Ken had prepared this fertile psychological soil. He'd complimented and re-complimented Craig, bolstering him, while tapping his nails with a distracting *clickety-click* gallop on the tabletop with each smiling and nodding ego-stroke. Then, he'd used this neuro-linguistic trigger to anchor Craig's mind with the task he needed him to commit to; the *clickety-click* sound helped him to drive home his proposition.

"I estimate we'll cram the illusion of three months of real life training into a three-day session; *you'll* come up with the pharmaceutical to do the job. Consider what your life will look like in three years when we float this success on the NASDAQ, Shanghai or London markets!"

Ken had painted a picture of gold gilt grandeur and Craig had envisioned the concrete foundation he'd yearned to give his family.

Always the master of manipulation, Ken had steadily smuggled the idea into Craig's mind, and by the end of the evening, Craig had been thoroughly convinced that it was his life's calling to solve the challenge.

Ken was a disciple of the notion that every man has his price, and he had been pleasantly surprised to discover how affordable Craig's had been.

The tariff that Craig had levied on the price of his conscience had been a bargain when weighed against the return that his expertise would yield.

"I'll sponsor you the entry fee," he had told Craig. "We can expect some resistance when getting your nomination past the board, and we'll have to dangle some bait to make it attractive for them. I'm going to transfer the entry money to you to buy your way in."

He'd then shrewdly plied Craig with more celebratory champagne before continuing with business. "Naturally, I'll have to protect the investment. My private attorney is drawing up the contract; I don't want you to skip out on me without first earning your keep." Ken had grinned widely as he'd sealed the deal with a backslapping embrace, his cunning tactics obscured by the friendly ambiance.

If Craig had possessed any modicum of business sense, he'd never have put pen to paper on the contract that Ken had produced. When the contract had been presented, it had been brimful of fine print, double negatives, Latin phraseology, and arcane word tangles that appealed to precedent laws that would give Ken all the power and reward.

The cleverly constructed wording had effectively overridden any estate or equity that Craig intended for his family to inherit through his will and testament. In short, in the event of Craig's death, Ken would inherit everything that he owned.

Within a few short weeks, the board had been swung, and Craig had begun spending his every waking moment wrestling with the problem. Sequestered away like a hermit, his family life had been in the tatters that Ken had manufactured in order to keep his mind on the task. Ken had run interference, keeping the company directors from pressing Craig into justifying his position.

Then the breakthrough had happened—Craig had arrived at the process for triggering the temporal lobe epilepsy.

"There are still some minor side effects, but we're almost there," he'd reported excitedly to Ken. "I'm still having trouble because the lab-chimps go into convulsions from fatal epilepsy if the dose goes even a fraction out of specs. I've got a suspicion that it's the beta-globulin in the formula. I'm pretty sure that after a couple more trials we'll be ready to test it on a volunteer."

They'd both been elated.

All of that had transpired during the previous year, and during the interim, Craig had succeeded in fabricating the prototype sample needed to achieve time dilation.

Together, he and Ken had secretly applied the product to the NASA patches. They'd flown to Brazil, via two separate travel plans, keeping the rendezvous utterly secret.

The elementary NASA patches—together with the hypnosis and software adaptations—had already achieved a degree of time dilation. However, the introduction of that first minuscule narcotic dosage—barely a detectable trace—had catapulted time dilation to an astounding four-fold increase in efficiency.

The results had been remarkable. So astounding, that they'd bordered on arousing suspicion; and since nobody but Ken and Craig had any idea of the true reason for the sudden breakthrough, the true hero of the accomplishment—Craig—hadn't received any of the praise.

The achievement had not gone without some appreciation from Ken. In lieu of broad praise, he had slipped Craig a hefty cash consolation prize.

Months had passed and the time dilation program had made it through the research and development phase. Against the cautions of the development staff, it was quickly being pushed through test marketing and into full production. The board and employees remained ignorant to the true magic behind the breakthroughs, accepting the simplified version of truth. The software department had also achieved breakthroughs, and the entire improvement in function was ascribed to them.

Profit projections were obscene, and the executive staff had been in overdrive, preparing for a commercial launch when disaster had struck...

The entire kettle of fish was now hanging in the balance, looking as if it was about to tip its load of wretched deceit.

There had been a meltdown; a high-ranking military client had suffered a severe psychological trauma.

Fate had picked the worst possible subject to visit its mischief on. The individual undergoing training was a top-ranking general on the payroll of the Joint Special Operations Command and the Pentagon. He was also a senior reconnaissance operative who had formerly trained with the battle-hardened Selous Scout battalions of old Rhodesia, weaned in wicked wars deep in the treacherous savannas of third-world conflicts.

The catastrophe had occurred when the general was online, undergoing a twenty-fold dilation experiment in a lengthy fifteen-hour stint.

From the general's perspective, the fifteen hours had translated into two weeks of intense jungle warfare. Until the point that he'd been brought out of hypnosis and the virtual world, back into reality, it had been a textbook procedure, perfectly on schedule and without any hint of a hitch.

Nothing had seemed untoward until he'd been in the recovery phase, undergoing stabilization and debriefing. Then, without warning, he had gone 'flashback' and unleashed his deadly hand-to-hand combat skills onto the medical staff.

They'd darted him full of sedatives, yet, terrifyingly, it had only served to inflame the situation. In-house security had been called, who then had tasered him with ten thousand volts, with little effect.

It had taken three point-blank rounds from beanbag projectiles to knock him off his feet, and he'd gone into arrest, convulsing on the floor, then had slipped into a deep coma.

The board of executives had been called to an emergency sitting, and since they had all been ignorant of the drug content in the patches, blame had been lobbed from department to department as though it were a live grenade.

The psychology department had been the first to come under scrutiny. They had been grilled but defended their electronic hypnosis routine, certain that it had been applied per protocol. Hundreds of thousands of lines of code had been picked over, seeking a bug. An industrial espionage attack was painstakingly considered, yet AI self-audits had come up clean.

Video and telemetry data of the routine were run through digital analytic and forensic protocols; procedures were rapidly reviewed. All had proved faultless.

Next to face examination had been Chief Information Officer, Max Schneider. Defending his department, he had asserted, "We've run every conceivable version of anti-virus and self-analysis several times over without the slightest hint of an issue. If anything, the files are surprisingly intact—far less so than statistical probability predicts," he'd stated confidently.

With no conclusion reached, the board meeting had adjourned with the vague verdict "extreme and unfortunate incompatibility of subject to content".

It had only been in the early hours of the following morning, back at Ken's mansion, that Ken and Craig could finally come to blows over the true cause of the afternoon's debacle.

"Yes, fuck it... YES!" Ken had boomed as he paced back and forth, shades of Athens looming again on their mutual horizons. "There are risks in everything—you don't have to waste time with the obvious. Stop fucking whining about the outcome for this asshole. I don't give a shit except that if he croaks, they'll stick their probe up our ass up to their elbows. Let me explain something." He was suddenly calm—too calm. "You are going to fix this, and you're going to fix it quickly. You're administering the antidote, and I don't care if it hasn't been tested and I don't care about its effects; you just get this prick down to Earth and walking out of there in more or less lucid fashion. We're about to run the PR campaign and I don't need your fuckups and shortcomings derailing this... understand?"

Ken's mood was inflamed by an evil hangover; a legacy left by the previous night's indulgence with Miss Catherine Kaplan.

"In spite of all of these problems, my other plans are still very nicely on track," he consoled himself.

He'd ensured that Nancy Mitford, his personal assistant, had dispatched a floral arrangement to Catherine at Kaplan Advertising & PR. In the attached note, he'd thanked her for her spectacular efforts in creating the commercials; it was more than the retrospective thanks, and she'd smiled knowingly when the flowers arrived.

"Worst case scenario," Ken continued, pacing like a caged tiger bordering on dementia, "If this fucker kicks it, what will an autopsy uncover?"

"The lab chimps have consistently showed nothing, not a trace. *Zero.* I went down that avenue a hundred times. I must have overdosed a zoo full of other primates, nothing has ever showed up!"

Craig was an emotional wreck, falling apart under the stress. *This could be murder!* The panic was rising. *What if they start digging and discover Athens? Interpol will have my prints from the site... Christ, I've got a child to think of. How the hell did I let Ken drag me in so deep again?*

The terror racing through his exhausted mind pushing him ever closer to a nervous breakdown.

"Primates? Fucking PRIMATES, not humans?" Ken thundered in a murderous rage.

Craig cringed away from the beast that had suddenly gripped the man. He'd never seen such a savage switch before, and he recoiled. "Jesus! You're not serious?"

Craig's illusion of Ken was splintering, the delusion of his blind respect for the man ripped away. He had always held Ken in the highest esteem, rationalizing Ken's vicious history as a symptom of an Alpha personality.

What raged before him now revolted Craig and shook him to his core.

"You're FUCKING RIGHT I'm serious, you dumb cunt!" Ken thundered. "I told you that we needed a terminal test before we went commercial."

He'd said it before, but Craig had never thought he'd meant it literally; now as the angry throbbing vein snaked across the Ken's forehead of thinning hair, there was no doubt.

The shocking memory of Ken pushing for this outcome was dredged back into focus; too late now, Craig realized he should never have glossed over it at the time.

Lounging in a fashionable nightspot near the city's center, Ken had casually broached connecting an unsuspecting drifter to test the drug to expiry.

Then—as had been the case too many times before—Craig's next recollection was of when they had connected a hastily befriended stranger up to the contraption.

It had been the early hours when the facility was unusually deserted. Ken had persuaded Craig to administer a dose of his new serum to the homeless man, one that far exceeded the understood limits.

The hard life out on the streets seemed to have steeled the man's metabolism, making him impervious to their dose. Insisting on a reaction, Ken had driven on, pushing up the dosage. The night had slipped rapidly by, Craig delaying as best he could until the day-staff were due to arrive, forcing an end to the experiment.

By the time the unfortunate man was dumped in a dirty alley— a block from the hospital, at Craig's insistence—the sun had been rising. The man had been barely breathing, but Craig had convinced himself that he'd pull through.

Now, being honest with himself, Craig wasn't that confident.

"If you'd FUCKING WELL LISTENED..." Ken was still ranting, charging himself into a frenzy. He picked up an ivory-handled, six-inch, sterling silver, antique letter opener and was brandishing it, hacking away at invisible demons.

Craig was terror-struck, mortified by what he knew Ken was capable of and might do next. They were two men reduced to their wild state; Ken, out of control with rage and Craig, blind with terror. He began inching toward the door, studying Ken, timing his dash to coincide with Ken's furthermost point away during his pacing.

They were in the banquet area of Ken's mansion and Craig's car was a corridor, two doors, and a flight of six steps away when he bolted.

The distance to his car was an infinite gulf; time slowed and the space stretched ahead of him with surreal elasticity. His timing was perfect and he caught Ken off-guard long enough to put another dozen paces between them before Ken gave chase.

As he ran, Craig fumbled with his keys for the ignition fob. He dived into the driver's seat, slapped the electronic fob into its recess and hit the Start button. The Maserati's engine roared to life. He stood on the accelerator and the engine bellowed mightily, the back end drifting wide and the tires spinning in place, trying to grip the surface. Ken slammed into the driver's side window just as the tires bit and the car slapped him aside, taking off in a shrieking, snaking plummet down the driveway, careening out of control toward the locked cast-iron gates at the exit.

With a deafening crash and a shower of sparks, the vehicle burst through the barrier, shearing the hinges off at the gateposts.

Chapter 4

Police investigators reckoned the mangled wreck was beyond posted freeway speeds at its point of impact. The steep descent of the driveway had caused the car to flirt with the limits of its acceleration.

Evidence of any attempt by Craig to slow or avoid the stone retaining wall across the street was nil. Speculation had it that his neck was snapped by the initial impact with the gate. The car had run headlong across double lanes and collapsed the chassis against the stonework, flaccid airbags hanging from every panel like oversized, spent condoms.

The coroner on scene disagreed with the police assessment. Craig's neck displayed a lateral force break from his right side, an inconsistent fracture with a head-on impact. Though his determination was noted on file, it was put aside as a strange curiosity. The police were more interested in the events that had led up to the catastrophe.

"Yes, we argued, Colonel. Another cup?" Ken, the high-ranking police officer and his lieutenant were alone in Ken's breakfast room. The staff, clearly shaken, were keeping to themselves in the scullery.

Twenty-four sleepless hours—among the worst in Ken's memory—had soaked his energy. He knew that it would be many more hours before he could hope for shuteye; he was running on caffeine and other self-medication.

The colonel, having been roused from bed at Ken's insistence, had personally taken over the scene. He was conducting the report in a friendly and efficient manner. As a police colonel, he naturally had received LifeGames certification; he owed his career to the company. So, he considered himself very fortunate to be in the presence of the man who had made his rise through the ranks possible.

He'd sped through the motions of the exercise without pushing for more answers than were plainly obvious to even a layperson; he had no intention of finding fault with a man he considered to be something of a personal hero.

Ken could sense the man's sentiments and felt comfortable now, confident that the incident was going no further than this report. He was more concerned with three major problems that might arise.

With Craig dead, the potential security risks of leaking the nature and function of the pharmaceuticals were eliminated. Now, the matter of tweaking the chemical formula to avoid further reactions was of some concern.

Ken had worked as closely as possible with Craig during the development phase so that he had a working knowledge of the active chemistry. He'd also taken the precaution of video recording all important developments; these were stored in his private vault. He could have new chemical batches re-synthesized to the existing specs; it was engineering the unknown problems the Pentagon subject was suffering from that might prove impossible with Craig gone.

Fortunately, he thought, a lab in China was on a secret payroll for just such an eventuality, and further developments could proceed at that location without too much fuss or the need for an ethical squint.

Secondly, the fact that Craig had died under questionable circumstances—at the mansion and during the early hours of the very morning following the unresolved catastrophe at work—would be bound to raise eyebrows.

It didn't pose any risk for Ken; he'd just rather not set tongues to wagging.

He put the worry aside. He'd work on a plausible story to out-maneuver any possibility of gossip later, after some sleep.

And finally, the general's life still hung in the balance; and along with it, Ken's and LifeGames' reputation. If the man were to die, he would pull them a long way down with him.

It was going to take finesse and a spot of luck to get out of this quandary, he thought.

The colonel finished taking his statement then departed with his lieutenant to inform Craig's estranged wife, Pat, and son of the tragedy.

After he'd left, Ken phoned the hospital where the general who had suffered meltdown was being treated; he desperately needed some positive news on the man's recovery.

"Yes, Sir—he's stabilizing. Would you like to speak to anyone in particular? The gentleman's family is down the corridor..." The nursing Sister had a pretty voice, brimming with compassion.

"Not to worry, Sister, I'll call back later." Ken hung up before she could ask him any more questions.

"Good," he spoke out aloud to himself. "One down, two to go."

He went directly down to the server room in his basement. It was now 9 a.m. and would be midnight in China, so he'd have to handle that last.

Ken pressed keys on a numeric touchpad on the wall and it slid back revealing a handprint reader onto which he placed his palm and fingers. Above it, a hidden mask flipped and swooshed forward. He placed his forehead against the pad and stared into the mechanism; his eye pattern matching the database, and a section of wall clicked and hinged open.

He walked through and the door closed behind him. Inside was a console encircled by several screens; this was his private, secure communications room. From here, all communications were 128-bit encrypted for maximum confidentiality.

He'd planned to put the issue aside till he could first get some sleep, but his mind wouldn't pipe down in its quest for a plausible story. *Why was Craig at my house?* The question repeated laboriously in the echo chamber of his exhaustion.

The scenario was falling into place, so he dialed Nancy's private line. "Hi, Nance. I've got some dreadful news, I'm afraid. You do need to sit down." He paused for a moment until she confirmed that she was ready. "Craig's been involved in an accident."

"Was it serious?" Nancy's voice quavered.

"*Very*, I'm afraid. It was... uhhmm... fatal."

"What? How? Where did it happen...? When?"

"At the bottom of my driveway, last night."

She peppered him with a flurry of questions, staggered by his coolness, but betraying nothing of any unspoken thoughts that attacked her. She'd become very fond of Craig; a little too fond, Ken thought.

"With yesterday's problems, neither of us were going to get sleep so we went to my place for a nightcap." Ken could hear her tugs of breath as the reality set in, and her sobbing began in earnest. "He had so many personal problems... just wanted a good friend, I guess. He hit the bottle a bit hard."

Ken knew without any doubt that the investigation would be quashed, so he reasoned that nobody at the office would ever know for sure what was in the police report. He figured he could pretty much say whatever suited him.

After a parade of condolences had been traded, Ken proceeded to discuss the business of the day.

"I won't be in today so do update me about the general's situation and anything else that I should know about. And— oh yes—set up a board review of the advertising campaign and PR review. Any time tomorrow or later will do. Also, get ahold of Catherine and make sure that she has the recordings ready."

He signed off with Nancy.

With the mundane business wrapped up, the larger problem could be attacked.

By late afternoon, Ken had been thinking about using the lab in China to prepare an urgent intervention, but the more he thought about it, the worse the idea sounded. The Chinese government was already working on a program in competition with LifeGames' option. One wrong meeting behind the bamboo curtain, and he'd be paying for their fast track to overtake him.

No... he needed a location somewhere less competitive, somewhere where he could control and eliminate anyone fool enough to leak anything.

From his private vault, he took out a well-worn address book bound in calfskin and thumbed through to the Ds.

"Kenny, Kenny... me old *mucker*... let's get something straight here. If you've got a nutritional problem, you'd go to Nestle. You've only come to me because you've got a narcotics problem. True?"

Ken could hear David Karcher smiling gleefully and counting a big payday.

There was a long and suspenseful silence; each man could hear the other's breath as it puffed through the handset's mouthpiece. Ken began to sweat as his mind raced for a way out of the dead end David had been so good at snaring him into. He tried a few angles.

David let Ken stumble on with a bunch of poor excuses before he decided to break the deadlock and let Ken off the hook.

"If you tell me about it Kenny, I'll put you onto the right people; otherwise, let's stick to pleasantries."

Ken had forgotten how the beach-bum attitude that David portrayed could instantly snap about, becoming a steel thrust.

"Ok, everything I've told you is half true," Ken admitted. "This is an idea that I've been considering since we started heating our subjects up a little too much with the virtual reality. I'm looking for something to make their transition back to reality... gentler."

Ken was a bath of perspiration; David always had a way of doing this to him. The acrid-sweet smell reeked of fear as he skirted the precipice of truth.

Ken claimed his Skype camera was malfunctioning, so that David could not view him in his unsettled state. He might be able to fake confidence in his voice, but David was a master in neuro-linguistic programming, having taught Ken all that he now knew about the technique. David would instantly have him at a vast disadvantage if he had a visual bead on him. Ken took refuge in invisibility.

There is a proverbial honor that exists amongst thieves. The trust between these two men extended beyond that to a mutual gun held to each other's heads; both knew the details of dirty dealings that would put the other into a deep, dark place for a long, long time.

"This must be bigger than I thought, old son!" David was enjoying his turn to rub in the advantage. "Still so guarded, Kenny..."

Ken was desperately seeking a way to relax David's grip. He guessed that humor, even weak humor stolen from Catherine, would buy him time to think.

"I trust *you* to keep the secret, Dave; it's the people that you tell that I don't trust!"

"Always the joker under pressure, eh? You've got to work on it, boy'o." David let the pregnant silence last for a torturously long period. "Ok, I'll allow you some privacy; what's your email? I'll pop some options over and asterisk the really wicked outfits; they're probably the ones you'll want to use... but it's five times the usual rate."

"Five times!"

"Bitcoin please."

"That's outrageous!"

"I was thinking twenty times would be outrageous. How about ten times the rate then?"

"Fuck's sake..."

"I'll still do five if you like…"

They settled on five times the already exorbitant rate for information and silence, and signed off.

An hour later, the email was in. There were six options, five of which were third-world dictatorships infamous for their narcotic exports. One of the six options immediately stood out; one of the two that had been asterisked: "*Paris*".

"Which way to go?" Ken began a monologue with himself, his nerves still frayed and jangling from his conversation with David.

"Paris is bound to be more sophisticated... and discrete if everything goes right. But if anything goes wrong, it'll be near impossible to keep the lid on it there."

Backwaters, he thought, *they're so much more convenient... you can pay off or bump off dissenters.* This made him smile, narrowing the options.

He began to lose concentration. It was time for a line of powdered inspiration.

Moments later, Ken felt invincible. "*Colombia*", the other asterisked option, now had his attention.

"I know the lingo… hmm… and if anybody could, *they* could certainly be persuaded to keep their mouths shut."

He paced, pondering it, back and forth, and then went back to the screen and stared at the list until a decision whispered to him.

"Ok, Colombia. If their lab's up to the task, this time they *will* run a human...." He didn't finish the sentence out loud.

His plan cemented in his mind. He'd take a short trip to make sure they followed through properly and bodies were suitably disposed of.

Early that evening, Ken went through various messages on his phone.

The colonel had kept his word by phoning with some information concerning the investigation into Craig's death. "They've picked up narcotics on the man's body, Sir. As you suggested, it looks as if Mr. Angelis had been using... cocaine... quite a sizable quantity... perhaps dealing."

Careful when making his statement earlier, Ken had led the colonel to believe that he was a deeply ethical and law-abiding citizen.

The picture he'd painted of Craig was slanderous.

"We'd been arguing about his deterioration at work, his absent-mindedness and so on. It already cost him his marriage. I put it to him that his career wasn't looking too rosy. Don't get me wrong, Colonel; he was a hell of a worker and well-liked, maybe a genius. That's precisely the problem, the *reason* it upset me to watch him toss his life away on drugs!" Ken had paused to worry at an itch near his eye with his index finger. "His wife knows nothing about this of course. The man was very secretive; tragic..."

He'd left the thought unsaid, looking down in the charged silence, pleased that the colonel and his aide were swallowing the story. He'd pretended to compose himself, looking slowly skyward, shaking his head hopelessly, tears welling in his eyes.

"I'm sorry, I get really pissed off with these idiots... some things you're supposed to grow out of."

"Of course, Sir," the officers had each sympathetically reassured him, acting as sounding boards for the man's grief.

"You know, Craig was worth more than this nonsense." Ken had laid it on thick, preparing fertile ground for escape routes if he ever needed them. "I kept this whole situation from his colleagues. That's *why* I asked him to my house to discuss it. I thought it would be better if the two of us could sit down, as friends, and thrash it out..."

Another theatrical pause had built up the empathy. "'You've got a child, Craig, a wife who loves you that you've driven away,' I told him."

As he spoke, Ken had acted out the bogus scene for the men, dropping carefully crafted neuro-linguistic actions into his pantomime to cement key ideas into the officers' minds.

"...And that's when he blew his stack, Colonel. I've never seen anything like it. I tried to stop him, but he was demented—he just took off."

Ken had carefully assumed open body language, leaning forward with his forearms on his knees and his palms open directly toward the senior, the colonel, in a picture of grief.

"Who knows a man's mind? Perhaps the pressure of becoming a father late in life. Could be coming from nothing and getting too much, too quickly, from me. I can't fathom it, Colonel."

As they'd moved to depart, while the lieutenant went to use the facilities, Ken took the moment to slip some advice to the colonel who had announced that he would personally break the news to the newly widowed Mrs. Angelis. "I don't think there's much point in revealing the drug angle to her... What good would it do?"

He'd assumed the colonel would convey the message to his underling.

The following message in his voicemail was from Catherine. "I'm really devastated for you, Ken. I know you were close to him. Hmmm. I hate situations like this—sorry, I really don't know what to say. I think I met him once... Well... very awkward; sorry all the same. Speak to you soon. Ciao, ciao."

Her Italian-style sign-off was a lovely touch. "Ciao, ciao," Ken repeated aloud, trying to imitate her voice.

Upon first hearing her voice, he had noticed a little stir in his loins. *No way!* he'd thought. *She's hot enough... but this is ridiculous.*

He laughed at himself, quickly trying to reject any possibility that there was also a lump in his throat. With concerted effort, he blocked the feeling.

The idea of actually feeling *emotion* for a woman terrified him. "Naagh... not me, mate!" He broke into song in the style of a young Cliff Richard at the dawn of pop music. "I'll be a bachelor boy, and that's the way I'll sta'ay'ay..."

He was still singing to himself in a jovial mood when the next message began to play with an ominous intensity that instantaneously truncated the melody and his happy demeanor.

The message began with an electric *click*, a popping sound that sounded to Ken like an international connection on a poor line, followed by a weird, dragging, static echo. Try as he might, he could not figure out what it was; it sounded deathly. Ken listened closer, switching from the handset to speaker and the sound filled his room in an eerie fog of intonation.

Something in the background made his hair stand on end.

Two seconds...three seconds of the driving, sonorous cacophony pierced through the veil, then suddenly, Craig's voice—tortured and stretched—cut crisply through. *"STOP!"* His voice was faint as a whisper, but charged with imposing authority. Abruptly, the line went dead.

Ken was appalled, staring agape at his handset.

A feeling of dread stretched out to every corner of the room, its unfamiliar sensation gripping him.

"Fuck!" he exclaimed aloud, not wanting to touch the handset as it lay where he'd set it, not sure what to do with it if he did.

How could this short message have shaken me to such a degree? His mind was somersaulting.

Gingerly he picked it up. The digital readout on the voicemail indicated that the incoming call had been logged at 16:36 that afternoon, a mere few hours ago.

Ken realized that at this exact time, he had been on the other line with David, and Craig's corpse should have been safely resting in its refrigerated drawer down at the mortuary, its slack vocal cords incapable of uttering another sound.

"It's some kind of mistake," he reassured himself confidently, preparing to replay the message again, intent on listening for any telltale transition in the message that might betray overdubbing.

Pop...the weird background activity... "STOP!" ...disconnection sound...pause...new message. "Hi Ken, Nancy here. It's five to five. Catherine's on for 10 a.m. tomorrow, I've confirmed it in an email to you. I hope you're okay and don't worry, everything's under control here. Bye." Disconnection sound...nothing.

Ken paused the replay. Nancy's message indicated 16:54, which was within a minute of her own time check. "How the hell did an old message from Craig end up in the middle of two current messages from today?" He was perplexed.

He skipped back and forth, running through the messages several more times. He maximized the volume to study the *clicks* and *pops* and other eerie sounds, but none of it made any sense at all.

Ken was no sound technician, yet what he was hearing seemed to gel and have a muddled pattern. Defeated in his attempt at trying to fathom it, he forwarded all three messages to his email, hoping something about their sequence might explain *why* they were improbably in this order. His IT department could take a look at it in the morning.

Exhausted, he made ready for bed, but try as he might he could not shrug off the mysterious dread that persisted and haunted him throughout the long, fitful, and exhausting hours until dawn.

Chapter 5

"Our Pentagon boy's stabilized, Ken. Looks like he'll pull through, but the press is sniffing around the hospital." Suspecting that Ken would be in the office early, second-in-charge, Henry Fowler, had been waiting for him to arrive since 7 a.m.

"He's conscious?" Ken was relieved; the extent of the man's recovery would dictate the depth of the military's investigation.

"Yep, but doing some strange babbling that nobody can make head nor tail of. Going on about demons and spooks... sounds rather like the *X-Files*... weird stuff. Oh yes, Leon says your name came up in his ranting. Your name... and Craig's."

Leon was the resident psychiatrist in LifeGames' employ—in charge of hypnosis.

A chill ran up Ken's spine, his mind immediately jumping to the recording on his handset and in his email.

Henry continued his rambling. "What seems odd to me is that the guy probably read about you in the press, but who knows *Craig's* name? Strange."

Ken was logging into the central server and didn't look up from his monitor, ignoring the speculation. "Any further clues about what put him in the hospital?" Ken thought it important to ask the question to steer the decoy away from the truth he alone knew.

"Nope, but we've still got the time dilation unit shut down. The good news is that the standard commercial side is going like hell."

'Commercial side' was company jargon for the ordinary, non-time-dilated virtual training procedure.

"Yesterday, I spent three hours on the blower to Lufthansa; they're expanding the crew analysis to executive management as a quarterly review! We're prepping modules to run executives through for dealing with mid-air disasters, missing planes and major collisions; told you they'd bite. With them in the bag, we'll pull all the others in. They've got an image to uphold *and* the right attitude toward technology."

Ken needed to concentrate as he navigated through the network into Craig's computer; Henry's babbling was distracting and irritating, and he tried to shut it out, giving no encouragement or feedback.

But Henry was oblivious to being ignored, and steamed on in a buoyant mood. He'd intensely disliked Craig and had not shed a tear. Today was just another workday.

Ken had spy software running on every computer used by executive staff; the software took a screen image every thirty seconds, and logged every keystroke made.

On Craig's desktop, he was running a search for a .wav file, a sound file; searching for any recording that might contain a sample of Craig's voice. Only the occasional word from Henry's rambling penetrated his mind.

Ken hated it when Henry tried to imitate his personal style of slick talk, which he was now doing. Henry was a suit, a nerd; he should stay within his own grey little personality.

Despite Ken's lack of enthusiasm, Henry was still happily prattling on about Lufthansa. "I told Jimmy to steer us their way. Once they've signed on, it'll be a flood. We won't be able to keep up."

He kept carping, and Ken kept ignoring his pauses begging for endorsement.

"...My money remains on Cathay or Emirates being next in line. I told Jimmy to forget the American airlines, forget British; their nose is going to be out of joint if the Germans do it before them. They'll only come into the program once they think that a dignified period of time has passed."

Ken accidently grunted on impulse, and quickly regretted encouraging the fool.

"Virgin may be the problem. If Branson sees that the training works, he'll probably try to copy our systems and go into competition before you know it!"

Ken was sick of it and needed to derail Henry before his anger popped, so he cut him short. "You ready for our ten o'clock?" It was clear that Henry was a frustrated marketer who couldn't wait to meddle in Jimmy Castle's marketing department.

Using any excuse that he could come up with, Henry was in on Jimmy's meetings, chipping in with his penny's worth of opinion. Jimmy hated the interference, but he had admitted that Henry possessed an instinct to spot a profitable market opportunity.

"I wouldn't miss it for the world," Henry beamed. There was relish in his eyes.

"Jimmy will be delighted," Ken said, just as Nancy stuck her head around the door. Her eyes were ringed dark with insomnia and puffy from crying.

"Morning," she said in a manufactured perky voice; she was not one to ever impose her sadness on others.

"Morning Nance, how're you doing?" Ken asked out of conformity.

"Bearing up," she assured, her mouth forming a forced smile.

"I received your email and voicemail last night, thanks. By the way, what time did you leave the message?"

"Just before five—didn't I give the time? I usually do."

"Yes, sorry... of course you did. I forgot." Ken smiled and then added, "What time did the general wake up?"

Nancy shrugged, but Henry answered, "Around eight last night. Leon called it through, but under the circumstances I suggested we not bother you."

"I'd like to have known... but thanks."

The strange chain of coincidences seemed to be escalating. Craig dying in the small hours, his voice appearing in a voicemail later in the afternoon, then the general finally waking and ranting about Ken and Craig. It was a silly correlation, but one Ken couldn't avoid noticing.

"How many dictation recordings of Craig do you have, Nance?" Ken asked.

Craig was a stranger to the keyboard and Nancy transcribed his dictations.

"Shew," Nancy blew through pursed lips and rolled her eyes. "Hundreds on my laptop. You after anything in particular?"

"Not really, just a voice sample. Silly... unlike me, but... I dunno... maybe closure? Bit of a history with him you know; guess I want to just hear his voice once more." He played the sensitive card masterfully as Nancy and Henry both nodded thoughtfully.

"I've got a ton—I'll email something over."

"Please."

Nancy disappeared to do his bidding.

"The police think that it could have been drugs, Ken; Craig's death," Henry solemnly ventured.

Ken was staggered by Henry's express knowledge of the incident. "Where the hell did you get that, Henry?!" Ken tried, too late, to obscure the alarm in his voice, but it rang through.

"Sorry Ken, I got sidetracked with Lufthansa, I was going to talk to you about it. An officer was here yesterday going through Craig's personals; he had a search warrant. Did you know they found a large quantity of cocaine in Craig's car?"

Ken feigned disinterest and nodded minor acknowledgement, focusing his attention back on the pile of papers cluttering his desk. In truth, he listened intently, tuned to every word and intonation Henry uttered, trying to get a measure of how much the man knew or was likely to figure out.

"Drug takers right here, under our nose. I never liked the guy—told you as much."

Ken formulated a response. He rose and moved to shut the door.

"I've known about his problem for a while, Henry," he began to explain. "Hadn't you noticed how absent-minded Craig had become?" As Ken spoke, he was nodding his head just perceptibly, lightly drumming his fingernails on the desk like a miniature horse galloping, affirming his lie, welding it into Henry's mind.

Henry began to nod in time. "You know, now that you mention it... but drugs? I thought maybe he was ticked in the head."

"I tried to keep it under wraps, Henry. It wouldn't have done team morale any good," Ken asserted. "That's *why* I had him round to my place last night... gave him an ultimatum to quit the drugs or resign his position."

"I know, the officer told me," Henry chirped triumphantly.

Again, Henry's insight stumped Ken, and a slight panic that he had misjudged the colonel began to grow.

"Was it the colonel or the lieutenant?" Ken quizzed. The answer would seal the fate and career prospects for the man who had broken his unspoken request to withhold these confidential matters from the office.

"Only a lieutenant came here; he said his boss had gone to break the news to Craig's wife... or widow, I should say."

I'll deal with him... Ken made a mental note. "Okay. Well, it's true; there's no point in stoking the rumors and bringing the man down, so just keep it to yourself. The whole situation blew up at my place; Craig went crazy when he realized that I knew about his addiction. He panicked, got out of control; I've never seen anything like it—he laid a strip of rubber the length of my driveway. God only knows how they'll clean it up, and he also destroyed my entrance way."

"His wife know about it?" Henry asked.

"I doubt it. I think that's what sent him off the deep end; when I brought up her name, he thought I was threatening to reveal...."

Nancy knocked.

"Come in," Ken called.

She stuck her head around the door, hesitating.

"Come on in Nance, we're not hiding from you."

"I mailed you four recordings."

It was quite unlike Ken to be sentimental, but she guessed that every man had a right to a change of heart in the face of tragedy. More curious was his interest into the specific times that different events had occurred; her call and the general waking. She knew him well and this was out of character. He was trying to cover something up.

"I think we all need to get on with other things," he stated, as if he'd read her mind trying to gauge his. His voice was suddenly brittle.

Both Henry and Nancy felt the tide of Ken's mood swing and Henry excused himself to go about his daily tasks.

"Coffee?" Nancy extended an olive branch.

"Please... and get Stuart Reese from IT up to see me without delay. When I'm done with him, I want to see Anton. I've gotta see both of them before ten; thanks love." Ken was fond of Nancy and her peace offering had instantly doused his irritation.

Once he was alone, Ken listened again to the emailed voicemail of the "Stop!" recording. Then he immediately listened to one of the four recordings of Craig's voice that Nancy had sent to him.

He re-listened to the extracts until Stuart's timid knock sounded at his door. "Come on in, shut the door. Coffee?" Ken smiled genially at the youth.

"No thanks, Mr. Torrington." Stuart was nervous and expecting the worst with all manner of persecutions flooding through his mind. *Could it be the problem with the general, or something with Mr. Angelis?*

Stuart was a sound engineer, and his specialty was looking after all audio aspects of the commercial side.

A summons to the executive suite was rare and the only time he'd ever spoken directly with Mr. Torrington had been at his sound-mixing desk when visitors needed to be impressed. Ken would generally ask him technical facts and other specifics regarding whatever he was been doing at that moment in the sound-mixing process; all fairly canned for the visitors' benefit.

"Are you sure you won't have a cup? I'm having." Ken couldn't have been friendlier.

"Ok," Stuart relented with a stutter. He didn't drink coffee. "I mean, yes please, Sir."

Ken saw his apprehension. "Don't worry Stuart, there's no problem. I've got a favor to ask of you."

Stuart relaxed slightly.

"Milk? Sugar?" Ken asked warmly.

"Two, please." Gingerly, the lad regained his nerve. "A... a little milk too please."

Ken dabbed at the intercom's Talk button, "Another coffee for me please, Nance. One for Stuart, two sugars, milk." He released the button without waiting for confirmation, shutting off the transmission as he continued to address Stuart in a lowered tone. "You know much about voice fingerprinting, Stuart?"

"I.... I'm sorry, Mr. Torrington?"

"It's a term I've heard, voice fingerprinting. Isn't that what you call it when you match a voice to a specimen to confirm identity?"

"Sorry, Mr. Torrington. That's right, acoustic fingerprinting. I mean, your term is correct; I misheard...heard you, that's all."

"Have we got the equipment to do that?" Ken asked. He'd never quite come to terms with the precise applications of all the gadgets within the guts of his own facility.

"Sure, Sir, we've got great stuff—the latest!" Within the territory of his beloved skill, Stuart's personality blossomed to life; his face was an ear-to-ear smile.

"Could you check something out for me?"

"Anything, Sir."

"You've heard about the tragedy with Mr. Angelis?"

"Yes, Sir." Stuart averted his eyes. "I heard he was a very good man. I'm sorry."

Ken saw that it was genuine grief and it provided him with an opportunity to capitalize on it.

"Stuart, I'm trying to help the police with their investigation and I thought that our lab might be more up to date than theirs. Craig was a great man and a close friend to me. Our company is going to miss him and I intend to do all that I can to help get to the bottom of the tragedy."

Stuart was gazing at Ken, almost hypnotized by Ken's sham sincerity. He too had fallen in line with the rhythm of Ken's nodding head and imperceptibly drumming fingers.

"The police have asked for absolute confidentiality on the matter and I gave them my word that they would have it. Now, I want you to promise me that no one else but you and I will know about this—not even inside the company. Understand?"

Stuart almost did himself damage in his eagerness to ratify the promise.

"Good," Ken responded, satisfied. "Take a look here. These four recordings *definitely* contain Mr. Angelis' voice. This other recording is from someone's voicemail and it sounds a bit like Mr. Angelis saying 'stop'. Think it's enough to go on?"

"Yes, Sir! Any word, in any language is enough… even humming and I could get a match. I can download an app with a modular analyzer that magnifies… that amplifies… the target sound. We can tease it from any background and eliminate auxiliary static through coaxial logic in a quadratic array of hyper-contained modular fragments that…"

Ken held up his hand to halt Stuart before he could really get going on his pet subject. "As long as we can get an accurate identification, that's all the police need."

He cut it short as Nancy arrived with the coffee and shared her finest maternal smile with Stuart.

Ken waited for her to leave before continuing.

"There's something else in the background, something that sounds to me like interference; the police want to know if it's a clue to location. See if you can make sense of it. They also suggested that you may want to see the sequence of the messages. I didn't know if it would be preserved, but I forwarded the voicemails either side of this target recording."

It struck Ken that he'd said "forwarded", and the contents of the message would connect the messages directly back to him. In an instant, he decided that the kid was too terrified of him to ever breathe a word about it, but he emphasized his earlier request again, to be sure.

"Now, remember… it's very confidential; I can't disclose why. But the cops are not certain that it's a direct sequence, as it seems that someone might have fiddled with it and replayed an earlier recording as a prank. Can you check for any super-imposing or editing? Anything."

Stuart was pretending to sip at the coffee. "When do you need the details, Sir?"

"As soon as possible, Stuart. I want you to make it a priority, and if Mr. Fowler or anyone else inquires, you tell him to talk to me. Now, I'm sorry, but I've got another meeting lined up."

Stuart left the office at a canter.

Five minutes later, the software coder, Anton Lim, arrived. Ken was on the phone but he held his hand over the mouthpiece and greeted him. "Morning, Anton. I'll be thirty seconds—arrange a coffee for me."

Anton disappeared out the door and moments later, Ken heard Nancy exclaim. She was a health nut and Ken knew he'd soon be having his ear chewed for his caffeine intake.

When Anton returned, Ken was done with his call.

"Close the door would you," Ken asked, still seated.

"Sorry to hear about Craig, Ken. I heard that it happened over at your place." Anton had been indifferent to Craig as a person yet Ken reckoned that his neutrality would probably have turned to aversion if they'd had more interaction with one another.

"Yeah, a great shame... but life's a sexually transmitted disease, you see—curable only by death." Ken shrugged.

"I suppose you want to know about the progress...? The cyber-sex development," Anton asked.

His voice had a habit of carrying and, as if hushing a child, Ken put his finger to his lips.

"Shhh... This can't get out, Anton. My connection's a freak. We don't want to piss him off with a leak."

"Shit... Sorry. I'm always too loud," Anton apologized in a whisper.

"Seriously, Anton. I told you, he's Saudi royalty—it's a favor for a favor. I can't even talk directly to him about it; he hinted, I suggested it could be done. It's a very delicate arrangement, but if we get it right, there's a whole lot of doors that will open. Understand?"

"Got it."

Nancy entered and set the tray down. She pointed at the coffee and wagged a cheeky finger at Ken.

"Yes, mom... sorry mom."

"Yah!" was her only matronly response.

After the door closed, Ken went on.

"The guy's got a kink; he wants something exotic. Think you can come up with something spectacular?"

"Something vintage maybe? Has he got any interests?"

"He's mad about the Roman Empire, if that's hint enough."

"It's done..."

"Just reiterating—it's not something I want Rigor Mortis sniffing around about."

Rigor Mortis was a nickname Ken and Anton had coined for Max Schneider, Anton's immediate superior and Vice President of Research.

Neither of the two men liked Max's painfully serious and dull outlook on life. He was dead but refused to lie down.

Anton grinned. "He won't know a thing."

"Treat it as priority, Anton, and if Rigor Mortis *does* get wind of it, tell him to come talk to me. That'll shut him up!"

Max wouldn't dream of crossing Ken as he knew Ken wanted him out of the company.

But, as one of the foremost authorities in the world on virtual reality programming, he was indispensable. Since LifeGames Corporation was right at the cutting edge of virtual reality technology, neither man could do without the other; yet, Ken still wielded the heavier and sharper sword by far.

"Sorry Ken, I haven't had a chance to mention it. Yesterday, I dug around a bit on the dark web and scratched up some useful code; it's AI enabled. I can deconstruct and knit it into something useful."

"Very good; excellent thinking." Anton's news brought the prospects for Ken's coming thrill with Catherine closer to reality by a huge margin.

"Let me make a run first before the plaudits," Anton cautioned.

"How long you reckon?" Ken wanted a number to focus on.

"Depends. These things never go smoothly."

"A week? A month... six months?"

The fresh scent of the chase was making Ken giddy and reckless, so he moderated his enthusiasm. "Sorry, I'm ahead of myself, I just want to impress the guy. Make it happen as fast as you can, Anton. If I can help you in any way... with a little cash boost... tell me how."

The intercom beeped announcing a message and Ken held up his hand for silence before pressing the On button, "Yes?"

"Stuart Reese in audio, Ken. He says that he's 'got a match'?" Nancy's voice was thick with puzzlement.

"Thanks, Nance." Ken immediately rose and moved toward the door.

Anton mirrored him.

"Keep me up to date," Ken instructed, reaching for the door handle.

Anton nodded, "Sure. Thanks for the coffee."

Ken drew pinched fingers across his own lips as if he were closing a zipper. Anton nodded again in acknowledgment.

Stuart's small empire was a world of humming servers and colorful, dancing monitor graphs. Ken watched the boy's fingers fluttering instructions into a keyboard, and in response, a ream of unintelligible data scrolled onto one of the screens. Stuart had been so thoroughly entranced by the data that he hadn't heard Ken entering the room. The click of the latch closing behind him made the youth leap to his feet. "Sorry Sir, I... I didn't hear you come in."

"Didn't mean to startle you, son." Ken gladly assumed the role of master to slave; a relationship Stuart was keen to amplify. "You've found something?"

"Sure, Sir. A bunch of things!"

Ken liked the boy's enthusiasm and noted how around his own subject, Stuart was a giant of self-assured maturity.

"I'll cover what I'm sure of first," Stuart explained as he busied himself in a blur of activity, punching keys and clicking his mouse. "The sequence is affirmative; in other words, there's *no way* that it's a collage or any other kind of superimposition. The cut-on to cut-off pulse of the voicemail was crisp with no shadowing or partial obscuring. Secondly, the voice is without question a perfect match. In the dictated recording, the subject says the word "stop" twice. I lifted each instance off into a separate file."

Stuart leaned across in front of Ken to dart a string of commands into another keyboard, but when Ken stepped backwards to allow him better access, Stuart suddenly leapt to his feet.

"S... So... sorry Mr. Torrington Sir! I lost myself in the data. Won't you please sit down?"

"Relax, Stuart," Ken soothed, as he guided a chair up next to him. "You carry on and don't mind me here."

"Thanks, Sir. Errr... where was I? Yes! The graph that you see on screen A." He pointed to a screen stack with its uppermost unit marked by a plaque labeled 'A'.

"That's the word 'stop' frozen in graphic animation. I lifted it off of the dictated recording." He tapped the appropriate recording on the desk before him. "Screen B, is 'stop' lifted from your voice recording."

Ken felt an icy chill shoot through his veins; Stuart had clearly said "your recording". He definitely knew it was from Ken's phone. But the boy was under obligation to maintain the strictest secrecy, so Ken forced himself to relax.

All the while, Stuart was excitedly continuing on about his findings, "...from the dictated recording."

Ken filled in the spaces he'd missed from Stuart's explanation while his mind had leapt in diversion. Screen C represented the second dictated 'stop' from Nancy's recordings.

"Even at a glimpse, you can see that they're identical. The small inclusions are noise or static from outside interference."

Stuart tapped a few keys and the screens re-scrolled in perfect synchronization with one another, making them look even more identical.

"I've applied a noise reduction filter, it's something like the Dolby option on your home stereo—eliminates the ambient…"

He frantically began to key away again, talking as he did so.

"I'm giving you a quick background, Sir, but I've already run a printout of all the screens and the information is backed up onto disk for the police. I can go around and explain my work to whoever is dealing with the case."

"Thanks Stuart, but that won't be necessary." Ken patted him on the back, slowly relaxing as Stuart enthusiastically reiterated that he knew it was a sensitive issue.

Then suddenly, speakers began to croak, repeating the stretched-out sound of a bullfrog at an exaggeratedly slow speed. The sound was chilling.

Stuart noticed Ken's fright and quickly apologized about the sound of the rendition.

"Sorry, Sir. I should have warned you. This is the modular analyzer that I mentioned earlier in your office. I've slowed the recording five-fold to get a visual on the three files."

He pointed at the monitor stack where a ballet of graphs was snaking in perfect synchronization, one above the other. When the surreal croak ended, Stuart paused the images. "As close of a match as I've ever seen, Sir."

"It's definitely the same person?"

"Definitely. Yes, Sir."

"What about the background sounds?" Ken was feeling jumpy.

"I'm afraid that I don't have a firm answer. That's why I left it till last. It's like nothing that I've ever heard before." Ken thought that he could see Stuart's forearm hair standing up. "That first *pop*, which you mentioned, Sir. It's definitely part of the message."

"In other words, you're saying that it must have occurred *after* connection had been made?" Ken squinted, trying to keep up with the technical details.

"Exactly, Sir! The strange thing is that it is ninety-nine percent the result of a static electrical arc—a short-circuit—yet, an energy release of that magnitude should have knocked out the entire circuitry! The only way that it wouldn't have done that is if the static burst had occurred before the connection and *we know that it hadn't.* Sorry Sir, this must all sound rather confusing, but technically it makes sense."

Ken was massaging his head, trying to make sense of what he was hearing. "How would you sum it all up, Stuart?"

"I don't know, Mr. Torrington. It's only a small detail but it definitely falls outside of any laws of physics and even quantum fluctuations within electronics that I'm aware of."

"And the rest? The background?"

"I've identified three separate sources; at least that's what it seems to be. Listen for yourself, Sir. I'll first run through them in real time. The sound will be blended and exactly the way you heard it before, but now you'll notice that I've taken away possible ambient *hiss.* The result should be a lot crisper."

Stuart hit the Enter key.

The sound was quadraphonic and underpinned by a sub-woofer. Pure as gently stroked crystal glass rim, it made Ken cringe with an army of spiders running up his spine—the most powerful sensation of trepidation he'd ever felt.

And alongside this haunting channel of sound, Craig's voice spliced through it, ethereal and at *one* with the underlying reverberations. It was an aurora for the ears—an enveloping sound advancing from all directions, enmeshed into a single overwhelming discordance of dread. The voice was not projected over the sound, nor the sound over the voice. The *dragging, ticking* and *droning* possessed a timeless quality. There was no comprehending the strange effects; they appeared to emit from a sole source.

A loud rapping on the door sent the two men leaping and their hearts jolted with three beats in one, and the empty hollow of a skip. It was Henry, busy with his morning rounds.

"Ken... what brings you here?"

Henry's cheerful demeanor suddenly infuriated Ken.

"We're busy with a very-private-matter! Would you mind closing the door," he snapped irritably, immediately turning his back on Henry to speak to Stuart. "Run it again Stuart."

The abrupt confrontation had terrified Stuart out of his wits and without looking at either of his superiors, he immediately jumped to the task.

"I am, all right—damned sorry," Henry grumbled with affront, closing the door from outside.

"Sorry about that Stuart, he spooked me, I overreacted," Ken apologized.

Equally startled, Stuart tried to formulate a response but choked on it.

The prevailing mood of alarm that had built up with the swirling sounds had fled from the room with Henry's intrusion, leaving a more fertile vacuum of emotion for objectivity.

Ken studied the sound graph's peaks and valleys frozen alongside a time scale. The total sequence had lasted a shade under seven seconds.

Stuart had regained his nerve enough to talk. "This is the base sound, the one that's most evident." He activated the recording.

It had the quality of a low and deep throb not unlike a very large diesel engine, a ship's engine, idling; its resonance had a timbre so deep it could be felt more than heard.

Divorced from interference sounds, it was unmistakably the dominant tone. When it was finished, Ken studied the screen. Each pulse length was shown to be 0.96 of a second, with a 0.72 second pause interval.

"Nothing too significant there," Ken said but didn't feel, his response rational in spite of the hairs at the nape of his neck telling a very different tale. Standing stiffly to attention, they echoed a deep superstitious chill that throbbed with caution, chiming to the very hub of his soul.

Stuart concurred with Ken's opinion, "This is the second sound, Sir."

It had an accelerating *tick-tock* characteristic of a mechanical clock, conveying movement and urgency.

Or perhaps insanity? Ken thought, as the crisp and deliberate notes stirred another cocktail of sickening familiarity within him, the origins of which eluded him. "No clues?" he probed Stuart for a hint to the solution.

"None, Sir. Sorry. The third's the strangest of them all."

Stuart was right; it was a high-pitched garble of sound, faint, only a whisper that terminated quicker than the other two sounds did. That fact was plain to see on the graphical display. Screen A displayed the *throb* sound. Screen B displayed the *tick-tock*. And screen C displayed the *pitch*.

Ken took a closer look. The *pitch* was shorter than the other two by precisely 0.7 seconds. "Any ideas?" Ken was pointing from one screen to the other, indicating the missing time.

"I saw it too, Sir. But I wasn't sure if it mattered. I was trying to figure it."

"Where does Mr. Angelis' voice fit into all of this?" Ken asked, almost rhetorically.

"I edited it out."

"Can you put it back in?" Ken probed.

"Easily," Stuart went straight to the task. At that moment, the phone began to ring and without breaking stride on the keyboard, Stuart scooped the handset up and wedged it between his ear and shoulder. "Audio... Yes... Yes, Miss Armstrong, he's right here with me," he handed it over. "For you, Sir."

"Thanks." Ken took the hand piece. "Hello, what's up Nance? Okay… hmmm, alright... God, I didn't realize the time already. Tell them to start without me. I'm here if you need me," he replaced the receiver.

"Would you like to carry on later, Sir?" Stuart inquired.

"Not a chance of it! We're on it, let's run it to ground."

Stuart was equally motivated to ferret out the elusive key to the mystery. "Two more ticks and I'll have it, Sir... Hang on... here it comes... okay," he hit the Enter key.

The high pitch sound echoed around the room again, but instead of stopping short, Craig's voice was neatly tagged on to its tail. The graph showed just shy of seven seconds—precisely 6.6 seconds.

"Gotcha," Ken punched his hand with his other fist in triumph, then looked perplexed. "But, what does it mean?"

Stuart shook his head. "It's somehow familiar, Sir. An old style of transmission... Shortwave?"

"No. It's not electronic sounding..." Ken was massaging his head, the detective work becoming a thrill. "Water? Maybe boiling water... a burbling stream?"

"I doubt it," Stuart spoke, absentmindedly nibbling his nails like the teenager he was. "Wrong waveform, wrong slope, the wavelengths are too abrupt."

The sound was familiar yet foreign.

"Wait a minute." A notion flashed through Ken's mind. "Can you slow the sequence?"

Once suggested, it was an obvious choice. "I'll slow it five-fold."

Moments later, the porridge of sound began. Slowed, it had morphed into a jumble of clipping sounds resembling swallowing or chewing. It possessed rhythm and pace, with a human quality. "Another language? It sounds like someone speaking underwater," Ken mused aloud.

Stuart shrugged, wracked by confusion.

They ran the sound through several more times before there was another knock at the studio door. It was Catherine and she was breathless. "Morning Ken, Nancy showed me down. I've briefed them and we're on a break. I'm about to run the commercials. I know you wanted to be in on it...?"

"Hi, Cath. Oh, this is Stuart Reese, our audio tech. We've had a hitch with a project I must work through, I'll be up in a moment."

Ken had moved across the room to her, instinctively blocking her view of the graphs on the monitors, ready to usher her out of the room if Stuart ran the audio again. Something within him insisting that she not hear a bar of it. Then he re-thought this irrational reaction and decided her opinion would be helpful.

"I told Nancy that you should go on without me," he re-affirmed, his voice stiff.

"She told me, but I knew that you'd invested a whole day for a preview and *really* wanted to be in on it when we revealed to the team, so I thought I'd better be double sure."

His jealously protective demeanor drove her to retreat through the doorway, but his attitude suddenly changed and he stopped her short.

"Just a moment, Cath. Give this a listen, it'll only take a second... Run it, Stuart," Ken instructed.

As the sound of the chewing obscurity began, Catherine cocked her head over to one side like an inquisitive dog. Something in it resonated with her at an emotional level. With each passing second, she craned her neck with ever more puzzlement, her forehead creasing into a scowl.

When the sequence ended, Ken put their best guess to her, "Human?"

"I think so," she remarked, adding, "sounds like it's backwards though?"

"That's it!" the two men sung in chorus. "Thanks, Cath!" Ken was steering her out the door. "You run along, girl. I'll be up in a moment."

Catherine stood for a moment in bewilderment, looking at the door closed in her face.

It took Stuart two keystrokes to invert the garble and the resulting sound was human all right, a yawningly slow human drone. A deformed inflection. The labored rendition of a weary old man intoning, "Our Father, who art in Heaven. Hallowed be thy Name..."

Euphoric at cracking the riddle, Stuart seemed untouched by the content. He paused the recording. "Damn!" he said excitedly, "Still too slow!"

The smile of triumph on Ken's face had melted into an ashen, blank gaze, plucked from his spot as master of his empire and dumped into the echoing halls of his Catholic upbringing.

Stuart saw the terror. "Are you all right, Sir?"

Ken didn't reply, but absently waved Stuart back to the task at hand.

"Our Father, who art in Heaven..." Craig's familiar voice began to recite, the tone a nightmare of foreboding, cascading from the speakers on all sides.

Something slid through Ken's gut—the haunting terrors preached into him since he was just knee-high now usurped his adult confidence.

Stuart was oblivious to the childhood stirrings and improbability of the message's impossible timing, recorded as it was on Ken's phone hours after the man should've been cold in a fridge. But he saw the naked terror in his master's gaunt face.

"Do you want me to audio finger-print it, Mr. Torrington?"

"Don't bother." Ken had stood up and started heading for the door. He was in a stupor. A look of glazed bewilderment and colliding thoughts overwhelming his expression. "It's him, I know his voice."

On the threshold, Ken stopped and turned back to face Stuart. He looked stooped, withering under the burden of shock and horror, but he found his voice of authority and instructed Stuart to "Send a report, up to my office".

He went out the door, without looking back.

Back in his office, Ken locked the door and set a large mug of coffee down on a low table before slumping into a sofa.

After tapping a quantity of white powder from a vial onto the tabletop, he cut it into several lines with his Black Card.

"This is bullshit." He shook his head as he worked. "There's a logical solution..."

He felt aggressive, cornered—frightened and stalked. His fists clenched until the nails bit into his palms. A lather of emotions had put him on long-forgotten shaky ground where Jesuit priests in long, black cassocks with leather lashes hanging from their belted rope cincture would stalk the cold, drafty corridors of his school.

He shook his head to clear the distant memory of it and checked his watch.

"Four past eleven. I'll go in at eleven twenty," he decided out loud. With his feet slung up onto the table, he shut his eyes and began to file all of the events into a logical perspective.

At precisely 11:20 a.m., Ken swung the board room's door open and strode in. The gathering within was a full house of hushed suits hunched in eager digestion of the screen's unfolding visual feasts.

Catherine stopped the image with the pause button and a sea of faces swiveled around as one to stare at Ken. "Morning," he greeted in a voice full of manufactured cheerfulness.

"Morning," the chorus replied.

"Forgive... urgent issues needed attention." He smiled at Catherine. "Continue."

He slid into his vacant seat as the image on screen burst into life then jumped to the start of the sequence so it could unfold for Ken's benefit.

"Our Father who art in Heaven..." Craig's voice crept back.

Chapter 6

Midday saw the review break for lunch. The afternoon session had been scheduled for analysis and comments.

Catherine pulled Ken to one side; by now, she felt familiar enough to be direct, "What's up, Ken? You're really not looking well."

"Nothing Cath, just pressure."

He'd almost fully recovered from the morning's emotional rollercoaster ride and had mostly shut out the repetitive voice.

Ken had slipped out of the review before the break to phone Alex King.

Alex was a private investigator to whom Ken paid a retainer that ensured he would always be at Ken's beck and call. In addition, Ken had always made a point of including Alex when sharing the spoils from his questionable deals. He believed that by mutually linking their fates, Alex was married into a vested interest if and when trouble brewed.

"Alex... it's Ken." He'd hit Alex's voicemail so he kept the brief fairly vague. "There's an issue in Colombia, scouting that needs doing. You can collect details from Jo. I scribbled a note detailing what I need. Sorry it's on such short notice, but it's mighty urgent."

Jo oversaw the security team at LifeGames HQ; her office was at the main entrance. Ken always utilized her whenever he needed confidentiality. She was ex-military with high clearance and low curiosity.

The brief to Alex was simple. Establish contact with the laboratory but maintain anonymity; pose as a businessman, review their capabilities for reverse engineering and duplication of patented pharmaceuticals, and gauge their willingness to and price for working anonymously. Left unstated was that the lab would be re-engineering the time dilation drug.

Catherine was still chitchatting with Ken when Anton breezed over bearing a smirk and good news. "The code seems good." He flashed a toothy grin. "I'm burning with curiosity so I'll pull an all-nighter to check it out. Care to sit in and see if it works?"

"No, but thanks anyway Anton, I can only get in the way."

After Anton's news, Catherine noticed a dramatic shift in Ken's mood. In her mind, she mulled the possibilities, *Code? They're like little boys with a secret.*

"What's that about?" she asked, as Anton moved on.

Ken's eyes twinkled. "You'll see, sunshine."

"Even more interesting," she commented. She was eaten up with curiosity.

Ken just grinned.

"At least it's cheered you up."

At that moment, Nancy entered, scanning the room. She spotted Ken amongst the crowd and briskly made her way over. Standing out of earshot of others, she beckoned him over.

"The hospital called. The general, Roger Daly; he's stabilized. But there are... *complications.* Leon said it could be serious; psychiatric anomalies, he said."

"Any details?"

Ken was gauging Leon's degree of discretion in the matter—whether or not he was disclosing privileged information. Nancy was wise to this. Even if he had, she wouldn't betray him.

"Not really, all I do know is that he's under observation and has extreme symptoms of schizophrenia. He thinks that he's some kind of priest," Nancy shrugged. "They've just appointed a new specialist, a psychiatrist, to look into it. I took down the doctor's name and put it on your desk; not sure if you want me to involve Leon?"

"Thanks, Nance, not to worry—I'll review the situation and brief Leon. I'll be up in a second." Ken returned to where Catherine was standing. "Just the ups and downs of business," he sighed, not wanting to kindle any more curiosity in her than was already evident by her expression.

Catherine checked her watch. "Time to get on with it."

"Don't wait for me Cath, I've gotta make a quick call, then I'll be right back."

Back at his desk, Ken had the phone to his ear. "Doctor Rupert, please."

A moment later, "Rupert speaking." The doctor's voice bore a beautifully modulated and cultured Etonian accent.

"Doctor Rupert, Ken Torrington; LifeGames Corporation."

"Ahh yes, Mr. Torrington, I'm honored. What can I do for you, Sir?"

"Please... call me Ken." Ken was not fond of titles, particularly once he'd been out-ranked by academia.

"Thank you, do call me Andrew. The Daly case no doubt?"

"That's right. My PA mentioned that he's surfaced, but is suffering a trauma? Schizophrenia, I believe?"

"Schizophrenic-like, yes. That's not a diagnosis, just the closest bead we have on it for the moment. General Daly is having rather a problem adjusting to reality."

The doctor's tone brimmed with the British penchant for understatement.

"I confess, it's perhaps the worst case that I've ever seen. The damnedest thing is that his file presents a perfect psychological profile. We don't understand how this could have occurred. The man's seen action in every corner of the globe and been through some real hellholes... a seasoned veteran."

"I believe he thinks he's a priest of some kind?" Ken queried, the dark ruminations from the sound room and flashbacks to cold corridors once more threatening from the shadows of his mind.

"Convinced of it, sir. The man has no inkling of reality and doesn't respond to his own name. Suddenly—and this is most vexing—ranting and raving, speaking fluent Latin. There is nothing about fluency in Latin recorded in his file."

"Very peculiar! Would you mind if I come down and see the situation for myself?"

"Of course. That won't be a problem, they'll track me down if you ask for me by name at reception. I'm here until eight tonight."

They said their good-byes and signed off.

A plethora of motives urged Ken to get down to the hospital as soon as possible; his eagerness to read the military's mood for investigating the cause of the incident, and the strange new coincidence of Latin and priests popping up yet again. *This was, of course, a coincidence,* he thought, *a strangely unsettling one.* These things begged him to investigate.

The shifting terrain of his day meant that Ken had lost all interest in sifting through the details of Catherine's review. It was a missed opportunity, but there would be others.

Instead, he spent the following hour sorting through various dilemmas that required his urgent attention. Only then did he return to the board room to see how the review was progressing.

The review was winding up and Henry—who had quit sulking about the earlier affront down in the sound room—summarized the findings for Ken in a whisper behind his hand.

The executive staff had come to pretty much the same conclusion as Ken had.

"I led a good team," Ken praised them and himself to Henry in one succinct opinion.

After the adjournment, Ken made his way over to Leon Goldstein, Head of Psychology and chief officer in charge of the hypnotism sequences.

"What did you think of the review, Leon?"

"Excellent, excellent! We've got a winning team in Kaplan. Brilliant work, Ken-o, just *bbbbbrrilliant!*"

During the creation phase of the campaign, Leon had been invaluable as an in-house consultant. His background in psychology had provided a vast depth and clarity for examining the machinery of a consumer's mind.

"There's an interesting situation that's developed with General Daly, our wayward subject in the hospital."

Leon's eyes popped wide open with interest. It was usual for him to appear nutty, but even the slightest surprise could make him look utterly insane. "Ooh..." His mouth formed a perfect circle.

"I'm going down to see for myself, care to join me?" Ken invited.

"Sure, sure. It's my department all right. Must do, *must* do." He always tended to repeat himself when his mind was running too fast. Indeed, with age, he'd allowed creeping idiosyncrasies to have their way with him.

"I have to go over a few things here and I don't know how long I'll be," Ken explained. "We'd better go separately. I'll see you there around five, is that all right?"

"Sure. Definitely," Leon bubbled away.

Chapter 7

"Calling Doctor Rupert, Doctor Rupert to reception please."

The military nurse snapped the public-address system off. "Doctor Rupert will be here in a moment, please take a seat." She indicated for Ken to proceed through to the adjoining waiting room where he saw Leon sitting, reading a magazine.

"Thanks."

The nurse smiled, unable to resist his charm.

"Leon... Ahead of time as always."

"Ahh.. Ken-o, isn't it strange how somebody always disturbs you as you reach the juicy bits in a waiting room magazine?"

"Shall I sit over there?" Ken pointed to the far side of the room.

"No, no. Definitely, no!" he answered, peering over the top of his glasses at Ken. Leon patted the seat beside himself. "What's Gerald's problem then?"

"Gerald?" Ken was stumped. "Gerald who?"

"Yes, Gerald... the one you wanted me to visit here." Leon removed his glasses and twirled them by one arm as he spoke, a puzzled look on his face.

"Gerald...? No Leon, not *Gerald*. General. The general with the issue... *Daly*... General Daly. You don't remember the *situation* we had with him; the *meltdown*?" Ken scowled in frustration.

Leon was a brilliant psychiatrist with a string of books on hypnosis to his credit and a mind like a sieve.

"Golly... General Daly... quite right, Ken-o! How did I get that muddled?" He shook his head and replaced his glasses.

Ken spotted a tall, regal gentleman marching up to reception. The nurse pointed toward Ken and Leon, and Ken immediately rose to his feet.

"Andrew?" Ken inquired of the approaching man.

"Yes, you must be Ken?"

They both extended hands to shake as Leon still discussed his own confusion with himself.

"This is our in-house psychiatrist, Leon Goldstein," Ken introduced, hesitant to mention Leon's official title at LifeGames. He thought it prudent to first gauge Doctor Rupert's reaction to Leon's peculiar mannerisms.

"It's a pleasure to meet you. Please, do call me Andrew."

"The pleasure's mine." Leon was still sitting, evidently lost in bewilderment.

"This way, please, gentlemen." Andrew signaled for them to move on. Leon scrambled to his feet and stole a moment to ask Ken, "... now who's *this* man?"

On their way up to the psychiatric ward, Andrew filled them in on the details.

"Roger, the general, has developed the notion—and is utterly convinced of it—that his name is Fernando Sanchez. That he is or *was* the Spanish Emissary to the Vatican in Rome. He claims that he was wrongfully hanged for the crime of preaching deism and it was—according to him—a plot to frame him, perpetrated by a subordinate who coveted his position. The strange thing is that a whisper of scar tissue does seem to encircle his neck. It seems to be something consistent with the trauma associated with hanging. But there's no note of that on his medical file. We, of course, record all prominent anatomic features of staff, but it's arguable that it's not prominent enough and could have escaped detection."

The lift doors opened and Ken glanced at Leon whose eyes looked as if they were about to be ejected from their sockets. They were wild and ablaze with excitement.

This smacked of his pet subject—*Reincarnation!*

As they made their way into the corridor, Leon grabbed hold of Andrew's arm. "Go on!" he insisted.

Leon's sudden impulse and ferocity startled Andrew and he stammered a moment, "Th... the Latin is another oddity."

Leon leapt at the clue, "*Latin?*"

Ken realized that it was time to explain. "Sorry, Andrew, this is my fault." He turned to Leon. "Leon, I'm sorry, but I haven't had a chance to fill you in on details; Roger Daly is somehow faking Latin and perhaps you should let go of Doctor Rupert's arm."

Ken pointing at the offending grip struck Leon like a bolt of electricity and he leapt away from Andrew then darted back to pat him on the arm. "So, so sorry, Doctor. Sorry, I get a little carried away with things like this."

"Not to worry, old chap."

Andrew made it sound convincing, but he maintained a healthy distance from Leon as they ambled onward.

"As I was saying, the only thing that I can think of is that he must have picked up Latin as a child. He went to Catholic school, that much we do know; it's plausible. Your people must have done a hell of a job on him to trigger a suppressed memory."

Ken kept silent on his own lapsed Catholicism and recent rebound of memories.

"No!" Leon lost control of his dignity again. His eyes were locked onto Andrew with the raptured concentration of a fanatic. "It's a past life regression; the first I've seen with our program!"

Bewitched by this possibility, Leon's mind galloped off in a new direction, rattling off a hypothesis of the benefits that might arise out of such an incident.

They'd reached Andrew's office and Ken used the instant of entry to momentarily hold Andrew back, allowing Leon to proceed through the door first. "Sorry, I should have warned you. Leon's quite brilliant in his job, he just gets a little carried away..."

"No problem, old chap," Andrew was no longer uneasy. "I've been thinking about his name. Leon Goldstein; not the author?"

"The same," Ken confirmed, grimacing slightly. Leon's books were controversial and each successive publication was known to be more outlandish than its forerunner.

"Doctor of Psychiatry, isn't he?"

"Indeed. He doesn't like..."

"Excellent!" Andrew cut in. "I've read all of his books. He's as mad as a March hare of course, but revolutionary; and that drives the profession."

With that, Andrew shot past Ken into his office to re-introduce himself.

From that moment, the character of the meeting changed. Ken became a spectator, his interest in esoteric matters was nil.

Since childhood, he'd lost all interest in everything but money.

The son of God-fearing wealthy industrialist parents, he'd fervently opposed everything they'd stood for. Then, as a troubled youth, his internment at a strict Catholic school had set his repulsion for the mystical into gear. No system, not even one that tried to beat spiritual matters into him, could match his devotion to money.

His experience with the monks had only cemented his revulsion for authority, and treading the established paths to wealth through tertiary education proved too confining as well. His path to cash had taken more devious directions and he'd become increasingly apathetic until he'd dropped out of university altogether. He'd gone travelling to find himself. He'd learned that the road away from inherited riches is a tougher one than the road toward his own quest for it. After some lean years in poverty, greed had stepped into the shoes of his rebellion and hiked him up a new ladder to success.

His family had become as important to him as the God he'd never seen. And to them, he had come to embody all that they despised in the modern world.

Ken's inadequacy for contributing to the fast-evolving discussion between the two doctors was painfully obvious.

Unaccustomed to being an observer, Ken began to seethe at being marginalized.

The doctors were like a pair of bantams flying at each other in a flurry of good-spirited disagreement.

Andrew argued that pure neurochemistry was driving the ailing general; Leon argued back, citing quantum fluctuations and entanglement.

"That is just absurd, old boy!" Andrew waved in frustration. "The purest nonsense... non-science nonsense."

"You cannot say that! Quantum entanglement and healing is a very well-respected field," Leon countered, taking off his glasses and twirling them in one hand.

"Then show me the mathematics for it... Ha!" Andrew charged for victory.

"You need to give it a chance..."

"I will, when you show me the mathematics! Quantum mechanics is *not* a branch of philosophy. It wasn't derived through contemplation, it is a science of mathematical probabilities. The advocates..."

Ken's ego could take it no longer. "There-is-a-patient-to-be-visited..." he spat, not even attempting to hide his peeved tone.

His interruption was like a bucket of ice water over the pair.

"Oooh, sorry, Ken-o. So sorry, old boy. It's philosophy, you see, the very essence of being!"

Andrew rose silently and indicated for them to follow him.

Roger Daly was trussed to his bed, hand and foot.

Andrew had explained as they moved from office to ward that, due to heavy sedation, it was unlikely he'd register their presence in the room.

He could not have been more wrong in his prediction.

Roger stirred as the trio entered his ward. His lids fluttered as he tried to make out the silhouettes approaching.

Ken was the last through the doorway. As he stepped over the threshold, Roger's expression snapped from groggy sedation to menacing intent. He raged into life, raising up onto his elbows, his eyes blazing ferocity, all of his attention fixated directly on Ken. A growling monologue of Latin antagonism began boiling from deep in the man's chest.

The unexpected confrontation drove Ken back on his heels in an uneasy retreat to the door.

Then, without warning, like a magnet's pole nearing its opposite, Ken flew forward in a murderous rage. They slammed into one another like a pair of wild cats. Both doctors tackled Ken as he hit Roger in the chest with his shoulder, and the bed overturned with all four tangled in a spaghetti of hospital drips, lines, cabling and flying equipment.

Roger's demented thrashing had broken one arm-tether and, as the two doctors tried to drag Ken back toward the door, Roger came clawing after them with the bed still strapped to him.

The commotion brought hospital security tearing into the ward. They packed onto the demented adversaries, smothering them with sheer numbers, cuffing them, only achieved a degree of calm once Ken had been far removed from Roger's presence.

"What the hell was that all about?" Andrew was bitching, as he dabbed at a fast-closing eye.

Ken lay mute, looking fixedly at the door and down the corridor through which he'd been hustled, longing to get back to the scrap.

They'd shot him full of sedatives and had him cuffed to the hospital bed. Two security personnel were posted at the door.

Leon was surprisingly calm, sitting on a chair alongside the bed as if just a visitor on a routine afternoon visit. "How are you feeling, Ken-o...? Relax, you can relax now."

After a moment, Ken's eyes defocused from the doorway and he relaxed, coming back to his senses;

"Better, thanks." His eyelids were drooping to half-mast as Leon's voice meshed with the sedative and took its hold.

Leon's voice had assumed its slow and deliberately warm rhythm, the same he used during hypnosis sessions. "Can you tell me what went wrong?"

"I, I don't know..." Ken was now completely relaxed and cooperative.

"Have you ever met this man before?"

"Never."

"Do you think he knows you?"

"I don't know. I doubt it."

"Why did you get so angry?"

"RAGE!"

Though it carried little volume, the onomatopoeic expression welled up from deep within Ken's body. If he'd possessed power over his faculties, he'd surely have growled it. And just as quickly, he slid back to docility.

"I saw your rage, Ken," Leon coaxed gently, "...why couldn't you control it?"

"I... I'm... I don't know..." Ken fought for reason.

Leon had hypnotized Ken on several occasions in the past and knew that he would be open to his best suggestion.

"I'm offering to help you Ken, but I'll need your help. Do you want me to get to the bottom of this?"

"Sure."

"I'd like to hypnotize you; do you feel strong enough?"

"Yes."

Since Ken was not military personnel, Leon had taken over his case.

All the while, Andrew had been watching from a distance, making sure to sit where Ken could not see him.

"All right Ken, I'm going to begin counting you down from five... the closer that I get to one, the deeper you'll go into a relaxed sleep. *Five*... your eyes are shut tight and you cannot open them... *Four*... you are beginning to feel very, very tired. All you want to do is sleep.... *Three*... there is warmth and peace all around you. *Two*... you're deep in sleep and you cannot open your eyes... Try, Ken, try to open your eyes. You cannot open your eyes, Ken.... *One*... you are in a very, deep sleep..."

His task concluded, Leon's voice changed from its slow and methodical rhythm to its normal intonation as he turned to Andrew. "Ok he's gone, how's your eye?"

"Feels like hell. I took a dreadful whack, didn't see it coming. Must've been this cretin's elbow. What possessed this lunatic? Suppressed resentment of some kind...?"

Andrew was guessing at the deep resentment Roger may have created in Ken for putting LifeGames under scrutiny.

"I doubt it, Ken-o isn't bothered by that sort of thing, very sanguine. He's money motivated; places no value on moral issues at all. Frankly, all the psychological angles we could ponder don't apply here. I know that you would probably expect this from me, but my guess is that it's something *faaaar* more sinister."

"Well, he's your patient—be my guest. Bloody man should be incarcerated," he grumbled.

Leon returned his attention to Ken. "Ok Ken, we had a little problem next door. Do you remember the incident?"

"Yes." Ken's answer was staccato yet still tinged with anger.

"You can relax Ken, it's all over, we're far away and there are guards here to protect us. Ok?"

"Ok." Ken relaxed.

"The man on the bed, Roger Daly; are you *sure* you've never seen him before?"

"Never."

"And could he know who you are?"

"No."

"Were you angry at him?"

Ken hesitated.

"I'm not asking if you're angry with him; were you angry with him before *he* became angry?"

"No."

Leon nodded to Andrew, and both men concluded that Ken was not covering up any resentment towards Roger.

"Roger was tied to the bed, Ken; he couldn't have really threatened you no matter how angry he got. Did you know that?"

"Yes."

"Yet you attacked him. Why?"

Words were trying to form on Ken's lips, his mouth moving spasmodically but issuing no intelligible utterance.

The two doctors looked at one another in puzzlement and shrugged. They both knew that hypnotized patients answered plainly and with unguarded honesty.

Based on the evidence, Ken's actions seemed motivated by something of which he was truly ignorant.

"Ok Ken, we can talk about that later. Is there something else bothering you? Something at work possibly?"

Ken's eyes filled with terror and he began to shake. "*Craig!*"

The response stunned Leon momentarily, as he hadn't expected such a clear reaction. "Everything is all right, Ken; you're safe."

As Leon calmed his gibbering, Ken slowly relaxed.

Leon quickly explained the circumstances of Craig's death to Andrew. Both doctors were further puzzled. The death of a work colleague, even the distressful circumstances of this particular case, shouldn't have had such a dramatic effect; particularly given Ken's personality.

"Homosexual? a relationship between the two men?" Andrew ventured.

Leon scoffed at the thought.

"You never know..." Andrew pressed it.

By now, Leon was prepared to try anything "Your relationship with Craig, was it *special* to you in any way?"

"No."

"Did you ever carry on a sexual relationship between the two of you?"

"No." Ken's answers were unimpassioned; they may just as well have been generated by a computer.

"Did Craig threaten you in some way?"

Ken hesitated a moment before responding, "No." His answer was certain, but it had been well considered and replied to with some angst.

The doctors glanced at one another again. "Significant?"

"Did Craig threaten you physically?"

"No." Ken's answer was again, definite.

"In what way *did* he threaten you?"

"It... it wasn't a threat." Ken displayed childlike honesty in his answers.

Leon wrapped his questions in all the understanding and support that his tone could convey. "What was it then, Ken?"

"The... the recordings," Ken said, becoming uneasy as Leon probed closer to the core of where his fear lay.

"The recordings? What about the recordings, Ken?"

"His message on the recording."

"Craig's recording?"

"My voicemail." Fear quavered in Ken's voice.

"Calm Ken, calm. That's good, very good." Leon gave Ken a moment to relax, then prodded, "What was the message, Ken?"

"A prayer." Ken maintained a long pause. It seemed as though his subconscious mind wanted Leon to drag the information out of him.

"And?" Leon asked.

"STOP!"

Both doctors were flummoxed by the brevity of Ken's reply, and even more so by his tone, which communicated that the threat was the word 'STOP'.

They knew that it was not Ken's own wish to terminate the session.

"Did Craig say 'the prayer' before he said 'stop'?"

"Yes."

"Stop what? What did Craig mean by 'stop'?"

"I don't know." A deep crease was etched into Ken's forehead, testimony to his genuine confusion.

Leon decided to address the other lead, "What prayer did Craig say?"

Ken hesitated.

"What were the words?"

"Our Father who art in... heaven."

Leon halted Ken. "Okay, that's good enough. Did Craig say anything else?"

"No."

"Are you afraid of prayer, Ken?"

"No."

Leon wanted to test if Ken had secretly converted to a religion; anything was possible. "Are you religious?"

"No."

"Do you believe in a god?" Leon widened the constrained definitions of religion.

"No... I... I'm not sure."

Ken's extended answer surprised Leon, so he broadened the definition even further. "Do you believe in a spiritual world, Ken?"

Ken didn't answer, though his frown suggested that he was wracking his mind for a response.

Leon could see that Ken was becoming increasingly uneasy. "Calm Ken, forget the question."

Ken immediately relaxed into his zombie-like state whilst the doctors discussed the unfolding enigma, concluding that headway seemed scant.

Leon was most perplexed. Ken had always enthusiastically denied any plane of consciousness beyond the physical. "Bullshit and crap," he'd always labeled Leon's hobby.

Indeed, Ken would find any opportunity he could to poke fun at Leon's books, all of which centered around the technique known as Regression Hypnosis; a method for patients to recall their past lives. As far as Ken had always been concerned, the claim begged for ridicule.

"From what you've told me Leon, Ken's newfound attitude today is rather a sudden and material change in his conviction," Andrew observed, without adding any solution to the riddle it posed.

Leon decided to dig deeper into Ken's subconscious.

"Ken, has Craig perhaps made you more aware that there is a spiritual world?"

Ken hesitated before answering, "Yes."

"And this fact frightens you?"

"Yes."

"Does your belief in the spirit world have something to do with Craig's message on your voicemail?"

Ken became edgy again. "Yes."

Suddenly, the Sister burst into their ward, exclaiming, "Quickly please Doctor, there's trouble with General Daly, he's broken loose!"

Andrew leapt up and bolted for the door.

Leon could hear the furor echoing down the passageway and he was overcome by the curiosity to investigate, but he thought it sensible to first end the session.

Then he had a second thought; he decided that it would be best to ensure that Ken got some induced rest.

"I'm going to count you up to *five* Ken, and as I count, you will begin to awaken. When I reach *five,* you will feel wonderful, however, you won't remember this conversation and you will be dead tired. All that you will want to do is sleep. All right.... *One...* you're slowly beginning to wake up... *Two...*"

After Leon had finished the routine, he waited a moment longer to ensure that Ken was comfortably asleep. Then he retreated to the door, watching Ken's chest rise and fall in an even rhythm of relaxation. He exited, taking the security guard into the corridor with him.

Beyond the closed door, he briefed them with his own set of instructions, "Mr. Torrington will probably be asleep until morning. Wait here until someone tells you otherwise."

He departed at a trot, itching to see what was brewing in Roger's ward.

The scene that greeted Leon was more akin to medieval barbarism than scientific medicine. Six hefty security guards were bodily restraining the patient who was struggling with every sinew against the constraints of the straight jacket that he was being bundled into.

Andrew was the impassive overseer who double-checked each broad, leather strap as it was fastened into place.

"What are you going to do with him?" Leon asked, his mind already imagining the worst.

"Nothing. We'll have to let him cool off." Andrew remained indifferent to his patient's terror as he tended to the bloated shiner that his eye had become.

114

"You've given him all that you can?" Leon mimed the use of a syringe.

"Unfortunately. I suppose that you'd like to have a go at him with your hypnosis?" Andrew guessed. He could see Leon's disapproval of the prescribed methods.

"Definitely, old boy... definitely." Leon's eyes were filled with challenge; the heat of battle with Ken had cooled and the quirky old genius was back. "I guess that he's too excited for hypnosis at the moment. Too excited by far."

"How's your guy?" Andrew hedged, too bitter about the knock he'd received to forgive Ken. He signaled his disdain by deliberately avoiding Ken's name.

"Out like a light, he is. Out like a light."

They stood a while longer, watching the tormented man's weakening fight against his restraints.

Back in Andrew's office, they dissected the evening's startling turn of events until Andrew checked his watch. "Wow, almost eight! I'd better get a move on."

"Doesn't time fly, when you're having fun! Such fun," Leon muttered as he rose.

Chapter 8

"I've been worried about him for some time, Nance." Catherine puffed on the electronic cigarette she'd taken to using, trying to wean herself off of the bad stuff. The management at the trendy restaurant had cleared her use of it.

She preferred Juicy, a brand with a distinct cherry signature; she called it her "juice-stick".

"I don't want to peddle rumors, but Ken seems to have quite the little problem—his Columbian marching powder." She put her juice-stick aside and added, "Not that it's any of my business, but he's got it all... he's *arrived*. Why gamble it on addiction?"

Her concern was sincere. She could speak freely with Nancy. The relationship between the two women had matured quickly; over the recent months they'd become close.

Nancy's expression looked pained; Ken had a manipulative way of welding people to him so that they cared for him as a friend.

"I've been wanting to talk about it with someone for a while. Two years ago when I joined, it wasn't so obvious, but lately— actually, over the past month—he's been out of control with it."

"Well, you know him a lot better than I do, Nance, so if *I've* seen the deterioration, then it's bad."

"And the mood swings? You never know what you're going to get. I used to accept them, thinking they went with the territory.

But it's become over the top." Nancy's expression and voice were despondent.

"I'm with you... Everyone says he's impossible. He's been great to me. He knows precisely what he wants, and he nitpicks—fine—I can deal with that. But since this incident at the hospital, it's like I don't know him. He's like a different person."

The way Catherine moved her eyes betrayed that emotion had crept in. *Shit... she's falling for him,* Nancy realized with alarm. She reached across the table to take Catherine's hand. "I've got a way with him, Cath..." then added, "whatever we speak of here, stays here... okay?"

Catherine smiled appreciatively.

They continued holding hands as Nancy went on.

"The real deterioration began with Craig's incident. The general was hospitalized the day before, creating bedlam at the office... long-knives in the board room."

"Sure."

"That could be very traumatic, but Ken's not a regular human in that sense; he'd normally *never* be phased by something like that. I'm sure you don't know his back-story...? A lot of trauma. Really, and I mean *truly* bizarre and gory deaths of friends and family—it's like he attracts it."

"Wow... that *is* news to me!"

The warmth of the bond between the women was elevated by their continued contact. The tenderness stirred something in Catherine, and it felt a little like the love of a sister she'd never had, but it was more than that too.

They'd been meaning to dine together prior to the Craig incident, but somehow had never gotten around to it. For months, their social calendars had been too frenetic for either of them to find a slot and make the time.

Eventually, the weight of the prevailing circumstances had made it necessary to share mutual difficulties.

Nancy resumed, "He understandably took the day off, the first day I've *ever* known him to stay out of the office. The place runs itself, but he won't stay away for anything."

Catherine agreed.

"Anyway, he took that day off. I left a message on his voicemail around five that evening. Remember? It was about your campaign review the following day."

Catherine nodded.

"Ken was in the office early the next morning, cheerful enough in spite of all the calamities with Craig and the general, but nitpicking over the precise time or sequence of one thing or another occurring. He insisted that I dig up an old sample of Craig's voice... made up a story about being sentimental and wanting to hear his old friend's voice again. Like, *seeeeeriously* out of character. I played dumb, acted like it was a regular thing for him to do."

"*Weeeird...*" Catherine encouraged, engrossed in the story.

"He asked me to call Stuart, our sound engineer, up for a matter."

"I met him when I went down to call Ken for the review."

"Of course, yes; I directed you. Odd thing was, Ken has nothing to do with the operations staff, Henry runs that."

Ken had impressed on Catherine the strict chain of command; his breaking of it was significant.

"I confess—I've got a naughty habit; I look at screens and I see every detail at a glimpse."

"I'll bear that in mind."

They both laughed.

"When I took coffee in, I saw Ken had an email from himself *to* himself with a sound file attachment. I'm an admin person, I know these things. And the file type was a voicemail from his mobile. Why would you email yourself a voicemail, I wondered...?"

"Probably to keep a record of it," Catherine ventured.

"Could be. I know Ken's patterns and the way he works, and something had definitely agitated him. He asked me to call Anton, our top programmer. Remember—Ken had missed a day and had a huge backlog, plus your review, yet he was cramming in meetings that break protocol. I thought it really strange and out of character, maybe some kind of prank that Anton's sorting out for Ken."

Ken had hinted to Catherine that good progress was being made by the "programming department" on their cyber-sex game. Now, as she silently connected the dots, she hoped that she wasn't blushing.

"Later that morning, Stuart called me, bubbling with triumph. He asked me to tell Ken that 'he had a match'. What kind of match?"

Catherine loved to solve puzzles and this was a mind bender that sent the cogs and wheels of her mind churning, trying to link information.

Nancy put forward her best hypothesis. "My guess is that there's a connection between the time of day that I'd left the message on his voicemail, Craig's voice on the dictation recordings, and the time that the general had woken up in the hospital. I just haven't figured out what it is."

"Whatever the *match* is, it didn't make him very happy," Catherine suggested. "I think that's the day I went down to the sound room. Ken and your sound man were playing a voice recording backwards and asked if I knew what it was; it was obvious, and when I'd said as much, they acted like they'd just won the lottery. Ken kicked me out of the room in a buoyant mood. Twenty minutes later, when he joined the review, his mood was very sour. Something must've gone wrong."

They considered that fact a while, failing to reach clarity.

"So... was he matching his voicemail to my dictation files?"

"Perhaps they didn't match and that's what upset him?" Catherine proposed. "I can't imagine what those recordings could contain that would upset Ken so much."

They pondered the point for a time before Nancy came up with another lead.

"It wasn't more than *twenty* minutes between you going down to the audio room and Ken emerging. Ken came up to his office within *five* minutes of me showing you down there. He seemed bewildered and grouched at me to get his tenth coffee of the morning. He looked like death, like he'd seen a ghost!"

Nancy's words sparked a memory flash in Catherine's mind. "I'd paused before I went into the sound room; I was in a bit of a rush, but the sounds were so weird, goose-bump stuff, that they transfixed me. Then, after they threw me out, I stood and listened again. They were up to something that gave me the creeps, Nance."

Nancy's skin was prickling, hairs standing on end. "You know what that is? Backwards speech? It's *Satanic!*"

"Come on… Ken interested in spiritual stuff? I can't see it."

"That's what it is though." Nancy was adamant.

"You think he's into a cult?" Catherine posed.

They looked at one another, each entertaining the possibility. Then, they simultaneously burst into peals of laughter at the improbability.

"Henry approached my desk earlier. He was full of mutters about Ken biting his head off. He said that the door hadn't been properly latched and he'd used the same word as you. 'The *weirdest* sounds', he said." She paused and cocked her head. "Now that I think about it, he said he'd heard Craig's voice, said it was an emphatic 'STOP', but was blended into a rumbling and ticking… the weird sounds. He also said that it gave him the creeps. Huh!"

Catherine was infected by Nancy's strange account, the sounds once again echoing in her mind.

"Sounds from one of your dictated recordings?"

"I doubt it Cath; for security reasons, all company recordings are locked and encrypted. I've never heard anything like what you and Henry described in Craig's or any other recordings."

Catherine scowled. "What else is there? The voicemail you saw," she deduced, "a message from Craig? Could that explain Ken's obsession with times and sequences of events?"

"Oooh… this is intriguing…"

They both took lingering sips of wine while they considered the plausibility of their conclusions.

"On the day the general melted down, the whole executive team holed up in the board room till nightfall. And we know Ken and Craig went back to the mansion. And then Craig's death. Would it be a recording from that day that rattled him? If so, then why? If not, what's the connection? I didn't think they'd ever socialized..."

"Beyond me... maybe it's nothing? We probably can't get to the bottom of this."

"But isn't it fun trying!" Nancy rubbed her hands gleefully. "Okay... here's another clue. Leon, our psych guy."

"Love him! Batty old coot."

"He was at the military hospital when Ken went loopy. Ken was off for three days, and for most of the next week, too. Leon spent a lot of time at my desk, picking my brain about Ken and what had transpired. I told Leon everything I know... everything I won't get fired for... and a bit more."

"I sense one can really trust him; good Karma."

"Very. Now, a penny's just dropped in my mind; Leon mentioned a recording that Ken was too nervous to talk about. Wow..."

"Big Wow!"

"Leon had him hypnotized... said he became agitated. Leon think's it's very spiritual... thinks Ken's somehow spiritually shaken."

"Quick recap—you said Henry also heard what I heard?"

"Gave him the creeps, just like you, just like Ken... *Fffflowers*!"

"Spooky..."

On impulse, Catherine took Nancy's hand and cupped it. They kept holding hands; it was comforting and warm—like sisters. Like sisters... and perhaps something more.

"Why's everyone so terrified of this sound?"

"Wait till you hear it."

"Don't think I want to... seems to have put the fear of God into Stuart, our tech geek. Both Leon and Henry said they can't get a squeak out of him, and here's the next twist; the only thing he'd volunteer was that it all has to do with a police investigation into Craig's death!"

They discussed the police connection and came to no firm conclusions, so Nancy continued.

"Ken hauled Stuart over the coals for that leak. Could have lost his job. In fact, he did; but Henry intervened and reinstated him. Said he had ordered him to disclose the details. So, there's now a bigger rift in the Executive staff; two camps."

"Sounds *grrrreat* for business; aren't you all just the happy crew?"

"Yeah... really! Since the incident, the poor kid evidently hasn't showed his face outside of his sound room. Ken also had an unholy blowout with Leon shortly after he came back to work."

"I got the impression that Ken thought quite highly of Leon," Catherine inserted.

"He does. I think this is a temporary squabble between them. Leon *definitely* wasn't fazed in the least, told me that it was just a 'perfectly normal reaction' that Ken was experiencing."

"Any clues about their argument?" Catherine quizzed.

"Yes, and I don't have to *suppose* anything. Ken's door is only three inches of solid teak and I heard every word. Let me correct that... I heard every word from *Ken!*"

"That bad?"

"That bad," Nancy agreed. "Leon instigated the meeting himself, and asked me to hold all calls for either of them. I knew that he intended to speak to Ken about the hypnosis session and Ken's drug problem."

Catherine withdrew her hand to fire up the juice-stick; it had been the first break since they'd touched, both so comfortable with the affection.

Nancy kept explaining what she'd learned, leaving her hand where it lay, waiting for Catherine's hand to return.

"There was no sound from Ken's office for about ten minutes after Leon went in, then I heard Ken's voice begin to rise, as he was ranting about his 'confidence being betrayed' and Leon's 'snooping into business that didn't concern him'."

"Yikes."

"Then Ken began using language that would make a sailor blush."

"Sounds like we need to discipline him."

They were both a little tipsy and strung out by the intensity of conversation. Catherine's silly innuendo sent them into a fit of delighted chuckling.

"In a nutshell," Nancy tittered, "Ken's not real keen to be hypnotized by Leon again. I think he's scared it makes him too honest."

Another burst of laughter.

Their giggling infected other nearby diners who periodically laughed in response to Nancy and Catherine's mirth.

"Ken's effectively banned all of us from talking to him or one another about the recordings or 'anything else that undermines his authority'."

"Oh... isn't that *nice*," Catherine joked. "The guy is losing it."

"Seriously, I'm worried," Nancy agreed, hoping she was putting a hitch into any further affections Catherine might develop for her boss. He was beneath her.

"And the general? News on him?"

Officially, Catherine was supposed to be ignorant about the incident. Ken had smoothed it over with the military top brass, so there was no threat of a leak or PR damage control.

"I *really* don't think that you want to know!" Nancy staged a shudder.

"With a reaction like that, I *insist* on knowing. I'll beat it out of you if you force me to!"

"Promises, promises," Nancy teased, the wine talking.

Catherine raised a seductive eyebrow. "Speak," she ordered in a deep voice.

Nancy obeyed. "Yes mistress. Leon's been down to the hospital... for God's sake, don't breathe a word of this to Ken. Visiting the general is on the banned list of activities, but the doctor at the hospital is intrigued and can't stand Ken."

"Scout's honor," Catherine saluted with two fingers.

"Well, Stephen King, *eat your heart out!* What Leon's uncovered is a real horror story..." she quaffed a swig of claret before continuing. "They've tracked down this Fernando Sanchez, the guy who the general thinks he is. He actually existed, was a real person. He was the Spanish Emissary to Rome during the reign of Pope Urban the Eighth, in... yep... the year of our Lord 1630 until his delightful colleagues executed him by hanging in 1638! The Vatican keeps extensive records of these things, and you know old Leon, like a dog with a bone."

Catherine's eyes grew larger with each alarming word that Nancy uttered. Finally, forgetting to breathe, she choked and exploded into a fit of coughing.

When she recovered her breath, Nancy proceeded.

"Leon's made great progress with Roger, but Andrew—the other doc—is arguing over diagnosis. Andrew feels it's either an extreme case of bipolar behavior, but Leon's sticking to an awakening of a personality from a past life."

"If Leon's right, my guess is that it's something in the LifeGames program."

"Andrew says they've found traces of antipsychotic medication in the man's blood, yet no prescription for it in his file. Leon says antipsychotics suppress dopamine receptor activity... whatever that means."

"And...?"

"I don't know enough about it, it's all third-hand and over my head anyway, but to them it's a big deal. Means there's a rat somewhere."

"At least the guy wasn't Cleopatra or Napoleon—that's the usual claim."

"Truly! But there's hope yet; besides Fernando, Leon has uncovered two other former lives that Roger can recall under hypnosis. He says he was an Indian squaw who lived around thirteen hundred and his other personality was in Genghis Khan's army."

"Well, the Genghis thing would explain Roger's current occupation," Catherine observed.

"Wouldn't it," Nancy agreed. "It seems that our Roger is quite the warrior."

"Has Fernando come up with any more revelations?" Catherine encouraged.

"Yeah, he's a regular mine of information, turning up facts that only a handful of specialist historians know."

They both shifted uncomfortably in their seats and Catherine suggested a change of scenery. "Night cap?"

"Good idea," Nancy agreed.

Settling their tab, they headed for a popular late-night jazz cafe where the aroma of brewing coffee mingled with the hubbub of festivity.

Time was of no concern to either of them as it was a Friday night and they were both traveling in Catherine's car.

Nancy continued her story as they drove along the highway. "Leon's slowly persuaded Roger to come to terms with the fact that he harbors a personality from another epoch. Leon tells me that it's the most detailed past-life regression he's ever encountered. I mean... it gets weirder and weirder. Roger's got Fernando's neck scars, there are the historical..."

"Neck scars?" Catherine looked appalled, darting her eyes from the road to Nancy and back to the road again, her face a mask of shock.

"Didn't you know about that, Cath? Roger has a rope-burn scar around his neck, but he doesn't have a clue how it got there and it isn't recorded in his military file!"

"God-Jesus... Nancy, you're giving me the creeps," said Catherine, shivering.

"You want me to stop?" she asked.

They drove on in silence for a few moments, each contemplating the unbelievable details.

"Actually Nance, there *is* something I was going to mention earlier. I was thinking of conducting an online run... at LifeGames. I'm a little hesitant now. I'm not really sure that I want to find a Fernando somewhere in my past! My mother certainly wouldn't approve."

It was a tonic and the air of dread evaporated.

"Don't be silly Cath, we've run perhaps millions of people through the program with no problems. Ken always says that you're much safer online than you are out in the real world. I can't disagree."

Between glimpses back to the road, Catherine managed to convey a look of "pull the other leg" and they giggled again.

"No, I'm not being paid to say it! Seriously, Leon went into a lot of detail explaining to me about Roger's regression and besides, Roger is the only person that's had anything go wrong."

"Oh, come on Nance," Catherine tut-tutted.

"Okay, okay. I must sound like a used-car salesman. I'll grant you that we had some teething problems, but then again, we're working with computer software which is notoriously full of bugs and viruses and God knows what else. Roger is the only one to have experienced any *lasting* problem. The Pentagon is our largest client and you know how finicky they are. They wouldn't endanger anybody's life; anybody from their own side that is."

Catherine offered her an incredulous look for the third time.

"Okay, okay. But face it Cath, you're a skeptic."

"For beware..." Catherine wagged her index finger in the air to lend her words solemn authority as she quoted the closing words of the *Desiderata*, "...the world is full of trickery." Her voice possessed all the philosophic resonance she could muster.

"You're right, I suppose," Nancy agreed. "Being a skeptic *is* good; I'm legendary for it."

"Sorry I sidetracked us—you were going to tell me about Leon explaining something?" Catherine refocused.

"I was?"

"Uh-huh," Catherine hummed in a seductive lilt.

"Oh yes, it's the wine. Leon was saying, that in a tormented spirit like Roger's, there's an enormous confusion. In Leon's version of it, the man's participation in the program must have brought all of his violent past to a head. There must have been a particular vision that triggered Fernando to come out of his subconscious. Who knows? Perhaps Fernando the priest wanted Roger to confess his sins?"

"Don't you think it's a little odd that it hadn't happened to Roger before? How much more realistic can the game be than a real war zone, where they say the guy has spent a lifetime?" Catherine argued.

"True." Nancy thought about it a moment. "Perhaps you can use it in the next phase of the advertising and PR campaign, Cath; 'A program so realistic, it'll leave you four times the man you were before'!"

They erupted into their umpteenth chorus of hilarity for the evening and Catherine was forced to halt the car short of the parking lot to catch her breath.

"We shouldn't be doing this, you know," Nancy said, suddenly struck by the fact that Catherine was driving intoxicated.

"So sorry, mom... I didn't mean it... it just happened—and it's only round the corner."

"We'll get a cab after this," Nancy insisted.

"You're right... I'll pay."

"We'll share the fare. What was it you were going to do online?" Nancy inquired.

Catherine spat out the first answer that leapt through her mind, "Ken would kill me if I told you!"

"If that were true then, I'd be a corpse ten times over tonight, Cath. I've been spilling the beans to you all night and I'll beat this out of you if you make me," Nancy plucked on Catherine's own line.

"Promises, promises," Catherine was not to be outdone.

They locked the car and made their way, arm in arm, toward the cafe.

"Well?" Nancy insisted.

"Well what?" Catherine responded cheekily.

For some reason not clear to herself, she was looking for a way out of telling Nancy about the planned cyber-sex game. Oddly, she could not understand her own uncharacteristic embarrassment.

Nancy gave Catherine a hard spank on the rump to prick her memory.

"Oh *that!*" Catherine made a remarkable recovery from her amnesia.

"Yes, *that!*" Nancy repeated firmly.

"All right, all right, I'll tell you when we sit. You find a spot, I'm going to the little girl's room." Inexplicably, Catherine still wanted to delay.

"I'll join you."

They spent a few minutes retouching tear-streaked mascara, sporadically giggling.

Then, having found a seat and with medical-grade espresso on order, the two settled in. Nancy rubbed her hands gleefully in anticipation of the details about the secret that Catherine had held out on.

She could delay no more.

"Cyber-sex."

"You are shitting me, lady!"

"I swear."

"Are you nuts?" she said with a laugh, tickled by the beverage. "I didn't know we had *that* program."

"You don't... well, not yet anyway. That's what your programmer and Ken are up to."

"Anton Lim?"

"I think that's the Anton that Ken talks about," Catherine replied. The dizzying sensation of disclosure slowly ebbed, leaving her invigorated.

A freshness and a conspiratorial level of friendship had now been reached; the pair tittered like pubescents, their professional caution hurled to the winds.

"I want details, baby... Where...? When...? How...? Come on, out with it."

"Not much I can say yet, Ken's very economical with details. I guess with all his problems, this one's not a priority."

"Hmmm..." Nancy remained flushed. "Don't worry, he's a dog... it's a priority."

"From the little I've gathered, they're patching some external code into a main sequence program, but there are some integration issues."

"It's kinda cold though, isn't it? Very premeditated, a very mercenary way to get your kicks."

"There's a charm in that..." Catherine suggested. "It's not the only way I'd like my sex, but for a lark, I'll try it once."

"I'm not sure I'd be that brave."

"With your boss...? On the other hand, it could pay dividends, I suppose."

"He's your boss too. Well... sort of."

"Hmm, way to go Nance, give me cold feet."

Their mood almost sobered, but neither of them wanted the buoyant atmosphere to end.

"So—who's your lover?"

Catherine jolted with shock at the directness; she'd never disclosed her orientation or private life. The moment to discuss it had never arisen before.

"What's your fantasy?"

Catherine's mind raced at the question. Usually, she was an open book, she'd tell anybody anything at any time; but something about this fragile sisterhood was too precious a gem to risk on truth's rejection.

"Really?" she'd said, before she thought it.

Nancy had seen the surprise. "Was I too forward?"

"No, you just caught me unaware. Don't be silly, I've got nothing to hide. Of course, I'll tell you."

Then Nancy realized her own error. "No... oh, no... not in reality. In the game! Who's your lover in the game? What's the setting?"

They both burst into laughter and it broke down another small barrier.

"I'll tell you... I seriously will, but you must promise to still love me." She laughed to pretend she didn't mean it.

"Scout's honor," Nancy saluted, and they laughed again.

"I haven't focused on it. I don't really think I'm getting that choice."

"Ken!" Nancy said it on impulse.

"What?" Catherine genuinely missed it.

"I suggested Ken... He's conceited. If he's choosing, that's who he'll pick." Nancy paused. Navigating a sea of morals was always hazardous, especially when alcohol has the microphone. "Honestly...? I saw *something* spark the very first day you came to the office."

"You're kidding!" Catherine looked mortified. "I don't think..."

Before she could finish, Nancy cut her off. "I don't think anyone else has seen it; both of you hide it well."

There seemed little point denying it.

"What's in it for him?" the alcohol asked. "Oops, sorry," Nancy apologized. "Too many questions... none of my business."

"Okay, time to stop being coy. Ask away, if I don't want to answer anything then I *won't answer*, ok? I'm a big girl." Warmth and trust was building between them. "Ken wants to watch."

"Just *watch?*" Nancy cocked her head.

"*JUST WATCH!* And only Ken. He said he can arrange it. I'm game."

"Men! Bloody voyeurs."

"Who isn't?" Catherine flashed a smile.

Nancy didn't answer.

"I'll confess it. I'm nervous. It's a boundary I probably shouldn't cross. Not with him and perhaps not like this—my first cybersex experience," Catherine re-emphasized.

"Probably the safest sex," Nancy quipped.

Catherine held back; her impulse was to say 'How about two women?' Instead, she offered, "I don't know, Nance. What if it sends me loopy?"

"A bit late for that!"

Catherine laughed at her exaggerated and crazed rolling eyes. But Nancy then snapped back to a serious expression.

"Honestly Cath, there's nothing to worry about."

"Apart from hospitalization...?"

"I'd do it..."

"Oooh... now there's something to watch," Catherine said reflexively, the alcohol lending her tongue its own disobedience.

"You're welcome," Nancy responded, following the lure of decadence.

They were reacting to one another's comments with knee-jerk honesty, and being so freshly initiated into full friendship, it continually fractured the flow of their conversation.

Catherine knocked their stuttering segues of mild embarrassment on the head;

"Why are we being so coy? I reckon most people are exhibitionists. *Damned to hell* and all that."

"You mean voyeurs, Cath; I'm not sure I'm an exhibitionist. But I think all of us like to watch, and look in on lives. It's spawned reality shows and celebrity obsession."

"What I'm thinking about is several steps past that."

They both laughed heartily and easily.

The two had come a long way in a short evening. They'd started as good acquaintances and the connection had blossomed into a real friendship and heady intimacy.

Their bond continued to grow from crescendo to concern, from laugh to honest revelation; every breadth of human emotion poured out and shared until the Eastern horizon grew pink and the arrival of a new day promised.

Chapter 9

The bearded man was dressing for battle. He donned a light smock made of smart fabrics, its weave impregnated by all manner of nano-telemetry microdots and Wi-Fi feedback gauges. Below the fabric, gel patches the size of halved Ping-Pong balls studded his body in strategic locations. He looked more like a hospital patient prepped for surgery than someone dressed to kill.

As she watched through the one-way observation window, Catherine noticed the man had a rare and unsettling intensity of lethal intent in his stare; his eyebrow, a single solid bridge. He looked at her through the glass, directly into her eyes; and as much as they assured her it was impossible to see through the mirror, his eyes still bored into her mind minutes later.

She guessed that he was in his mid-forties, yet with muscle tone that appeared twenty years younger. Before they'd dropped the slip over his head, they'd seen that his alley cat body was a network of deep scars and thick welts; a battlefield of healed trenches and old impact sites where projectiles and shrapnel had done their work.

She'd nudged Ken, horrified and asked, "What's this guy been up to?"

"Stamp collecting," Ken whispered.

"Seriously...!" Her tone revealed the urgency for a reply.

"He's probably been in more skirmishes than you've had shopping trips."

"Jesus! He sure bought some nice souvenirs."

Earlier, Ken had briefed her that this would be a Spetsnaz building-clearing exercise. Spetsnaz were the elite of the elite in Russia's Special Forces who have undergone countless grueling training programs to earn their stripes.

As Catherine watched, they slung the man into a webbing of straps that were then hooked onto a set of enormous hoops, all connected to form a massive double-volume gyroscope.

The construction had the appearance of Copernicus' model of planetary motion with the Commander strapped in its center as the sun.

This would be a commercial run, not a time dilation trial, Ken explained.

"Why the gymnastics equipment?" Catherine frowned. "I thought you said they just lie there and twitch?"

"The gyroscope? You do remember details," he complimented. "This is going to be a very physical routine. We could do it with the God Helmet, with transcranial stimulation, but then we wouldn't be able to assess his musculoskeletal condition. He needs to be in peak physical condition and this is still the only way to test that to breakdown."

The team was ready and the exercise could begin.

Once he had secretly placed the re-engineered drug into the patches, Ken had given his permission to resume trials, bringing the time dilation facility back on track.

For Ken, the previous six weeks had been overwhelming and stress-filled.

Alex King, the private investigator charged with setting up a Colombian connection, had needed access to far more technical data and specifications for the pharmaceutical re-development than Ken had on hand. Ascertaining them through third-party consultants while trying to retain anonymity had proven almost impossible, but eventually they had been delivered.

Ultimately, when the deal was struck and the Colombians invested, Ken was able to step from his own shadows, into their murky world.

During their argument, in the minutes prior to his death, Craig had mentioned what the solution for the drug's problem would be.

Ken had passed the information on and the fault had quickly been found and eliminated.

Alex had arranged for the drugs to be manufactured in bulk; Ken's only task was to attend the drug trial. To remain incognito, he'd prepared an elaborate disguise and faked a broad Scottish accent. As far as he'd been concerned, remaining undetectable was the only test necessary for the use of the drug. The drug was a three-part concoction, entirely benign and of no interest to any food or drug administration. Only once the two active ingredients were mixed and spun through a centrifuge would the catalyst be added, and take on its required neuropsychotropic characteristic.

He'd observed two trials performed on unsuspecting subjects. Their doses had been massive, and they'd died in hallucinating terror. Ken had watched the autopsies where, thankfully, no trace of the drug had been revealed. Once satisfied, he'd paid the laboratory in the blood diamonds they'd requested before slipping out of the country on a private jet.

With the adapted formula for creating the psychotropic under lock and key, Ken would have no need for anybody else to know the true secrets of time dilation. Each of the components could be manufactured in separate facilities and stored apart. The drug was potent enough to only require infrequent brewing. Vast quantities could be affixed to gel patches in a very brief time.

In a single day, an unskilled worker using an automated applicator kept in a locked strong room could prepare enough patches for a year's requirements.

"Ready online. Audio."

"Ready online. Visuals."

"Ready IT..."

"Subject prepared; hypnosis sequence launched..." The intercom speakers in each monitoring booth repeated the checks with drilled regularity. All were in general announcement mode and every department involved in the run was hearing the call.

It was much like the launch sequence of orbital rockets, as Ken had explained earlier. "The program can either be controlled centrally from up here or by using the tablet running a control app."

He'd shown her the interface.

"With it, a single operator can run the entire show, but we generally man each station to fine-tune aspects of the subject's experience."

What he had failed to mention was the safety aspect of running unmanned.

"My run's not going to be with a full house, right?" Catherine had whispered with alarm.

"I wouldn't share it for the world, darling," Ken assured.

Not fully understanding the technology, and assuming it integral to the virtual reality, hypnosis was the aspect that most troubled Catherine.

She was certain that Ken was no hypnotist, so how was he planning to put her under when it came to cyber-sex? She'd met and liked Leon, but she was definitely not going through with it if he was to be present.

Hearing her terms of engagement, Ken soothed her fears with a thorough explanation.

"As you can see, everything's computer controlled and monitored. Each booth has its own screen and audio repeater that displays *only* their exclusive responsibility. They've got an override to correct errors that might be made up here." He gestured to the main control room. "Look, Leon and Mark are down there."

He pointed to a windowed room where the two men sat with earphones about their necks and a microphone between them as they hunched over a screen.

Oddly, although Leon's voice had been counting the subject into trance through the intercom, the two men were chatting at their own pace.

"Who's doing the talking?" Catherine asked.

Turning to the operator, Ken ordered, "Kim, show Catherine the repeater."

Kim immediately executed a few keystrokes and one of the screens on her monitor console split into a number of windows.

Within each window, was a different aspect of the words being uttered. One window contained the written text complete with a tracking cursor, keeping tempo with the spoken words. Other windows contained graphs and data that pertained to the voice quality, modulation, and feedback from the wireless telemetry smock worn by the man in the gyroscope.

"My God!" Catherine exclaimed. "I had no idea." She was no stranger to technology but the extent of it staggered her.

"See," Ken pointed to another windowed booth, "there's Stuart; this screen is a split responsibility. Stuart in audio must ensure that all of the technical aspects of the sound quality are maintained and are authentic."

"Is it a recording?" Catherine had asked.

"No, it's AI, the Artificial Intelligence I told you about. Computer data parsed through a neural network." Ken smiled. "Impressed?"

"Impressed doesn't come close... it's overwhelming. Hang on," Catherine inserted, scowling, spotting a flaw. "If this is pre-recorded, when Leon isn't here, why is his voice necessary? What if you want to give a command that he hasn't pre-recorded?" she posed.

"What a clever little thing you are," Ken said, then pinched her rump.

It was unexpected—inappropriate—and Catherine whirled on him, offended. But something in his look obliterated her furious response, so she smiled idiotically instead and hated herself once more for doing so. He could do things nobody else could, and consistently get away with it. It was like he had a grip on her mind.

"Everything is computer controlled, that's not Leon's voice that you're hearing."

"It's not?" She was perplexed.

"Well, in a way it is. We used his voice, or rather its intonation. He has the perfect modulation. We synthesize it, build up each syllable, inflection by inflection, so that whatever we key in will be reproduced in audio."

"And other languages? Could this synthesized Leon say it in other languages?"

"Absolutely. The unit is online, taps into the cloud and draws from the characteristics of any language we need."

Catherine's mind leapt to consider the implications of what this aspect of the technology along might mean for political diplomacy; the media could put words in *anybody's* mouth without them ever having uttered them!

As if reading her mind, Ken added, "More than that, the voice will stand up to identity analysis. Nothing will distinguish it from Leon's actual voice."

The existence of this technology had previously caused Ken to entertain whether Craig's voicemail to him had been just such a hoax, fabricated in the studio.

It wasn't inconceivable. Delivery to his phone would be easy for the computer to initiate through VOIP, voice over internet protocol. The only question was who would have had the motive to create such a bizarre ruse, and to what end?

All of the routine checks were complete and the hypnotized subject hung like a helmeted crucifix in a futuristic torture rack.

As she stretched to touch the main screen set into the console before her, Kim spoke into her microphone, "All systems are a GO!"

The instant her finger contacted the touchscreen's pulsing Start window, the speakers erupted into a cacophony of sound and the man in the web raised his head off of his chest.

From their elevated viewpoint, Catherine watched as television repeaters around the stadium complex burst into life.

"Let the games begin," Ken announced, heralding the unfolding drama; Catherine's mind jumped to the Coliseum in Rome.

This modern scene was, for her, an unsettling echo of that dark age when the persecuted fought beasts in a pit just as the warrior would now face his fabricated adversary.

For a twenty-first century woman, it was a strange vision that felt almost like *Déjà vu* and she forced herself to snap out of the momentary trance.

"He's seeing all of this?" she asked, startled by the life-like images on the monitor screens.

"You sound surprised Cath; didn't you work with these visuals in the commercial campaign?" Ken queried with a sarcastic flavour.

"Yes, but when you hear that it's computer footage, it just doesn't seem possible. I know it's dated thinking, but 'virtual reality' conjures up grainy animated images in the arcades."

"If it makes you more comfortable, think of this as just another multi-billion-dollar arcade game."

Catherine ignored his gibe. Minutes later, still in awe by the activity that bustled around her, a reckless thought bounded into her mind. "Can you hook me up? Now?"

Ken turned slowly to face her, his mouth agape. "Do you want me to get you a doctor?"

"Why?" She felt admonished by his reproach.

"Maybe you took me too seriously, Cath... This program is not a game. None of our programs are."

Jilted, but not defeated, she fell silent; brooding a few moments on his justified point.

"What if you don't hypnotize me...?" she came back, at her most persuasive level. "If I can sample it while my nerve is strong, there's more chance of me trying it some other time." She was blackmailing him into giving her a tryout, at the peril of the sex game.

Ken caught the drift of her none too subtle threat and wasn't prepared to call her bluff.

"I suppose we could tone down the tempo... Kim—we got any down-time today?"

Kim opened the bookings roster on an auxiliary screen. "There's a space from sixteen thirty to nineteen hundred, Mr. Torrington."

"You're on!" he informed Catherine.

As she looked down from a level above, the lightly dressed gladiator tumbled with the ease of a trampoline acrobat and Catherine's heart surged with mixed emotions of dread and elation.

Like a child swept away in the war of his imagination, his every move was a balletic response to his private vision. He dangled weightlessly in the rigging, evidently hiding, crouching, crawling, rolling, running and peeking around the next non-existent corner, telegraphing no warning of what he might do next. In isolation, he looked demented, but the monitor offered a glimpse of sane redemption for his actions.

Glancing from man to monitor was a queer study of the interplay between an event and its victim.

Catherine watched in fascination as the object of the tunnel vision with which she had worked so much during the production of the commercials, unfolded in an unceasing sequence of action.

After a few minutes, they departed the spectacle and made their way up to reception where they'd part ways until their four o'clock rendezvous.

As they moved along, yet another memory kept playing through Catherine's mind. It had its foundation in a procedure that Ken had given her the option of not watching.

She had considered the option as a challenge, a test of her will, and she'd declined the option to avoid watching. But watching that aspect of the ritual had been horrifying and simultaneously stimulating.

The man had stripped completely naked and a female doctor had inserted the catheter and a rectal bag apparatus. The scene had continued flashing through her mind in deliciously decadent flashes of voyeurism.

Now, unable to control her aching trepidation anymore, she asked Ken if she'd have to undergo the same procedure later in the day.

"Of course, you don't have to, sunshine," he replied cheerfully. "Just don't wear your best underwear!"

Catherine's heart sank and they walked on in silence for several more minutes. During that interim, she steeled her heart against the predicament that she was soon to be in, consoling herself with the fact that at least it would be a female performing the task.

Ken walked with her to the car. He had been wearing a sadistic grin ever since she had asked the question, and finally she tired of his amusement at her expense, lashing out with a playful blow that caught him harmlessly in the middle of his chest.

She punctuated the action with a stern rebuke. "Enough!" she pouted, her face pinching into a dramatic sulk. "I'm not going to play anymore."

Ken plucked at his lower lip in the manner of a childlike taunt and Catherine made as if to chase him. "All right," he cried in a laughing retreat. "I'm only kidding with you. You won't be time dilated, you'll be able to take care of your own potty training."

Relief washed over Catherine, yet she growled with sham furry at being hoodwinked. Then another penny dropped. "*If*—and only if, mind you—I do play the sex game, what then?" she asked, raising both eyebrows.

Before answering, Ken moved to a safer distance, out of her range.

"Don't worry," he paused, letting it hang as he increased the gap between them, "those bits will already be occupied."

He'd begun to run before finishing the sentence, but Catherine had anticipated something vulgar and she was quicker over the distance than he'd reckoned, planting a glancing slap on his back as he tried to dart away.

"*Bastard!*" she shouted after him as he fled, then she turned back to her car.

"See you at four!" he taunted.

Chapter 10

The bed was jackknifed to support Roger Daly's torso. His face was serene and when he spoke, his voice gentle.

This was not the man that his comrades-in-arms would be familiar with; they knew the brooding Roger, the deadly Roger, the Roger whose voice on the rare occasions it did breach his self-imposed reclusion, was gruff and monosyllabic.

Throughout his life, Roger had been a man of few words and precise action. He had been trained to follow orders and not to partake in careless chatter; in his vocation, there had been little need to communicate.

Leon was Roger's alter-ego; his world, one of unceasing communication, and talk, the tool of his trade. A trained communicator, Leon was quickly winning the battle against the warrior, Roger's intense character crumbling to the superior armaments.

Leon's unorthodox treatment had begun causing consternation in military circles; training men up to Roger's extreme capability did not come cheap, and the military bean counters had their calculators out.

Roger increasingly looked like a write-off; he'd soon enter their balance sheet as an 'acceptable loss'—an innocent sounding euphemism for quantifying a life through statistics.

Like any business, the military had their budgets and lives were either an asset or liability. In this equation, death was a less expensive option, funerals being cheaper than welfare.

A classified report on the Roger incident had been written up; the negative outcomes weighed against the savings of field-training causalities. LifeGames training remained the preferred method. "Acceptability rates for resulting mental disorders may be allowed to remain at elevated levels while the company overcomes teething challenges associated with the time dilation technology."

Ken had managed to lay his hands on the report. "My kind of businessmen!" he'd chirped happily.

Once Roger's psychological analysis disqualified him from ever retaining his former status, his file was officially closed. Roger had been no ordinary soldier drilled for marching and cannon fodder; he was an elite killing machine, a stud bull amongst the herd.

Roger knew he'd made the shift onto the debit side of the military budget. This left Leon scrambling to shore up the depressive void and collapsing self-worth that the man was tumbling into.

"How are you feeling today? More chipper I see," Leon observed, patting Roger's foot through the blanket.

Although no sound breached his lips, Roger offered a brief nod to confirm the conclusion. Deep within the troubled eyes, stirred the promise of a smile.

"Good old boy, good." Leon squeezed the foot with camaraderie.

Just then, Doctor Andrew entered the room. "I heard that you were in, Leon. What's on the program for today?"

"Oh, I thought we'd put a few more historians out of business... put them out of business, yes," Leon bantered cheerily. "How about that, Andrew, you up for it?"

The two physicians had developed a good friendship. Though Leon was officially not supposed to be in the wards, Andrew had declared *"To hell with them!"* when the signal had come through from Operations Headquarters.

According to the signal, Roger was to be stabilized expeditiously using only prescribed and trusted psychological and pharmaceutical methods. "This," according to the signal, "will affect his most hasty discharge from the armed forces."

Official word was that Roger had become a burden that the military no longer intended to carry.

The entire dehumanized affair had caused Andrew to respond angrily. He'd openly flouted ops authority over him.

"I don't know quite how and it makes no sense to me, but Doctor Goldstein is achieving results which far exceed the prescribed patient recovery rate that Operations expects of me," he'd told the hospital superintendent. "I don't give a continental damn what they think, but on my watch, Doctor Goldstein is quite welcome to proceed with the good work that he has been doing!"

The superintendent was a true military man who was more than a little cautious about crossing swords with a psychologist. He had dismissed Andrew with a clear instruction that the official line should be toed; it was clear that a blind eye would unofficially be turned.

"So be it!" Andrew had punctuated the *status quo* with a victory for justice.

"Defeat at last!" Leon cheered.

Andrew hadn't intended to ignore answering Leon's question regarding his own plans for the day. His failure to answer was only due to distraction from the details of the graphs and statistics that hung on a rather dated-looking clipboard at the foot of Roger's bed.

"Defeat!" Leon repeated.

"What was that?" Andrew inquired, puzzled.

"No time to appeal the decision, old boy... no time." Leon enthusiastically sealed his latest victory in a tussle between their opposing philosophies.

This claim was based on Andrew's failure to oppose him on the question of putting historians out of work through regression hypnosis. Andrew's distracted omission was tantamount to tacit acceptance that regression hypnosis was bona fide; a silly perpetuation of the mind-sparring the two had engaged in from the moment they'd met.

"Someday, I really must stretch you out on my couch for counseling old chap, you're more senile with each passing day."

Leon ignored Andrew's counter offensive as he hummed a victory tune to himself while maneuvering a chair into a comfortable position to begin his session with Roger.

"Don't listen to a word he says, Roger," Andrew instructed, circling his own ear with his index finger, hinting at Leon's derangement.

A hint of smile touched the corners of Roger's mouth.

"Run along then, run along," Leon called after Andrew as he left the ward on rounds. "Now, where were we Rog, where were we?"

Over the weeks and many hypno-sessions, Leon had all but removed the Fernando character from Roger's conscious mind. It had been an arduous task made more difficult by Fernando speaking with a heavy Spanish accent in a sixteenth-century English dialect.

Through long and in-depth negotiations, Fernando had accepted a retreat back into the recesses of twentieth-century Roger's mind, where he dwelled with the two former personalities. Each of the three additional personalities that inhabited the mind called Roger had their own clearly defined memories and outlooks.

Leon had dabbled into the ones who'd pre-dated Fernando. He'd discovered some promising results, yet only Fernando held the link between Ken and Craig and the terrifying prospects of demonic dabbling that Fernando growled about.

In this regard, Leon had discovered that extracting information from Fernando was an excruciatingly slow process.

Fernando was a minefield of irrational ranting; if Leon made the mistake of mentioning either Ken or LifeGames, then the session had to be terminated.

Fernando would begin to work himself into a tirade that would invariably explode and then degenerate into a wild-eyed string of Latin curses and prayers. The prayers, in turn, would give way to ritualized chants and a climax of uncontrolled epileptic convulsions would grip the man. When that point was reached, Leon's only option was to banish Fernando, bringing Roger back to consciousness.

The epilepsy was a clue that Leon had followed—but there was much more to it.

"All right, Roger."

Leon pressed the 'record' button on his dictation recorder and checked to see if both spindles were turning, drawing the old mini-cassette ribbon through the recording device. The machine was ancient, and the tapes that it played were obsolete; but Leon fiercely rejected moving on to digital media.

"I'm going to begin to count you down from five, okay?"

Leon took a sip of water while Roger nodded and obediently closed his eyes in readiness for Leon's first command.

"*Five...* you're becoming drowsy, very, very drowsy. *Four...*" Leon was at work, and all hint of senility evaporated. "I'd like you to remember a time, Roger. It's your first day of school. Can you remember your first day at school?"

"Yes, Sir." Roger's voice was soft and timid, unmistakably the voice of a six-year-old.

"Very good boy, Roger. Let's go even further back in time. You are just born and you are being washed by your mother..."

The man in the bed transformed into a helpless and feeble infant, his limbs flopped as if paralyzed, his toes and fingers curling, in the manner of infants. His face contorted and a moan gurgled in his throat.

"Good, Roger. Now, you are not yet born; you are inside your mother's womb where it is warm and safe and you feel *verrrrry* peaceful."

The face relaxed from the trauma of birth, becoming content. Roger's thumb plugged into his mouth and his knees drew up to his chest, his eyes fluttering lazily, the lids turning them to slits.

"Very good Roger, very good... You feel very loved." Leon re-positioned himself for the task that lay ahead.

The man-sized fetus in the bed was to all appearances asleep, the cheeks gently pulsating against the thumb.

"All right Roger, I want you to remember another time, a time that came even before you were inside of your mother. Can you remember this time?"

Roger's thumb fell limply from his mouth and his limbs went slack, his facial expression blanked as though he were dead.

"Good! Think again, this is a different time, a life that you remember. Who are you?"

Nothing.

"Who are you?"

Still nothing... and then the eyes began to track behind the closed lids.

"Tell me who you are..."

The eyes opened and tracked around, looking for its interrogator.

"I humbly ask, sir... what is your name?"

The body came roaring back to life, assuming a presence of great authority.

In a throaty grumble, course from a guttural Spanish accent came the reply: "I am Fernando Sanchez, Bishop of Andalucia and Spanish Emissary to the Holy Vatican in Rome."

There had been an uncanny metamorphosis of Roger's body, face and aura. So thorough had been the man's transformation that, to the un-initiated, the scene would appear to be a disturbing possession by an invading spirit. Alternatively, it could be a most professional hoax indeed, but few would be fool enough to suggest that this was Roger at all.

"What is the period in which you live, Sire?" Leon always began the session with the identical line of questioning; it was his method of verifying that his channel to the former personality was open. Fernando Sanchez's authority demanded very specific protocols or he would refuse to answer.

"I was born in the village of Mijas during the year of our Lord fifteen hundred and seventy-two. I will die in the year sixteen hundred and thirty-eight."

Leon was familiar with regressed personalities viewing themselves as current beings.

They would speak of themselves in the present tense, yet they would simultaneously have the curious habit of mentioning their date of death as matter of fact.

For them, the transition between terrestrial life and the spiritual world appeared to be no more than an academic point of departure.

"I seek the salvation of many good souls, Your Eminence," Leon continued. He'd found it an important ingredient to first make these assurances of his intent before questioning Fernando.

"*Bendito seas,* my son," said the Bishop, blessing Leon for his devotion.

"There is a friend who has left our world, he was known by the name of Craig Angelis."

"I have knowledge of this soul." Fernando folded his arms.

"He has imparted a message to yourself, Eminence?" Leon carefully navigated the waters of heretical suspicion.

"Much evil my son, much wickedness," his voice growled. So soon into the session and Fernando was already fierce. "Beware, for your own position is stalked by the demons of Hell."

Leon's skin crawled with the sincerity in the man's voice. "The evil takes what form, Sire?"

"The evil surrounds you in your place of work. Heed my warning!" Fernando boomed, close to the precipice that would quickly give way and slide the whole session to its premature end. "For you are *not* in a position to control your destiny."

Leon averted his eyes from the crazed stare of his patient-become-confessor, and an ironic notion passed through his head.

"Here he was, a Jew, circumstantially thrust into an impromptu session of confession with a Catholic priest who hailed from the most oppressive epoch in humankind's history.

He wondered how the intolerant Bishop would accept talking with a 'heretic'. Although not a practicing Jew, Leon was painfully aware of the bigoted mind. He knew all too well that in Fernando's limited outlook, the stigma would be damning.

There was a crackling silence in the room, and slowly Leon raised his eyes to find the Bishop studying him intently, inclining his head, frowning as if seeing Leon's thoughts. "And do not believe that your *false* religion will gain your admission into the Kingdom of God."

The Bishop's voice crashed into Leon's mind, bringing a new dimension to Leon's experience. Never before in all of his vast experience had he known any subject to read a hypnotist's mind.

It was a shaking experience for Leon as Fernando continued haranguing him with his admonishments.

"Your salvation will only be achieved when you guard the thoughts of *your* heart against Lucifer; the Prince of Darkness creeps through the chambers of your den!"

Leon had never penetrated this far into the enigma, which Fernando's riddles perpetuated. Maintaining an attitude that he hoped would convey his deepest gratitude for the great man's advice, Leon tried to restore calm.

"I am grateful for the advice that you offer me, Sire," he ventured.

But calm was not to be, and he watched helplessly as his words had little effect on the building momentum of the Bishop's slipping rationality.

"The Beast is in league with your master. It uses foul balms and sweet words to recruit soldiers into the armies of the Antichrist! *MADRE DE DIOS, PERDONA TUS PECADOS...* You are as one blinded by the darkness! You bring great perils to all of mankind! Let the inquisition cleanse your sins!"

The session was over in that instant. Fernando continued to build his outburst toward a crescendo of bed-rattling wrath until the tirade exploded into savage chaos, forcing Leon to assign him back to his own period, and bring the memory of Roger forward to its self-awareness.

After he had ensured that the conscious Roger was in a relaxing sleep, Leon made his way toward the hospital's exit. The route took him past Andrew's office.

"How did it go today, old chap?" Andrew was secretly hooked on the saga.

"Short but sweet. Too short. That's the trouble with religious nutters, can never get a word in edgeways. Not a word."

Leon filled Andrew in on the scant progress made, rewinding his cassette and playing the interesting bits.

When done, they began to consider the riddles that the session had borne.

"My guess is *drugs* and *you*, old boy!" Andrew offered triumphantly.

"What on earth do you mean by that?"

Leon was bewildered. Their constant and ongoing duel of wits extended to diagnosis, and by not reading Andrew's cryptic clue, Leon had forfeited a point in their game.

"The 'balms'? They're *drugs,* old chap! I saw it on that fellow the moment I met him. He's an addict if you ask me, always at his nose." Andrew mimicked Ken's constant fidgeting with his nose.

Whenever Andrew referred to Ken, he said "that fellow".

Leon knew of Ken's cocaine addiction, but it was prudent to deny Andrew's charge.

"Not a chance of it... not a chance. With all the pressure he's under, Ken couldn't afford it."

Andrew eyed him suspiciously. "If that's what you truly believe old fruit, then your diagnostic skills *definitely* need brushing up on. I can give you pointers."

The banter continued unabated as Andrew completed his analysis.

"And drugs, of course, cloud that fellow's thinking. They make him employ the likes of you, you see; *sweet words*."

"Sweet words, sweet words," Leon repeated over his shoulder as he made for the door.

Though it had taken him another point down in their jousting game, he'd graciously accepted defeat by bowing to Andrew's playful insult. Theirs was a subtle humor for the duration of which both men generally maintained deadpan faces.

Andrew reveled in his victory and went back to his papers.

"God be with you," Leon closed the door and departed for his car.

As he drove, Fernando's words looped through his mind with nagging persistence.

Andrew was correct; two phrases stood out from the entire litany: 'foul balms' and 'sweet words'.

But what was the significance?

Foul balms meaning drugs? Possibly.

Sweet words meaning hypnosis?

That, he conceded, was possible too. But the more Leon thought about it, the more he became convinced that there was a sinister meaning lurking there.

Chapter 11

"As the hydraulics engage, keep your eyes on the HUD—the heads-up display—as a digital countdown will be running. If you're ready, give a thumbs-up to command when they call for it. Look straight ahead, head back, chin tucked and brace for the hydraulic ram."

"To abort, I pull up on this lever?" Catherine asked, to confirm what flight instruction prep had drilled into her all morning. Though she fought to portray a nonchalance she wasn't feeling, her eyes were stark, staring ahead in terror.

"You're not going to abort," Ken assured, and something forbidding slid through her gut. He signaled the control room with a thumbs up and Kim's voice immediately transmitted to every corner of the operations complex.

"Standing clear for a GO! I see a green light at launch command—do I see thumbs from the simulator? Delta-foxtrot-lima—the simulator—Miss Kaplan—do I see your thumbs?"

With an effort that felt like pushing against clinging mud, Catherine forced her hand within the glove to respond with the thumbs up sign. Her vision was hopping to the thunder of her heartbeat, so loud in her ears that it blotted out the launch announcements.

"And it's a-counting... a-seventeen... a-sixteen... a-fifteen... ignition sequence start... a-twelve... an-eleven... a-ten..." a man's voice spoke.

Ken continued standing alongside the open cockpit, watching her prepare for takeoff; an erotic entree to the promised cyber-sex that drew closer by the day.

All the hardware necessary to produce the required bodysuit had already been assembled and was in surreptitious testing and undergoing software interface. Anton had promised to have it set up and ready for use within a fortnight.

Ken watched Catherine's breasts heaving with the hyperventilation of fear. It appeared that they might at any moment burst their way out of the lace bra restraining them.

Catherine at least had several hours of practical instruction under her belt in an abandoned bid to gain a pilot's license. This was the reason she'd chosen the fighter-pilot program from the ones they'd offered. Flying was the closest matching skill she had to the library of possible options.

"Delta-Foxtrot-Lima... it's a-seven... you're ready for takeoff... six... a-five..."

Catherine was looking down the impossibly short deck of an aircraft carrier. Ahead, out beyond the bow, lay a turquoise army of wind-flecked swells marching in long lines under the driving hull.

Disbelieving her eyes at the realism of the image, she looked to her left, and there was the launch officer in his ship's control turret where Kim should be, his mouth perfectly synchronized with the strong Southern drawl of his count.

"A-four... a-three..." He winked at her, not missing a beat in the count. Winked! She couldn't believe the level of realism.

She looked fixedly ahead and gritted her teeth for the slam of the thrusters; the *thud-thud* of her heart slowing time, the pounding in her ears obliterating the count.

Something to her right where Ken had been a moment earlier appeared in her peripheral vision and her focus snapped to it; a flight crew member's sleeve was flapping as he crouched in the blustery wind.

"A-one... *Launch!*"

At "launch", Catherine was hoofed in the back by what felt like a stallion; the deck exploded into onrushing acceleration, the

153

deck markings a blur as the end of the deck zippedunder her. Gone with it, the familiarity of a base beneath her undercarriage fell away to the ocean.

It was only her spasm of terror that kept the throttle wide open.

The swoop of the aircraft and its sudden roll to starboard galvanized Catherine into action.

Until that moment, she'd been paralyzed by fear, but the treacherous tilt had her on an instant collision course with the waves that flashed by her dipped wing-tip only feet away. The cockpit heeled over to one side and she was compressed into her seat by gut-wrenching centrifugal forces. Instinctively, she leaned against the stubby joystick and pulled the plane out of the turn and into a rattling climb.

The sensation was like none she had ever imagined. The craft jolted and snapped in response to the stick, shuddering with the pummeling forces of overcorrection. Her vision was filled with the blue of heaven and she remained jammed into the near vertical climb.

"JEEEEEES-U-S!" she yelled over the deafening thunder of the jet engines. Then, in the far reaches of her mind, she heard flight control confirming her successful launch. He had gone on to question her piloting skills.

Get fucked, she thought and then wondered if the computer flight controller would be programmed to deal with that sort of message.

Every sinew and fiber in Catherine's body pulsated with shock, every finger felt capped by a throbbing golf ball. Terror supercharged adrenaline through her.

She'd managed to roll the jet into level flight and attempted to maintain a steady heading, knowing that fear paralyzes and she must fight to regain her nerve.

After a few minutes of level flight and a few giddy, sickening swoops when her concentration slipped, she began to relax. *I'll be a passenger for the rest of the flight,* she cunningly decided.

Flight control piped up cheerfully, confirming her headings, the weather and her position according to his radar.

Nobody had told Catherine that she couldn't simply admire the view from her bubble in the manufactured sky.

And besides, she thought, *it'll be the best way to take my mind off of the inevitable landing.*

She started hankering for the comfort of her cherry-flavored *juice-stick*. Or, better yet, "a real cigarette"; it was now all she could think about.

Looking about and above her, she observed fine clouds wisped over the dome and around the wings. Nothing about the experience betrayed that this was all an illusion, taking place within four walls. So, she formulated a plan to trick the computer, reasoning that if she moved quickly enough the sensors that monitored her movement wouldn't have time to relay her actions to the processing unit and feedback images in other directions.

She chose an obscure place to look, reasoning that the computer would be least likely to have insignificant images in its data bank.

She leaned far forward then suddenly whirled her head to look behind her. There, true to real life, was the seat's upright back, complete with all the paraphernalia of oxygen pipes and wiring leading to the simulated helmet she was wearing. She hadn't expected this attention to detail.

When her eyes left the horizon, the plane yawed and swooped. Catherine quickly caught the drift and righted the path once more. Then, after a while, she decided that it was time to execute a slow 180-degree turn and return to ship.

Gently, she coaxed the thoroughbred into a long, banked sweep, and the sensation of G-forces gently pinned her into the seat. The compass rolled lazily as the nose came about, making the sun's shadows swing around within the cockpit until they faced in the opposite direction. With the new course set, she settled into the homeward run.

Catherine had time to consider her predicament and, dreading the approach and landing, she instinctively backed off on the throttles. Immediately, there was a sensation of deceleration. Intrigued, she bumped the throttle open a fraction and watched the gauges respond by several clicks as the gentle thrust from behind her seat confirmed the increase.

The ice of Catherine's trepidation was now broken and a host of conservative experiments begged to be tried. She gave the joystick a minute wiggle and the plane jerked. She elevated then descended in quick succession and the plane dolphined. "This is *fun!*" she squealed with delight.

"Say again? Delta-Foxtrot-Lima."

"Err... tha... that's a negative transmit, o... officer." She'd forgotten that she was being monitored. "Out."

The computer copied transmission receipt.

Catherine felt like a fool talking to the computer, but all the same she hoped that her terminology was authentic. *What does one call a naval flight controller anyway?* she wondered. *Admiral?*

Reminded that this was only an illusion, she had another idea to trick the computer. Without warning, she suddenly looked up toward the sky and sure enough there she saw her own helmeted image reflected back down to her by the canopy. "Well, I'll be buggered," she mumbled under her breath.

The radio crackled into life once more, "Say again? Delta-Foxtrot-Lima."

In her quest to trick the machine, this time she decided to run another test. She said nothing at all.

"Delta-Foxtrot-Lima, do you read me... over."

Still Catherine maintained radio silence.

"Delta-Foxtrot-Lima, please confirm you copy me... over." As if the statement were the product of an intelligent mind, the voice had conveyed a sense of urgency.

It was a major effort to avoid instinctively answering the urgent request, but Catherine bit her tongue.

"Delta-Foxtrot-Lima. Kindly establish..." Suddenly the voice of the computer was cut out and overridden by Kim's concerned voice. "Miss Kaplan? Are you okay?!"

It gave Catherine such a fright that she jumped, making the aircraft swerve. "Y... yes Kim. Sorry, I'm being silly. I've been trying to outwit the computer."

Kim abruptly signed off, apologizing for breaking into the illusion.

Remembering that the entire complex had witnessed her childish folly repeated on every monitor, Catherine cringed with embarrassment, glad for the helmet to mask her shame.

She sat for a while feeling as awkward as an adult in a child's playpen with a stadium full of onlookers, but before long the illusion overtook her senses once more.

The HUD indicated she was flying at three thousand feet over an ocean and the aircraft carrier appeared like a toy just over the horizon on her starboard side. With all the deftness that Catherine could manage, she carefully tickled the throttle back, watching her airspeed drop away. fearful to avoid a mid-air stall, she eased the plane into a long, gliding descent.

The carrier was in full view as she leveled out at eighty feet. The blistering pace of the swell running under her belly was an initial frame of reference by which to judge the plane's breathtaking speed. The image was paralyzing, but worse lay ahead; *much worse.*

Ken had been standing on the surrounding scaffold of the mock plane's cockpit. He'd scrutinized every movement that Catherine had made, noting how the whites of her knuckles had grown more prominent with each passing moment.

The contraption had hissed and shook on its pneumatic mountings. As the unit had rolled to its right in a nose-downward approach, he'd tried to judge the feeling that Catherine might have been experiencing. He'd correctly guessed that she'd misjudged the end of the runway coming up in the launch sequence.

Then he'd seen her wrench the joystick over and back in an effort to correct the craft's nose-dive. Watching the cockpit tip severely, coming to stand on its tail, he'd again guessed correctly that she had been seeing blue sky.

He'd watched her a while longer, but since he knew what adrenaline had been doing to her time perception, he'd quickly bolted up to the control center to have a view of the flight from Catherine's perspective.

The main screen in the control room had been displaying an image that correlated with Catherine's view. Ken had entered the room as Catherine had exclaimed what fun it was. He'd pulled up a chair and continued to watch, chuckling at her stammering reply to the computer 'officer'.

When she'd suddenly looked up at the canopy, he'd asked Kim, "What's she up to?"

"She's trying to fool the computer I guess, Mr. Torrington. Most of the first timers do it, they don't believe that the computer can be so true to life."

"Not a bad little pilot either!" Ken had pointed out and Kim had nodded in agreement.

"Delta-foxtrot-lima, your heading is A-OK but you're closing too fast. Trim airspeed to one-eight-a-zero knots. Over."

Catherine checked her airspeed. The dial read two hundred and thirty knots.

"Do you read me, delta-foxtrot-lima? Over."

"Yes! Err. Affirmative, Sir!" Catherine was beginning to panic. "O... Over."

"Drop your under-carriage, delta-foxtrot-lima. Over."

Catherine checked and realized that the computer was correct. She pulled on the knob and felt the clunky machinery engage. The additional air-drag made the plane shudder and slow. She studied her horizon; the carrier loomed in the center distance but the gap was closing quickly.

"Delta-foxtrot-lima, your range is two miles. Your ETA, forty seconds."

Those forty seconds took forever to pass by and felt more like a week as Catherine ran her final approach checks. Her airspeed was down to 185 knots and the cockpit shook violently as the plane skipped over the wind eddies that kicked up white horses and chop on the water's surface, close and fleeting below.

"Delta-foxtrot-lima, adjust your altitude to seven-zero feet!" the voice said with urgency again. "ETA touchdown, thirty seconds."

Catherine's heart was pounding. A bead of sweat tickled her tear duct before finding its way into her eye. Her vision blurred and the eye stung from the salt. She shook her head violently but the unpleasant irritation could not be dislodged.

The plane began veering dangerously and the controller shouted a string of commands that she tried to obey, "ETA, ten-a... nine-a... de-throttle. Seven-a... descend! Five-a..."

In a moment of panic, Catherine slammed the reverse thrusters into operation and instantly the plane stuttered and began to plummet out of the sky, giving Catherine the sensation of riding inside of a glass elevator.

"THROTTLE-UP! Two-a..." the controller yelled.

In that flit of a second, she remembered her flight instructions: land under full power. Strangely, she also remembered seeing a television documentary years before about landings on carriers. The narrator had said the same peculiar thing, "Planes must land under full power because if the catch cable doesn't engage, the engines must be ready to execute an instant takeoff."

She rammed the throttles to full power as the deck came rushing up to meet her and the last glimpse of ocean disappeared out of sight beneath the nose cone. The backbreaking jar of hitting the deck was an explosion of sound that drowned out the final count of landing.

Catherine was slammed into every bulkhead within the cockpit and the restraining crash harness bit deeply into her flesh. The mayhem of her broadside trajectory took her crashing through the catch barriers that had been pneumatically sprung to slow her momentum. She felt like a casual onlooker watching the scenery go by with resigned acceptance.

After what felt like minutes, the plane slid to a halt. The under-carriage evidently sheared, the cockpit lay canted over to one side with the wing tip propping up the fuselage.

A deathly silence prevailed, broken only by the muted sound of running footsteps. Catherine looked through the cockpit dome to see a figure clambering up onto the listing wing. As he unhooked the canopy, the sound of the wind was the first thing that she could remember... the sound and the face of the man who had run out to meet her—it was Ken who beamed down at her.

Then, without warning, he lunged deep into the cockpit making as if to kiss her full on the mouth. On reflex, Catherine twisted away from him in an effort to avoid his greedy tongue.

Suddenly, there was a touch on her arm and Catherine looked sideways to see the hand, but there was nothing there! Only then did the realization strike her that the *touch* was real, yet her visual perspective was *not*.

She unclipped and removed the helmet. Ken was still leaning into the cockpit of the micro-screen's image. With the world of computer stripped away and the world of reality once more revealed to all of her senses, Catherine felt groggy and disoriented.

The flesh and blood Ken was standing over the open cockpit. "After a landing like *that,* I thought that you'd at least be pleased to see me," he remarked.

Catherine was bewildered, her emotional mind not synchronizing with her intellectual one.

"And to think that I ran to rescue you," he teased. "You'd pull away from my kiss, would you?"

"It looked more like you were about to eat me!" She was forcing her mind to assign the illusion to its proper context.

"Stick around!" he promised, extending a hand to help her out of confinement.

Catherine looked about at the sea of fans smiling down on her through their control room windows. It felt like being on Wimbledon's Centre Court.

"Bumpy landing?" Ken inquired sarcastically.

"Where should I send my doctor bills?" Catherine quipped, massaging her shoulder; he laughed. "Good God Ken, I'd no idea that it could be like that. Christ, I nearly wet myself every second that I was up there."

As she spoke, she instinctively looked skyward where, four stories above, the ceiling of the complex concealed the sky. Catherine was still finding it impossible to reconcile the fact that all of the action had taken place inside a sealed room.

Ken identified her puzzled expression. "Imagine what it would feel like once Leon's finished convincing you that it's not a game. Imagine what it will feel like when you believe it's reality."

She thought about Ken's comment as she walked. *A lucid nightmare,* she guessed. "How long was I up? It felt like an hour," she asked.

"Twenty-three minutes exactly," Ken confirmed. "Imagine again that this wasn't a real-time program. Imagine that you were time dilated. What would it feel like if your mind had been sped up ten or twenty times; where would *that* take you?"

"To Hell!" Catherine answered without any hesitation.

Chapter 12

Catherine was exhausted to her core, aching in muscles that she never realized existed.

"I thought that you went flying?" Jacky queried suspiciously, as she massaged arnica cream into the blue, swollen bruises that blotched every part of Catherine's body.

"Not your kind.... Ouch!" Catherine pulled away as Jacky probed a particularly ugly welt traversing her groin, the handy-work of one of the safety harness.

"It looks like you crashed!" As an airhostess, Jacky was qualified to know a little about aviation. She had been shocked by the seriousness of Catherine's condition and found it difficult to correlate the physical evidence with a flight simulator.

"Actually, I did," Catherine admitted.

Jacky had just arrived home and Catherine hadn't had time to brief her on the afternoon's events.

The stiffness from her physical abuse had begun to set in while Catherine was still on LifeGames' premises.

She'd excused herself and made a run for home before her muscles seized completely. Not being in the mood to cook, she'd treated herself to sweet and sour from her favorite Chinese take-out. Permitting herself the luxury of such oily and batter-heavy food was an agonizing self-conflict vacillating between guilt and reward.

Today, the excuse had been simple: *I've already spent the calories.* Achieving a credit on the calorie count was always the objective.

Jacky had arrived home to find Catherine sitting at the dining table, nearly naked, tending to her injuries between mouthfuls of food. Jacky had taken over the chore, allowing Catherine to finish eating.

As Jacky cleared the table, Catherine's conscience crept back so she repeated the same calorie excuse to Jacky that she'd earlier told herself.

Misery loves company, so once her appetite had been satisfied, she began to feel remorse for her indulgence.

"You're not going to eat, Jacks?" she tempted. If Jacky would partake, it would diminish the weakness in her own mind.

"No thanks Cath, I ate on the plane." Jacky smiled knowingly, letting Catherine stew in guilt.

After tidying up, Jacky went upstairs to find Catherine in a piping-hot bubble bath. Only Catherine's head was showing through the growing tide of bubbles, and the increasing volume of snow-white froth was expanding as the Jacuzzi jets boiled the water into lather.

"Jump in, it's great!"

"I think I will," Jacky answered, already unhooking her bra and letting the straps fall away. Estimating where Catherine's legs might be below the obscuring blanket of white, she stepped in.

"OUUUCH!" Catherine let out a howl; Jacky had guessed wrong.

"I hardly even touched you!" she apologized, then recoiled. "Oh-my-God! I really am sorry." She gently caressed the swollen shin that Catherine produced from below the bubbles. "I'm so sorry, Honey... sorry!"

They lounged in the steamy waters for a while, the herbal salts and an overdose of anti-inflammatory tablets beginning to work soothing miracles. All the while, Jacky maintained her inquisition, extracting every detail of the day's events from Catherine's weary mind.

"I'm going to have LifeGames program you into a court room scene. You can be the prosecutor!" Catherine warned playfully.

"Don't tell me that they've got a court program too?" Jacky asked excitedly. It had long been her yearning to become a lawyer, but cost and the lure of travel had put an end to the idea.

"It's not a *single* program," Catherine pointed out. "LifeGames has every major case in history... or, at least the facts of the case, and how each case turns out is up to the delivery of arguments by the subject."

"You mean I could defend Manson and if I'm convincing enough, he'll go free?"

Catherine nodded and added, "Or you might equally lose a case that has been won in reality!" Following her day in the complex, she considered herself something of an authority on LifeGames' repertoire of options.

Jacky's jaw was hanging slack, her mind envisioning herself in court. "What on earth are they doing for lawyers?" she puzzled.

"Not only lawyers; they're training and assessing most of our judges, teachers, politicians, engineers, doctors... We're going systematically through professions; we'll be targeting the entire legal profession in the next phase of my campaign."

"You can choose to be either defense or prosecution?" Jacky was fixated.

"Sure." Catherine assumed an air of wisdom. "You can also be the judge or on the jury bench, or defense. Roleplaying is your choice."

"Fantastic!" Jacky's mind was racing again as she thought of all the cases in history that had produced an unjust judgment, imagining how she would remedy their outcome.

"Computers are all about choices. That's what LifeGames is really in the business of selling: *choices.* Of course, this is no ordinary arcade game. It's the most advanced facility of its type in the world, with branches in every major city." Frustrated that she was unable to ad-lib the explanations, Catherine was regurgitating verbatim what *she'd* heard.

"Do you think that you could organize a run for me?" Jacky asked with childlike excitement.

Catherine cringed, realizing how silly it had been to build Jacky's excitement to such a pitch, only to have to disappoint her.

"Phew, sorry, but I don't think so, Jacks." Then she realized that there was a perfectly legitimate reason she could give that Jacky would readily accept without feeling hard done by.,

"LifeGames *had* to run me through the program, to help me understand the product."

Jacky looked painfully shattered. The short-lived dream of fulfilling her legal ambition—albeit only to the accolades of a hallucinated audience—had been dashed.

Catherine could see the lingering despair that she had caused so she sought a way to sweeten the bitter pill.

"You wouldn't believe what they're charging... I heard from the secretary that it's thousands of dollars per hour!"

Jacky had a violently jealous nature, and Catherine never personified her clients to her lover by name. She always implied a more distant relationship: the big boss, the accountant, the secretary.

In this case, it was increasingly awkward. Her recent intimate dinner with Nancy was hard to play down and her forthcoming experience with Ken might equally play havoc with spoken truths.

She was too far into her lie to break the silence and needed to keep all parties separate.

Catherine's ploy worked as Jacky's beaten illusions withered in the light of the exorbitant costs.

"I suppose it's outside my budget for this month then..." she sighed, crestfallen.

Most of the pilots on Jacky's airline were constantly undertaking refresher courses at LifeGames to brush up their skills. Considering the costs that Catherine had just revealed, she tried to estimate how much money it must be costing her company. The figure would have to be staggering.

It irked her anew that the pilots could be so blasé about flying the simulator. Yet, she could remember a time when it had been the newest fad and had created an instant hierarchy between those who *had* and those who *hadn't* participated.

It had wedged the gap between pilots and crew ever wider, making many of the pilots more aloof and condescending than they already were. They considered LifeGames training to be far beyond the scope of the crew's needs or understanding.

Despite the internal politics, it had recently been rumored that the entire crew would soon be put through their paces.

"Imagine, Jacks... that's only the price for the older commercial online run, the kind I just did, with all the paraphernalia. The moment you start training with time dilation, using neural linking, it begins to get *properly* expensive!"

Since Ken had just explained the pricing structures to Catherine, the details were fresh in her mind. The steamy bath and champagne they were sipping began to loosen Catherine's tongue.

"A hard cost is a very sophisticated nutritional plaster they've developed. The plasters are one of the secrets of the time dilation; without them you'd be like a car without a gas tank. They're amazing little devils! NASA uses them on spacewalks, but these are..." she checked herself before she spilled more beans. "They're... it's complicated and I forget the details. Anyway, the company also charges a percentage of the rate, which I mentioned earlier, for the time that you *experience*, regardless of how much *actual* time you're hooked up for!"

Jacky was trying in vain to grasp what Catherine was saying; accounting had never been her strongest subject.

"It's really very simple," Catherine proceeded carefully. Let's say that you're a soldier and the military wants to test you on an exercise."

She felt a small pang of guilt as she repeated Ken's words verbatim. She hated parroting someone else's thoughts, but her depth of knowledge on the subject disqualified her from explaining it in her own words.

"You could physically go to the site and do the exercise in the traditional way, but it may take several weeks and the entire staff, companies and battalions... and of course, assessors, would have to be there with you," she explained. "It may also be dangerous and the repercussions on our environment would certainly be costly."

Jacky was smiling at Catherine, enamored with admiration at the grasp that Catherine had of the subject.

"With LifeGames, the soldier can be assessed under battle conditions for a fraction of the cost. There's no danger involved and the computer spits out its assessment whilst the generals or admirals sit back and watch in comfort. But weeks of real time would cost too much. You're still following me?"

Jacky adjusted herself off the jet of water. The area that it had pummeled was numb and beginning to itch with the increased blood-flow. "Only just," she replied. Her mind had wandered and she wasn't following but she agreed anyway, enjoying Catherine's exuberance. "Carry on."

"Time dilation is LifeGames' latest available option. They can speed up your brain twenty- or thirty-fold. The highly sophisticated software and hypnosis makes it all possible." Catherine explained the dynamics of time dilation exactly as Ken had explained it to her. "Got it?"

"Uh-huh…" Jacky grinned, finding a new and particularly pleasurable jet of water.

"Come on Jacks, be serious..." Catherine prodded her playfully in the ribs with a toe. "Where was I? Oh yes. You get nothing for nothing, so besides the cost of the nutritional patch, the army must pay a premium for the technology and the value that *they're* getting out of it."

Jacky sighed with pleasure in response.

Determined to finish, Catherine prodded her again and continued relating her story.

"Although they're only using twenty hours of computer time, their man experiences thirty times that... and thirty times twenty is..." Catherine ran some quick mental arithmetic, "six hundred hours! So even if LifeGames charges them half of the hourly rate, the bill would be a fortune. But the training would be half price with much more gathered data. And it only costs LifeGames one patch and twenty hours to sell three hundred hours at an exorbitant fee! It's no wonder they're the top profit earner this year in Forbes!"

Catherine's words hung in the air as she watched Jacky arching with the pleasure of the water's pulse. She had become wrapped up in her explanation and only now realized why Jacky hadn't been concentrating. She waited silently as the final waves of her spasm washed through Jacky's body.

The experience left Jacky glowing and grinning with contentment.

The warm water and salts had invigorated Catherine's aching body. For the time being, her limbs were free from pain.

"You dirty little rascal! You didn't hear a word of what I said, did you?!"

She leapt across the tub, launching a playful attack on Jacky.

After play wrestling, the two wrinkled prunes climbed out of the bath and patted each other dry with luxuriously thick towels before preparing for bed. In bed, they chatted quietly on a range of subjects as the strains of Mozart filled the cavernous bedroom with the unobtrusive power that only expensive sound systems can deliver.

The low voltage lights were dimmed to a canary yellow and the setting was idyllic with large marble busts atop their stone columns assuming the role of erotic guards of honor.

Set into one wall was a huge exotically stocked fish tank, and through its mood lighting, a kaleidoscope of colors danced to the tune of its softly humming electric pump. The light caressed the lush greens of the potted palms and deep reds of the Persian wall rugs.

Jacky tended Catherine's injuries, her soothing touch in harmony with the surroundings. When the Mozart playlist ended, only the fish tank's gurgle was audible. Jacky rose from the bed and glided naked across the room to pull the patio door closed, her taut body drenched in soft light that accentuated her deep mahogany tan. Catherine stirred, feasting on the vision of her lover. The aches that Jacky had recently massaged still throbbed to the memory of her touch.

Jacky slipped back into the bed and cuddled up close. "I've been thinking..." she whispered next to Catherine's ear, "imagine having sex with that computer!"

Catherine jolted awake, guilt charging through veins, but she lay very still, wondering if Jacky had noticed her response. She didn't have long to wait because within minutes, Jacky had slipped into oblivion, leaving Catherine to watch the fish tank's light making fiery dragons fight on the wall. Fueled by the guilt of her planned infidelity, her aches began to seep back.

Finally, sleep came; bringing its tormented psychedelic nightmares, a serpent bearing Ken's face was trying to force its way into her cockpit. Standing impassively by, watching her feeble struggles, were Nancy and Jacky, arm in arm. By their side, stood an old, hooded priest shouting damnation for her soul.

Jacky awoke from Catherine's tossing and thrashing. She pulled Catherine to her naked breast and consoled her like a mother to her child. "Don't worry baby, I'm here. I'll always be here for you. There's nothing to fear. Sleep baby, sleep."

Catherine's dragons transformed into romping cubs as the fish tank gurgled a soft and comforting lullaby.

Chapter 13

"In league with your master," Nancy repeated.

It was lunchtime and Leon had been playing the recording of his latest session with Roger for her. She was using her spare time to type transcripts of the sessions, a task that had cost her many sleepless nights as the Bishop's words began to invade her dreams.

"You've got a restless spirit," an old friend who claimed to be psychic had once told her. "It's a gift you should develop... learn to understand the spirit world, just open your mind."

The thought of it creeped Nancy out, and she'd ignored the advice.

Reading accounts of the paranormal or watching horror movies was one thing, thrilling even. But it was quite another thing to pursue the supernatural and not know what calamity it might bring. Nevertheless, as time had worn on, like it or not, the Bishop *was* opening a door that Nancy had intended to keep shut.

"In league with your master," she repeated. "Well, we've said *'to hell'* with Ken enough times. I suppose the spell finally worked," she laughed. "Then again, I've always suspected that he's sold his soul to the Devil. *This...*" she indicated, sweeping her pointed index finger around to encompass the empire that Ken had accumulated with her statement, "...doesn't happen for everyone."

Leon grinned. "Now, now, Nancy. Jealousy will get you nowhere." He chanted the child's lyric.

"*Jealousy?* No thank you! We both know what it does to you." Nancy was referring to Ken's moodiness and drug problem. She abhorred moodiness and had made an art out of being cheerful.

"Tut-tut," Leon clicked his tongue at her in jest.

Nancy pushed the play button to resume the recorded session. "Who uses foul balms and sweet words to recruit soldiers into the armies of the Anti-Christ!" She paused the recorder. "My guess is that it's Ken's aftershave that the Bishop is referring to. He bathes in the stuff, you know?" Nancy nodded, confirming her explanation to herself. She joked on, "I've spoken to him a hundred times about it, but it's no use Leon; it's absolutely no use..." She let her voice trail in mock weariness of her fruitless struggles.

Leon chuckled at this lovely lady whom he had come to care so much for.

"And *sweet words*," Nancy continued. "Do me a favor! If that isn't Ken, then I don't know who it is... *Sweet words...* He's the smoothest operator I've ever come across and believe me Leon, I've come across a few! Ken could actually slide *up-hill*, that's how smooth he is."

"Who's smooth?"

The voice was like a gong in a temple; Nancy felt giddy.

"Afternoon Nance, afternoon Leon. Can I see you in my office, Leon? Any messages for me, Nance?" Ken kept talking, as he walked from the entrance past them and into his office.

"Ken..?" Nancy's voice quavered slightly as though she'd seen a ghost. "Afternoon, I thought that you were in Korea today."

"I couldn't make it Nance, something come up. Are you coming, Leon?" Ken didn't looked back as he strode with purpose, speaking over his shoulder as he went.

Neither Nancy nor Leon could hear whether he'd said anything else as he disappeared through his door into his office.

"*Faaaaaark*.... Did he overhear us?" Nancy mouthed to Leon, her eyes wide with fright.

The instant that she had heard Ken's voice, she'd scooped up the recorder and transcript from her desk. The flurry of action had drawn extra attention to their otherwise innocuous presence on her desk.

"Coming... just coming..." Leon sang in a relaxed voice.

He shrugged as an answer to Nancy before shuffling away towards Ken's office.

Halfway to the door, he leaped into the air, clicking his heels like Charlie Chaplin.

"Come in, Leon." Ken was wading through the notes on his desk. "Close the door."

Leon kept eye contact with Nancy as he closed the interleading door, moving with chameleon speed, making horrified faces at her.

Nancy wriggled and twisted, trying to hold back laughter borne of terror. Ken watched Leon's performance from behind, accurately judging that his eccentric colleague must be up to something crazy.

All that he could do was shake his head in amazement at what made the little man tick. Not wanting Leon to know that he had seen the goings on, Ken timed his returned attention to the paper shuffling perfectly with the latching of the closed door.

"What's up then Ken-o? What's up?" Leon was as sprightly as ever.

Since Ken's blow-up over the hypnosis issue, their relationship had begun to repair itself; they'd had dinner together and Ken had accepted that Leon had meant him no harm and had in fact uncovered very little damning information.

"A small problem, Leon. I know that I can trust you and I thought that I'd open up. Something has been getting me down lately."

Leon studied Ken, realizing that he betrayed all the symptoms of insomnia. For several weeks, deep rings of exhaustion had encircled his eyes and he'd been experiencing uncharacteristic lapses in concentration.

Ken had come to the realization that he was in desperate need of psychological help.

He'd weighed the pros and cons of using Leon against involving an outside private practitioner. It wasn't a question of cost. Rather, by nature, he was untrusting and suspicious of psychologists and psychiatrists, and Leon was the only exception to his paranoia.

He'd further rationalized that he need only tell Leon what he felt comfortable imparting. By remaining in control of what he said, he knew that there would be no way for Leon to uncover the web of deceit that he had carefully woven.

Ken had also decided that he needed to share the burden of his secret recordings with someone. He felt that Leon would have a deep understanding for the inexplicable phenomena.

"Let me start by being honest with you," he began. "I know that you're visiting the hospital to conduct a study on the general."

Leon covered his genuine surprise. He didn't deny what Ken had stated, neither did he ask Ken for his source of information.

"At first, I was angry; I felt betrayed that you went to the hospital against my express orders." Ken stroked his chin. "I must admit, once I discovered the results you're getting, it made me proud to have a man of your caliber on the staff."

Sweet words, Leon thought, seeing straight through Ken's buttering him up. "Thank you," he replied.

"You know that I've always been a skeptic about the super-natural, the after-life... things that go bump in the night."

"Not you, Ken-o? Surely not you?" Leon kidded.

For years, Ken had been ragging on him about his interest in the occult and those jeers had accumulated within Leon's memory. Now, with Ken rattled by something in that same vein, it provided Leon with the perfect opportunity to administer some of the medicine that Ken had liberally dished out over the years.

"Please Leon. I'm serious, I *need* your help."

There was a genuine plea there, a desperation in Ken's voice that Leon had never thought he would hear, and he snapped into his professional role. "I'm sorry Ken, I didn't realize."

"As I said, I must get something off of my chest," Ken resumed. "I need your promise that you will keep this all to yourself."

Leon weighed Ken's words carefully, taking them seriously. "Ken, let me explain something. I flit around here in my own little world and it's relaxing for me. I'm at my best when I can work in an easy atmosphere. But when the chips are down," he paused dramatically, "when they're down, then I'm a hell of a good psychiatrist."

Ken knew Leon's words to be true and there was a moment of silence as each man focused on what they would say next. Ken spoke first.

"I've never had an interest in religion or the occult, that sort of thing; you of all people know that I'm a dyed-in-the-wool rationalist. You know that I've always rejected that nonsense, Leon, yes?"

Leon allowed Ken some time to recap what a thoroughly shallow, money-grubbing lout he'd always been.

Ken's self-centered views were most certainly *not* news to Leon but what *was* news to Leon was the incident that had sparked Ken's reformation.

Ken confirmed that the turning point in his views had come with the death of Craig.

"As you know, I'd been distraught all day because of the police investigation, backed up work, security being down because of the gate—all that. I was exhausted so I took a couple of sleeping pills around lunchtime and went to sleep. After I'd slept, I found that there were quite a few messages waiting for me on the voicemail." Ken continued recapping, "It must have been around seven or eight in the evening."

Leon observed as Ken scratched vigorously at the lower lid of his eye; the action that always betrayed his lies. The more vigorous the scratching, the bigger the lie. The scratching always commenced with the first words of the lie and ended simultaneously with the last.

This scratching routine lasted for the entire duration of Ken's account.

You weren't really sleeping, so what were *you doing?* Leon silently pondered.

"There had been a few *personal* calls, one from Nancy and another from Craig. There had also been some less important ones after that." Ken cleared his throat. "Nancy had called at precisely five minutes to five o'clock. Twenty minutes earlier, Craig had called at twenty-five to five. Both calls were from the late afternoon on the day of Craig's death, except... Craig should have been cold and stiff and in the morgue for God's sake!" Ken's voice rose to a squeal.

Although Ken had laid out all of the facts in his protracted build-up, Leon had been so busy trying to sift for lies that the story didn't gel in his mind until he heard Ken's final summarizing sentence.

It took a moment for the implication to sink in, then the significance struck Leon like a blow.

"Are you sure, Ken? Are you positive that the message was recorded *after* Craig was already dead?"

"Absolutely. I had cleared voicemail the day before. The call log and date stamp on the message agree... it happened. Nancy even confirmed the time of her call and, according to Stuart in IT, they were definitely in sequence." Ken ground his teeth. "Before Nancy's call, there had been a message from the police officer investigating the case with a message about a dead man, before the dead man's call. It doesn't take a genius to see there's something wrong with that! Then Catherine called a few minutes after this weird call from Craig that shouldn't have been possible, and both *she* and the log also confirm the date and time. It's impossible... but it's conclusive."

Ken was very rattled.

It was cruel of Leon, but it was payback for Ken's many years of dishing out skepticism and ridicule; now, with Ken terrified, it was amusing to toy with him, make him work to prove he wasn't mistaken or insane.

"A hoax?" Leon suggested.

Emotionally, he loved the evidence that Ken was painting a picture of; if it proved true, it would provide concrete support for the view that he'd spent a lifetime and so many books trying to legitimize.

But as a scientist, Leon had a commitment to initially find a logical solution. He was professionally bound to plod through the obvious solutions first.

Ken became defensive, his voice rising yet more excitedly. "Not a chance of a hoax! Stuart checked for that too."

"What do *you* think it was?" Leon wanted Ken to commit himself to an opinion.

"I don't know, that's why I've come to you." Ken was too cagey to put his head in the noose. Admitting to an after-life would bring too many questions to bear on his personality and his actions in his present life. "What do you think?"

"Do you want a doctor's answer, or the answer of a crazy old man who believes in ghosts and goblins?"

"Both." Ken's answer was no surprise to Leon.

"As your doctor, I know what you have always thought of these things. I'm talking here about you being an agnostic, maybe an atheist. Am I right? It seems something about this experience has changed you."

Ken began to answer Leon by filling him in on the content of Craig's recorded message. He had brought the recording with him to let Leon assess it for himself and together they ran through it, Leon listening intently.

Something about the strange cacophony captivated Leon yet he couldn't place what it was.

Ken attempted to put his own impressions into words, "It had a very strange... an unfamiliar emotional effect on me, Leon. I've never experienced anything like this before."

It seemed as if Ken was telling a lie when he said "before", but Leon wasn't sure. He considered what significance there could be if Ken had told a lie, without perhaps realizing it himself. What if he really *had* previously had an experience like this?

Would the answer to that question be the solution to an even larger puzzle? Leon wondered.

By telling Ken a white lie of his own, and thereby tricking his subconscious mind into revealing some of its secrets, Leon thought that he might achieve clarity.

"Sorry to interrupt Ken, but are you *sure* that this was the first time that something like this has ever happened to you? I hate to have to bring it up, but it may be important. When you were hypnotized at the hospital, you started to tell me about other experiences that you'd had. Can you remember ever having other supernatural experiences before this?"

Leon was watching Ken's body language, watching for that scratch of the lower lid, seeking to reveal answers to his suspicions. What he did see was Ken's genuine attempt to ferret out the elusive threads.

"I think," Ken spoke as he sifted through his memory, "Don't hold me to this, Leon—but I *think* that it may even go back to around the time that I started LifeGames. It seems strange, now that you mention it, but *I do* recall having had an experience like this before. It's weird!"

He shuddered—Leon saw it and decided to question Ken laterally in the hope that by not asking direct questions, but rather associated ones, he'd be able to build up a profile of Ken's experiences.

"Did the stress of LifeGames give you a different perspective on the meaning of life?"

Ken thought about Leon's question; it made little sense. After all, he'd faced enormous stresses prior to launching LifeGames. "Sorry Leon, I'm not sure what you mean."

"All right Ken, that was a little vague." Leon carefully rephrased his question, "Sometimes, during periods of great stress, the conscious mind becomes exhausted. Meanwhile, with all of the excitement and adrenaline present, the subconscious becomes *overactive* during sleep. Have you ever found that when times become stressed, you start to dream a lot more than usual?"

Ken began to nod and the nod gained momentum as he searched his own mind, becoming vigorous; much more vigorous than Leon would have thought appropriate to the question.

It was a good sign. Ken was uncovering something about himself, so Leon pressed the point further.

"Dreaming can be a symptom. By simultaneously contemplating the..."

But Ken had ceased to listen, his eyes glazed with introspection and he continued to nod as memories ran through his mind. "Dreams..." he murmured.

"Dreams?" Leon repeated, dropping his own line in favor of spurring Ken to dredge deeper.

"No... no, not dreams; they were nightmares!" Ken replied, reconsidering his initial definition.

Leon could sense a breakthrough about to occur. "What kind of nightmares?"

"I... I don't know. Honestly. Th... they..." Ken sighed, unable to focus on the elusive recollection. "Damn it, I can't remember," he growled. "It's right there, but I can't get hold of it."

"It's ok Ken, we'll get there," Leon reassured, well aware of the role that positive affirmation could play in assisting a patient.

Hypnosis would be the ideal method to circumvent this impasse, but for Leon, it remained a frustration to have the tool so readily available yet be banned from suggesting its use.

"What is the first word that comes to your mind when you think of the nightmare?" Leon posed.

"Terror." Ken did not hesitate in his answer, then added, "I know, that must be kinda obvious."

"No, no." Leon cautioned, "Don't spoil the thought with a negative. I want you to clear your mind. Here, catch..." He threw Ken a priceless crystal ornament that had been lying on the desk, and as Ken scrambled to save it from breaking, Leon fired off a question, "When did you play ball last?"

Ken was furious. "What kind of idiot thing was *that* to do?" he yelled, incensed by Leon's recklessness.

"Good," Leon chirped happily. "Your mind's clear."

Ken looked at him in bewilderment, disbelieving his own ears at Leon's strange methods for achieving results.

Leon seized the moment to strike, peppering Ken with a barrage of briskly asked questions. "Your nightmare. Terror! What do you feel? What do you hear? What can you see? What?"

"The sound." Ken sprung from fury to elation, "That's it! *It was the same sound as on the recording!*"

Leon tapped Ken's mobile lying on the desk, which contained the uncanny sound recording on it. "This sound?"

"Yes, exactly the same sound. No wonder it gives me the creeps when I hear it!" Ken shuddered anew with the memory revealed.

Leon wanted to recheck his own response to the sound. "Do you mind if we hear it again?"

They ran the recording through several times and, although it was a creepy experience, it revealed nothing more.

There were various people that Leon could think of who might be able to throw more light on the recording. The only way for him to investigate any further would be to have a copy but he judged that it was not the time to ask for one.

Instead, he'd find a way to get his hands on it some other time.

"Let's recap," Leon suggested. "You *were* a confirmed skeptic, but now I guess that you'd call yourself... *open?*"

Ken agreed.

"And the change is the result of nightmares?"

Ken agreed again.

"Anything more?"

Ken shook his head.

"I'm afraid that it doesn't give us much to work with Ken, but its progress nonetheless. Its progress..." Leon maintained affirmation.

"You're finished playing doctor?" For the first time ever, Ken seemed anxious to hear a theory from the crazy old man in Leon's personality.

"Finished as finished can be."

"Coffee?" Ken offered, feeling a hankering to clear his mind.

"Why not... why not indeed."

"Nance. Two coffees, please," Ken spoke into the intercom.

"O..." Nancy's reply was cut off mid-word when he released the button.

"I am bursting for a leak," Ken said as he stood up; he scratched his eye again. "I'll be a moment."

When Ken left the room, Leon tapped the phone with his index finger and asked, "What secrets do you contain?"

He wished he could risk taking a peek, but there was no way he could dare. Besides, it was sure to have a password, and there just wasn't time.

The automated coffee was quick, and Nancy came into the office before Ken returned. Hurriedly, she whispered in an urgent tone, "What's up?"

"I'll tell you later," Leon promised.

"Did he overhear us?" she insisted, as she'd been sitting on pins and needles.

"No..."

Just as Leon started to answer, Ken entered the room, forcing him to finish his sentence with a decoy.

"...sugar for me, thanks Nance. I'm trying to cut down... cut, cut, cut..." Leon detested sugarless coffee but he needed to throw Ken off any hint that they'd been discussing him.

Instantly realizing what Leon was doing, Nancy provided him with an escape out of his stated commitment. "Are you sure?" she asked.

"Actually... no; why suffer? Two as usual," he said, following her lead. "I'll start my diet tomorrow. Tomorrow's a better day."

As she passed out the cups, Nancy marveled at Leon's ability to think quickly when he needed to. It was an ability that ran contrary to every other aspect of his personality.

It was obvious to Leon that during his cloakroom visit, Ken had achieved a miraculous lift in his energy. It was also clear that he was anxious for Nancy to leave the office.

The moment that she was gone he asked, "You still in crazy-old-man mode? Jekyll or Hyde?"

"Absolutely unadulterated Jeklyll," Leon said cheerfully. "Ab-so-lutely, Ken-o."

Leon proceeded to fill Ken in on what he'd gleaned from Bishop Fernando and, although the crazy old man mode was evident, Ken was glad that Leon hadn't resumed the worst of his over-the-top style of eccentricity. It was a trait of Leon's that generally irked Ken, since he couldn't come to terms with what it was that made the trait ebb and flow.

Leon noticed something as he related Roger's hypnosis session to Ken. He stopped mid-sentence and asked Ken to have Nancy bring in the recording and the transcript she'd worked on.

When she entered, Nancy looked startled. Not aware of all that the two men had discussed, she assumed that trouble was brewing over Leon's unsanctioned visit to the hospital and her unauthorized participation in it. She left, her stomach still knotted with trepidation.

After she'd gone, the pair listened to the Bishop's ranting, then Leon put his hypothesis to the test with Ken.

"If we take his words literally, then 'your master' must be referring to *you*. Correct?"

"Correct," Ken replied.

"And the 'Beast' is presumably... worst case... Satan."

"Presumably," Ken answered hesitantly, unconvinced.

"'In league with' in the Bishop's parley; that would approximately mean *working with* or *working for*, I presume?"

"I guess so." Ken frowned, trying to understand what exactly Leon was driving at.

"So, *he* thinks that *you* are working with... or maybe for Satan."

"He may, but it wouldn't be much of a theory, Leon. I reject all that tripe... we're just ordinary flesh and blood doing its thing... no magic. I'd hardly be much of a candidate for this Satan guy to impress."

"Actually, the Bible-thumpers would say that you're his *best* candidate," Leon corrected him. "And you may indeed be the best candidate, but that's another story."

"That bunch of nuts..." Ken scoffed.

"There may be something to it, Ken. They say the Devil does his most successful work with those who believe he doesn't exist."

"Very convenient," Ken shrugged scornfully.

"What on earth was my point," Leon sighed. "Ah, yes. Fernando says that you're using 'foul balms'." Leon watched for Ken's scratch, and it was vigorous. "...and 'sweet words' to recruit soldiers. Any idea what he's on about? *Foul balms*?" Leon said it again, the trigger word that had set Ken off a second earlier.

"It sounds like ordinary ranting."

Ken's newfound openness was suddenly beginning to close. Leon could see him fighting to keep his voice steady and strong, and keep his hands from fidgeting, but his forehead was prickling with sweat, with stress.

"Do you *really* think this guy is genuine, Leon? It sounds like bullshit."

In the tone, Leon sensed that there was something even more going on, but he thought it wise to let it pass and file it away for another day.

"These religious loons do tend to go on, don't they Ken-o... they sure do go on."

Leon realized that he was quickly painting himself into a corner; Ken was smart and would realize he was onto something—his only refuge would be to exaggerate senility and act the buffoon.

Just then, fate came to his aid in the form of the intercom beep. Ken held his hand up for silence.

"Yes, Nance?"

"Ken, is Leon still with you?"

"Yep," Ken snapped.

"They need him in operations; could he please get a hold of Henry? It's urgent."

"Will do, thanks Nance." Ken turned the intercom off. "Thanks for your time, Leon."

"Only a pleasure, Ken-o. Only a pleasure old chap; I'm sorry we couldn't get to the bottom of it."

As Leon was leaving the office, Ken called after him, "Where'd you learn to distract someone by tossing priceless crystal around, just to uncover what's on their mind?"

"I didn't, Ken-o... just thought it up," Leon replied nonchalantly.

Then, as he reached the door, he turned back to Ken, absently repeating to himself loud enough to be overheard, "Foul balms and sweet words..."

Ken scratched.

Chapter 14

It was nine fifteen in the morning when the phone rang. "Cath Kaplan," she answered, with her lyrical signature greeting.

For the next four consecutive days, butterflies flitted around in Catherine's stomach and she barely slept at night.

Every time she thought of it, her breath caught in her throat and the palpitations in her breast came in tantalizing waves. Agony and ecstasy intertwined, forming a knot below her belly button.

The source of this great heady rush were just two words, *"It's ready."*

Those had been the only words Ken had spoken when she'd answered; he'd said it and hung up.

Determined to outlast his patience, Catherine refused to react to his mind game by calling him back. Hour after gut-twisting hour ticked by in a procession of glacial procrastination.

"So, you *are* still alive." Ken's voice was sarcastic, but there was lust below the surface.

"Apparently." Catherine was haughty in response.

"Oh, come on Cath." Ken's resolve failed him; swamped by desire, it crumbled away.

In that instant, he realized that a change in tactics by quitting the charade was his only chance to fulfill his desires.

"When are you coming out to play," he whined like a child.

Surprisingly out of character, Catherine thought.

It was the moment of truth. It had been weeks running into months since he'd challenged and she'd accepted... innuendo filled emails, conversations and private quips passing between the two in front of colleagues.

And now the day had dawned.

He'd invested hugely to get it ready; she had pondered long and hard about the ethics of it. She dared not do it, but she couldn't pull out either; it was too far gone.

What to do? How to respond?

She could hear him breathing on the other side of the phone—how long could she say nothing?

"I've been expecting your call since Friday."

"Oh!" she exclaimed in a caustic tone, trying to hide the relief in her voice that the childish game could be over. "Was that *you* who called on Friday? and here I was thinking that it must have been a wrong number."

She took refuge in Ken withholding caller-ID from recipients.

"I wanted to see if you would be free," Ken began to reply feebly.

"You wanted to see if I would be free?" Catherine mocked, controlling the conversation, still scrambling for the final decision that would need to be made any second. "Do you think I'm a fast food take-out?" She said it playfully, carefully.

"I won't know that till I eat you," Ken ventured awkwardly, the delicate negotiation stripping him of confidence.

"Who says I'm edible?" she replied, but her loins had their own agenda, an image bursting in her mind and a rushing sensation deep in the cocoon of her pelvis seemed to suck with the insistence of a light vacuum making her breath quick and shallow.

"We've got down-time tomorrow. Any chances?" Ken asked offhandedly, as if the reply didn't matter to him.

"Well, let me see..." she leafed noisily through her notebook as if it was a day-planner, keeping the phone close to the pages so he'd hear them turning. "Gee... it looks so busy... I doubt it. Let's see, how about Thursday the twelfth?"

Catherine could easily make the arrangement for the following evening and in truth she had every intention of doing so, but now it was *her* turn to play a waiting game and make Ken suffer.

Catherine could hear the pages of Ken's day-planner being turned, seeking that date far in the future.

"You're joking!" he responded sounding peeved, "...that's almost three weeks' time!" There was shrill alarm in his voice; it was out of his control. "No Cath... *Come-on!* Christ-Jesus, you can't do this."

"And why not?" she answered, maintaining the upper hand. "I'm also a professional."

Ken saw his plans floundering, tripping over ego and knew he must tone it down.

"How long has it taken to come up with the game? What are a few more days?" Her digs at Ken were driven by fear and awkwardness.

"I know... I know, it's been almost three months. We had problems, but that's exactly my point. Why must we wait *another* three weeks?"

Animal desire blinded Ken to any vestige of pride, lust making him drive an otherwise degrading bargain.

He begun begging.

Catherine wondered how long she could tolerate his suffering before lust turned into aggression. *Not long,* she assured herself.

"Ok... There's a chance that I can cancel my date for tomorrow night but I can't promise you anything. This is short notice, Ken." She milked whatever she safely could from her advantage. "But if I *can't* make it tomorrow, you're the boss... I'm sure you can arrange another convenient time?"

"I'm well aware that I'm the boss, Catherine," Ken responded bitingly, "but I can't simply put a booking into the roster because the computer will automatically assign a team."

By the sound of Ken's voice, Catherine guessed that she had stretched his patience to its absolute limit.

Ken continued bellyaching, "Unfortunately, it's very difficult to find the gaps for down-time we need to set up our equipment. Short notice is the *only* way that we can arrange it, Cath... This is just as awkward for me." He tagged the apology onto the end, trying to remove the friction from their proposed engagement.

"All right, I'll see what I can do," Catherine relented.

"I'll try to keep the booking open," Ken promised and Catherine wanted to burst into laughter. He sounded like a teenager on a first date desperately trying to maneuver through all of the obstacles making him as awkward as a duck climbing stairs.

"I'll be in touch." She closed the conversation.

They hung up with the issue still a hot potato.

There had been neither intention nor hint of romance from either side in their negotiation; it was full of naked lust and both of them knew it. Products of the liberated age, the promise of raw thrills had driven the pair onto the marshy bog of carnal desire.

Contemplating it privately, each concluded that lust for lust's sake was not an entirely bad state to entertain; lust and romance were entirely distinct emotions they could deal with separately.

Catherine pondered it all day. *It was rather like her first visit to the school doctor,* she thought, *inevitable and terrifying, yet deliciously decadent... I must be warped.*

Ken phoned again at lunchtime but Catherine could offer him no confirmation.

His call at four thirty caught her in a meeting. "Catherine..." the intercom on her desk piped.

"Yes, Jenn?" Catherine responded; Jenny was Kaplan's receptionist.

"Mr. Torrington called *again*, he sounds distressed." Not understanding the situation, Jenny's voice had been infected by Ken's insistence.

Still, Catherine remained determined to draw out his agony a while longer. "You told him that I was in a meeting?" she queried.

"Yes. But he was *very* insistent, and said that he was leaving his office and going home. He mentioned that he might pop by *here*, on his way."

Catherine flared with anger at Ken's presumptuousness. She had no desire to see him; she was relieved to be forewarned.

She quickly estimated that with no traffic, it would take him half an hour to travel the distance. But since he would have to push through the evening rush hour, she was content that time remained on her side.

"Ok Jenn, buzz me at ten to five. I must get a move on before he gets here. I'm not going to see him without an appointment." She signed off, then began to wind up the meeting with her staff.

By five o'clock, Catherine was on the road and very pleased that Ken was ignorant of her home address.

He was also not in possession of her unlisted home phone number. She knew that she would be safe from his harassment. Then, after thinking about it, she realized that she would have to call him anyway lest he label Jenny as a bad receptionist who didn't pass on messages.

With a sigh of annoyance, she scrolled to his name and hit the Call button;

"Torrington," came the authoritative voice in a tone that poorly cloaked a lashing of irritation—he'd obviously seen her name come up.

"*Ken?*" Catherine barely recognized his voice.

"Catherine?" he barked back. "*Where the hell have you been?*" His irritated snap betrayed a spoiled personality of someone accustomed to getting their own way.

"*Don't you dare use that tone with me!*" Catherine fired back, instinctively going on the offensive; her anger was genuine. Client or no client, she wasn't going to let him get away with brash rudeness.

"S... s... sorry Cath, I... I've had a hell of a day," Ken retreated.

All day he'd been unable to focus on anything but his lust, he'd become obsessed with it. The irrationality of animal instinct had gone so far as to make him jealous over the whereabouts of Catherine, his fantasy lover.

"I've had a hell of a day too but I don't harass Nancy and then bite your head off!" Catherine had also done little more than fantasize the day away, and expressed it now in anger.

Now unfolding, was the strangest mating ritual that two people could play. The forces of instinct were at fever pitch, making the two victims of lust cannibalize each other's emotions in an unholy orgy of dominance.

Each had spoken their mind with all the finesse of wrestling porcupines, but Ken knew that bringing the tussle to a conclusion would be a process of cautious negotiation.

"Where *are* you?" Ken inquired, referring to their particularly poor connection. "It sounds like you're calling from the moon."

His question had been delicately phrased, as though he were dealing with the finest china that might shatter at the slightest mishandling.

"I'm in my car, on my way to deal with a big problem we're having across town," Catherine lied.

"Any chance of seeing you later?" Ken asked, not sure if he could bear the tension of seeing Catherine or hearing her refusal. Yet, he had to broach the subject of their proposed date.

"No chance I'm afraid, they're going to press with this job in the morning so it *must* be completed by tonight. I'll have to push through this problem even if it takes all night."

"I'm being silly even asking," Ken backtracked, attempting to redeem his pride. "I've also got a few things to get through."

The phone crackled with his distress and his gut wrenched as his mouth refused to speak the words that he demanded of it.

Catherine could sense his anguish and she surmised its source. She would not yield, or give him the confirmation that he desperately desired. *Stew, you bastard,* she thought; *stew!*

Ken sensed that the conversation was at its end. With all of the coercion that he could muster, he dragged out of himself the question that they both knew he'd called to ask—trying to make it sound like an afterthought.

"Hmm. Oh yes. Anything more about, maybe... tomorrow?"

"Unfortunately not," Catherine replied, battling to wipe the grin off her face, "but I'll let you know tomorrow."

Her fence sitting cost both of them a sleepless night.

Chapter 15

"Goodness gracious!" Catherine exclaimed. "Couldn't you find anything more revealing?!"

Her crotch felt sodden and heavy and the blush she'd carefully been restraining since her arrival became a glowing beacon.

Never in her active sexual pursuits had such a height of tension escalated for so long, leading up to an event.

For three days, as the bristling negotiations around the cyber-sex had pressed on, Catherine had sought sanity and release from the madness of it through private means. When that hadn't worked, she'd turned on Jacky.

"What is it with you, girl?" Jacky had sighed between wracking orgasms. "You're insatiable!"

Each idle moment had been an opportunity not to be missed; driving became a hazard as she weaved through the traffic, guiding the car with one hand and reckless abandon.

"It's not exactly standard IBM peripherals, Cath. Anton did the best with what was available," Ken explained, defending the creation.

Anton was a programmer first, an integration engineer second, and an amateur model builder as a distant third. He had constructed the entire mechanism from spare parts, some bought through online pornography catalogues.

Catherine blushed her deepest scarlet at the mention of his name; the way he looked at her, she was positive that Anton had figured out for whom he had been constructing the suit.

The contrivance termed a 'suit' was nothing more than a connected tangle of webbing straps and attachments that had little in common with anything vaguely garment-like.

Ken was trying to act calm and appear suave in a clumsy attempt to convey the impression of 'all in a day's work'.

He would have done much better, Catherine thought, by dropping the bravado act and immersing himself into the novel thrill, which it really was for each of them.

"Champagne?" he offered, handing Catherine a glass.

The surface of the honey liquor was a'tremble; a loyal transmitter of the hand that held it out to her.

"Thanks." Catherine took it with no greater steadiness.

"To Caligula."

Ken's tactless toast to the Roman Emperor, infamous for his orgies, brought images of the Coliseum rushing back into Catherine's mind.

For a reason alien to her knowledge, she shuddered with the familiarity of the thought and a chill ran up her spine.

Like two cats circling each other, neither wanting to make the first challenge, they drew out the moment, skirting the business at hand.

This is weird, Catherine thought, unable to decide whether she was enjoying or loathing the prolonged buildup. Ken's frayed nerves were making him drone on tediously as he explained the technicalities of the program.

The delicate precipice of stimulation threatened to crumble under the load of his dreary waffling. Aware of his awkward approach, he was desperately scrambling, seeking to take charge of his own mouth and the situation.

With the vehement intensity of two magnetic like poles, a hidden hand invisibly held them at arms' length and neither could breach the wall of the other's intimate space. Both were acutely aware that the situation could no longer be sustained.

Unable to withstand the tension, Catherine drained the dregs from her glass and took the initiative; alcohol had become her kind assistant dulling the keen edge of her inhibitions.

"The show must go on!" She almost gagged on the cliché that spilled from her mouth.

She took Ken's hand and gave it a squeeze, making his Adam's apple turn a somersault and his complexion turn instantly pale, his voice equally insipid.

"Let the ga... games begin," he croaked and had to clear his throat mid-way through the tired and overworked line.

Intending to distract her mind from what lay ahead, Catherine had purposefully worked late that evening. Once home, she had taken a long warm bath and only with a will of steel did she resist the urge to relieve the aching sexual tension that incessantly nagged at her.

She had taken her time soaking and douching herself, wanting to be meticulously fresh when the time for being exposed would inevitably arrive.

Her drive to the LifeGames premises had been an indistinguishable blur. All the excitement of her fighter jet simulation now seemed insignificant to the heart-pounding that spurted adrenalin into the tiniest capillary of her being.

Now, the time to make ready was upon Catherine and her heart was a leaden anchor pounding out her ecstatic agony.

They were two strangers about to partake in the most pre-meditated act of sexual exposure possible.

What the hell am I doing? Catherine's mind cried out, cartwheeling in opposition to her shaking fingers as they fumbled for endless seconds to unfasten each button on her crisp, white blouse.

The silk garment fell away, exposing a heaving rib-cage topped by two lace-cupped protuberances of breathtaking magnificence. "Errr, must I take this off too?" she stammered, any hint of voice control eluding her.

"Afraid so." Ken was suffering the same vocal malady.

Her bra slipped off but the flesh that it had retained stood proudly erect with turgid nipples, moist from the sweat of anticipation. With his peripheral vision, Ken ogled Catherine's first exposure of naked flesh as her skirt fell to the floor and she stepped out of it.

He could hardly bear the sight as she peeled away the silken, moistened G-string. He tried to cling to his casual manner, failing dismally, fumbling with the body strap that he was preparing.

The scene had become all that he could handle as he moved cautiously to avoid displaying his achingly engorged manhood. His erectile dysfunction had become his greatest frustration in life. Once so strong and virile, it had become almost impossible for him to achieve an erection without stimulants or perversity.

His vision hopped with each thump of his heart; it felt like he should sit before he fell down in a faint. But time ran out on him.

"Ready!" Catherine's voice was clear and confident.

Deciding to stop the deadly serious pangs, she had taken charge of herself and let her inhibitions fly from her.

She was stark naked, her hands held skyward and her back arched in the pose of a female gymnast. Nuzzling from a neatly trimmed pubic tuft was a slightly protruding flange. Ken gulped audibly at the vision.

Catherine first knelt, then lay back with legs splayed as Ken fitted the equipment. It was a necessary procedure that they both pretended to endure, yet secretly found to be an aching stimulation.

"What a way to get to know each other!" Ken croaked, his voice breaking up as he spoke.

With all the wiring, pipes, bags and paraphernalia plugged in and ready to go, she stood alongside the contraption that would play midwife to her coming fantasy.

Ken dared for a second to gorge on every minute detail presented to him, but it made him all thumbs as he struggled to adhere the time dilation plaster onto her skin.

"Th... the worst is over," he stammered, trying with dismal capacity to make small talk.

Catherine stepped into the harness that clasped into a girdle that would fit snug up under her, forming a modern chastity belt for a kinky new age.

"No need for lubrication here!" Ken exclaimed as he brought the phallic focus of the contraption into contact with her.

The seating of the thick and knobbed implement was an explosive sensation that made Catherine wince as it nestled close to her G-spot, strumming her hair-trigger sensitivity. With two fingers, she adjusted the mini-phallus hinged onto the larger one inside of her. Identifying the blood-engorged bead of flesh that she sought, she placed the small stimulator into contact with her throbbing delight.

"All ready?" Ken's voice was husky.

"Yes," she sighed her answer, once the contraptions had settled delightfully into position.

Minutes later, she was rigged onto the same gyroscope that she'd watched play host to the war game weeks before.

The affixed nipple stimulators began a gentle and insistent tug of suction.

Ken had said there were too many skin-contact straps for the nano-infused smock to provide feedback; she'd have to remain in the buff—it was something she hadn't anticipated. Instead of the smock, monitors on her temples and sternum would wirelessly feed the computer data back and forth. Ken would use the remote-control tablet to stay close at hand and monitor the event.

With her helmet on, Catherine became the helpless and blind victim of Ken's voyeurism as he circled beyond her synthesized world. Ken prepared for the show of a lifetime.

Chapter 16

The fire crackled and hissed in its hearth and two women lay sprawled before it. A boxer was watching them over his crossed front paws, his eyes moving from one to the other as they took turns speaking.

Lying on her side, Nancy had assumed a fetal position, wrapping herself around Catherine's body and Catherine was using Nancy's thigh and hips as her backrest. Her own legs lay flat on the ground before her.

Thin and poignant strains of oboe drifted on the air, embracing them in currents and eddies of sound.

"God Cath, you look like death, girl!" Nancy's initial greeting to Catherine on her doorstep hadn't been intended as an insult; it had been a plain and shocked assessment.

The Catherine that had appeared before her was gaunt and pale.

"It looks like the life's been drained out of you."

Nancy had taken Catherine's hand and guided her through the door, into her inviting cottage and warm maternal arms.

"I think that it has," Catherine had agreed.

"Now you relax, I'm about ready to start dishing up. Wine?"

"I can't even bear the thought!" Catherine held her hands up in surrender. "You carry on."

Nancy had shown Catherine her half-full glass in response. "What have you been up to my wicked friend, playing truant? That much I do know. I tried to reach you both on Thursday and yesterday."

"I got your messages, thanks Nance. I've been resting, I'll tell you all about it over dinner," Catherine had promised.

"I'll bet it has to do with Ken." Nancy couldn't help but fish for clues, she wasn't a patient gossiper. "He's been like a man possessed, Cath; on at me all of the time to call you," Nancy had chuckled.

Catherine had laughed too, but it was shallow and only a social conformity, not driven by any modicum of amusement.

"It was ridiculous the number of times that I was *supposed* to phone through but I didn't bother... I just told him whatever came to mind. 'She's in a meeting', 'She's on a plane', 'I left a message'. What did you do to the man?"

Catherine had seen what Nancy was up to, prompting for details. "Wait till dinner Nance, I'm not going to tell you before."

"You know what?" Feigning deafness, Nancy had badgered onward. "He wanted your home number and... *sheeez*... did he blow his stack when I told him I didn't have it!"

Catherine's home number was little known beyond family and her closest friends.

Catherine's unyielding stance against imparting more gossip till she was ready had been motivation enough for Nancy to dish out the meal in record time.

If Catherine looks this tired, she'd assured herself, *it has to be a hell of a story!*

It was Saturday night, seventy-two hours since Catherine's cyber-sex episode.

Over dinner, Catherine had kept her promise, breaking the news and giving the details.

"I thought that I was going to watch," Nancy had pouted.

"That was my line," Catherine had corrected her.

It had taken the entire meal for Catherine to describe the delicious build-up to the game.

Nancy had been transfixed, stimulated to distraction. She had continually forgotten to eat until finally she gave up altogether, leaving the bulk of her meager portion untouched.

Her exhaustion forgotten, Catherine had risen to the occasion, leaping in and out of her seat to demonstrate every detail.

At the end of the meal, they had retired to Nancy's living room where the fire was raging. With food in her stomach and the excitement invigorating her once more, Catherine had decided to accept a sherry.

Nancy had stretched out and Catherine had accepted the invitation to cuddle close beside her. Now that she'd finished laying out the buildup to the event, the events she'd encountered beyond the cyber curtain could be told seated.

Nancy was visually aroused, her nipples announcing the fact through her light cotton top. "A Roman orgy—Oh... my... God!" she gasped. "Where on earth did he get that idea from?"

"He said that I gave it to him." Catherine sipped at her sherry. "That day when I watched the soldier. Ken said that he'd quoted the opening of festivities at Roman circuses and I had looked 'as if I were reminiscing'." She framed it with her fingers in the air, as Ken had when he'd said it.

"Could you remember the incident?"

"Clearly. The strange thing is that he is right, although I haven't the foggiest idea why I feel that way," she replied, and sipped again. "Come to think of it, I've always been drawn to anything vaguely Roman. The orgy didn't help matters," Catherine huffed.

"You'd better not let Leon get wind of it; he'll want to regress you."

"Aaaagh, the visual on that... Not Leon, please, Nance. I like the man, but Leon and sex... No!" She took a minute taste of the sherry. "Anyway, Ken got it into his head that The Lupanar in old Pompeii would be *juuuuust* the place for me to strut my stuff."

"The Lupanar—should I know it?"

"I hope not. It was the most famous brothel in the ancient world, which might be a clue as to why the volcano blew its stack."

They laughed heartily.

"I'm jumping ahead there..." Catherine was enjoying drawing the story out by setting the scene; watching Nancy wide-eyed with anticipation and burning with curiosity was a treat.

"Yes?" Nancy prompted.

"Once I'd put the helmet on, all I could see was that snow that you get on TV when the station goes off the air. There was a hiss billowing in my ears."

"The bastard had you in that position? Blind and deaf to the real world?" The idea kind of excited Nancy but she felt she should show outrage.

"It was great," Catherine confirmed sarcastically. "I felt like a market chicken with all of my glory displayed for Ken's leisurely inspection."

Alarm bells suddenly rang loud and clear in Nancy's head. "He couldn't have videoed you?" she asked casually.

"*SHIT...* I didn't think of that. Shit... SHIT!" Catherine hissed angrily. "How could I have been that stupid... I was so carried away... all the excitement, I didn't even think about it! *SHIT!*"

Catherine was stunned into silence, trying to comprehend her own naiveté. Nancy gave her the moment and Catherine brought herself out of it.

"Well, what's done is done. The consolation is that he could only have filmed me once the helmet was covering my face, which means my reputation is still safe." She consoled herself with a laugh she didn't feel.

Nancy thought it best not to point out that CCTV cameras riddled the building, filming from every angle in the operations room. That would be like closing the proverbial stable door with the horse long gone.

"On that pleasant note, I propose we should draw another vat of sherry." Catherine upended her empty vessel.

Nancy recharged it along with her own.

"To *uhhmm...* To no repercussions," Catherine toasted, referring to what was foremost on her mind.

"To no repercussions," Nancy agreed, trying not to look as worried as she felt.

With the silence between them, each was considering the predicament as the fire hissed and crackled with indifference to the world of humanly affairs.

"As I was telling you," Catherine continued, "the bastard took forever to turn the damned image on. I could feel him circling me, studying my nether regions."

Nancy had blindfold fantasies of her own and lived in the moment. "How did it feel?" she asked.

"Spooky... terrifying... but mostly, plain kinky."

"Eventually I started to feel cyber sickness... disorientated and nauseous, like I couldn't find my bearings. Total visual and audio deprivation. It was awful to not know which way was up or down; the weirdest sensation, Nance. For the amount of time that the bastard made me wait, it really wasn't pleasant." Catherine sneered in distaste. "I don't know if he picked up on my irritation, but as I was about to remove the helmet, VOOM—everything burst into life around me. I was in a small winding cobbled street full of two- and three-story buildings crowded together on it."

Catherine took time out from the story to take a lingering sip.

"Come on, Cath!" Nancy jabbed Catherine in the ribs with her finger.

Catherine spluttered from the tickle, nearly spurting a mouthful of liquid over Nancy. A dribble ran down her chin that they both reached to dab at and the first round of laughter for the evening erupted.

"It's astonishing," Catherine marveled. "I remember every detail. I'm talking detail I'd never normally retain; the street names, the graffiti, the names of people I met."

"That's how they say it is," Nancy confirmed. "Everyone on the program says it's like your brain is in hyper drive and retains everything. That's why LifeGames certification is essential to get anywhere in life—once you're certified, you *really* know your stuff."

"Wow... I'm sitting here now, and I can see it before me. I was in the cobbled street and must have been looking a bit bewildered, and this lovely looking man came over. Not at all threatening. He put his hand on my arm, and I swear I felt it. I started, he apologized then introduced himself as Aquilinus. Beautiful—chiseled jaw, cut arms; my, oh my, what an accent, Italian. I was thinking, 'this is nuts, the guy's a hallucination, he's only a screen image,' but he was there, he touched me."

She looked dreamy, like she was seeing it all over again.

"And...?" Nancy prompted urgently.

"He said I must come with him... we were going to The Lupanar. You see—how would I remember a word like that? Lupanar! I asked him what it was. 'The brothel district' he said. So, this was Ken's idea of a turn-on, take his first date to the brothel district."

Screeches of laughter followed.

"Down these narrow alleys we went. All cobbled. Beautiful. And there on the corner of Vico del Lupanare and Vico del Balcone Pensile was the strangest building, like that odd corner building leading into Times Square. Sort of a triangular jut with the roads forking on either side; the upper floor bigger than the lower floor, like it was added on, like business maybe got so good that they went up a level without town planning."

"You really do have the detail!"

"The walls were like that slate flooring, slasto, from the seventies. Anyway, in we went. As we walked, he told me about it, about the Lupanar, the brothel we were going to, very matter of fact. Now—I must remind you that I had that *thing* inside me, so walking in the gyroscope had me very aware of it..."

"Uh-huh..." Nancy was transfixed, transported two millennia back in time.

"Calidrone, Forunata, Mertis, Fasa, Fabia, Nika—these were the fine ladies I would meet. Januaria specializes in oral sex, he told me. She's very, very good, he said. Male prostitutes too— one Lubraki... Maratimos was his name, specialized in servicing virgins."

Nancy let out another, "Oh-my-god."

"I'm not really a virgin, I assured him. Aquilinus smiled wryly, assuring me that today I would be. He could arrange gladiators who turned tricks on the side; they're sports stars of our day, he told me. The elite Roman women were their clients, satisfaction guaranteed, or your money back."

"And we thought we'd invented the concept," Nancy joked.

"So, we went in. Small rooms off the corridor, dimly lit with lanterns, the sounds of rutting behind doorways screened by curtains. My heart was thundering, but up the stairs he led me. His hands, his touch, soft as a warm breeze.

"He stopped to show me some graffiti in Latin, translating it for me. *Hic ego puellas multas futui;* 'Here I fuck many girls'. *Felix bene futuis;* 'Lucky guy, you fuck well'. The man's eyes danced like an imp."

"You're getting me all hot and bothered, darling," Nancy admitted.

"Oh, we haven't even begun yet," Catherine promised.

"I'd better sober up then before I do something unbecoming. Coffee?"

"I'm dying for a pee."

Nancy went off to organize the first, Catherine to resolve the second.

They settled back in.

"So we get upstairs, and it's palatial—a lot bigger than it looked from outdoors. Drapes on the walls, tapestries, mosaics inlaid on the floor, beds and cushions everywhere—reds, golds, royal blue—marble columns, baths with rising steam. A table swaying under a sumptuous feast, and people going at it everywhere—I mean *everywhere*—in every known position and some that have never been written down yet."

"*Ohhhhkay...* and Ken's watching all this on the monitor?"

"Fuck! I forgot about that. I'm telling you, Nance... this is witchcraft, it captures you. It's a parallel universe going on down there."

"Some universe you were in."

"I didn't want to leave! Now suddenly, I realize I'm naked. Guess virtual reality's handy like that; one minute you've got a toga on, next... well... I've got a towel around my waist. Like, *how did that happen?* I'm thinking... and then I realize my breasts are very firm."

"They look it."

"No silly. Yes, they are, for thirty-five; fine, they're not bad. But this set was for an eighteen-year-old. Great! nice upgrade I'm thinking, but that towel is not hanging like it should. I'm turned on, obviously I'm feeling pretty horny, and then I see the evidence of it..."

Catherine paused, debating in what order to impart details for the best shock value.

Nancy poked her in the ribs again. "Come on... just tell it as it happened. What evidence?"

"In a minute... I see someone notice me, he's wearing a centurion outfit, and starts making his way toward me. I freeze. He's got a bod like you wouldn't believe, I mean *godlike*; and there I am, staring... gaping. Peeping out the bottom of his kilt is his..."

"His what?"

"You know what."

"No... no way! How long's the kilt?"

"Mid-thigh."

"And this is attractive?"

"I guess whoever programmed it thinks so... and there might be a clue to why—the man's face, Mr. Bickus-Dickus' face...? Who else, but Ken-bloody-Torrington."

The two exploded in laughter, Nancy blowing a plume of misted coffee from the mouthful she'd just swigged.

For the next ten minutes, every time Nancy stopped laughing and tried to gather her breath, Catherine would say it again with a Monty Python intonation, *"Bickus..."* and the carnival of laughter would begin all over.

Finally, the joke wore to a chuckle. "What an asshole," Nancy eventually managed to say with a straight face.

"But you gotta brace y'self, Sheila." Catherine's eyes twinkled with mischief. "'cause the next little detail's *reeeeally* gonna blow your mind."

She sipped from the sherry glass again. She loved playing with Nancy's excitement, building it to a crescendo.

Nancy elbowed her with impatience. "*Come-on*, girl. Quit stalling!"

"All right, all right," Catherine giggled. "Remember I said that the towel round my waist was hanging strangely? That I was terribly horny...? Well... when I took a peek under the towel, what did I see, but... yes... not a pussy at all but a very, *very* large cock."

"A cock!!" Nancy was staring at her with an open mouth.

"Well, it was either a cock or the biggest clitoris in all of creation!"

When Nancy had recovered enough of her ability to talk, she inquired, "Up, or down?"

"Halfway... But after I took a look, did it ever react—started looking at me, the thing did," Catherine bumped one hand from a low angle to the ground to the horizontal in a few staccato twitches.

Nancy collapsed again, gesturing for mercy, pleading for a halt in the story, laughing till she cried. She remained a quivering mass of convulsions for several minutes.

"So there I was, locked and loaded... an ocean of backsides and boobs bobbing and bopping. The positions, oh my, oh my... You wouldn't believe it possible. Somebody in your programming department owns the Kama Sutra!" Catherine had to wait for Nancy to calm again before she could proceed. "Now what's an innocent girl with a twelve-inch cock to do with the thing? I mean, what do you *do* with those things? Seriously? I wandered through the sea of banging flesh, and picked out a particularly delicious, well..."

"That has got to be bizarre. I can't get my head around it. The thing *in* you... and sticking out of you? Connected?"

"You bet. A gender-bender. It felt like some kind of pneumatic vibrator mimicking every detail that I dished out. Weird! I felt like a guy... I guess?"

"And you were time dilated?"

"Ken said it was ten-fold, but it felt like a lot more than that. Jeez... I saw two sunsets."

"How much real time were you on for?"

"Only an hour and thirty. There was going to be a midnight run, so we had to quit an hour before the shift arrived."

"You should have experienced about fifteen hours on the machine, not enough time for two sunsets."

Nancy pondered what she knew about time dilation, privately deciding that Ken must have run Catherine on much more powerful software than a first-timer should be exposed to.

"You sure? Not fifteen hours? Two sunsets?"

"Nance, if I'm sure of anything then I'm *positive* that I had more than fifteen hours. Much, much more. I'm not joking when I tell you that I waddled out of there like a cowboy!"

Nancy knew that now she would never see a cowboy without thinking of Catherine. "And Ken?" she asked, "I've got to know. What had he been up to during all that time?"

The look on Catherine's face told a story.

"Silly question, wasn't it?"

"Very silly..." Catherine agreed. "Let's just say, I didn't have too much trouble from him when the game was over. Don't get me wrong; it's not that he didn't try. But not to put too fine a point on it, much to his despair, his mind and body were no longer in agreement."

"Now that I think of it, he *was* rather slow on Thursday morning. Looked haggard, like he'd been busy the entire night!"

"Busy; *alone*," Catherine assured her. "Once the game was over and Ken unhooked me, it wasn't such fun anymore. I mean, I'm a big girl; I didn't expect to feel romantically swept away by my knight in shining armor. But with the lust extinguished, the atmosphere switched to *very* clinical, ugly, *sordid*, and terribly awkward. Horrible to be naked while he fiddled with helping me to *carefully* undo the hardware from my poor abused, and very disinterested body. I suddenly got slammed with real perspective; that we were strangers and he was my client! Like... faaaaaark... what was I doing? It's strange how a sex drive can be so strong that it obscures reality."

"Would you do it a second time?" Nancy wanted to know.

"Not with Ken! But the game was fun. Be honest... who wouldn't try it, even if they won't admit to it?"

As Catherine went on and the earlier hilarity gave way to introspection, it became increasingly clear that Catherine was suffering serious regrets. Talking it through was a tonic and a trigger.

Once Catherine had said her piece, they sat in silence for a while, each contemplating the event and its consequences.

When she felt the timing to be right, Nancy put a question to Catherine, "Where to from here?"

"For the first time in my life Nance, I really don't know." She looked disheartened. "I've been a bad girl. Okay, that's nothing new for me. This though," she huffed, "it's extreme... insanity. A serious error."

Nancy nodded sagely, not wanting to inflame the discomfort of truth any more than it was already agitated. The descriptions had been so vivid and stimulating that she had entered Catherine's world, living out the scenarios. The illusions had raised her own excitement levels to a point that the story had begun to feel *normal*.

The virtual reality was an illusion, while its consequences were suddenly all too real.

A hint of a forced smile now trembled on Catherine's lips. "It was fun while it lasted, but I get the distinct feeling Ken isn't satisfied to leave it at that. I think he wants more and I don't exactly feel that way. If I'd ever fantasized that it would be fun to get it on with him, now that the fantasy has been somewhat lived out. It's over—fantasy gone. I'm seriously repulsed by him, can't face seeing him."

Nancy agreed. *Would it help to add to her woes?* she wondered.

Nancy knew Ken's character, and his character dictated that if he desired Catherine, then he would have her at any cost.

"I don't think that I've jeopardized the account." Catherine tried to convince herself out loud of something she really didn't believe. "Hey, we're both adults, we'll see past a silly prank like this."

"You can be sure I'll update you on anything around the office," Nancy replied, giving the only weak assurance she could bring herself to give. She stroked Catherine's leg affectionately.

"Thanks Nance, guess I've been very stupid but you know how it is," Catherine shrugged.

"Girls will be boys," Nancy joked, which managed to raise a light chuckle from the ashes of Catherine's recent laughter.

"Something else." Catherine suddenly went serious; troubled. "You can imagine how Wednesday night—actually, Thursday morning—after we'd finished, I went home broken, dead tired."

"Sure; that many hours in the saddle would be rather taxing." Nancy hoped to rescue Catherine's crashing mood once more.

Catherine smiled with her mouth, but her eyes couldn't bluff it.

"Strange. I just couldn't get a moment's sleep. Every time I'd doze, I'd jolt awake with the most vivid nightmares, kinda like I was still trying to put Ken off; with him trying to *do* me and me trying to push him away,"

Nancy was silent, inexplicably fearful beyond the story she was hearing.

Catherine shook her head in disbelief at what she had to say.

"Every time I woke, I could swear that I smelled his aftershave in the bedroom. My conscience was playing tricks on me, I guess. I think of myself as sexually liberated, gracious... I act it out, but the old demons of childhood..." she left it unsaid.

She paused, clicking her juice-stick on. The tip glowed to life and a pencil line of cherry aroma joined the smoky tones of Patsy Cline's voice as it massaged the stumbling piano chords of "Crazy". The melody waltzed a *pas de deux* with the hearth's crackling, dancing tongues of flame.

"I've read all the psychology and jabbering about 'suppressing the learned inhibitions from my conscious mind.' I can even believe that this sort of a fling is bound to scratch away the surface of what I *actively* want to feel and believe." Catherine was putting on a brave front, showing pragmatism.

Nancy was silent, unable to add anything, and not trying to. In the absence of consoling words, she offered her touch, running her fingers through Catherine's hair.

"The odd thing about the smell was that I'd washed thoroughly when I arrived home. I didn't want any reminder of the memory near me. My clothes went straight into the laundry downstairs, and I went directly to the shower without touching or sitting on anything else. After that, I had a quick snack and a whisky to unwind, soaked myself in a bath of salts for an hour. The entire time, I had the bubbles going so it would really get me as clean as could be."

Nancy heard "bubbles" and thought *Jacuzzi*. She loved jet-baths and hoped for a try-out sometime.

"Nothing, absolutely no smell could have survived that. Hell, I hadn't even touched Ken, but somehow..." her voice trailed off.

"Foul balms," Nancy said absently to herself.

"What? *Bombs?*" Catherine couldn't quite make out her murmers.

"Balms... sorry Cath. Ken's after-shave—he uses too much."

"Dreadful, isn't it! *Yech...* off-putting."

Catherine had previously enjoyed his scent, but by association, she now felt revolted at the thought of it.

"Well, at least you'll be off the hook for the next seven days, he's in Russia from Tuesday," Nancy consoled Catherine.

"Good news at last!" Catherine sighed.

Nancy's diversion had given Catherine a chance to momentarily cast off the shadow of dread that had become her constant companion.

What she'd refrained from telling Nancy was that the reek of Ken's scent was still constant and persistent.

Worryingly, she realized that it was strongly associated with her recurring nightmare of him. It seemed to manifest during the later hours of the night and on into the early hours of the morning.

What Catherine had also omitted was that in reality, Ken had meekly accepted his sexual advances being turned down, while in the nightmare, he was far more insistent. She felt as though he was beginning to possess her.

She cuddled closer to Nancy.

Jacky would be away on a five-day international flight and Catherine had no intention of returning home to lie awake... alone.

Chapter 17

"I seek the salvation of many good souls, Eminence." The ritual of introduction was almost at its end.

"*Bendito seas,* my son," replied Fernando, bestowing his ceremonial blessing.

"Your Eminence, I am a man eager to learn more of what your great wisdom can teach. I beg your patience with me, for I am your humble and devoted servant."

Leon was carefully attempting to unwrap the Bishop's fragile trust, baiting Fernando in order to verify an interesting fact that he'd gleaned from the recording of their previous session.

Fernando's voice twanged with threat in response, the irrational personality constantly seeking any opportunity to seize control. "*You would serve me before Good?*" he accused.

"No, Sire! I serve only God, but in so doing, I serve yourself as is His Emissary."

Fernando had followed but not taken the bait so carefully set for him. Instead, he'd crossed himself with ritualized formality and—eyes to the ceiling—muttered Latin payers.

Still, Leon was pleased that the conversation had shifted quickly onto the subject of God, since it was in the definition of the word 'God' that he sought to uncover something that appeared to be of significance.

He decided to risk asking the question directly, cautiously conjuring all the humility he could muster.

"I noticed, Eminence, that you speak of 'Good', whilst when I say the word 'God', you do not correct me. How can this be?"

Fernando smiled for the first time since Leon had become acquainted with the man. "They are one and the same, my son."

It was a beautiful smile; it spoke volumes of love and peace, yet it was an entirely different expression from the smile that Roger would offer from the mask of that same-shared flesh.

"Thank you for your patience, Sire. I ask in good faith why your earthly brothers in the church speak not of the Good, as you do? Rather, they use the word God as I do." Leon studied Fernando, having carefully tailored every word according to the minute eddies in the man's mood.

The priest showed no obvious change in emotion, yet sadness began clouding his eyes as he answered.

"Because, my son, these men of the cloth are but human, and like yourself, they speak only what they are taught. The books given unto them contain words depicting lofty ideals but with the passing of time, rigid words betoken many and varied realities. Inevitably, men will not understand a word to signify the same meaning as its scribe had intended. Therefore, the ancient writings, which have become incomprehensible to the populace, will require interpretation. But men of power find benefit in dividing, not in uniting. Good transcends interpretation. God does not."

Leon remained silent, allowing the truth of Fernando's wisdom to soak in. He maintained his silence in respect for the solemn prayer that Fernando offered up in Latin to Good, that all men may unite in their beliefs.

When the Bishop had finished his prayer, he continued with his explanation.

"In your time, the mere mention of the Almighty has become a tool of seduction, dividing the nations of the Earth. Should it not be enough that the name Good defines that essence that all can invest their faith into?"

Leon was fascinated by the uncluttered logic of this otherwise suspicious man. It puzzled him how calm clarity could suddenly emit from one so dogmatic in his suspicion.

"But Sire, was this not also true during your time on this Earth?"

"It has always been true. *Que Dios nos bendiga.* The Beast has always sought the souls of men." Fernando's eyes sank to half-mast.

"Forgive me Sire, for I require your great knowledge in order that I might fight all that is evil. If all men *do* truly believe in good, then how can the Beast profit from only the name upon their lips?"

Leon had found that he needed to keep Fernando talking; giving the man time to brood always degenerated into ferocity.

"When the *name* a man gives to his Creator dictates his character; when another name for that same Creator comes to another man's lips, it will cause a taking up of arms, one man against his brother."

Fernando was speaking carefully, laboring over his words.

"When leaders have fallen into the camp of the Evil One. When all the populations of the Earth are roused to murder for names only; in that time, men's hearts will be devoid of reason and they will not be in a position to support Good any longer. All will be lost."

The rational Fernando covered his eyes with his hand in a manner of much introspection. When the hand was removed, a transformed Fernando had taken hold.

"The times in which you live are like none that have gone before!" he thundered.

"Evil has many tongues within every home. Evil grips your leaders and the Anti-Christ will unite men under a false banner." He gasped for breath.

Leon wanted him to continue speaking.

The priest found his breath.

"Those who follow this earthly decoy will drive the shackle-pins of their own bondage deep into the Earth. And this Earth shall become the final abode of their bondage."

To this point, the monologue had been excited yet neutral but now the Father was becoming incensed. He fixed his rabid eyes—suddenly smouldering with all the fires of Hell—onto Leon and his voice was deep and threatening.

"Men like yourself assist darkness more than you can know! Beware, for evil puts on its finest face and wears the turban of Good! The true testimony of Good has been anointed with the balm of lies."

Fernando's body began to convulse with rage and Leon knew that he would soon have to bring the ranting to a halt.

"Those that joust on your fine steed will soon bring un-surpassed Evil to bear on good. With their souls in bondage they will turn their actions against their own salvation!"

The commotion had grown too great and grudgingly, Leon was forced to return Fernando back into the deep recesses of Roger's mind.

Chapter 18

Leon hawked the session's recording to his usual sources of opinion.

"That's got to be television, Leon. That part about 'tongues in every house'." Nancy was delighted to find an apparent ally in Fernando. She had instantly been convinced that Fernando was expressing a cryptic opinion of television's power to influence public sentiment.

Leon and Nancy became sidetracked, discussing the thorny issue of the power of the media in general.

"On which side of Nostradamus did your Bishop live?" Andrew asked with his tongue firmly in his cheek.

Leon ignored the jab. "What do you think of the last part of the session, old chap?" Leon had been keen to hear Andrew's sage advice. "What do you think?"

"The 'fine steed' business?" Andrew used the question to buy himself time to think.

"That's the part, that's it," Leon encouraged.

"A steed for jousting to him would mean a place to practice. Or possibly an animal or mechanism to practice on?"

"Could be, old chap... could be."

"Your offices," Andrew continued. "What your company does. You provide a place for people to train. They're trained to fight in the Nostradamus Armageddon. True?"

"True... too true."

"The way that I interpret it, you continue holding trainees in bondage with your hypnosis. It's probably *that fellow* of yours and his megalomania; he's the type that always wants to dominate everything, don't you know? Probably got something subliminal stuck into your programs... bending minds to his will! Too bloody rich and powerful by far."

It was a thought that had crossed Leon's mind, yet the idea was ridiculous. Even for Ken, it would be too big a dream.

Leon also glossed over Andrew's opinion of Ken. His words had clearly been meant to ensnare Leon into passing public judgment on his employer.

"'Turn their actions against their own salvation'. Now, what do you make of that, old chap?" Leon ventured.

"That's a piece of cake, old fruit. Obvious!"

Andrew scoffed triumphantly.

"Your participants will gladly follow whoever or *whatever* organization allows them to practice what they're trained for. They'll put aside morals and their own best interests. How many individuals—who would otherwise be passive—are you training to drop atom bombs on their fellow human beings, sanitizing it with your clever tricks? And how many of them will 'just be following orders' when they are called upon? And of course, you carry the culpability, you have a hand in making them more efficient at it than never before. Will you be any the less guilty of your own destruction?"

Leon pondered the hard-hitting analysis. There was plenty of savvy in it, but the scale of irrationality was beyond proportion.

After he left Andrew, he took some time to quantify the sheer volume and status of individuals that LifeGames was training.

He mentally went through a list: all of the world's elite military forces, with the prospect of lower levels of soldiery soon to be on the books; most of the world's top politicians and lawmakers; prominent businessmen and scholars; pilots—less influential in the greater scheme, yet they remained vital for the modern migration of populations—and now university lecturers and school teachers, as well.

Reviewing the evidence, as improbable as it was, he was forced to concede that total world domination by "Ken the Terrible" could, in the not too distant future, be a distinct possibility.

The vision remained disturbing and he decided to test the hypothesis on Ken at the next opportunity.

"Ken-o, you got a minute to spare? Just a minute."

He played the recording for Ken and they discussed various aspects of it before Leon casually dropped the question.

"How about world domination? What if we put a subliminal in the sequence to get the participants to react to a trigger--don't you suppose we could, you know, influence them per our needs?"

Ken really liked that idea, and said so; that old tickle that made him dab at his eye suggested something sinister. "That's a great idea, Leon! I'll make you my assistant when we take over."

"That's all, thanks. I must run along now, Ken-o, must run along." Leon leapt to his feet and hurried to the door.

"By the way, Leon," Ken called after him. "I've been having the most vivid dreams."

But Ken's attempt at keeping his attention was futile; Leon was in a world of his own. With a few hops and skips, Leon was gone; gone off in his own world and out the door.

Chapter 19

The fire was burning in its hearth and the boxer was asleep, his breath gently slapping at his jowls.

The two women were naked, curled together in a passionate embrace. The delicate smell of washed bodies blended with the dancing light and whispering flames; the scene a symphony of harmony. The couple's every sense was aroused and stirred to a velvet smooth consistency.

Their limbs entangled, they were one.

Then Catherine caught that unmistakable waft on the air. Her body jolted, rigid with fear.

Nancy gasped, startled by the lurch of the woman in her arms.

The sudden commotion woke the dog. His head turned toward them; he had Ken's face.

Catherine leapt to her feet, her eyes blind with terror. It took Jacky several minutes to calm her hysterical sobbing and bring her out of the nightmare.

"I'm taking you to a doctor!" Jacky resolved.

"I don't *need* a doctor," Catherine insisted.

"I don't care, I'm taking you!"

Catherine shivered and shook violently throughout the rest of that long and sleepless Sunday night.

Come morning, Jacky bodily dragged Catherine out of the house and into the car, determinedly resisting all of Catherine's refusals to be taken across town to their practitioner.

When Jacky had arrived home at noon on Sunday, Catherine had claimed to have had an early night on Saturday. Yet, she was utterly exhausted, shattered, as if she hadn't slept for a week.

"Honestly, Jacks. I went out to dinner with a client, then I curled up *before* midnight and slept like a baby."

Catherine's account was entirely true; she did have dinner with a client, and she had slept like a baby, just not in her own bed. She'd bunked over at Nancy's house. They'd talked until just before midnight when both had fallen asleep in front of the fire. At dawn, they had awoken in front of cold ashes.

Catherine had experienced the best night of uninterrupted sleep that night, since waking on Wednesday morning.

Jacky was distressed, and wasn't buying any of it.

"What's going on with you? I've never seen you look so washed out."

"I don't know. I've been like this since you left."

"But Wednesday morning you were fine." Jacky was vexed.

"I know." Catherine slumped in despair. "I've been suffering constant nightmares, every night. I find I'm dreading going to sleep."

"But why? Why the nightmares? I've never known you to have a nightmare, Cath. Never."

"It must be the stress, I don't know.... Work's rough at the moment," Catherine hedged. She was finding it brutally difficult to keep her secret.

"It must be! I'd never imagined you'd let it get to you like this."

As Jacky spoke, she was coaxing the car into an open parking bay outside of the doctor's office.

"Is it something *I've* done? Maybe something that's happened to you?"

At this speculation, Catherine prickled with fright, an adrenaline bomb bursting in her gut. By a wisp of a thread, she dangled over the cliff of confession.

"*No,* Jacks! How can you be so silly? If it was anything, anything at all, I'd tell you. I... I don't have a clue what it is."

"That's a *very* good reason for getting professional advice." Jacky swung Catherine's own logic against her.

"I don't need this," Catherine argued, crossing the threshold. She hated doctors.

"Come on!" Jacky beckoned firmly.

The doctor ran a course of elementary physical tests.

"You're as fit as a fiddle," he pronounced, writing a prescription for a course of sleeping pills.

The prettily coloured pills made matters much worse, trapping Catherine in her nightmare. She fought like a shark in a net, thrashing and kicking, lashing and biting, Jacky battling to control her.

She was in a world of her own, the powerful sedative denying her the relief of consciousness. She battered Jacky, convinced she was the attacker.

"This can't go on. Please, Cath, this can't go on," Jacky repeated, tears cascading down her cheeks as she rocked Catherine deliriously in her arms, consoling her through the night. *"This just can't go on!"*

When the birds began to sing, the heavy musky smell was still dank on the air. Both women were sitting huddled on top of their covers feeling like refugees under their own roof. It was Tuesday and Jacky had been scheduled for a late afternoon flight. She called in sick and called a doctor for Catherine who provides house calls—he offered no improved prognosis.

It would be Catherine's fourth working day at home.

"Stop. Please stop!" Jacky softly begged Catherine's unseen and clandestine tormentor.

Catherine buried her face in Jacky's bosom, sobbing from exhaustion and fear of sleep.

It was while Jacky prepared lunch that Catherine's fear of sleep became irrelevant. As she lay resting, the unmistakable sound of footsteps approached.

She had been about to roll over, intending to beam a well-deserved smile of thanks at Jacky, when the footsteps halted short of the room.

Catherine hesitated.

Anxious moments; no sound.

Then, on the air, floated the unmistakable scent.

The pitch of her screech carried to every corner of the house.

Hearing the shriek, Jacky abandoned the plate she was holding in mid-air, fright lending her feet wings, flying three stairs at a time to Catherine's side.

The doctor's house call once again proved fruitless. He prescribed the heaviest possible dose of opiate.

Catherine was locked in a world of deception, unable to disclose the identity and circumstances of her stalker. It made her feel sordid and filthy for her cheating.

To add to the calamity, her office had relayed several messages asking her to urgently respond to Nancy's escalating calls. Jacky had intercepted these and was becoming suspicious. Catherine was desperate for a gap to respond and halt the unraveling circumstances, but Jacky was magnificently attentive, not leaving her side for a second.

Chapter 20

Night had fallen and the two women were sitting in bed watching old movie re-runs, delaying the inevitability of sleep. The more potent pills stood, untouched, on the table alongside Catherine's pillow; sleep was still the main enemy.

Catherine was the first to slide out of consciousness, leaving Jacky sitting sentry for another hour; eventually she too succumbed.

Television's uncanny ability to rise suddenly in volume, and invade sleep, wrenched Jacky from her dream world. She woke with a bolt of shock, disorientated.

Wrapped deep in the warm and comforting folds of sleep, Catherine remained oblivious to the world.

The time on the bedside clock read 03:39. They'd been asleep for more than six hours.

Jacky cut both the television and bedside light, and covered Catherine properly before turning in.

In four hours, she would be welcoming passengers aboard the flight.

The nightmare was over.

"Where on earth *have* you been, Cath?!" Nancy was verging on anger, fueled out of concern. "I've been going out of my mind calling your office!"

"I'm sorry, Nancy. I've had a hell of a time with those nightmares. It's really been very bad."

"Well, why didn't you return my calls? I would have phoned you at home but I *still* don't have your number, and your office won't give it to me."

"I think it's best if I see you to explain. Will dinner work?" Catherine had come to the conclusion that to remain friends, she would *have* to disclose her personal life to Nancy.

"Great. That will be absolutely super. My place again?" Nancy responded.

"No, mine this time. You won't find it on GPS, the area's too new. I'll message you a map now."

Jacky would be abroad for two days, providing Catherine the ideal opportunity to reveal her secret. She'd first show Nancy the warm and nurturing home she had built; and let the conversation unfold from there.

On her drive in to the office, Catherine pondered the mysterious stalking episodes. If they did not soon resolve, she felt she had little choice but to reveal her indiscretion to Jacky.

Tough days lay ahead, but fortunately the good sleep from the previous night had sharpened her wit and she felt competent enough to cope with the prospect of either predicament.

With her private life partitioned off and put aside, she prepared for a full day at the office.

With five days of unattended work piled on her desk and every electronic device screaming for her urgent attention, the hours evaporated.

Looking at the mountain of work, she was on the verge of canceling the dinner date, when the uneasy sense of being watched crept back. She surrounded herself with people all day long, but every time she went to the toilet, the terror returned.

Doubt crept back, her confidence quailed and her productivity plummeted. She simply could not go home alone tonight.

Suddenly, in the late afternoon, the uneasy feeling went away, and she felt fine. Testing it, she went to the loo—nothing. She got into the lift alone, rode two floors and returned—fine.

Again, those piles of files and insistent electronics insisted she cancel, but when she looked out the windows, the sky was already darkening. To cancel with Nancy now, would be too rude.

Chapter 21

The entrance to Catherine's villa was majestic; it had an imperial presence to it.

"I can see the Roman connection, all right. No wonder Ken organized that," Nancy mused.

"He's *never* seen this, Nance." Her hackles rose at the mere mention of his name. "I'd *never* let him know where I live."

"That's strange..." Nancy frowned suddenly, her mouth hanging slightly open in dismay. "I know that, of course I know it. But now that I think about it, he *somehow* gave me a *real* impression that he'd been here, told me how it looks... just like this." She stood back and gestured with her palms.

Catherine felt an explosion of anger within, which she bottled. Then, a ridiculous thought sparked in her mind, and she asked, "When did you get that impression, Nance?"

"I'm not sure, it just dawned on me... I don't know... maybe... maybe two weeks ago? Can I come in?" Nancy tagged the timid request onto the end of her statement.

"Oh, of course; yes, of course. Sorry Nance... so sorry, I got side-tracked."

As they made their way from the foyer into the double-volume space of the house, Nancy's head swiveled in a continuous scan and she issued a procession of disbelieving exclamations.

"I've only just got home myself, Nance; I hope you don't mind but I grabbed take-out," Catherine apologized.

"Of course! Don't be silly," Nancy lied. She hated the idea, as she despised take-away food.

Catherine opened the microwave and placed the boxes inside.

"Why not look around while I re-heat it and shower. The entertainment center's in the corner, put anything you like on. If I'm not down yet, come upstairs when you're ready."

While Nancy went off exploring, Catherine ascended the stairs for a quick shower. She needed to do this, to have Nancy there as a backup yet feel alone and little isolated; a mind-game to beat the fear and madness overtaking her.

As the water cascaded over her, she contemplated the two-week estimation of Ken's insight.

It had been around two weeks earlier that Jacky had complained of a sleepless night. Catherine could remember having slept particularly deeply on that occasion.

Jacky had *insisted* that she had felt a presence enter their room, where it had lingered throughout the night. Jacky was not normally superstitious, so it had struck Catherine as odd at the time.

"There was a lot of activity, constant small noises," Catherine recalled Jacky complaining. "I couldn't quite figure out where they were coming from. There was definitely no wind."

"It must have been your mind playing tricks," Catherine had proposed.

Then Jacky had said something that had sent a pang of guilt rushing through her. "I was sure that I could smell the scent of a man, Cath. It really got me spooked so I checked the security board... nothing."

At the time, her guilt had been unfounded; back then Catherine had still only been *planning* infidelity.

A few days after that incident, Catherine had given Ken a greeting hug at work and Jacky had later caught a whiff of the scent on Catherine's clothing. Her nostrils had flared and her eyes had widened with recognition. "That's *exactly* the smell, Cath! I could swear it's the same smell that was in our room the other night."

Jacky had proceeded to interrogate Catherine regarding the scent, but she had disregarded it. "I'm in contact with a lot of people in a day, Jacks."

Perhaps it was the improbability of it, but Catherine had somehow not linked these coincidences. Even under the heat of her shower they now gave her a shiver.

As she toweled off, she called down to Nancy, "All okay?"

"All fabulous."

"I'll be down in two."

Dropping a T-shirt over her head, the flotsam of evidence kept washing through her mind, and she waded deeper into the waters of her recent delirious, sedative-induced dementia.

She was positive that Jacky had remarked several times about the same recurring scent on each occasion that Ken's phantom had come to haunt her.

"This is a palace!" Nancy was still overwhelmed.

"Thanks, Nance. I picked it up half-built from a divorce auction. Those were the days..." Catherine reminisced. "Shew... I had to stretch the company's budget to the limit to secure it—not really ideal, but there was no other way. We very nearly didn't make it."

"You started Kaplan from here?" Nancy guessed.

"I didn't actually *start* it here, no. The place we started in was a real dive with cracked walls and roaches. You name it. It was horrible. I've got some photos somewhere that I can show you. Wine?"

Still shaken from her earlier thoughts, Catherine reached for her juice-stick to calm her nerves.

"I brought a red."

Catherine continued as she uncorked a chilled white. "I got this place nine years ago." She was pleased to talk about anything other than her current problems.

Her rise through the ranks of the advertising community was a local legend of which Nancy was familiar.

Rumor had it that her late grandfather had bypassed all contenders in his last will and testament, gambling on the fine character and astute mind of his favorite granddaughter to make good with the winnings of his life's work. It had cleaved the

225

family like a ripe melon but his gamble had paid handsome dividends.

Where rumor and fact diverged, was in Catherine's subsequent actions. The moment she had turned a profit from her inheritance, Catherine had maintained her personal commitment to reimburse those who she'd estimated to have forfeited from her gain.

Catherine had recently branched her company's purely above-the-line advertising out to below-the-line contracts. Ken had convinced her to take on PR functions as well, believing that the three disciplines were indivisible in the modern world.

They toasted everlasting friendship, the clink of fine crystal wineglasses ringing crisply.

"We'd grown too big for the dive. The moment I saw this place, I *had* to have it," Catherine continued, filling Nancy in on the accurate details of the legend. "I moved Kaplan in downstairs and—don't tell the IRS—*I* moved into the upstairs."

Her comment produced their first mild chuckle. Tonight, Catherine needed light and calm.

"Working from home was great, but eventually we outgrew this and we needed a proper commercial environment. That was two... two and a half years ago."

"It sure is magnificent, Cath. You can be very proud of it. Hail Caesar and all that."

"I see," Catherine was trying to make light of it, playing along, "...that you're still fantasizing about my Roman experience."

"Don't be silly, Cath. I'm sorry... shew, that was out of taste, I didn't even mean it that way at all. It's just. Wow! All of this is *really* breathtaking... it kind of just came out."

Nancy was trying to find the right moment to fill Catherine in on Ken's manic behavior and obsession with talking to her along with saber-rattling about pulling the account.

With insight from her Saturday dinner with Catherine, Nancy had gotten a better grasp on the situation and had tried to intercede. "Pulling the account seems very harsh, Ken. They've delivered, and the staff are hitting the objectives in her absence. It would be punishing her for being off sick."

"Actually Nancy, this has got *fuck* all to do with *you*!" Ken had never sworn in front of her before—much less *at* her. His door slammed behind him.

"Then why the *fuck* did you come and talk to me about it?" she'd screamed after him.

Yanking her desk draws open, she'd tipped her personal items into a bag and was midway through a resignation email when Ken had reappeared with a post-cloakroom attitude, cheerful and acting as if nothing had happened.

Twenty minutes later, he'd convinced her to stay, but his vulgarity had cost him a twenty percent salary hike and an apology. *Sweet words,* she'd thought; *his sweet words and his foul balms.*

His obsession had continued from Russia. Her phone rang off the hook with all manner of poorly cloaked excuses, each punctuated with his real reason, "Kaplan call yet, Nance?"

Eventually Catherine found the courage to ask, and Nancy filled her in, downplaying and softening where she could to reduce the stress.

"Actually Nance, I've been thinking long and hard about the situation. You've seen the revenue your account means to me... this has been a hell of an expensive mistake, but I'm going to have to walk. We'll survive, but we'll have to dig deep and probably cut some positions at first." Catherine fidgeted. "The price of experience, I guess."

"We'll still be friends." Nancy couldn't argue the rationale.

"Damned sure we will!" Catherine insisted.

Their eyes met and held.

Catherine's confidence waned as the thought of the things she still had to disclose came rushing to mind. "Always... I hope."

"Always!" Nancy agreed.

Nancy had seen Catherine's aversion to Ken's name when she'd mentioned it earlier, so she'd omitted to mention his latest call. With him in Russia, the time zones were pretty far apart. He'd just woken very early Wednesday morning in Moscow, while it had been late afternoon in Silicon Valley.

After his usual "Any word from Cath?", he offhandedly mentioned, "I just woke from another really vivid dream about her."

Come to think of it, Nancy thought, *that's why I assumed Ken saw this house... he mentioned dreaming about it, described it perfectly.*

"Chicken a la Chong." Catherine was knocking the microwave-warmed and batter-encrusted apparitions out of their Chinese takeout cardboard boxes onto delicate Meissen porcelain.

Nancy cringed but faked a polite anticipatory smack of her lips.

After the first mouthful, she realized her folly and was pleasantly surprised by the flavour.

During dinner, Catherine tackled the subject she'd invited Nancy around to discuss. "I've got something to say that's a bit awkward." Catherine looked slightly ashen with stress.

"More awkward than a giant cock?" Nancy tensed. "How much worse can it get?"

"Well... funny you should mention it," Catherine was relieved by Nancy keeping it light. "Seriously... it's something I've got to tell you..."

Nancy saw her stress and reached across the table, taking Catherine's hand and holding it. "You've killed someone, right?"

"No... it's the value of our friendship. I have few friends, and they're precious to me. I consider you a friend."

Nancy squeezed her hand, affirming the same sentiment.

"We're both adults, Nance. I'm positive you'll understand... I don't want to injure our bond."

Catherine took a long and deep draw on the juice-stick, studying Nancy's expression.

Nancy was holding her breath, her face growing flushed, infected with trepidation for the big and building disclosure of great import.

"I'm... uhhmm... when I was twenty-five, I'd had enough of men's lies and abuse. I'm... well, Nance, I'm gay."

Nancy's long-held breath came out in a whoosh.

"*Sheeeeuwww!!*" And she started to laugh, doubled over with hilarity and relief. "I thought you were going to tell me something important, Cath... got me all worked up... I'm gonna give you a good spanking, my girl!"

A relieved Catherine did as she was told, stood up for a smack and Nancy stood with her, wrapping her arms about Catherine's neck and looking into her eyes.

"Why would I care? Why would it be any of my business?" she asked plainly. "What gives you the notion it's a secret?"

"I give it away?" Catherine asked, surprised.

"No, not to just anyone, but... come on... I didn't fall off the turnip truck yesterday. You and I are pretty close; when you talk about your partner and not your *husband* or *boyfriend,* well..."

"Well... I can't go around talking about my wife... can I?"

"You're married?"

"Not yet. In this mad state, you never know if it's going to be annulled at the next election."

They laughed; laughed as old friends who hadn't known one another very long.

"So you knew I was a lesbian all along? A dirty dike."

"Such ugly words, Cath. You're neither."

"So that's out of the way. A real relief. Next disclosure, you've sort of figured out. Yes, I have a lover, been with her five years. She's a little... she's a bit jealous."

Catherine described how they'd met and the circumstances that they'd endured through the years. It opened the path to discuss the predicament her liaison with Ken had put her in, the threat Ken posed in terms of coercion, in terms of any hint of blackmail.

"He knows about Jacky, I told him."

"He's kept it quiet; not that it's something he'd talk to me about anyway." Nancy confirmed. "Ahh... That's why the big cock." She started to laugh good-humoredly. "A cock and boobs."

And Catherine joined her in hearty laughter.

"Anything he can do, I can do better," Catherine cracked.

"Well, I guess it's truth or dare evening over at Catherine's house," Nancy suggested. "Truth from me? I've had the fantasies too... of being with women. Just never bothered to or been in a position to act on it."

"So happy Nance... so happy you understand."

They sat down in the open-plan lounge.

"No. Thank you for trusting me. Why not show me a pic of this lucky girl? She's not about to come through the door and scratch my eyes out..?"

Catherine was jubilant, euphoric to have the burden off her shoulders. If she could play this right with Jacky, the three of them could become friends. Catherine obliged Nancy's request and went upstairs to get her iPad with lots of pics.

As she reached the threshold of her darkened bedroom, she hesitated, suddenly afraid to leave the light and Nancy's presence.

"Ridiculous!" she admonished herself and resisted the urge to snap a light on. She crossed the shadow-drenched room by the light of the full moon streaming through the window. The room was peaceful, devoid of any negative atmosphere.

The battery on her iPad had recovered to thirty percent so she unplugged it and made her way back to the lit stairway.

"How much time have you got?" she called, descending the marble steps.

"All night. You've must have a lot of pics."

Nancy detected a hint of plea in Catherine's voice—the poor girl was still rattled and wanting to stretch company.

Catherine laughed.

Nancy knew it didn't matter how late she'd get to bed. Her only commitment the next day would be to Ken, and in the Moscow time zone, he'd be asleep well into her afternoon. She had anticipated an all-nighter and had organized for Jo, the security administrator, to cover for her.

"She looks lovely. What's her name?" Catherine took the liberty of flicking on into the album.

"Jacky." There was affection in Catherine's voice.

"Are these modelling shots?" The photos looked too professional to be casual snaps.

"Yes—pics of photos in her book. She used to dabble; now she's on air-crew so there's no more time."

"Well that explains how you can have me to dinner," Nancy winked. "How long's she away for?"

"Till Thursday morning. She's not *really* jealous... well... no more than a man would be."

"A man would be jealous of *me* visiting his girlfriend?" Nancy poked fun.

"True," Catherine conceded. "But then, they are rather naïve, aren't they?"

They laughed a lot more as they flipped through the albums which included some photographs of Catherine's former male lovers.

"Jacky doesn't mind this?" Nancy inquired.

"That they're men? Or that they're in the book?"

"Both, I suppose."

"She's also had boyfriends before, so there's no room for complaint. In fact, she'd never had gay inclinations; they only came about from dealing with a *situation* with a photographer. She really doesn't like men much. She's got a real issue."

"It's sad."

"And you...? Got a love of your life?"

"Alas... lost."

"Oh dear."

"Years ago... I'm well over it. Drunk driver."

"Oooh, no," Catherine grimaced. "The other evening?"

"Uh-huh... bad girl. You gotta stop that nonsense."

"Sorry mom... I really don't do it much, was just the company."

"Enough of that already. You were going to tell me about her lack of jealousy. All these pics of lovers; *shewee* girl, you have some taste!"

"She doesn't mind the pics, they make me who I am, she says."

"Mature... good. Nothing worse than a skeleton in a cupboard; it begs for blackmail."

Nancy's sober words resolved Catherine's mind; she had to make it right with Jacky, she had to come clean about Ken. She'd make it her first priority come Thursday.

Whatever the consequences, she thought, *they can't be worse than having a man like Ken holding a gun to my head.*

She told Nancy of her intentions.

"I didn't mean it as a judgment."

"I didn't take it as one, Nance."

"How will she take it?"

"Honestly... I don't know. Probably not good... but it can't be worse than this. I can't live like this."

"I'll be here for you."

"Thank you." Catherine rose. "Coffee?"

"Please. I must use your facilities."

"Straight up the stairs into the bedroom, use the en suite." Catherine could just as well have directed Nancy to the guest toilet on the ground floor and closer, but she wanted Nancy to feel like family.

Downstairs alone, she felt comfortable, not a hint of paranoia anymore. "Thank God," she sighed softly to herself. "The nightmare's over, it's over!"

That night, the two friends lay together, embracing like sisters in Catherine and Jacky's bed.

There'd be no need to tell Jacky about it—it was meaningless. If Jacky asked, she'd not deny it, but there was nothing to report.

She was certain Jacky would see it that way.

Chapter 22

Her nipples were erect buds of desire. The curve of her back as arched, as achingly beautiful as an arch could be. Her carefully trimmed pubis jutted with all the pride that the human form could offer.

Altogether, she projected an appeal more alluring than lust could accommodate.

She held the pose of confidence for long seconds. "Just look at me," her stance exclaimed. It was not an arrogant exclamation, just a self-assured one.

Her audience was three, one by her side and two transfixed by the screen. All leered, spellbound by the visual feast. The man by her side *and* the man ogling the scene that unfolded on the monitor were the same individual.

The plush hotel room was equipped with a giant flat screen monitor that auto-detected Ken's MacBook, and wirelessly displayed its bidding.

A betrayal of trust was rolling across the screen.

Ken had his feet up on one armrest, his body stretched across the sofa and his head reclining on the opposite side. During the seven days that divided the event from tonight's parade, he'd watched the secret recording more times than he could count; it consumed him.

Watching her take pleasure was his fantasy of the moment, a tonic to a flagging libido corroded by chemical abuse. Convincing her into going through with it a stroke of genius enjoyed twice; the event and its recording.

Ken had stood the staff down for the event, sowing different assertions, orders and claims into different ears to ensure the operations block kept it private for just Catherine and himself.

The CCTV was a problem; he couldn't allow any possibility of footage showing a naked service provider performing nefarious deeds with him ogling and shooting his own footage, leaking onto the Internet and social media.

"I can't risk anything being leaked to the tabloids, Anton. Just one leaked frame and the press will be all over Saudi Royalty and his concubine in our facility."

Before leaving that evening, Anton had cancelled the recordings to that sector of the building and physically pulled the plugs on the cameras into the recorder. Ken had watched and re-checked that they were disconnected right before Catherine arrived.

Ken had shot it high definition with his iPhone—it was all he could risk. The footage danced, shook and shuddered from beginning to end; adrenaline an unsteady base.

The re-watching of it had haunted him, waking him early each morning, like a drug, unrelentingly urging him to watch it.

"Ahh... my favorite part," he pointed.

The girl stared, her eyes bulging, unblinking in disbelief. "This client must be an actor! Look how he appears on the film."

The girl had rarely seen a television monitor before; there was only one in her small village in Siberia. Her eyes were glued to the screen, transfixed on the beautiful woman actor who was kneeling naked, this man doing something to her rear end.

What a funny sight for a child to see—it made her giggle.

Ken checked the time—it was nine-fifteen. Jetlag still had its grip on him. He'd wake early again, so tonight he'd limit how much of his obsession he'd watch—just enough to excite the girl.

Tonight, he'd sleep well. She was such a pretty little thing, she'd be a great help.

No doubt his slumber would be filled with dreams of Catherine again. Dear, sweet, uncooperative Catherine.

Chapter 23

It was Thursday evening and Catherine's troubles returned with a vengeance.

Tuesday night she'd slept alongside Nancy with no hint of a problem, and Wednesday afternoon had also been without incident. Just for a brief moment alone in the private toilet adjoining her office, she'd suddenly felt a walked-over-my-grave shiver, and then it was gone.

She'd tested the air and there seemed to be the slightest whiff of him. *Probably just a memory*, she'd mused, *a memory and a paranoia*. "Toilet spray," she'd said aloud, "...shit smell," and laughed.

Wednesday night, she returned home alone and caught up on admin, then slept alone. She was relieved.

Thursday had been without incident.

Jacky was due home by six and Catherine had decided to surprise her with a three-course meal and for once cooked it herself.

She'd stolen some hours from work and was home cooking by five o'clock when she heard Jacky.

"Hi Baby... you're early," she called, silently cursing the spoilt surprise.

No answer, so she called again.

Nothing.

Battling her worst fears, she walked toward the entrance hall where a Roman Centurion was admiring his own image in the mirror.

She dropped the earthenware bowl she was holding and fled back to the kitchen.

A little before six, Jacky came through the door to find shards of pottery and liquid spread across the hallway. Her noisy entry prompted a fresh round of terrified sobs from the kitchen.

Catherine was a twitching mass of anguish, beyond tears, her face a swollen red tomato with two pig-eyes too terrified to open.

The doctor shot her up with a maximum dose of *benzodiazepines*, a potent sedative.

"That'll take her through till morning," he assured. "I'd like you to bring her in to Santa Clara tomorrow. I'll meet you at psychiatrics, floor six, around eleven. I'll need to keep her under observation for a few days I'm afraid."

He scribbled the details onto a prescription leaflet to ensure that Jacky wouldn't forget.

"This is important Jacky, she may resist—force her to come."

Catherine woke at nine on Friday morning.

Both women looked like they'd been in the same scrap, their eyes were similarly puffed, their complexions similarly drawn.

"I don't need observation, Jacks. I'm not nuts! There's something more than hallucination going on here. You've felt it too... Come on... you've even smelled him! Christ, I..."

Jacky was at the end of her tether, strung out and explosive. "Smelled *WHO*?" Jacky cut her off, her tone threatening. She knew something was up, she'd known for weeks, she could feel it.

Catherine startled. "Th... the smell that you've smelled... The person." She hadn't intended for her confession to be uncovered in this way, she wanted to break it boldly, building up to it with perspective, feeding Jacky information one fact at a time.

Bolts of furry were jagged sparks in Jacky's eyes. "What person?!" she spat. "You said *him*. Who is *he*? Who is this *man*?!"

Catherine was weak, crushed, emotionally destroyed and woozy from the sedative. She was outgunned but she tried to slow and divert the pace of the deteriorating situation. "Jacky, please darling. Please come and sit down, I've got something to tell you."

Catherine's call for reason was the trigger, and Jacky exploded. Sleepless nights of her own and the sickening suspicions of what she assumed was to come detonated in the most primitive part of her brain.

The more Catherine struggled, the deeper she sank into the quicksand of conflict. With every defense she offered, with every context she appealed for, the more devious and sly her position appeared.

When Ken's name was brought into the conversation, Jacky snatched it up and ran with it. Catherine had slept with him... she'd been sleeping with him for months.

An hour later, Catherine was no closer to defending her innocence. She'd admitted to everything that she had done, but Jacky was not interested. "It's the weakest excuse I've ever been insulted with."

Catherine would not admit to it. Would not admit to the month or more of working late to fuck the guy. Eventually, she collapsed from the accusations into a blathering heap, sliding to the floor, crumpled against the skirting board with her will emotionally kicked out of her.

"You are a real stupid little bitch..." It came like a growl, Jacky's voice as low as a panther in a dark wood. "You think I haven't seen this all before? Hello... Darling, I fly with pilots every day of my life, in a different port every night. You think I don't know every story? That when I'm in the other port you... well..." She stood over Catherine and lashed her with her tongue. "His smell's on your clothes, his stench in our bed! You're being stalked! *Bullshit!* The cover's blown, baby, he's in and out of here; *in and out of YOU* every time I turn my back!"

After every breakable ornament within reach had already been hurled across the bedroom, Jacky began throwing personal belongings back into her travel bag.

Catherine was beyond arguing. She lay facing the skirting board, her tear-soaked mat of hair piled over her face, but it was no protection from the merciless tongue that pulverized her;

"Oh yes, dear; there's not much I don't know!" Jacky latched the case, snapped the telescopic handle up and made for the door where she paused a moment. "And by the way, slut... a *Nancy* called." Jacky's voice was suddenly honey and roses with sarcasm. "She said, 'Why aren't you at work today, bad girl? And... thanks for dinner Tuesday'." She laughed; a nasty, cruel and scornful laugh. "Oh, and 'you'll be pleased to know' your Nancy said, 'Ken will be back tomorrow'."

The door slammed closed for the final time and a deathly silence seeped throughout the house.

The phone rang at ten thirty.

It rang again at eleven.

By eleven thirty, Catherine had peeled herself off the floor. She was the living dead, her voice no more than a parched groan when she answered, "H... hello."

The barely human croak sent Nancy into a panic. "Catherine! What's the matter? Are you all right?"

Nancy careened along the highway, barreling through traffic snarls and running streetlights, the trip a blur all the way from the office.

Catherine was on the front steps, at high noon, sitting in her nightgown.

"I'm not going in, Nance. *He's* in there." She was calm, dangerously calm, punch-drunk calm and numbly accepting whatever fate threw next.

Nancy went through the house in a savage mood. "Show yourself, you bastard! Be anything *like* a man and show yourself!"

Her challenges bellowed, the sound of her voice a weapon, a projection of her spirit that bounced off the cold stone pillars.

Only Ken's smell remained as testimony to his presence. Nancy's reconnaissance took her through the scenes of the earlier battle; the bedroom a shambles knee-deep in remnants of once beautiful artworks.

Catherine's bedside table was the only corner of the room not destroyed. It stood out as an island of neatness in an ocean of bedlam. On it were two pill bottles where Nancy had seen them on Tuesday night. One of the bottles was weighing down a leaflet and beckoned Nancy's attention. She picked through the debris and discovered on one page the instructions that the doctor had left.

A few minutes later, Nancy came triumphantly out the front door carrying a hastily assembled overnight bag. Catherine was still sitting on the steps, hugging her knees to her chest, gently rocking. "I've spoken to Doctor Johnson at the hospital, he's waiting for us. Come on."

"I don't need psychiatric help." Catherine's protests were emphatic but trailed to nothing as Nancy took her firmly by the arm and led her to the car.

With her cargo stowed and buckled in, Nancy returned to lock the house. Curiously, it seemed fresh, the scent of spring blossoms on the air.

"You'll never hurt her again, you bastard. Never!" she shouted into the emptiness of the structure as an oath.

Back in the car and pulling out of the driveway, Nancy patted Catherine's leg. "We're meeting Leon there," she reassured. "He knows these things better than anyone."

Chapter 24

The evening traffic was choking the city's arteries and Nancy was in Leon's car.

As they joined the river of steel snaking its way homeward for the weekend, they'd both accepted that this would be a frustrating crawl.

"Ken's back tomorrow, and there's a lot we should talk about before we see him. Is there any chance for us to have dinner tonight?" Nancy had suggested to Leon as they were about to depart the hospital.

"Today is...?" Leon had queried.

"Friday." Nancy could never be sure whether he was serious about being bamboozled by the task of keeping track of life's trivia.

"Ah-ha!" Leon had clapped jubilantly. "Not a problem then, not a problem at all. We've got a date."

It had puzzled her that the day of the week factored into it; as far as she knew, Leon was a bachelor with a limited social life. It seemed unlikely that any other day would be more or less convenient.

She'd just shaken her head and chuckled. "It's almost five, perhaps we go in one car? It's not far and the traffic's horrible."

Without answering, Leon had been brusquely off, heading for the exit. "C'mon Luv," he'd called to her in a loud and fake Yorkshire accent. "The train's bloo'y leav'n."

The busy reception foyer had come to a halt, passersby stopping in their tracks to stare at this strange noisy foreigner in their midst.

Now what's come over him? Nancy wondered, shaking her head as she trotted in hot pursuit, shrugging perplexedly to bystanders who'd cleared a path for Leon's purposeful passage.

She could well understand their dismay and alarm. He'd developed a hunched back and an exaggerated crab gait and proceeded muttering and grumbling to himself.

"What's that all about?!" she'd enquired when she'd caught up, not entirely certain whether or not to be concerned.

"Weekend!" He'd said it as if it was an astonishing and delightful surprise, adding in a perfect rendition of Queen's English, "Give the masses some entertainment I say, give them some fun, what!"

"Sometimes I really wonder, Leon... I wonder and I worry."

"Jump in," he'd invited, holding the passenger door open for her.

"With *you* driving?" She'd screwed her face up.

"Never..." he'd paused dramatically, "judge a book by its cover! I'm the safest driver on the road, I tell you. I get my frustrations out in other ways. I'll be no statistic, no statistic at all!"

His words had struck a deep chord in Nancy's soul and she'd swallowed back the welling emotion for the man she'd adored and lost. "I'd like to go via Catherine's house, if we may," she'd asked Leon. "I'd like to check something out... I've got the keys, Catherine won't mind."

Someone had been in the house. It was far from tidy but the breakages had been swept aside and Nancy also saw that some areas were denuded of ornamentation.

The scene was poignant and bleak; where warm rugs had once hung, were acres of cold white wall. Where warm hearts had once beaten, an icy chill brooded in silence.

Gooseflesh rose all over Nancy's body and Leon put a comforting arm about her shoulder and steered her toward the door. "There's nothing that we can do tonight, Nance. Nothing at all."

They returned outside to the world where the rhythm of life still throbbed. They entered the highway and merged into a lane, becoming another set of headlights.

"He's an evil bastard, Leon."

"Now, Nance..."

"He treats people like dirt. Money... money, money, money... and now this!"

"Nothing's proven," Leon cautioned, against his own deepest instincts. "Nothing's proven."

"You don't mean that..." their starter courses was arriving. "You're a bloody devil's advocate—no pun intended."

The waitress was studying them, a quizzical look written on her face begging the question, what was an eccentric, dotty, old man doing out dining with a fine-looking filly?

They spoke at length, establishing what each knew about the fast unfolding situation at hand. During their commute, Nancy had filled Leon in on the details that she thought he might need to help Catherine's recovery. Santa Clara's psychiatric department had agreed to allow Leon to treat Catherine as a private consulting specialist. It gave him full access to her at any time, for the duration of her stay.

Earlier in the day, while driving Catherine to the hospital, Nancy had casually inquired about the preparation procedures that Ken had implemented prior to her cyber-sex incident. Something in Catherine's original relating of it had bothered Nancy, it hadn't sounded right. Her suspicion was triggered more by an instinct than a detail.

"I know it's awkward to talk about, but I think it may be important for treatment, Cath. I'll keep details in confidence."

"Leon can't know about the cyber-sex, okay."

"Of course," Nancy had promised. "I need to know all of the precise details of how Ken *ritualized* you—you know we call the prep a *ritual?*"

Catherine had nodded "I know exactly what it is you want to know... the same thing's been plaguing me."

As Catherine had spoken, she'd taken to the juice-stick, its glowing LED tip dancing, exaggerating the tremble of her hand.

Nancy wasn't fond of the cherry aroma in the confined space of the car, but she didn't have the heart to deny Catherine the crutch at such a difficult moment.

"I wasn't hypnotized, yet I experienced an enormous time dilation."

Nancy had done a poor job of covering the shock of confirmation on her face. Hypnosis was the key to time dilation... everyone knew that. So, if there was no hypnosis sequence, then...?

"I should've thought about it when I accepted the game, damn it." The smouldering tip between Catherine's fingers had accelerated its dance. "How was I going to be time dilated if he'd promised to not run the hypnosis sequence?"

The implications were horrifying.

"*Sooooo*... Where was it, if it wasn't in the hypnosis? A subliminal?"

"What about something in the champagne? Maybe that plaster?" Catherine had puffed nervously. "I'm a God-damned fool... Shit, Nance... I'm more street-wise than this! That bastard and his filthy habit; Christ knows what concoction he could have spiked me with? Two sunsets! It must've been strong as all hell. *FUCK!*"

Catherine had slammed her hammer-fist onto her thigh, sending her juice-stick cartwheeling through the air and down between the seat and door.

"Oh damn, I'm sorry Nance. It's won't burn anything." She'd begun awkwardly fishing around to retrieve it. "I don't normally use it in a car, I wasn't thinking."

"Relax sweetie, if this was our worst problem today, we'd have no problems."

By the time Leon had arrived at the hospital, Catherine had already been admitted and was in the ward under the care of Doctor Johnson. Nancy hadn't yet had time to brief him; all he knew was that Ken was somehow involved in her nightmares following an online time-dilation run beyond the fighter jet simulation that Leon knew about.

"I'll explain why later Leon, but have them draw blood and run a full battery of tests; it looks like Ken slipped her a Mickey Finn."

"Chloral hydrate?"

"No idea, Leon... just something that would have exaggerated the time dilation."

He'd raised his eyebrows and whistled. "Better we talk first. That's a pretty darned big haystack to find a very little needle in, Nance. A darned big haystack."

Through Leon's mind had been meandering all the previously meaningless tidbits he'd run into. Anton had come to him for advice on aspects of sexual motivation, wanting to know what deviations he could prompt in the Artificial Intelligence Due Diligence routines for a hush-hush program he'd been working on. Ken had also casually inquired about the psychological effects of gender switching.

Now, revelations of a clandestine game involving Ken, Catherine and narcotics had left Catherine with pathological fears of Ken. Leon was pretty certain he had the situation figured out. Catherine was suffering as a victim of guilt, her deep morals in conflict with her excessively liberated actions. He decided that this was not a case of doping. *Not exclusively doping*, he'd re-qualified his thoughts.

He decided to appease Nancy and have them run some elementary tests to check for the more common hallucinogens.

Time had fled ahead of all the details that needed sharing, and the pair was well into dessert already.

"I'm thinking of leaving the company, Leon."

Sadness crept into his eyes. "Surely not just because of *this*, Nance? Surely not?"

"It's part of it, a big part... but mostly it's the attitude. My stock options are worth a fortune, but they're not worth my conscience. Look what he's done to Cath..."

"But he's not treating Catherine badly Nancy, she willingly chose, nobody forced her. She got emotionally hooked, her emotions are frayed, but she'll pull through."

"It goes beyond this single affair, Leon." She didn't want to argue it all over again, it was getting late and she felt beat. "I'm bored with my work, it's time to move anyway."

"Bored? You're *bored* at LifeGames? Impossible, Nance, impossible!" Leon exclaimed. "You're right at the cutting edge, it doesn't get better than this. Our clients don't get bigger. You're not bored, Nance. That's impossible."

"I am," she said plainly and with finality. "The company might be doing fabulous things, but *I* do the same thing every day."

Being Ken's right hand was *not* her passion; she wanted to be an artist. With what she could cash out, she estimated that she could now just about make it happen.

"I've sold my passion to buy survival," she explained to Leon. "I'm an intellectual prostitute."

Chapter 25

"GET AWAY... GET AWAY FROM ME...!" Catherine was screaming, overturning tables and crashing through chairs toward the hospital restaurant's open patio.

Patients and visitors scrambled to clear a path out of the way of the deranged woman's headlong dash for outdoors.

It was visiting hour and Catherine was having tea with a friend when Ken had materialized in the crowded public place. She could scarcely believe her eyes as his phantom boldly approached, a smile on his face, undaunted by witnesses.

Catherine's sudden reaction had stopped him in his tracks, frozen and mystified, unsure whether to keep walking or retreat.

Two men tackled and restrained Catherine before she could vault over the parapet wall around the third story patio.

Within moments, more bystanders ran to help until staff arrived. She fought like a woman possessed, and the area rapidly cleared as people recoiled from the insanity of it.

The incident momentarily stunned Ken. It was the second occasion that his visit to a psychiatric ward had resulted in general mayhem the moment he'd entered the patient's presence. He milled about, bewildered by the reaction.

A few minutes later, the hospital superintendent approached him.

"I'm sorry sir... are you Mr. Torrington?" His photo had been circulated to all staff on a no-visitation list. Much as Ken tried to keep a low profile in the media, most people knew him on sight anyway.

Ken agreed.

"Forgive me, but I am going to have to ask you to leave sir."

Insulted and shocked, he left the hospital grounds in a shriek of rubber and under the power of sixteen cylinders of Bugatti thunder. The instigators of his rude public ejection were clear, and he was on a mission to avenge this insult. Leon's name had been mentioned as Catherine's consulting specialist, so Leon's house would be his first port of call. It was Sunday and Ken was positive that the old fool would be home.

On Friday, when Ken had called into the office from Russia, Jo had informed him that both Nancy and Leon were at the Santa Clara Hospital tending to Miss Kaplan who had suffered an emotional breakdown.

After touching down on Sunday morning, he'd called the hospital, claiming that his sister had been admitted and they'd confirmed the ward number. He'd found the room vacant and correctly guessed where to find her.

He was now tearing through traffic without respect for rules or sense, aggression stripping him of the last vestiges of sanity.

The Veyron screeched to a halt outside Leon's door, announcing his arrival with a prolonged blast of its horn. A pedestrian and three neighbours stared in shock and irritation at the arrogant stranger who disturbed the harmony of their day. Ken saw nothing beyond the blind rush of assumptions fueling his tyrannical focus.

During the hell-ride, he'd neatly pieced together the conspiracy that Nancy, Catherine and Leon had concocted against him. In his mind, all of the little incidents he'd witnessed between them over the weeks and months had accumulated, culminating in this final betrayal.

The exchanged smiles between the women... their dinner together, which Nancy had accidentally mentioned. Nancy and

Leon plotting together at her desk when they thought he was in Korea. He'd seen Nancy trying to hide the evidence of their devious whisperings on that occasion. Nancy's aggressive defense of Catherine when Catherine was plainly avoiding him.

Oh, yes, Ken thought. *Now I see where allegiances lie.*

He strutted up Leon's pathway, his fists clenched tight. He beat his knuckles onto the door until they bruised and the skin smeared, yet Leon did not appear.

By the time he abandoned the door and spun his wheels the length of the quiet cul-de-sac, the street was deserted.

The little frail man must be cowering inside his house. He laughed out loud at the assumption. "Quaking with fear, too fucking terrified to confront me."

Ken blasted back onto the highway, putting his beast of a machine through its paces, but when he arrived at Nancy's door, she had already departed to rendezvous with Leon at the hospital. Ken had missed her by one cycle of the streetlights.

Again, he leaned on the car's horn until nobody in the leafy lane's vicinity could have missed his presence. It was a pointless and childish act as her car clearly wasn't in the driveway. But he didn't care—he was nose-in against her gate and intended for the neighbours to report the incident to her.

Giving up, he drove away, still blind with rage. But enough sense had returned to know that he needed to slow down, so he found another secluded street farther down and pulled over.

He removed a vial from the ashtray and fished in it with the extra-long nail of his smallest finger, retrieving a measure of powdered relaxation for his left nostril to vacuum away.

With his fury anaesthetized, he could head for home at a leisurely pace. There, he consoled himself that he would watch his beloved recording almost to punish this woman that gave him so much grief.

It was a possession of Catherine's that he alone had the power to control, all day and all night if he so wished.

Chapter 26

"It was the man's sister, Superintendent, I can't check every credential that people give to me," the security guard explained.

"You have the photo—there," the superintendent pointed past the guard into the recessed security office, "...on your wall. If you can't identify a person from their photo, what are you doing as a security guard?"

The superintendent stormed off before he created more of a public scene; he'd deal with it later.

"I'm terribly sorry about this fiasco, we've circulated the man's photo. It's on the wall at security, yet he somehow walked right through."

"He's like that," Nancy sneered, understanding that a guard would have a very difficult time with Ken even with the authority of the hospital behind him.

"I'll see to it there's an inquiry," the superintendent fawned; it was a private hospital that couldn't afford scandal.

Satisfied, Nancy thanked the man and rushed back into the private ward where Leon was attending to Catherine.

"How's she doing?"

"Stable," Leon reassured her.

"What now?" she insisted.

"We'll just have to wait a while. Soon as she settles, I'll probe a bit to see if there's any chance of making progress today."

The hospital staff continued finishing the task of making Catherine comfortable. They'd installed a drip to maintain a conduit for intravenous *diazepam* to quieten her anxiety. She'd also been lightly tethered to the bed, a requirement she'd grudgingly accepted so long as Nancy or Leon promised to stay.

"What will 'making progress' depend on?" Nancy pressed Leon.

"That's subjective, Nance. Catherine is very intelligent, very in touch. She's slowly accepting that this was *reality*... he was really here and not a hallucination."

On Saturday, twenty-four hours earlier, Leon had spoken at length with Catherine and formed a psychological profile on her. He'd confirmed the character profile that Nancy had described to him during dinner on Friday night; Catherine was lucid with a solid grip of reality.

His findings left him with another dilemma. Without prompting, Catherine had decided to volunteer details of the cyber-sex and when speaking about it, she'd displayed no sign of embarrassment or moral conflict. This behavior neutralized his earlier hypothesis about the underpinnings to the trauma.

Now he was without any viable alternative hypothesis or clue as to what might be going on.

The disruption Ken's visit had caused had temporarily derailed Leon's task of rehabilitating Catherine. For the first hour, Leon had acted more like an ordinary visitor than a physician, gently gaining her trust until she could handle a more exhaustive session.

Nancy watched as Leon's usual flippant, playful mannerisms slowly morphed into controlled professional conduct.

"How did today feel compared to the other occasions when Ken appeared?" Leon was purposefully avoiding the use of certain words, including 'visitations' or 'visions'.

"I don't really know," she answered, pausing, a light frown slowly creasing her forehead. "...but... hmmm, you're right, it did *somehow* seem different."

"Alright. Now, you mentioned previously that you could smell him before you saw him; what about this time?"

"Huh... that's true. No, I couldn't. Then again, he was pretty far away when I spotted him, and there were a lot of others around; perhaps that's an interference?"

"Maybe. Did he look the same? His face, his body?"

"He normally smiles at me." She shivered at the memory. "But this time... yeah... this time the smile was different. More... compassionate maybe, if that's possible for him. The other times his smile was..." Catherine searched for the word, "well, *evil*, malevolent maybe; with a sense of domination to it, lustful. So many words but none really sum it up completely."

Leon could see that she had more to say, so he kept silent and waited patiently.

"And his body..." she cringed. "I don't know how to put it, Leon—sometimes it's very different. I know you're going to laugh at me when I tell you this but he sometimes has the body of a... a..." Words failed her.

"Say it," he prompted. "Whatever comes to mind. It's very symbolic, not literal."

"Well, I suppose then... an *antelope*—hooves—somehow hooves come to mind. And don't laugh, I'm not delirious."

"We're not laughing, Catherine; don't block it," Leon advised.

"A goat?" Nancy offered.

"Yeah... that sort of a feel. I generally don't stick around to study his appearance, but that's the sense of it, Nance."

"Okay. So let's stay with that. Sometimes he seems different. So, does he sometimes have his own body, his actual appearance in *real life*?"

"Again, hard to just say 'no'. But his body does seem distorted, weird. Do you think it's important?"

"It could be Cath. I'm looking for patterns in these non-physical contacts; if we find patterns, we'll find solutions."

It was clear to Catherine that he thought she was hallucinating, and it annoyed her; her voice pitch started to climb with the frustration of it.

"What difference would that make to me, Leon. When he's here, he's as real as either of you two; he's flesh and blood, okay! I don't care if you believe that it's a 'non-physical contact'; I'm telling you that he's real. I'm not mad and I'm certainly not imagining it!"

Catherine's mood was unraveling and Leon realized that he would have to be more cautious.

"Catherine, Catherine, Catherine..." he said warmly and with affection, like a father to a daughter. "I'm not trying to discredit you, I'm trying to get to the bottom of this. And since I prefer not to do it with pharmaceuticals, the only tool I have is my questions and your trust."

He spoke slowly and carefully in his most hypnotic tone.

"If I accept here and now that this is some paranormal entity—and I'm prepared to do that—where do I start looking?"

Catherine and Nancy exchanged glances. It was a good argument.

"I must first establish or eliminate *all* of the rational possibilities. We *will* succeed but we can only do it with trust and sincerity."

"Okay, Leon, I'm sorry."

Catherine was calm again, won over by sense and skill.

"Is there any report back on my blood tests?"

"Afraid they won't come in till late Monday afternoon at the earliest," Leon answered.

Leon had thought at great length about Catherine's claim of being time dilated without a hypnosis sequence. The only possibility of this in his mind was a psychosomatic response, an autosuggestion self-hypnotizing her to think she'd been time dilated.

Catherine huffed irritably; she hated waiting for results.

"Now, there is another way to get to the bottom of this." Leon hoped that Catherine would agree. "I could hypnotize you."

Catherine looked horrified at the suggestion; she had a pathological aversion to it. Images of becoming a zombie, an eternal cerebral slave, crowded into her mind.

Leon had dealt with the irrational fear against his profession for decades; he'd anticipated and seen her expression;

"You'd be surprised, Cath, how much insight we'd get. It's not what you think. All I would do is facilitate your conscious mind to rest while your subconscious imparts perceptions without the noise and distractions from thinking and analyzing too much. Nancy can attest to it."

Nancy nodded in agreement.

Catherine listened intently, finding herself unable to resist; she loved the funny little man and was already under his spell.

A few minutes later Catherine was responding evenly, as calm and relaxed as Leon had instructed her to be.

His first questions were simple, and her answers corresponded to the ones she had given when the same questions had been posed to her conscious mind.

Satisfied, Leon branched to more in-depth questions, searching for any possibility that she had been self-inducing Ken's image. They proved that possibility to be negative.

"Leon, we've both already told you!" Nancy spoke softly for fear of influencing Catherine. "I smelled the bastard in her house on Friday morning too, even though he was still in Russia! Why won't you believe us?"

"Nance, I couldn't call myself a scientist if I didn't probe every probability. It's my job to be thorough." Leon thought a moment before adding, with a sly grin, "If I wasn't skeptical, then what would my career and books be worth?"

She thought about it and he was right; his books immediately went up in Nancy's estimation.

Leon returned to the task.

"Now Catherine, do you notice anything strange about Ken? Anything at all?"

Catherine's face began to distort with fear. She was in a state of regression back to the most recent incident when Ken had appeared as his most true to life; the time he had her cornered and could torture her without interruption.

Leon assured her that she was completely safe, and just an observer at the event.

"I want you to scan him with your mind, every detail; the way his hair falls, the shape of his ears, even his eyelashes. Is he as tall as he is in reality? Does he move the same way? Every detail. Take your time…"

Her eyes were staring wide open, tracking nothing in the ward, instead monitoring Ken's every move in the recording of her mind. "His... his hands... they're different. His nails, all his nails are the same length."

Pointing to one of her small fingernails, Nancy indicated Ken's habit of keeping one nail longer, mimicking him snorting off of it.

Leon frowned, a puzzle piece falling into place in his mind. He'd seen the nail, but had thought nothing of it.

"All right Catherine, calm again. Does he try to touch you at all?"

"Yes..." she replied, eyes wide, watching him. "He's following me, I'm backing... backing away." She was becoming agitated, but not as agitated as Nancy, infected by Catherine's terrified eyes that were tracking the invisible intruder moving about the empty hospital room.

"There's nothing to worry about, it's only a memory... he can't hurt you." Leon persuaded Catherine to withdraw from her memory. "He's gone now, you're back here, you're with us."

Catherine's eyes stopped their tracking and her body and face relaxed.

"Does he ever physically touch you?"

"No," Catherine answered immediately.

Leon checked a counterpoint in favor of hallucination.

"Can you tell me *why* he has never touched you?"

"I run, I hide. He *wants* me to suffer, he comes close and tortures me with his words."

"What does he say?"

"...I'm going to fuck you! You know that I'm going to, don't you? You won't be able to hide forever. I have you and I watch you every day. You can't take that away from me, you bitch..."

She paused, but before Leon could speak, she went on.

"...I've just watched you. I possess you... you are my right... I have *earned* you. Don't resist too long Catherine, or I'll bring friends to help me... don't you think my friends should have fun too?"

And then Catherine laughed, and it was Ken's voice; a rendition so real that it sent a shock wave through both observers.

"Craig is with us, Catherine. He says he's always had a thing for you. Don't you dare resist me anymore or we'll all rut you like dogs!"

The memory was harrowing and Catherine was beginning to shudder with fear. Nancy was no better; even Leon looked shaken, but he maintained an air of professional objectivity.

"Calm... calm Catherine, the memory is gone... it's gone. You're safe."

Her face went peaceful again.

Nancy's didn't. It was as if the terror had leapt from one woman to the other. Her eyes swum with the tears of terror, bulging in fright; she looked ready to bolt for a hiding place. Leon was too focused to notice.

"I only want to ask you one more question, Catherine. Ok?"

Catherine nodded as an automaton.

"Please think *very* clearly. You are in the kitchen cooking, it is Thursday evening, and there is no sign that anything is wrong. You haven't heard anything and you haven't smelled anything."

Catherine appeared relaxed; in her mind, she was preparing Jacky's surprise dinner.

"I want you to remember every small detail; a bird singing or a leaf rustling... everything is important. Take your time and tell us what is going on around you."

"It's been a lovely warm day..." she began. She was almost childlike in her rendition, replaying the events as if they were happening. "I wonder if Jacky will be on time? I should check if there have been any flight delays... just as soon as I put this in the oven... Where's my phone? Darn, still plugged in upstairs, I'll fetch it in a moment..."

She stopped and smiled, the movie of recollection rolling on. Seconds passed and a curious raise of an eyebrow as she recognized something.

"Sounds like the next-door kids have friends over... yep... a baseball game, I hope we don't lose another window. Darn it, I must get the garden service in to clear..."

Suddenly her mundane chatter ceased, cut down in mid-thought, her head tilting, listening intently for something. Leon and Nancy reflexively leaned inward as if the sound might leak into their ears too.

Her brow furrowed, examining her memories closely. "That's an odd sound... wow, it's faint... where on earth is it coming from? Everywhere, it's all around me, it's in my head... so familiar... I just can't place it." Her face was a picture of confusion.

"Does this sound always occur before Ken appears?"

"Yes."

She said it emphatically and without hesitation.

"Are you normally aware of it? Do you think about it? Focus on it?"

"No."

"Have you ever heard these sounds otherwise?"

Catherine thought, hesitating, matching sounds in her mind. "Yes... sometimes in dreams." Then she added, "It frightens me... it always leads to a nightmare... the sounds frighten me, it's like something being dragged."

"I'm just going to say it, Leon... it's Satanic."

"Now Nancy..."

"Look at the facts. What does your General say? Your regressed inquisitor... *foul balms*... *in league with the Beast*—a goat's body."

"Antelope; goat was your suggestion, Nance... your suggestion. We must remain objective."

They'd moved to the hospital's restaurant, a modern atrium full of palms and ferns. Catherine was peacefully sleeping upstairs. She'd asked to be moved to a shared ward, trading privacy for witnesses.

Leon had closed the session, instructing her conscious mind to forget the memories that her subconscious had disclosed.

"But still," Nancy suggested as she sipped, "A *beast* is a pretty strange form for an apparition to take."

"*Image*," Leon corrected her.

"You still think that it's a hallucination, don't you?" Nancy fixed Leon with an accusing stare.

"I did... I don't want to... I'm conflicted." Leon was in the grip of a bitter struggle between calm reason and the sentiments of his instinct. "But you are right Nance, it's becoming a difficult dogma to maintain, very difficult." Within him, reason was beginning to crumble under the advance of sentiment.

With no intention of inflaming Nancy's passions any more than they already were, Leon carefully considered what he was going to say next.

"There's something else, something that I really shouldn't tell you." He looked troubled. "Indeed, never in all of my career have I broken patient confidentiality. Never."

Nancy could see his conscience wrestling with itself, one dire situation outweighing another related incident.

"The recording we discussed a while back, the one with Craig's voice..." Leon went on to describe the technical details of Stuart's analyses.

"Backwards? The Lord's Prayer?" Nancy scowled. "Now there's a contradiction!"

"It's actually bothered me, Nance. I know I'm one weird eccentric hippie, one foot grounded, the other in the mystical. It's not an easy fence to straddle. I give logic and evidence every first chance, but when they run out, well..."

He shrugged and Nancy knew she had him in retreat, moving toward the esoteric which she held in high regard, so she pushed her advantage.

"Like I told you earlier, Catherine mentioned too many convincing details: 'Craig's with us'? 'I've earned you'? 'Possess you'? Come on Leon, what's with all that if it's not spooky and real?"

Then she played the highest ace in her deck.

"And don't forget, when she told us these things she *was* hypnotized!" She could see it had worked, Leon was on the run. "And *you've* always told me that a hypnotized patient will quote verbatim. So, if it was verbatim and Catherine added no interpretation of her own, it *must* have been Ken's apparition and those *must* have been Ken's actual words."

"I don't know, Nance. I agree that it is a tempting argument, but I really don't know."

"And another thing Leon. I know that Cath told you about her mischief. If I know Ken, he used the security cameras to make a recording. Would that have been possible?"

"Certainly," Leon responded. The thought had never entered his mind. "He could have done that, but I doubt if he would; the risk of it! But maybe on his phone?"

"Oh... great!" Now that it was said, it was so obvious. Nancy generally didn't automatically default to the devious option.

He could see her concerns and thought it best to minimize them.

"There's not much he could do with a recording like that, Nance."

"Oh, come on Leon. How much illicit pornography is out there?" She could see that he genuinely didn't have a clue so she expanded on her rhetoric. "Plenty. The web's overflowing with it. Child sex, snuff films, bestiality—you really don't know this, do you?"

Leon was divided from reality by several generations and a mind too busy in its own obsessions to be bothered with the conduct of others.

"Forget what someone can do with it, filming it is bad enough... what did he say? He watches her 'every day... possesses her'. You recorded the session; give it a listen."

"What...? Now? Here?" Leon looked about them at the assortment of visitors and staff in their immediate vicinity.

"You're surely not embarrassed? The real Leon wouldn't notice strangers. You're not also an imposter, are you...?" Nancy teased.

She was right; Leon wasn't feeling his usual self. The recent events had shaken him more than he'd care to admit.

He ran the recording and they strained to listen together. It was exactly as Nancy had characterized it.

"What do you make of 'possess', now?" she challenged. "It can *only* mean one of two things; possess her *image* or possess her *spirit*. Either way..."

Leon tried, but he couldn't fault her conclusions.

"And the part about Ken *earning* her? Spawn of Hell! She's probably a bone for this 'good dog' who has been serving his Master well! I don't know anything about Satanists, Leon, but it's the only conclusion that I can draw. Unless you outright discount the reliability that you always insist hypnosis guarantees during a recount."

"You sure drive a hard bargain, Nance. A very hard bargain," Leon was rattled. "If it was anyone but Ken, you'd have me convinced about Satanism by now. But not him!"

"You think that he's incapable?" Nancy challenged. "You give him too much credit."

"Not incapable Nance, he's a spiritual void. Not incapable. He doesn't believe in anything but his own supremacy."

There had been hesitation in Leon's voice and Nancy saw it. He was still trying to resist capitulating to her speculations, but his armor was crumbling fast.

"You're sure of that... that he has no spiritual side to him at all?" She forced him to question himself.

"To be honest, I don't think that *he's* even sure of that himself, anymore."

"Ah-ha," Nancy cried triumphantly. "And what makes you say that?"

"Well, the recording of Craig from his voicemail, it had him rattled. Some very odd stuff there... some pretty creepy background sounds." He saw her ready to leap.

"Creepy sounds hey? Now we're getting somewhere. Catherine hears a sound that announces Ken's presence, Ken hears the identical sound in his own nightmare, and Craig's recording has the identical sound on it."

"*Identical?* That's subjective," Leon said, pleading reason.

"Oh, identical's balls!" Nancy exclaimed. "We've got this bastard stone cold and you know it, Leon... you know it."

She excused herself to visit the ladies room. When she returned there were two fresh cups of coffee waiting.

The tide of Leon's opinion had turned and he was making no attempt to wind up their discussion. "You're still thinking of leaving us, Nance? Resigning?"

"Definitely. After today... after all we've uncovered?"

"That's a pity... a great pity."

It was clear to Nancy that Leon had something up his sleeve; she could sense it in his tone.

"It's always a great pity to see someone run from a fight," he added, clearly baiting her.

"Run from a fight?" Nancy repeated, taking the bait. "Is that what you think I'm doing?"

Seeing a grin beginning to spread across Leon's face, her hostility dissipated as quickly as it had arisen.

"Ok, Leon. I'm catching your drift. I've won you over, haven't I?"

"Not won." Leon wouldn't admit to being defeated at his own game of mind-play. "But you have persuaded me to agree with you... and that brings me to you, specifically. You can't change this situation if you divorce yourself from it. If you leave us, nothing changes, but if you and I work *together* we can change it."

Nancy couldn't dispute Leon's argument and with it, he extracted a commitment from her to hang in and fight.

"But what can I do?" she asked.

"I'll need that recording of Craig. I've got a hunch that it's the key."

Chapter 27

"It seems I caused a little stir at the hospital yesterday," Ken conceded.

If Nancy didn't know him better, she'd have thought there was a hint of apology was in his tone.

"I heard something had happened. I figured it had to be you, Ken." It wasn't easy feigning either ignorance of the ruckus he'd caused or geniality toward him, but she forced a lighthearted laugh, as if it was all quite amusing. "Terrifying patients is becoming rather a habit."

"Hey, that hurts. I've got feelings too, you know." Ken bought the sham reaction.

The pair had been playing out the charade since their first greeting ten minutes earlier, each obscuring their true feelings toward the other.

Leon had coached her. He'd said the best way to manipulate Ken was to appeal to his ego, avoid confrontation and diminish any negative connotations attached to him.

When Ken had arrived at the office that Monday morning, she'd treated it as another mundane start to another unremarkable week; getting him coffee, updating him on the most important messages, and asking about his trip abroad.

When the time was ripe, she'd mentioned to him that Catherine was in the hospital for a nervous breakdown, evidently triggered by an unknown stress.

Ken had lapped the charade up, offering his own responses of mock surprise for the reception he'd received at the hospital. He'd been pretty sure Nancy was part of the problem.

And what to do about Nancy?

He'd been pondering that for the better part of a week. She knew too much for him to just let her go. It would be easier to pay her off handsomely, give her an early retirement, and connect her future payouts to her cooperation; all easy to do. But how to sell it to her? *She needs a hobby,* he thought. *After a few months or years of happy retirement, when the heat was off... well, accidents happen.*

This idea made him smile.

Their game of wits was an opaque veneer over a rotting core of mutual repulsion.

Ken had put aside his rage of the previous day in favor of a tactical response to his employees' betrayal.

The first item on his agenda was to uncover precisely what motivated them. "What's the objective here?" he'd asked himself. "How're they planning to move, and why?"

Every answer had led to jealousy; if they were him, they'd be like him; if he was them, he'd be like them. They wanted to be more like him, with wealth and power; so he'd feed it to them— or the illusion of it.

"What exactly is wrong with Catherine? Some asshole on a power kick told me I'm on his little *banned* list... that's all he'd say. Ugly sod too. I'd have thought it a liability to have him running the lunatic wards; his face must be terribly injurious to the fragile little minds around there." Ken sighed in amusement. "Guess I'm gonna see how much *he* likes being banned from playing king of *his* castle."

The threat was chilling; Nancy had seen him crush careers before.

Nancy couldn't produce a smile. "Catherine's been having nightmares about you, apparently." She made it sound matter of fact.

"Me?" Ken seemed aghast. If he wasn't, he'd put on a good show.

"That's right." Nancy's tongue swished, poking against the inside of her cheek.

She estimated that Ken would have found out that she and Leon had visited afterward. The way he was acting, she realized he'd have already put out feelers and gotten feedback.

"You sure got the staff agitated," she teased, pretending it was amusing. "All that I could get out of them was that someone had come into the restaurant and that it had upset Catherine. I guessed that it must have been you; you know, because of the nightmares."

"Me—of all people, me?! I can't believe it!" Ken's attempts at mock exclamation were as weak as his humor.

"It really surprised me Ken... something about you stalking her."

"Good God, how would Catherine get *that* into her head?" He seemed to ponder it a moment and then tacked on a question. "And Leon's part in all this?"

"When I heard about it, I suggested he see if he can help. They allowed him to probe a bit, with hypnosis."

"He find anything?"

Nancy had to think quickly. "I don't know, Ken. Patient confidentiality. He hasn't said anything and I didn't ask."

Ken's mind was at full pace. He didn't want the cyber-sex issue to become public record; it was private. It was another ace that Nancy might hold that he'd have to pay for if she chose to play it.

"Sure. I'll chat about it when I see him. I tell you, you never really know a person. Catherine... of all people, I never imagined that she'd crack up."

"It's just stress, Ken. You know you're a taskmaster and a perfectionist; you did put a lot of pressure on her. I'm no psychic, but... 'why you'? Well, you're at the front of her mind, her big break—and she can't afford to disappoint you." Nancy felt like she'd gag on the butter she smeared on it.

"Hmmm..." He'd bought it. He finished his first coffee and pushed the discarded mug toward her. "I'm a little disappointed, though. You'd think my stunning good looks that she wants a piece of and can't get would really have done the damage."

It was his attitude that made him ugly, she thought.

"Have Leon contact me immediately when he gets in."

As Nancy reached Ken's door, he called after her, "Another bad night; I could use a refill."

Nancy called the hospital. Not surprisingly, Catherine had *also* experienced a bad night.

Ten minutes later, Leon called saying that he would be going by the hospital on the way. He'd be at the office within the hour.

Nancy quickly briefed Leon on key points of her conversation with Ken, reminding him that she knew nothing about any further conversations he may have had with Catherine. Only then did she connect him with Ken.

Five minutes later, Ken buzzed through on the intercom to relate what she already knew; the fact that Leon would be another hour, and re-emphasizing that he wanted to see Leon the moment he arrived.

He paused a moment and added, "Catherine evidently had another attack last night. I'm quite concerned about her, it's almost like I should feel responsible..."

Leon arrived bearing happy news. "A woman visited Catherine, I think her name was Jacky? Catherine told me to bring you the message that they had 'cleared up their problem'?"

Nancy doubted whether Leon would guess the nature of the relationship.

Ken couldn't have been more apprehensive as he ushered Leon into his office and seated him in one of the easy chairs. He'd given Nancy the instruction to screen all calls and serve two coffees.

Leon took note of Ken's one excessively long nail, estimating its growth exceeded that of the other nine nails by perhaps two months.

"How's Catherine today?" Ken was itching for details.

There was urgency in his voice that piqued Leon's curiosity. "Oh, a jolly lot better, Ken-o, a jolly-jolly lot better. Plenty of improvements today... plenty."

"I believe I'm the star of her nightmares? Sugar?"

Ken never forgot a detail, and he was pretty certain that some time ago when Leon had lied about cutting his sugar, he was in fact covering for something else he had been saying to Nancy that related to a conspiracy the two were plotting against him.

"Down to one now... cutting back slowly." Leon was wise to Ken's tricks, yet he was not prepared to suffer the full sugarless burden of his own trap.

Ken handed him the cup, not convinced that his suspicions were groundless.

Leon continued talking;

"I haven't yet established what precisely is wrong with her, Ken-o, but you're the focus alright. She's pretty fragile, and I couldn't risk scratching too deep into the problem. My guess? You're a scapegoat for her frustrations."

"They're pretty hostile toward me down at the hospital. Was it your idea to keep me from seeing her?"

"Given the circumstances..." Leon suggested. "Sorry you got bitten, Ken-o. I had no idea you were back or I'd have warned you not to go."

"So, it's a yes," Ken stated, staring at him long and hard.

Leon shrugged. "Sorry again. You saw her reaction Ken-o, it wasn't for nothing. She thought she was in a nightmare." Leon couldn't duck the question, so he rode it.

"I actually feel rather bad, Leon," Ken responded, sounding convincing alright, but his hand came up to his cheek and half-heartedly dabbed at an irritation. "Going for a chat is out of the question, so not much I can do to remedy it."

"Ken-o... didn't you mention you'd also dreamed about her... Catherine?" Leon had said it to track for revelations from that all-divulging finger. "You remember?"

"No... nope, I don't. Maybe... because the details of dreams slip out of my head just about immediately."

Leon could see that Ken remembered all too well, so he pressed him.

"Surely you remember, Ken-o? You mentioned those sounds... those same sounds from your recording.

"Hmmm..." Ken pretended to ponder it.

"Any more episodes?"

"If I have, I can't remember them," Ken answered, looking Leon directly in the eye, a practice he most often employed when trying to appear convincing.

"About the sounds on that recording..." Leon thought he'd try his luck. "I've got a friend who's very informed on that sort of thing, the paranormal and all that. Mind if I give him a listen to it?"

Ken assessed the request; there wasn't much the little man could do with the recordings. He agreed to forward the file.

"How long do you estimate it'll take to get her right... Catherine?" Ken asked.

"Tough to say. The mind's complex; could be weeks, could be months. Difficult to say."

"And nothing that I can do?" Ken wanted to smoke out any suspicion of his culpability.

"From what I can see—no," Leon answered, and instantly realized that here was an opportunity starring him in the face. "Unless, there's something that you're up to that's triggering the poor girl." He made it sound like an absurd and whimsical notion.

Ken didn't intentionally react, but Leon could see something eating at him. The ball was rolling, so he gave it a light push. "It's odd though, Ken-o. Seems Catherine's experienced some kind of sound associated with her hallucinations. Most peculiar... most peculiar indeed."

"Well now, maybe it's nothing to do with me then. Probably old Craig dicking with both of us, hey. He did fancy her, you know?"

"Could I miss it?" It wasn't true, but Leon humored the lie to milk it for truth.

Leon didn't miss much; only this morning, he'd watched Jacky pretend to be only a casual friend of Catherine's.

Leon knew Catherine was severing ties between the companies, so he decided to give that conversation a light nudge too.

"I've been rather hesitant to bring something up Ken, but I suppose I've been silly. When I hypnotized Catherine, she told me some details about your game... the sex game."

Ken went ashen.

"Does Nancy know?" There was a brittle edge to his voice.

"Oh, Lord, no, Ken-o... not from me... no, no, not at all. And there's no judgment either; lips are sealed and all that. Lips definitely sealed."

Ken recognized the advantage of suppressing his distrust of the little man, in favor of exploiting him instead. After all, there would be no way of banning Leon's private contact with Catherine. Threatening to fire Leon wouldn't work, as he had all the wealth he needed, and the competition would pay handsomely to have him. If Leon had Catherine's ear, as he appeared to, he could be an invaluable tool.

No, Ken thought, *I must guarantee his loyalty, I must keep his trust.*

"It was a hell of a ride Leon, your pacemaker couldn't have handled it," he said.

Leon put on a good show, pretending to find it amusing, chuckling. Ken was looking for solidarity, so he gave it to him with a small ego boost.

"Frankly Ken-o, I think she's hung up on you; you gave her too much of a good time, you see. Completely obsessed with you now... and trying to suppress it." And then he thought to twist things a little. "This is off the record, I'm afraid, but she's suffering rather significant delusions, terrified you've photographed or filmed her..."

Ken turned ashen again and dug at that old irritation, he looked ready to excuse himself to the cloakroom.

"Can't say I'd blame you if you did. Who wouldn't have, eh... who wouldn't?"

"That would've been a great idea. I of course had the CCTV pulled, so it's highly unlikely." Ken rose to his feet. "I'm bursting, arrange for two coffees, would you?"

267

Ken remained dead silent, listening from the inside of the door to the private toilet adjoining his office. He could barely make out the sound of Leon talking with Nancy.

"It's still just one sugar, Nance... just the one," Leon said, as he held up two fingers, pulling a disgusted face for the previous one-spoon cup.

Ken was none-the-wiser of the exchanged nods and quickly scribbled notes that passed between the pair as they made insignificant small talk.

"Better out than in, Ken-o?" Leon asked on his return.

"Much."

"As I was going to say," Leon began, returning to his brief. "The Chinese have picked up where the Russians left off in ESP research. You know... all that stuff about thought transmission."

Ken's face spelled curiosity. *What quirky new tangent was Leon onto now*, he thought? He feigned uncertainty. "ESP?"

"Ah... sorry; extra sensory perception, Ken-o. It's when I think something and you can read what's on my mind."

"Ahh... yes. All the rage when I was a kid. And...?"

His information was from an obscure piece of tabloid journalism Leon had read in a waiting room somewhere, but what he wanted to drive at was the principle of it.

"I heard they're training battalions to receive orders via ESP. Not just ESP; they're also tinkering with electronics and Wi-Fi, making it more reliable. They send out the orders to a device, and the subject receives ideas in their heads; orders, maneuvers, and the like. The Wi-Fi tinkers with their brain waves. The old Tibetan monks were supposed to be at it for centuries, of course, without the Wi-Fi."

It sounded ridiculous. "What are you trying to tell me?" he challenged Leon.

"Well... it's a crazy notion, Ken-o; it's from a tabloid after all, but what if your intimacy with Catherine has you somehow... linked like that?"

"Like I'm a radio transmitter and she's a receiver?"

"Possibly? But you do both carry one, you know—a radio. Your mobile, it's got Wi-Fi, transmits, receives; always connected."

There was no more doubt in Leon's mind that Ken had a video recording of the event. Perhaps, he thought, whenever Ken watches the recording, some kind of a bridge connects their minds. Sort of a quantum entanglement. It was a wild and crazy idea, even by his standards, but he decided to give it a go.

Guilt and a glint of worry had crept into Ken's voice. "Do you give it credence, Leon? You think there's science in it?"

"Proof... scientific proof? Now that's the tough one. A tough one indeed." Leon tugged absently at his own ear, as if loosening some details. "You've heard of quantum entanglement?"

"I just know it's confusing."

"Quantum entanglement is a measured physical phenomenon. What they've measured is that when pairs or groups of particles interact in certain ways in the quantum state of each particle, they entangle and can no longer be described independently. From that point forward, a quantum state exists for the system as a whole. In other words, they're entangled; what happens to one, influences the other over distance."

"You understand this stuff, Leon?" Ken was scowling.

"Not the details, Ken-o, not the details, nobody does. But I know enough to sound good and be dangerous. I read a little on quantum information science, how information transfer relies on quantum effects in physics."

"I think you're going to lose me," Ken admitted.

"Well, we're all a little lost, Ken-o. I guess the message is that you have a connection and it's bothering both of you. Give *it* up a while and see."

Leon swallowed the last of his coffee and cheerily made for the door.

"Toodeloo, Ken-o, there's work to be done... *Toodeloo*." And he was gone.

Ken hadn't missed the emphasis on 'it'—the wily old coot had probably sniffed his deviousness out. He decided to give the advice a try; he'd put that obsessive video aside a while and see how things went. Because, if it worked, *then it worked*—and the thought made him smile. It opened a whole new arena for manipulating others. Quite possibly, there would be money to be made in it.

Chapter 28

"Negative?" Nancy was angry. "That's impossible Leon, they've made a mistake. I'm going to *insist* that they re-run it."

"Why? Because you didn't get the result that you wanted?" Leon cautiously challenged. "Come on, Nance. You'd only be wasting Catherine's money; I'm convinced she's clean."

"Then how do you explain the time dilation?" Nancy challenged.

"She's a level-headed girl alright, of that I'm certain. But she's as susceptible to autosuggestion as anybody. Just as susceptible."

"Then what *are* you suggesting? If it wasn't a drug, then what…? You think she just imagined it?"

"It's likely that Ken didn't put her on full dilation. Without the hypnosis, the metabolic boost from the patch alone would have given her quite a jolt... quite a jolt indeed. If he'd tweaked the program even a little quicker, it would have felt much, much longer."

There was a lot of logic in Leon's analysis.

They were chatting as they drove from the office to the hospital. Leon parked the car and they made their way toward Catherine's ward.

It was Tuesday evening and, thankfully, Catherine should be in much better shape. Nancy had confirmed via telephone that she had not experienced any further encounters since Sunday night. It seemed a curiously significant fact in light of Leon's chat with Ken on Monday morning.

In addition, Catherine's relationship with Jacky seemed on the mend.

"I don't think that Cath will accept that theory of yours, Leon. She's very headstrong about what she knows."

"I'll tell her that the results aren't in yet. There are some things I'd like to ask her if she'll let me put her under again; interesting things."

Catherine was somewhat rejuvenated; her old smile was cautiously sneaking back. She seemed confidant, more self-assured, with a hint of enthusiasm for a new chapter without LifeGames in it.

"There's no need for a treatment, Leon," she insisted. "The problem's resolved. I can just *feel* it! And I'd just as soon leave it... forget it ever happened. When can I get the hell out of this place?"

"Discharging you isn't up to me, Cath. I can encourage it, but it's not my decision. If you're truly convinced it's over, you'd make me feel a lot more confident that I'd be doing you a favor if you'd give me one more shot, one more quick session; much more confident."

"I can't tell you how much work I have backed up; it'll just put me back in here if you don't clear me out of here soon."

"Come on, Cath," Nancy pleaded, casting her vote in Leon's favor. "You're his responsibility—please make it a little easier on him, please."

"I see; I have a team of doctors," she huffed, then looked injured. "I'm not getting the green light until I cooperate, is that it?"

"Something like that, Cath... something like that." Leon was nodding. "No green light I'm afraid."

Fifteen minutes later, Catherine's face was serene and calm as she described every excruciating detail of the cyber-sex session with matter-of-fact frankness.

"I am strapped onto the gyroscope. Inside the helmet it's black... Ah, now there's a snow effect and the hiss in my ears, I can feel Ken circling me, he's studying my body, it... it's *very* uncomfortable... awkward... This is probably a bad idea... Jeez, it's very sexy though! Come on Ken... What's taking so long? This is ridiculous. Should I take this goddamned helmet off? I'm really starting to feel disorientated. If I don't re-orientate myself soon, I'm going to throw-up! What's thi...? Oh, thank God, the snow's gone! What is this place? Good God, it's strange... some kind of village! Wow—is that a palace... looks almost like the entrance to my house...? It's a hell of a lot larger. Ooh...? That guy's seen me, he's coming over. Quite the bod too...

"All right, Catherine. The memory is over, you're still asleep. Before I wake you, when the helmet was on, did you hear my voice at all in your ears hypnotizing you before the game?"

"No."

"See!" Nancy whispered urgently.

"Hmmm... okay... alright..."

"Convinced?" Nancy challenged.

"Almost," Leon replied, turning back to Catherine. "Catherine, after you put the helmet on, are you absolutely positive that you did not hear my voice or any form of hypnosis? There's a rapping sound we tag all subjects with, like four fingers drumming on a table. Sounds like a horse gallop; you should remember it if it had run..."

"No..."

"Did you hear it at any time? Anything like it? It would have sounded like this..." And Leon clattered his fingernails in a fast gallop on the tabletop, *druumph, drumph, drumph.*

"No," Catherine answered, her eyes now lazy slits, the half-exposed pupils devoid of emotion in an unfocused stare.

"You were not hypnotized at any time?"

"No."

"How many hours of game did you experience?"

"Two sunsets, one sunrise."

"Are you sure... absolutely *certain* that you didn't experience an hour or two?"

"Yes."

"How many hours of real time did you use?"

"One hour and six minutes."

"Are you sure? Only sixty-six minutes?"

"Yes."

"If you were not hypnotized, how do you think Ken would have time-dilated you?"

273

Catherine did not answer, confusion painting across her face.

"All right, Catherine. It's all right. Forget that question."

Nancy nodded, as Leon grudgingly shook his head in amazement.

"All right Catherine, I'm going to count you awake." He began the count.

Catherine had described in minute detail everything from the moment she'd set foot on the LifeGames premises to the undressing sequence. It was a necessary and legitimate intrusion into her memory; imperative because Leon needed to remove every last vestige of doubt from his own mind.

It seemed inconceivable that Ken had used some method other than hypnosis to achieve time dilation, but the evidence was irrefutable.

During Catherine's most intimate recollections, neither Nancy nor Leon could look at one another. Both were blushing for her, a sneaky arousal lurking within each of them.

Ahead of the session, knowing what was likely to be revealed and feeling the need to clear the air, Leon had declared his intentions, "Don't worry Nance, I'm not going to record this." He had held up his ancient recorder to display its static cogs, no recording tape running through the mechanism.

Nancy appreciated his commitment to integrity.

"I must thank you for your cooperation Catherine. So sorry I had to put you through it, but I had to be certain of something."

"Sure, it was painless." Catherine shrugged.

"I owe you an apology," Leon admitted, his expression serious and sincere. "Until this session, I did not believe that you could have experienced dilation. The session's convinced me... I'm wrong, dead wrong. What you've disclosed makes no sense, makes no sense at all."

"Shew! Well, that's a bit of a relief, that you now believe me." She said it sarcastically, ironically.

"Sorry."

"I was pretty upset with him for doubting you Cath," said Nancy. "Think about it though—Leon's alliance is worth more now precisely *because* he was skeptical. If he'd believed whatever was concocted, without first trying to disprove it, his opinions and loyalty wouldn't carry any weight."

"So, it's a drug then... in the champagne? We drank champagne before the run."

Leon nodded. "Thank you Cath, you told me under hypnosis."

"If it wasn't in the champagne, then where? The patch?"

Leon was hesitant but no longer adamant.

"In the champagne? Possibly. Maybe in the patches? I'm no chemist, but that would take some *very* sophisticated alchemy."

"So what! Everything LifeGames does is sophisticated. Our business *is* sophistication and technology," Nancy argued.

"True... Nance... true. You know what kind of investment that would take?"

"You know what kind of dividends it would pay? You know what dividends it *is* paying?" Nancy retorted.

"So, where's the R&D in the budget?"

"Oh, come on, Leon. You're not serious?"

"Until it's proven..." Leon insisted.

"When the two of you are done, there's a patient who needs discharging."

"Nothing we can do till your primary physician signs off on it, I'm afraid, but I'll put in a good word... a very good word."

There was a momentary silence and then Nancy provoked Leon with her ace. "Foul balms, Leon, very foul balms. This sure gives Roger's words some meaning."

"Fernando," Leon corrected her.

"But it was *Roger* who said it. Fernando isn't a *proven* personality."

"Okay, point made, Nance—very good point indeed. I'll tell you... fiddling with drugs would explain why Ken was so adamant to bring Craig in. His only qualification was pharmaceuticals, he really had no designation."

"And after he joined us, we had the big breakthrough," Nancy smugly confirmed.

"Well then, I'm the outsider. Who's in on it?"

"Ken!" they sang in unison.

"And?" Leon insisted.

"Craig's death... an accident?" Nancy pondered.

"They found drugs in his car, remember?" Leon added.

"Planted drugs," Catherine scoffed. "I barely knew him, but wasn't he a real family man?"

"He was, but it became a real mess when Ken came back into his life. But a family wouldn't exclude drugs," Nancy added. "Haven't you heard the rumors? Craig had quite the addiction and more than a bit of history with Ken."

"The police report read 'no foul play, accidental death—case closed'," Leon emphasized.

"Police get bought," Nancy observed.

"As soon as he got the concoction right, Craig became expendable!" Catherine added.

"More than expendable. I'd say even a security risk to Ken," Nancy inserted.

"Not necessarily, ladies, not necessarily," Leon remarked. "The timing—on the same day, we lost Roger to his past and Craig died, all within 24 hours. If the key is a formula and the formula's got a flaw, Ken-o would need him."

"Unless he needed a scapegoat more," Nancy threw in.

They plumbed the unknown waters, on a tangent, dowsing for a probable cause for Roger's regression.

Every line of deduction they followed doubled back on itself, leaving them as bewildered as when they'd begun. Only one thing was clear; something sinister was going on, and Ken looked to be the only one with the answers. He had a vested interest in keeping them secret and the money, power, influence, cunning, and lack of scruples to achieve it.

When all seemed to have reached a dead end, Nancy recalled a new detail.

"You know... Jeez... do I feel stupid! A few weeks after Craig's death, he had me arrange to have some hardware moved from a small facility I didn't even know we had. We have so much hardware on so many properties, it's easy for something like this to slip through unnoticed. But there were some breakages in transit, and I had to put in an insurance claim. It was for laboratory equipment. I didn't question it, but I did think it odd; especially because it was being delivered to an address pretty close to Ken's house, a residential building."

"Hmmm..." was all Leon would commit to.

"When're my blood results going to be ready? Surely they'll show something?" Catherine demanded.

"Oooh, Catherine... now that's another apology owed, another apology indeed," Leon admitted. "The tests came up negative. I was so convinced that drugging was improbable and I didn't want you to waste money, so I only had them run elementary analyses."

Catherine was upset but pragmatic, and only gave Leon a light chewing out.

"So the jury's still out then; it's a definite maybe."

"I'm truly sorry, Catherine. Truly, truly sorry."

Catherine blew a defeated huff. "No matter. More tests then?"

"I'll pay, it's the least I can do, the very least. But I do have another angle—I want to play a recording for you, Catherine. Tell me the first thing that comes to your mind, the very first thing."

At the first strains of the puzzling sound, Catherine went rigid and gasped, "Christ Jesus!" Her breathing became ragged as if she'd sprinted up a flight of stairs.

Leon cut the recording. "What is it?" he asked.

"I... I don't know!" She was stricken with panic, back in the room with phantoms again, no longer lucid, her eyes darting, and her shivers returning.

Nancy rushed to console her, "Relax honey, nothing's wrong. It was just the recording."

"My nightmares... they're... it's like they're back."

"Because of the sound?" Leon probed.

"It... it must be. I don't know. Fuck... I'm suddenly jumpy."

"All right, Catherine. I'm not going to put it on again, I know what it is now."

The Pavlovian response had brought Catherine to the threshold of a nightmare, a stimulated suppressed memory; evidence that ripped the last shreds of doubt from Leon's mind. The sound was the common thread that ran through all of the madness and intrigue, triggering or accompanying specific paranormal episodes.

Each time he heard it, Leon realized it stirred something peculiar within him too.

But all of the recordings had been played to lucid victims; Leon had not yet tried it on a hypnotized subject. It was a final test he was keen to make, and he'd conduct it on his star patient—His Holiness, the good Bishop of Andalusia.

Chapter 29

The instant he opened his eyes and saw the two women sitting before him, Fernando, the cantankerous and ferocious Bishop of Andalusia, looked away.

"I would be obliged to have these women removed from my chambers," he said with disdain and disgust.

As if the brooding lethality of his Special Forces demeanor was steadily being siphoned away by his precursor personality, Roger Daly's temperament was slowly being humanized.

When Nancy and Catherine had earlier entered Roger's room, before he was hypnotized to become the Bishop, and Leon had introduced them, Roger had smiled genially, glad for the feminine interruption to an otherwise dull evening of television. He'd chatted easily with them, and slowly a spark of gallantry had crept in, softening him yet further.

Leon had played Craig's recording to Roger.

Although it had made him agitated, he'd remained adamant that he could not identify the origin of his emotional switch, nor could he say if or when he'd heard the sounds before.

At the sound of the recording, Catherine had again found herself overwhelmed by terror, fighting against her impulse to hide.

It had been eight days since her release from the hospital in Santa Clara, eleven glorious days since Ken's last attack two

Sundays ago. During that interim, she had recovered her old self, becoming absorbed in both her work and her fully restored relationship with Jacky.

Her hatred for Ken was now without bounds. She'd severed all ties with him and officially withdrawn as advertising and PR consultant to LifeGames.

From what Leon had established through cunning cross-questioning and general observation, it had also been eleven days since Ken had last dreamed of Catherine.

Jacky's acceptance of Nancy had vastly improved when the trio had dined together.

Catherine's second intensive blood panel had turned up negative. The only remarkable notation read, 'abnormally high red corpuscle count', consistent with increased metabolism due to the nutritional patch.

Similarly, Roger's panel showed 'certain impurities' that eluded identification. All talk about the inquest to take the matter further suddenly evaporated and everybody Leon talked to had developed amnesia regarding the earlier speculations.

In light of the negative blood panels, a patch would be invaluable if they were to move forward with the suspicions, but it could also pose a great difficulty. Every patch, whether used or unused, was barcoded and tracked all the way to the incinerator.

To this end, the company went to great lengths, even delivering used patches by courier from around the globe to the head office where they were checked off the books and committed to the furnace.

But Ken had unwittingly opened a door. Kampala was his headache branch, regularly fouling up administration. Nancy had selected an incomplete inbound consignment, and removed one more used patch from a package that was already short by three items.

She'd kept her illicit actions from Leon; if he was ignorant of the fact, he couldn't be considered guilty by association.

They'd passed the stolen patch on to Kevin, a friend of Catherine's who worked at a local university. He'd warned that it would take him some time to establish a result for the analysis.

Although Roger had been welcoming to the women at his bedside while sliding into hypnosis, his alter-ego personality, Fernando, had only disdain and indignation when he'd awoken to find them sitting before him.

After the curtain had been drawn around his bed, with the women on the other side, the Bishop had grudgingly become marginally cooperative. Their presence within earshot continued to rile him and he grumbled about it, about how Leon had insulted his deepest sentiments. How dare he give these women an audience without consent? How dare he only mask them by a simple curtain... it was intolerable!

The Bishop veered off into Spanish, making no apology for chauvinistic outrage. *"QUE DESGRACIA! PONERME EN LA COMPANIA DE MUJERES!"* Did Leon not know that he was a high-ranking official in the church? Did Leon not realize that if respect were not forthcoming, he would *impose* it?

And then it got worse—the Bishop looked through his window, across the courtyard and into the opposite wing where the flickering movements of a television caught his eye. He pointed it out to Leon and refused to continue their interview until it was removed; the closure of his blinds would not suffice.

With folded arms and pouting lips, he fixed his eyes toward the ceiling. Before he would speak another word, he demanded this "...diabolical evil, this tongue of Satan, had to be entirely cauterized... removed from the building."

As he waited patiently for hospital staff to remove the offending monitor, Leon realized that it was going to be a trying session.

He hoped that Fernando wouldn't realize that, just beyond the curtain, stood his very own 'evil tongue', in the dormant state of being switched off.

Explaining the delay to Nancy and Catherine, Leon had whispered softly, "We could be here all night if he gets wind of the other two hundred sets in the building!"

Returning once more to Fernando's presence, the quarrelsome clergyman's aloofness had become exaggerated even further; how *dare* this man abandon his presence to talk to women... to *women*—it was downright insolent!

Leon had to grovel in apology.

After what seemed an age, action was taken across the courtyard in the offending room. Leon watched as confusion and irritation unfolded when the television was turned off, unplugged and carried away. Fingers were pointed at Fernando's ward across the divide, and hands were raised in consternation and heads vigorously shaken in dismay.

All the while, the distinguished cause of the problem sat regally watching proceedings with detached satisfaction. He'd cleansed the world of one more great evil... he'd teach these ignorant heathens a lesson in decorum.

"May we precede, Eminence?" Leon eventually inquired. But nothing would be that simple tonight. All of these disturbances had caused the Bishop to suffer a dreadful thirst and water should be brought.

Naturally, when he called for water, no electric bell could be used. Leon's attempted use of the button roused too much suspicion. Fernando had a much simpler solution.

The women should be put to work. They should serve him the water, and serve him with all haste. "And please don't put ice in it—I don't even want to start trying to explain that!" Leon advised.

The tepid water arrived, and the Bishop satisfied himself that it was acceptable.

After Holy intentions had been assured, matters at hand could proceed.

"You spoke previously, Sire, of 'foul balms'. In my tongue, this term arouses much confusion."

Fernando eyed Leon unblinkingly; this underling was trying his patience. He was unaccustomed to such insistent badgering for answers.

Leon saw the battle glee in his eye, but forged ahead.

"Is this balm a preparation used to bring time into reduction, so as to..."

"Nay," the Bishop cut him short. "The balms of which I speak invite Lucifer into thy heart." His voice was calm and low, visibly governed with restraint. "By their acceptance, comes certain hell-fire and damnation. Savior from this certainty is only possible through devotion to the Good."

Fernando's reply begged more questions than it answered.

Beyond the curtain, both women were wide-eyed and attentive.

"May I ask, Sire, whether these balms were imbibed by the very body that you presently occupy? Did the man known in my time as Roger Daly imbibe these balms?"

"The same Evil is always offered to each soul at your black mass," Fernando responded, increasing in agitation.

"Yet *your* soul did not accept this Evil, Sire?" Leon prompted cautiously.

The Bishop detected the impertinence and insult in the man's question but he decided to overlook it; heathens could not always be expected to know the depths of devotion.

"The balm was offered to my form, but *I would never* stand idly by as darkness seized its hold."

Leon couldn't miss the chastisement that the grave voice conveyed; he reminded himself to re-double his efforts to proceed with caution.

In preparation for his next question, Nancy had showed Leon how to use his mobile phone as a recorder for today's session—he had it recording from the breast pocket of his cotton shirt.

This had freed up his ancient reel-to-reel cassette recorder. He'd held it next to the speakers of his computer to record the voicemail with the strange sounds and Craig's voice that Ken had emailed to him.

"Sire, I have here an instrument. It employs a method to make a record of sounds for the ear, much like writing records the details from the mouth and heart."

Leon hoped that using a cassette tape recorder rather than a digital one would at least provide some mechanical mechanism for Fernando to observe turning. It might quell the inevitable accusations of witchcraft and evil that would certainly otherwise be leveled at them.

For safety's sake, he had rehearsed some qualifiers that could justify the workings of the antiquated device.

"There is a cord that you will see move. This cord is not unlike that of a violin bow, which releases sounds according to its movement."

The description seemed to do the trick. Fernando took the recorder from Leon's hands the moment that it was produced.

"Where is this cord?" he demanded.

When Leon ejected the cassette, Fernando grabbed it and held the clear plastic case up to the light. He flicked it with his nail, then shook it and tapped it on his teeth, trying to establish if the material itself perhaps held the hidden mysteries that were promised.

"It is a fine cord, Sire," Leon gingerly pointed out the magnetic tape. Then, realizing that the Bishop was about to hook it out and begin unraveling it, he quickly added, "...that may easily be damaged *irreparably* by touching it."

Instead of touching it, Fernando sniffed and shook it more vigorously to hear if it would utter anything in protest, but only a common rattle emitted.

Satisfied that there were no captured souls evident, he handed Leon the two items.

"Let me hear this sound," he commanded, watching suspiciously as cassette and recorder were married again, one into the other.

Leon realized that further suspicion of foul play may arise when the spindles began to turn, so, as he clipped the cassette cover into place, he paved the way by explaining more wondrous facts.

"Please do not be alarmed, Eminence. Not unlike a time clock, this instrument uses springs and weights to achieve its movement that produces sound."

At the sound being played, Fernando sat back as far as the bed would let him, and for good measure, he crossed himself twice with a mumbled prayer. It was the mechanism that seemed to bother him, not the sound itself; for, as it went on, he moved cautiously forward, listening intently. Strangely, the sound of Craig's voice did not startle him either as it had everyone else.

When the recording had finished, he commanded, "Where did you come by such a sound?"

It had been the one question that Leon had not anticipated. Battling not to stumble over his words, Leon carefully formulated his reply.

"This is something that I wish to ask of *you*, Sire. I believe that this is not a sound common in my world, and it appeared within this instrument by unknown means."

Leon knew it was a floundering explanation, one that courted suspicion, yet inexplicably Fernando remained relaxed and collected despite this unsettling event, appearing to possess some insight.

He was perplexed by the Bishop's unpredictable character; generally overreacting to perfectly innocuous and innocent occurrences, yet ignoring what others found disturbing.

Committed to the explanation, he stumbled on.

"This sound would seem connected to strange occurrences of late, sire. One of the ladies present has been much troubled in this connection. She seeks to resolve her suffering; it is why I have brought her for an audience."

Fernando ignored Leon's allusion to Catherine's suffering. Indifferently, he continued on his own tack.

"This is the sound of the spirit world, it is associated with the movement through the planes... from your world to the next. The voice is of one who has been seized. I was in attendance at his departing your world. In order to save his fate, I offered absolution, but his deeds of this past existence had been too great and he became overwhelmed by the dark."

The Bishop spoke as if he were addressing a child, his patience ebbing as he proceeded.

"He did confess to me foul deeds before he was *taken*. And in repentance, he resolved to return and make amends in the name of Good. It will serve his justice more peace, yet he will surely burn all the same."

Leon could see that irrationality was boiling in the cauldron, Fernando's control of it slipping.

In the hopes that the small token would quench the powder keg threatening to ignite, Leon offered more of the water that had been brought earlier.

The Righteous Father quaffed the tumbler to its end.

"Send a woman for more," he brazenly instructed.

Leon did his bidding, passing the empty jug to Nancy. She took it and departed in a huff.

Outside of the ward, forced to miss the unfolding intrigue, she hurried past the scullery where she'd previously collected water. A group of passersby sensed her mood and stood aside.

"The Bishop can drink water from the Ladies' toilets," she told them with satisfaction.

Fernando brooded a while, thinking. Then, at his leisure, he spoke. "Show me this woman who is troubled."

Keeping her eyes averted, as Leon had instructed, Catherine dutifully appeared.

On seeing Catherine full in the face for the first time, Fernando sat bolt upright in his bed. "This soul is *ancient!*" he moaned, suddenly gracious.

To Catherine, the Bishop's words were not words at all, they were an emotion; an introspective the likes of which she had never before experienced, as though a pedigree she didn't know she had, had suddenly been shoved in her face. The instant cartwheeled her emotions backward through time to another age, another place, a place where she heard the clash of arms and the cheer of crowds.

Catherine had gasped at the sight of Fernando. Coming back to her senses, she realized that this was not the same youthful Roger whom she'd recently exchanged pleasantries with, nor was it the six-year-old Roger on his first day at school. As she studied him, she noticed the way he held his face and body, that they seemed entirely altered to that of a withered old man.

His eyes forced her a half-step back, mesmerizing her, searing to the depths of her soul.

At that precise moment, beyond the curtain, Nancy came silently through the door. Hearing the Bishop speak, she froze in her path, hesitating to round the curtain and break the flow of conversation.

"This soul has grown ahead of itself with confidence. A test is failed and the instant to move onward is imminent...."

Fernando's tone was haunting as he pointed a gnarled accusing finger at Catherine. Fanaticism overtaking him, he began to convulse with intensity, a torrent of warnings belching from his gut.

"Beware... BEWARE...! For the evil is upon you! Take my heed and repent against the power that already possesses you. I stand as a pillar at your back but tendrils already have you within their grasp. The Great Goat will have his way with you."

The old man began to froth at his mouth and Leon leapt in to end the session.

A few minutes later, the young and oblivious ex-General, Roger Daly, smiled pleasantly at the distraught pair of women he had just terrified out of their wits.

Among the thoughts racing through Catherine's mind, was one silly and insignificant fact. Today was Thursday the twelfth.

If she had stuck to her original date with Ken three weeks ago, tonight would have been the Big Date.

At the very least, she thought, *I'm three weeks better off.*

Chapter 30

It was eight o'clock on that stormy Thursday night when three figures huddled together against the driving storm, broke rank and scattered, each to their own vehicle.

Windshield wipers flogged out a losing battle against the torrential downpour and headlights barely dented the smothering blanket of sleet. They stopped once to collect supplies, then, never braking convoy, the three vehicles picked their cautious way out of the city, on into the wooded suburbs.

On reaching their destination, the occupants piled out of their vehicles when they were ready, bolting for the safety of unity and the warm comfort of the palatial villa.

"Have you ever seen a night like this?"

"Never! And—my word—I have *never* seen a house like this either Catherine, never a house like this!" Having yet to venture beyond the entrance hall, Leon was already in awe.

During Catherine's hospitalization, after her fight with Jacky, he had been to the house, but on that occasion the house had been like a construction site; a disaster charged with a negative pulse. He had been utterly focused on the unfolding saga, taking in none of the surroundings.

He was stunned to see how it had changed, its mood transformed with lights and re-injected with the zest for life.

Nancy completed the trio as she came skidding through the door, pursued by another squall. She was drenched to the bone from her short dart across the distance of a few feet.

After deserving hot beverages had been served and gladly gulped down, Nancy took Leon on a tour of the rest of the house.

When Catherine called "Dinner's on the table!", they returned to partake of another Oriental delight bumped from its cardboard container, garnished by a good dollop of Catherine's apologies.

The Bishop's ranting had fired the bogeyman into one and all and they had not discussed the details any further, none of them wanting to further fray the exposed nerves that his outpourings had tweaked.

Earlier in the evening, at the hospital, the unabating storm had created the ideal excuse to mill about in the hospital's foyer, none of them wanting to return to lonely dwellings apart. Even Leon, the seasoned veteran of things mysterious, had not escaped the supernatural horror that seeped into the stormy night's tone.

The longer they had stood in the foyer listening to the crashes of thunder in the heavens above and watching the backlit sheets of rain lashing the windows, the more the tang of apprehension brewing within each of them grew.

"I don't know about you lot, but I'm not going home alone. Either you follow me or I'll follow you," Catherine had said in a quavering voice.

A chance lightning bolt had punctuated the end of her statement, and it had swung the vote unanimously in favor of her large white-walled rooms and modern decor.

Back home, with the meal over and a round of coffee served, they cautiously waded into the murky waters of Fernando's parables.

Catherine checked her watch. It was nine forty. *Jacky should have been in some time ago,* she thought, hoping that the storm wouldn't delay her in-bound flight. She felt uneasy, a dreadful feeling of foreboding trying to further suppress her mood Then again, it always felt like this when Jacky was out in this weather, she reminded herself.

"I told you that the tongues were television, remember Leon—you laughed at me. I told you. Just call me brilliant." Nancy tentatively kicked off the proceedings.

"All right, *Miss Brilliant*; then tell us what a 'goat with tendrils having his way with me' or whatever it was that he said... what does *that* mean?" Catherine insisted.

The statement had terrified Catherine. She dealt with fear by challenging it—her challenge was a gauntlet thrown down to tempt fate.

"Stop it Catherine!" Nancy admonished her. The provoking of fate scared her to death and on this dark night, with Fernando's direct predictions so fresh in her mind, her willingness to continue was deflated.

"Stop what?" Catherine laughed out of fear, not humor; her laughter a surrogate for tears.

"Don't be silly, Cath. Let's not fool around with our emotions. They're raw, far too raw."

Even Leon was uneasy with the affair, struggling to get a grip on his own galloping emotions. He took Catherine's hand.

"We're all edgy tonight. We should talk through everything and plan the best solutions, but there's no need to put on a brave face between friends."

Suddenly and without warning, Catherine lost control, bursting into sobs of terror.

Leon and Nancy moved as one to embrace her.

Moments later, the door blew open, admitting a sodden apparition wrapped in an icy blast of wind.

The tight huddle of three spooked in unison, then Catherine broke away and ran toward it the instant she recognized who it was.

She stopped short. "Jacky?" she cried, hesitation suddenly in her voice.

"Sorry Cath, did I scare you?" Jacky dropped the drenched jacket held over her head. "I was wondering whose cars... oh, it's Nancy."

The grip of fear that had held them was broken and Catherine moved quickly to Jacky, hugging her furiously, overjoyed to know the ill omen of impending disaster was diverted.

Jacky headed off to shower and top-up beverages were poured.

When Jacky returned, they played her the recording to get a more objective opinion. The peculiar sounds proved meaningless to her, but the recorded voice of Fernando and the content of his ravings chilled her to the core.

'Foul balms' triggered Catherine. "Darn... someone remind me to contact Kevin tomorrow to see if he's found anything in the patch."

"Ooh... sorry Cath, I chatted with him last night," Jacky piped up. "Forgot to tell you, he said he's found something that 'doesn't seem nutritional'. Mean anything?"

"Is that it?" Catherine quizzed.

"He's still trying to refine it; thinks he might have more by the weekend. I hope that it wasn't too important."

"Is this something to do with the missing patch?!" Leon asked, puzzled.

"Yikes... I'm busted," Nancy laughed. "You heard about it?"

"Heard about it? I had to put up with Ken-o for three days; totally off his head about it. Crazy."

"I know, new protocols now—they're weighing packages to the gram on both ends of the route. Every patch is getting an RFID tag. They were already three short from Kampala; I thought a fourth wouldn't do much harm."

"It's been a witch hunt alright, a real witch hunt."

"I know, I got in the neck too. Really sorry, I had to keep it quiet. The excitement seems to have blown over."

"Not really. At the last board meeting, Ken hit the roof about security. We're outsourcing to offsite CCTV monitoring round the clock now. Big Brother all the way, Nance... all the way."

"Sorry for the shop talk," Nancy apologized, "we interrupted. Nutritional results?"

"Yes, and something about adrenaline and endorphins. It went over my head."

"What time is it? Do you think that I should call him?" Catherine asked, checking her watch. "What! It's almost eleven!" She was stunned.

Opinions were divided whether to phone or not, but curiosity was too persuasive and Catherine took the less intrusive option and messaged:

> *"Per the patch... Plse call ASAP regardless of time. Wont be sleeping. Plse don't forget VERY important"*

When Catherine hit 'send', Leon was on his feet.

"I'm off to club duvet, ladies... where the pillows are playing; definitely club duvet."

There was a general round of dissatisfaction that the star analyst was deserting. Jacky, the most superstitious of all, was also the most vociferous.

"You do know what tomorrow is?"

Leon laughed at the reminder. "Friday the thirteenth—what poppycock, Nancy; utter poppycock."

"Come on, Leon. It's a bad one out there, don't tempt fate. We've got five bedrooms, under-floor heating, breakfast in bed..."

"I'm off, cheerio," he said in parting, and was already halfway to the front door, pulling on his jacket. "I've left the recordings; don't want to spoil your fun, now do I?"

"Oh, Leon!" Nancy scolded him. "Come and sit down here at once! You're not going to be able to sleep anyway."

"Is someone going to make sure that I close the door properly?" he called back. "Nance, please don't forget to bring the recordings to the office."

They could hear his hand turning the door handle. Like a man possessed, he was unstoppable.

"Toodeloo!" His farewell sounded like the final note of a last post bugle call.

Catherine had followed in hot pursuit to see him out. She smiled and shrugged as she returned; uncharacteristically, he hadn't even stopped to hug her goodbye.

The sound of his motor, departing, left them in a cloud of dread.

"More coffee, cocoa, something stronger?" Catherine offered, raising the light dimmer to its maximum intensity. A severe uneasiness had crept in and it took a while for them to ease back toward the conversation.

"What I've been most curious about is this general who is also a bishop," Jacky posed. "I think that's a strange act of Karma. I mean, from a reincarnation perspective, you're supposed to *improve* as a person with each passing life. Does that mean then that a soldier is a level *above* a priest in the hierarchy? I mean, he's back as a soldier..."

"I'm sorry that Leon's gone, Jacks. He explained it so well." Catherine took up the challenge of explaining it. "Your spirit amounts to more than just your brain and the chemistry that gives you thought and memory. Your spirit *is* you. It's what makes you who you are. That's why *you* are not *me*."

It sounded so silly now that she'd said it. She racked her brain a moment, searching for Leon's exact words and excellent examples.

"Look, if my body's organs are transplanted into you, then they will become part of you, they won't be part of me anymore. If they ever get brain transplants right, then we'll be able to answer whether we really do amount to more than simple chemical reactions. But..."

She stalled, running out of facts, second guessing whether it was anywhere close to what Leon had said—or just what she'd hoped he was saying;

"I don't know. It sounded so simple when he described it."

The dead of night was pierced by a siren, the threads of its wailing woven into the howls of the wind through the trees, until the sound was swallowed by a ferocious volley of hail against the window panes.

In spite of the central heating, Nancy pulled her cardigan tighter about herself. "I'll be using a room if you don't mind."

"No chance of that, you'll sleep in our bed!" Jacky insisted, confirming it with a nod from Catherine.

A strange scent wafted into the room; it smelled for all the world like lilacs. Three sets of nostrils flared, testing its odd appearance against the improbability of its existence. Catherine was the only one to verbalize their collective thoughts.

"That's odd..."

Nancy took a turn at the explanation that had defeated Catherine.

"Karma says that the personality that you *are*, in spite of your experiences in this life, is an indication of who you were *before*. Your experiences during this lifetime will alter you in certain ways and you'll then carry those traits that you learn—loyalty and aggression, hunger for power—onward to your next life."

"But that doesn't explain how Roger, the general, could have slipped backward from the apparently higher ideals of Fernando the priest," Jacky insisted.

"I'm getting there," Nancy said, and then hoped that she would. "Roger, the soldier, was born to a country at war, and even though he'd apparently been a shy and gentle child, the discipline and authoritarian side of his former personality turned him into a natural warrior leader. Killing is wrong, according to Fernando's insight in the spirit world. Despite that, it hadn't given him any qualms about burning people at the Inquisition's stake during his own lifetime! At that time, he had been operating according to, and as a victim of, the prevailing wisdom of his age."

Jacky was bewildered by the complexity of the nebulous hypothesis and seeing this, Nancy tried to sum up her explanation as concisely as possible.

"The spirit world is like a locker room where you review what you're going to do on the playing field of terrestrial life. You plan your strategies of how to achieve the goals. God is..."

"*Good* is..." Catherine corrected her.

"You're right, Cath, sorry. Good is the prevailing wisdom that holds together the team, comprised of the rest of us. Good invented the game and made up the rules." Nancy indicated all of creation as symbolized by 'the game'. "And, like in a locker room, the character that we *hope* to be when we're planning to be brave and strong and smart, is not necessarily the player that we discover that we *are* when we're faced with all the problems that life throws at us. Money, religion, power; whatever it is that motivates us can be represented by a ball in this parable. But the ball doesn't always bounce exactly right and our teammates don't always pass straight or defend properly."

Since they appeared to understand, Nancy pressed onward.

"Sometimes when our game's over, we think we've won according to our rules and we win in the eyes of others who have the same rulebook. Yet in reality, according to the true rule book, which we don't get to see during our terrestrial lives, we might have lost."

This wasn't how Leon had explained it, but Catherine thought that it had nonetheless been a fine analogy. She spurred Nancy for more understanding.

"So, according to the Gospel of Saint Nancy, we're all—and I mean *all* of the teams... errrr... all the nations and religions of the earth—playing without being able to refer to the total rule book here on Earth. We only get to discover whether we've won, lost or been disqualified once the game's over and we're back in the locker room of heaven." She frowned, looking at Nancy for confirmation.

"Yes... sort of... I don't really know, because I'm making this up as I go along," Nancy admitted.

"And all that without a nightcap; it sounds pretty bloody inspired to me. Perhaps Leon's jumped into you," Jacky teased.

"Let me continue then... why don't I..." Nancy assumed Leon's voice and mannerism.

When they were done laughing, Nancy went back to her ad lib narration and amateur philosophizing.

"Perhaps all the world is playing the game with *extracts* from the rule book. Each *team*, or religion or nation, has got some chapters. Some of the rules overlap, others appear to contradict one another. But if they could all be condensed and put into perspective, then the whole thing might work out..."

She thought for a moment, finding a universal example to illustrate her point better.

"If you took the tennis rule book and divided it up between various novice players, you'd be sure to have confusion. Assume they knew nothing of the game. One fellow's rules would state categorically that hitting the ball on the tramlines is *out*. Another would have the rule about serving. It would speak of a ball bouncing beyond the service line also as being *out*. He would also be correct to apply that rule."

A light bulb illuminated in Catherine's head and she filled in the rest of Nancy's explanation. "But hitting on the tramlines is in *if* you happen to be playing doubles. And hitting beyond the service line is okay *if...*"

It was silly talk now, and they all knew it—lighthearted fun; something to take their minds off of the storm and forbidding gloominess of the afternoon's events and weeks that preceded it.

Jacky wasn't to be left out either; she jumped in to override Catherine, completing the final sequence of the comparison.

"*...provided that you're not serving*! Dead right, Nance! We should launch a new philosophy, 'Tennisssssaism'. No, better yet, make it a religion! Launching a religion is the best way to make money out of desperate people."

It put them all into fits of laughter.

"What we need to do is compare our various parts of the rules. That way we could get on with the game and quit fighting about the rules!"

"Definitely! That's why, up until now, this game we call *life* has been a fiasco. We keep on identifying opponents and calling their ball '*out*', or *'foul'*, without bothering to assess how their rules relate to ours."

Nancy laughed at the goofy ideas that kept rolling forward, but somewhere in them were nuggets of truth.

"The problem is that the referees are corrupt and they've got no intention of helping us piece the game together. Remember that those in control of the game are getting paid by the hour. The longer they sustain the confusion, the more wealth they accumulate; the more of the game they own."

"And the more irreplaceable they'll appear to be," Jacky added, "sorting it all out for us."

"Sure... they've also got the microphone and you can never argue with the person who has the microphone," Nancy observed.

"So, what we need is a players' organization?" Catherine suggested.

"Organizations are committees and committees *always* get hijacked because it's back to *money*. Does a *'democracy'* exist around this globe where the umpires *don't* siphon money away into private accounts?"

Nancy's words brought their high ideals of moments earlier crashing down onto the dusty earth of reality. They sat in silence, each considering the world's problems through the prism of tennis.

"What's the solution?" Catherine eventually posed aloud, asking what they had all been thinking.

"Individual players must wake up to the fact that it's a game with one overriding aim. Playing *together* makes it all worthwhile. Rules will always be necessary in order to play but the rules are not the *object* of playing. Religion is not the reason for living, it is supposed to be a way of achieving a better life on earth. And there need only be one overriding philosophic teaching: Uphold that which is productive, fair and just." Nancy paused.

Catherine picked up the baton of wisdom that Nancy had carried thus far.

"Umpires need only be obeyed if their calls are fair, not simply because they benefit one side for the moment. The next bad call is likely to go against you, because the umpire's playing to remain as umpire, he doesn't care whose on court or who wins and who loses; *divide and rule.*"

They were pondering the impossibility of the world overcoming the odds, when the phone rang.

The caller ID said it was Kevin, and Catherine answered.

She went serious, monosyllabic, frowning—and then she got up and began to pace with the phone at her ear.

When she came to sit down, she had worrying news.

"He's isolated something which I can't give you many details about because it's all Greek to me, but there's *definitely* something in the patch that isn't kosher. It's powerful and it's highly compatible with the body's own adrenaline. He said it would therefore be almost impossible to trace in the blood. And guess what; from what he could see it seems to be *highly volatile*. I don't know what that means, but it doesn't sound good."

They went on, poking and prodding at the fresh subject, and by the time their discussions were at an inconclusive end, it was the very early hours of Friday morning. Far too late to tackle the originally intended subject of Fernando's hypnosis session.

Catherine had determined that she would follow the matter of the narcotic through to its legal conclusion. She would subject herself to a more rigorous medical examination and have Leon advise the military to do the same.

In addition, she would brief her attorney to prepare documents to sue both Kenneth Torrington and LifeGames Corporation.

When the exhausted trio finally bedded down together, the perfume of lilacs was still lingering in their nostrils.

Chapter 31

Petals rained in a beautiful shower of purple and white hues. They settled onto the lid of the plain pine coffin that was already sinking into the thick mud at the pit's base.

Lilacs had been Leon's favorite flower and these petals were all from his own private garden.

Today was Friday the thirteenth; the same-day funeral honored the dictates of Leon's Jewish heritage.

Catherine surveyed Ken from the privacy of her largest pair of sunglasses. The certainty of his presence at the funeral had been a large reason for her selection of this pair; the balance of her reason had been to screen her eyes. They resembled the eyes of a boxer at the end of a brutal match, swollen and bloodshot from crying.

Ken circulated through the milling crowd like a forlorn hyena, searching for an opportunity to close in on his prey. Yet, his skulking was no match for Catherine's shrewdness, and she kept him at bay with her deliberately unpredictable movements among the mourners.

The dominating topic among the crowd centered on the mysterious circumstances of Leon's death.

Although it had been raining hard, police detectives did not link the cause of the accident directly to the weather. The stretch of road where the crash had occurred had been flat, straight and well lit. In addition, it had been very well drained, with no puddles or drifts.

Skid marks on the road surface had indicated heavy braking and swerving by the driver, and finally, the vehicle had body damage that would be consistent with an impact from a medium-sized animal. The hair caught in the front grill of the car had been coarse and had evidently matched with the description that Leon had made to paramedics before he had died.

"A goat?!"

The revelation had stunned Catherine; the entire area was suburban with no chance of livestock for dozens of miles in any direction. Besides, it was not the ideal climate in which to raise goats and the appearance of one would be a mystery.

"He was evidently quite insistent, Cath," Nancy had told her. "He wouldn't hear of it being a dog. To be certain, they're going to analyze the hair and a sample of blood that they also found."

"Let me guess... no trace of the animal?" Catherine had asked cynically.

"No," Nancy had confirmed.

A shudder of fear had gripped Catherine and she'd tried to act blasé about the details. "Perhaps he saw a goat and ran it down for me... to save me from my fate."

Nancy had taken the comment for what it was, the reaction of a brave but terrified woman.

The strain and circumstances of Leon's death plaited with the fresh prophesy for Catherine were too haunting to hear it verbalized. She'd held Catherine close and omitted an even more disturbing enigma in Leon's closing chapter.

The district coroner had been perplexed. The vehicle had only light damage; damage consistent with a slow speed collision into a mid-sized mammal. The airbags should not even have deployed and there should have been no injuries, much less a fatality.

"A 59-year-old male suffering acute death resulting from upper cervical spinal cord injury caused by cervical hyperextension— cervical *spondylosis* suspected.

Victim attended within 11 minutes of collision report; police report indicates collision with unknown mammal approximately 75 kilograms mass.

First responder paramedics report victim alive and able to talk, unresponsive physical animation below line of clavicle. Victim reports horned possibly goat-like mammal appearing in roadway in wet stormy conditions. Vehicle airbags deployed.

Intensive care immediately provided, victim became comatose, remained in unconscious state for an additional 12 minutes until cardiac arrest.

Findings of autopsy: Externally, excoriation on the forehead and the left eyebrow and slight subcutaneous hemorrhage in the dorsum of the nose observed. The intervertebral disk and the anterior longitudinal ligament between the 5th and 6th cervical vertebrae severed with hemorrhaging in the region of the injuries observed. The 6th cervical spinous process fractured in the direction to the major axis. A part of the posterior root filaments torn and the bleeding points could be observed on front of the 6th cervical spinal cord. On the histopathological examinations, in C2, C5-C6 regions marked ischemic changes and hemorrhagic necrosis could be observed. From these post-mortem results, we determined that the victim died from upper spinal-cord trauma due to a stretching consequence of the hyperextension injury..."

The funeral was at its end and the mourners drifted solemnly toward their cars, departing sporadically as the dwindling groups splintered.

As Catherine steered cautiously through the parking lot, Ken moved into her vehicle's path. Her initial instinct was to run him flat but sense took a hold over her and she halted.

Wearing his most disarming smile, he began walking toward the driver's window. Not wishing to create a furor at a funeral she cracked it open a fraction, leaving a letterbox slit for him to speak through. An army of ants ran over her body.

Ken removed his sunglasses and Catherine did not reciprocate. She noted with distaste that his glasses served as a mask to hide clear eyes reflecting no evidence of sorrow.

"Hi, Cath... Very long time, no see..."

"It's hardly the time or place." Her foot holding the brake shook violently, wanting to press the accelerator to the floor.

"Don't be silly, Cath. We're adults. Let's get over this. Let's have a drink. It's what Leon would have wanted."

The emotional blackmail made her want to vomit. Her wrath was detonated, weeks of terror and grief turned violent in an explosion of hatred. Not even the decorum of a funeral could dam the tsunami of her derangement.

"The only thing Leon wanted was *YOU* behind bars; preferably dead, you pig-headed bastard."

The uncharacteristic tirade had begun as a low rumble boiling from deep inside her chest, but her rebuke rapidly built up in volume and pitch to a haranguing assault.

"...We've turned out your filthy trough, you fuck. We've found the drugs that you're using for your fucking time dilation. You, my evil friend, will talk to me in the future *only* through my lawyers!"

The last of her words were drowned by the screech of spinning tires as she roared away.

In the silent wake of her car's departure, all stunned attention was focused on Ken. He re-donned his glasses and shrugged. At a glance, he saw that none within earshot could contradict him so he raised his voice just enough to reach them only.

"So sorry, lover's quarrel... she's taking the split rather badly. Bit of a drug habit I'm not prepared to fund anymore."

His friends and work colleagues were some distance away and out of hearing range. Ken breezed over to them, preparing an amended story for their ears.

Ken's sexual appetite had been dormant for weeks, but something in Catherine's aversion had re-strummed it.

She was a real challenge and he loved nothing more than dominating a defiant woman.

On the drive home, he decided it was time to view Catherine's recording again. The ritual of reliving his possession over her was the only relief for the charging sexual tension he felt building within.

She would be *his*, no matter how hard she'd struggle.

Catherine drove directly from the funeral to D. Edelstein & Partners, her company's law firm.

En route, she called ahead to ensure David was still available, and predicted she'd be there in half an hour.

It was a little after four in the afternoon when she parked.

"Miss Kaplan, how're you doing?" the receptionist greeted her as she came through the door like a whirlwind. "That was quick, you must have driven like the devil was after you."

"You have no idea, Jean... can I go through?"

"Go ahead, Mr. Edelstein's expecting you."

As Catherine tore down the corridor, Jean buzzed David, and he met her at his door.

"Hello, Cath... Good God, Jean's right. You look like death. Let me get you something?"

He led her by the elbow to his desk and pulled out a chair for her. "Jean... Tea for me, coffee, milk and two sweeteners for Catherine, there's a darling."

Catherine had always been entranced watching David's double chin as it jiggled when he spoke.

Standing a head taller than her and with the presence and character of a hulking bloodhound, he was a bear of a man.

Usually Catherine hated bumper stickers, yet she couldn't resist the one that David gave out to his clients: "My Lawyer Can Beat Up Your Lawyer!"

No truer statement could be written in jest, so she'd affixed it inside her desk drawer to look at when life looked bleak.

David reached across his table and engulfed both of her wringing hands with one of his great hairless paws.

"What is it, darling?"

His voice rumbled through the folds of his jowls. Though his doe eyes brimmed with gentleness and concern for her, she knew that a raw savagery lurked in their depths, reserved for whoever was bringing suffering to one of his flock. Today he was like an all-protecting father figure.

"Tell Papa..." he coaxed—it was precisely what she needed to hear.

She broke into monologue, summarizing the previous months. While the great bunch of bananas that was his left hand held both her hands in a communion of solidarity, his right hand scribbled notes and facts.

When she'd finished, her untouched coffee was cold so a second round was ordered.

Although Catherine was exhausted, David fired a new spark of life into her with his rousing can-do attitude;

"When will the blood results be available?"

"I only had specimens taken this morning, I guess it'll still be another week."

"What's your doctor's name? We've got to get this ball rolling."

Expecting that she would have the chance to first brief Doctor Johnson of what to expect when David reached him, Catherine gave the name and number, but it was too late for intervention; David was already dialing.

"Good day... Doctor Johnson?... good... David Edelstein here, I represent Miss Catherine Kaplan in legal matters, she's sitting with me now. We have a favor to ask..."

His words were crafted and voice carefully modulated to tolerate no questioning of his authority; there could be no doubting his habit of getting results and resolving matters without fanfare or delay.

The conversation finished as he recorded the telephone numbers of the pathologists who were analyzing Catherine's samples—he dialed again.

"Good day, my name is..."

Catherine sipped her coffee and watched David implement a blend of persuasive requests and cloaked threats to cut a swathe through the bureaucracy of the laboratory's administration.

"I appreciate these are not the standard tests, ma'am, that you've had to fly the samples to Germany, but my client's situation is dire... it is life threatening. I cannot disclose the details, but there is an implication here of an international incident..."

His applied pressure reduced the wait from twelve more days to a firm promise of a result by late Monday.

"So far, so good..." he reported with a smile. The receiver in his hand looked like a toy from a child's playpen, and the index finger of his other hand held down the cutoff button. "Now, this Kevin fellow... how do I contact him?"

The boom of David's admonishment, threatening and coaxing the pathologists was still ringing in Catherine's ears, so before giving the number, she made him promise to be gentle and go easy.

"Please, David; he is a good friend, it's a favor in his spare time."

David was enjoying himself and grinned like a naughty schoolboy as he jabbed at the telephone digits with his sausage fingers.

"Good day. Kevin Langley, please. Oh... Kevin? Super. My name is..." he gave Catherine a thumbs-up and a shrug, his expression asking if his approach was right.

She nodded affirmation.

He ran through the introductions in a voice more befitting a koala than the grizzly that he was.

When he'd finished, he winked at Catherine. "See... better?"

"Much, thank you," she smiled, marveling at his ease at role-playing.

"Okay, you heard most of that. He'll email me his report within the hour. He also promised to bear witness in court if it comes to that. We'll need more of the unused patches—can you get them?"

"*Shew...* dicey," Catherine said, giving the rocking hand signal of uncertainty. "These guys have locked up tight as a submarine. I don't think my outburst today is going to help."

"Perhaps there's something else I can do then." David prodded at the intercom again.

"Jean, please get me Alex King on the line would you, there's a darling."

He rang off, turning back to Catherine. "This guy's the best private investigator in town; if anyone can get their hands on something, then he can."

His phone began to ring.

"Edelstein... Oh, Alex. Where are you? Yes, yes. Good, okay... pop round now. When can you be here? Perfect, I'm waiting." He replaced the receiver. "Satisfied?"

She smiled her thanks.

Sounding like a Rasta, his joy for the fight rolled off his tongue, "Yeah my *sist'a*... I like it, things *a'moovin'*..."

They chatted for a while until the intercom announced Alex, then David met him at the door.

Alex was a shady character with shifty eyes and Catherine instinctively disliked him. He wouldn't look at her and barely made eye contact with David.

He sported a mustache and a loud Hawaiian shirt, suggesting he'd watched too many episodes of the Private Eye television series from decades before. Unfortunately, none of the charm of those protagonists had rubbed off.

It was a whistle-stop meeting, no more than a briefing, which was all he required. He only needed to know what a client needed, not why they needed it.

Moments later, Alex was in his car and backing out to perform David's bidding—his negotiated fee handsome.

He knew both his destination and the facility very well, and already had a well-formed plan in his head to lay his hands on an incriminating patch from the very man who was his benefactor. It was selling barbed wire to the enemy, but it was a sale, not a moral conundrum.

What was his job, he pondered? It was a question he had asked himself countless times before; the answer was always the same. He was an information whore, a mercenary. He delivered outcomes, not romantic notions of chivalry and justice. *It's all legal*, he thought, *as long as I don't get caught.*

"He's the best, Cath," David assured her. "I hope you're not offended; I'm afraid he won't talk in front of strangers, but we'll have the patches by Tuesday, at the latest."

"By Tuesday... wow. I noticed, he's *real* friendly."

"Yeah... bit of a loon, convinced everyone's as crooked as him." David aped Alex's shifty eyes and slinking body language then barked with laughter.

The guy had given Catherine the shivers. *So, what was I expecting?* she quizzed herself. A shark looks like a shark, not like a goldfish.

Something about him was so like Ken... Ken without the charm or humor.

"Another hyena," she said absently.

"Exactly!" David roared with laughter.

Fitting adversaries, Catherine thought. *Ken the hyena against this bear, David. Or was David a lion? A lion could kill a goat.*

Chapter 32

It was Monday morning and Catherine was back in David's office.

She removed the same dark sunglasses she'd worn on Friday, but now her eyes were more than puffy from crying, they were pinched closed.

"What in God's name happened to you!!" He flew out of his seat and around his desk. "It looks like you've been through a windshield!"

The whites of both eyeballs were a relief map of coarse and broken blood vessels. Her right eye was closed with thick bags of ugly blue swelling forming its lid.

Catherine was struggling to talk through grossly swollen, torn lips. Jacky shushed her and became spokesperson.

The short distance from her home to David's office had been a tortured trek for Catherine. Her head still spun from her concussion, its nausea constantly threatening in the swirl of lingering impacts.

David was a personal friend of Jacky and Catherine, occasionally socializing with them. Catherine was more than a client and her beating was more than just another case.

"When I arrived..." Jacky was relating to David how she had found Catherine. "...it must have been midnight or twelve thirty. I heard a hell of a commotion upstairs. I could hear it was violent, with screaming and smashing..."

Listening to the account, Catherine shuddered, remembering her experience.

"Before running upstairs, I grabbed a fire iron. Unfortunately, I had my high heels on and they slowed me down and made such a noise that by the time I reached the bedroom, a man was halfway out of the window," Jacky reported.

"Do you know him?" David asked urgently.

"No, I only got a glimpse, I'd never met him before. But I... I did recognize him though... I'd seen him in a picture. Catherine had a picture of herself with him at their campaign launch."

The memory of once having stood so close to Ken made Catherine wince and gasp in pain as the fractured rib bit sharply into her side.

Jacky slipped her arm about Catherine's hunched shoulders, agony from her condition written in her expression.

Although he spoke to Jacky, David continued to look at Catherine with aching sympathy.

"Okay, good, Jacky. Very good. You reported this to the police?"

"Yes, they were there within minutes."

"Have you got the case number?"

Jacky consulted her mobile and gave it to David. He immediately phoned the investigating officer; it was a very short call.

"Regrettably, he's not in, but I'll stay on top of it," David related.

"Now, Mr. Torrington is sure to have been informed of the case against him, so let's have a little fun, shall we? You have his number?"

David keyed in Nancy's exchange line.

"Mr. Torrington, please..." There was a brief pause. "Well, I'm afraid it's a private and confidential matter. I am Miss Catherine Kaplan's legal representative."

His connection to Ken was immediate.

After formal introductions and putting forward the charges to Ken, it became clear to both Catherine and Jacky that the conversation was turning ugly.

There was no mistaking Ken's shrill, petulant voice gaining momentum, until it was clear and audible from across the large desk. The rapid escalation in volume continued until the tinny treble of the miniature handset distorted; David tapped the speakerphone option on the base, allowing them all to enjoy every threat, curse and disclaimer that Ken was yelling.

But David hadn't called to hear Ken's opinion on the matter; his objective was to get Ken rattled, to force him to make a mistake.

When the string of rasping abuse came to an end, David clicked back to the handset and proceeded in a quiet, measured, menacing voice.

"Now listen here you lizard-breath. I don't give a fuck if you think you're Lord God Almighty... I don't like little boys who hurt little girls... understand? Ask around to see if your army of lawyers is keen to tangle with me. And if they're not, call me back. I've got a little battalion of asshole attorneys around town you can use. They're just your type, they also could do with a good whipping. Because, believe me brother, this case is going to provide that whipping for you and anybody who is stupid enough to represent you, that I can assure you. Now, have a nice day."

He said it cheerfully, with matter of fact sincerity, and replaced the receiver onto its cradle without emotion. As it went down, the handset speaker was a blizzard of distortion.

"Well, that should spoil his afternoon," David said to the ladies with a smile. "Now. I'm in the mood to put a fire under the pathologists."

Ken came storming out of his office to where Nancy was working busily at her desk, pretending not to have heard anything.

She could hardly avoid having heard his explosive rant through the closed door; her mind was furiously guessing every direction other than the one that had actually unfolded.

What she did know was that it was Catherine's lawyer, and this meant it would most likely have something to do with the patch. She'd braced herself to remain calm and sensible when the storm broke, to not betray any awareness or care in the world.

Catherine had insisted that Jacky not contact Nancy with news of her attack over the weekend, leaving her in blissful ignorance about the dreadful beating her friend had taken.

"There's nothing that she can do for me Jacks, come Monday morning she'll have all the problems she can cope with. Ken's going to hit the roof because of the incident at the funeral and Nancy's association with me."

LifeGames had closed at lunchtime on Friday for employees to attend Leon's hastily arranged funeral. During the graveside service, Ken had shot several evil glares at Nancy and she had returned his anger with interest added. She'd held her chin up and had spent the entire duration by Catherine's side.

After the funeral proceedings, just before Ken had approached Catherine at her car, the women had gone their separate ways.

Because Nancy had parked on the far side of the lot, she'd remained none the wiser for the explosive incident until she had arrived at work on Monday when she'd heard the rumor.

She'd called Catherine's mobile and tried Jacky too, both went to message. She'd called Catherine's office, but the only statement given was that she was "at her lawyer," and they could tell her no more.

"*YOU!!*" Ken hissed at her.

She looked up, to see him pointing accusingly at her.

"*Get into my office, NOW!*"

Turning on his heels, Ken stormed back to take up position behind the fortress of his desk; he'd missed her sarcastic grin behind his back.

It had been neither a good morning nor a happy weekend, and Ken was as mad as a rattlesnake in a tumble-dryer set to 'hot'.

His mood was directly related to Friday's incident; the Catherine debacle involving her statement about drugs in the time dilation had blown his lid open. He'd replayed the confrontation through his mind over and over.

The bitch had definitely said *drugs*. "How the *fuck* does she know? And if she knows, who else?" He'd tormented himself unrelentingly with the same question, the details he'd given up on that dinner date, when so much alcohol and lust for the woman had loosened his tongue were now sketchy in his mind.

There was also the matter of Nancy's insolence at the funeral. *That deranged little sow,* he had thought. *To snub me in front of my entire staff by showing her allegiance to Catherine?*

Watching Catherine's recording had brought on another sleepless and dream-filled night, and out of sheer frustration at not being able to get any peaceful sleep, he'd thought back to his discussions with Leon and had nearly erased the recording. Then he'd decided not to be rash. "When I'm less emotionally charged, I can always view the recording. It's worth keeping."

He'd thought long and hard about the possibilities that the recording somehow brought on the astral travel, the extra sensory perception that Leon had told him the Chinese were tinkering with. *What was the mechanism again?* He'd searched his memory banks; somehow Wi-Fi triggered something to do with quantum entanglement. It had seemed plausible when Leon explained it, but now it all seemed outlandish and too complicated to figure out.

But, he couldn't get away from it. There certainly seemed to be a connection between watching the recording, dreaming about Catherine, and her persistent bleating about being stalked.

Maybe his film of her was a dream catalyst; that made some form of strange sense. But his dream and her experiences seemed irrationally far apart, and he sneered at the thought.

Yet, the strange thing was, he'd admitted to himself, that his head hurt—like he'd been hit; as if the dream he'd had about being clobbered with a fire iron were real.

And then, as if to confirm his worst suspicions, on Saturday morning the police had come knocking at his door. He was to face charges of an assault on Catherine.

Alex, the private investigator he kept on retainer had called him at home with a disjointed request to get into the operations complex. There was something not right about his story, and Ken had refused him entry. For good measure, Ken had then called security to tell them to keep a wary eye open. Sure enough, Alex had been duly caught trying to gain access into the complex under the guise of an electricity department technician. He had told the weekend's skeleton staff that he had come to gauge their draw of current.

Ken would deal with him later.

And now, there was this bullshit. Nancy had *deliberately* put through Catherine's self-opinionated lawyer, without first creating a buffer for Ken to prepare himself.

"Where the hell is that girl!" he shouted at a volume that half the complex could hear. "*NANCY!*" he boomed again.

She did not appear.

He leapt from his chair and stormed back through their connecting door to where Nancy was calmly packing her belongings. "What the fuck do you think you're doing? I'm waiting for you!"

"I don't *think* what the fuck I'm doing," she answered, her voice clear and calm, an antagonistic lopsided grin like a banner painted across her face. "I *know* what the fuck I'm doing. I'm fucking... leaving."

She scooped her belongings under her arm and was gone.

Chapter 33

"Hello Jenny, Catherine please."

"I'm sorry but Miss Kaplan won't be in today, can I take a message?"

Nancy began to worry. "Is she all right, Jenny? I've been trying her and Jacky all day on their mobiles with no response to calls or messages."

"Is that you, Nancy?" Jenny sounded shocked at Nancy's entirely strained and altered voice.

"Yes."

"I'm sorry, I didn't recognize your voice at all..."

"I'm a little upset. You say she won't be in today?" Nancy asked a second time, the most diabolical thoughts racing through her mind.

"I'm sure I can tell you. She's been at the hospital and with lawyers; badly assaulted, Nancy. Sorry I didn't tell you earlier when you called, I've only just found out myself."

"Where? When?" Nancy was frantic.

"Friday night, in her bedroom."

"A robbery? Why wasn't I called?"

"Uhhmm, not a robbery, no. I think it best she tells you herself."

Jenny had been briefed that it was Nancy's boss who had assaulted Catherine. With no idea of the prevailing loyalties, she opted for caution.

"Is she definitely at home?" Nancy inquired.

"I think so, two hours ago they were both home. Jacky said they'd be out for a while, but didn't say for how long."

Nancy could sense Jenny's anguish and there was no need to prolong it, so she wound up her questioning. "Is Jacky still with her?"

"I think so."

"Thanks, Jenny. If she calls, *please* tell her I'm looking for her. I'm at home, she's *not* to call my office."

Nancy hung up and tried both mobiles, then phoned their home number where voicemail took her umpteenth message.

Nancy continued to check her phone for the following hour. Periodically, she'd try Catherine's number, only to be disappointed by the recording. When her call was finally answered, it was Jacky.

"What's going on?" Nancy was devoured by worry.

"Ken attacked Catherine on Friday night. I had a late flight and arrived home just in time to stop him short of killing her."

"WHAT?!!" This was far worse that Nancy had anticipated. "You mean that he actually came into your house? How did he get in?"

"The police don't know. Everything was locked and the alarm was fully armed. It's a mystery. Catherine reckons that it was his apparition."

"Oh sweet Jesus, no. How is she?"

"Bad, very bad. But she's starting to recover," Jacky sounded exhausted. "I'm sorry to cut you short Nance, but I must get a move on, I've got a flight in two hours. I'll be out of town till Saturday, but there's a nurse coming in for Cath."

"No!" Nancy stated emphatically. "I'll stay over. I... I mean, if that's all right with you?"

"Of course it is! It would take a weight off of my mind, I hate strangers in the house but it's impossible for me to take off any more time. I've about used up my leave for the year and besides, lately I haven't been at my best when I have worked."

"Cancel the nurse. I'll be right over."

Nancy threw together a change of clothing and headed for her car. On her way out, she had another idea and doubled back. For good measure, she packed in her .38 snub-nose 5-shot revolver with hollow points.

When she arrived at the house, Jacky was about to leave.

"Brace yourself... you're going to get a bit of a shock when you see her, Nance. But don't worry, the damage is only superficial, the swelling's already mostly gone down."

As Nancy entered the bedroom, Catherine croaked a greeting from the bed, forcing a smile onto her puffy face.

It took all of Nancy's self-control to cover the shock of seeing Catherine in such a desperate condition.

She produced a large bouquet of flowers that she'd bought en route. The flowers took Catherine's eyes off her long enough for Nancy to study her propped up on her pillow with what looked like a case of elephantiasis.

"Oh Catherine! What has he done to you?"

They spent the rest of the afternoon discussing all that had occurred during the previous three days.

It was an arduous task for Catherine to talk, but eventually she managed to communicate everything she wanted to say. She was suffering from severe concussion, a broken nose, multiple rib fractures and a suspected hairline fracture of the cheekbone.

The charges against Ken included attempted rape, breaking and entering, and assault with grievous bodily harm.

"Do you know how to use one of these?" Nancy produced the revolver from her bag, rechecking its load.

"Yes, I've shot before. I don't really like guns, but right now I do."

"Good... there's one in the chamber. I'm going to tuck it in here behind your head." Nancy pulled the mattress slightly away from the headboard and checked that the weapon would come out easily in the event it was needed.

"Can you reach it?"

With a bit of pained wincing, Catherine managed to get at it.

"If I really need it, I won't feel a thing; I'll get it, don't you worry," she stutteringly assured Nancy.

They went on discussing the problem that Ken still posed in both of their lives.

"Are you sure that he still has the fingernail?" Catherine asked.

Nancy racked her brain to remember.

"I'm certain it was gone because I felt for it," Catherine explained.

On Friday night, even after a combination of blows and strangulation, in the dream world of semi-consciousness, Catherine had been grimly determined to establish whether her robust attacker was indeed a phantom or flesh and blood.

She could clearly remember desperately feeling for the nail in a death-wrestle to break away from Ken's grip.

The shock and adrenaline had made time slow down, as if fighting in treacle; every blow performed in slow motion, every movement to duck stuck in the wrong gear. Peculiarly, she'd seen the comical side of what she was trying to do—groping for a nail while a man tried to murder her. And then the shock and horror of finding a trimmed nail where she'd expected a protrusion.

It had been *that* shock that had doubled her strength, allowing her a tiny gap to momentarily break his steel grip and catch a breath of air.

"At the office, was he at least cut or bruised?" she asked Nancy hopefully. "We're both positive Jacky managed to crack him really hard across the temple as he went through the window. The blow made him lose his grip and fall." Catherine was feebly pointing toward the window through which Ken had escaped.

Nancy moved across the room to look down the ten or more feet onto the spiny table of thorn-laden bougainvillea, the logical place onto which Ken would have fallen.

Nancy shook her head in disbelief.

"I'm sorry to have to tell you this Cath, but from what I could see, he was unhurt... and those thorns would *definitely* have ripped him to shreds."

The bush was particularly thick and spiny and unmolested; Nancy could see that each branch was studded with inch-long talons. There was not a broken twig to be seen.

Beyond the hedge, was thirty feet of open grass and beyond that was the perimeter fence, topped by spikes.

"Jacky said that she watched him go straight down into blackness. Neither of us heard him land and she didn't see him again!"

As Catherine spoke, her head shook with methodical denial of the facts that her mouth spoke.

Even under the cover of pitch darkness, nobody could cover that distance without being seen or heard, Nancy thought.

"Nance, I'm at the end of my tether, look at me! This *wasn't* an illusion. Hallucinations can't do this!" She touched at the swelling of her own face. "Jacky saw him here. She identified him in a picture. Yet he claimed to the police that he had been at home and asleep by eleven o'clock!

Catherine began to sob softly to herself.

"It was the same old nightmare all over again," she lamented. "But nightmares don't beat you to a pulp, and witnesses certainly can't see your nightmare!"

Chapter 34

David Edelstein had a serious problem.

It was Friday, four days since he'd taken on the cut and dried case of attempted rape and assault. The medical evidence was plain for anyone to see, medically detailed and reported by the police.

His chief suspect had both motive and opportunity, and had formally been identified by a witness and the victim who knew him well. Not surprisingly, because this suspect did not have an alibi, he claimed to have been warmly tucked into his bed at the time of the assault.

At its outset, it had appeared to be the easiest criminal case he'd ever be asked to prove. It had seemed far simpler than the civil case of violating Catherine with illicit drugs through an undetermined medium that he'd brought against him on her behalf less than a week earlier.

The police report of this assault charge, though detailed and thorough, left David with no more than bare bones upon which to build his case.

There had been no forced entry, and there had been no signs of an exit through the window as alleged. The accused assailant's body presented no identifiable bruising or scraping, which it *should* have sustained during the claimed reprisal and escape.

And finally, there had been no hair, skin, prints or blood anywhere on the property in spite of the victims' claims that the attacker was not wearing gloves.

"If I didn't know these girls personally," David had told his colleagues during the morning briefing, "I'd be certain that they were pulling our chain. This looks a hell of a lot more like a two-story fall and a subsequently opportunistic attempt to frame some wealthy innocent guy."

Fortunately for Catherine, David's instinct told him that something far more sinister was afoot than met the eye.

Then, during the ensuing week, all of their evidence relating to both cases had quickly evaporated like mist ahead of a warm wind.

When it eventually did arrive, the emailed report from Kevin concerning the patch had been vague. He'd revised his findings in their written form, the contents being remarkably different from his previous verbal assurances.

It read:

> "A chemical of unusual structure was identified, but proved too similar in its structural components to common human hormones, particularly ATP $C_{10}H_{16}N_5O_{13}P_3$ to be deemed a narcotic. The concentrations of the active ingredient proved too obscure to be properly identified..."

Kevin had also developed a strange aversion to the idea of testifying. Neither David nor Catherine had any success in altering his resolve on that score.

"I'm sorry Mr. Edelstein, but I've got my career to consider. When I spoke to you previously, I hadn't realized that the university has arrangements with LifeGames to use their facilities. I made inquiry and it was impressed upon me that my future prospects might be... well... *limited* if I did testify."

Kevin's cold feet had caused a red light to pulse brightly in David's own mind. He'd rummaged through back-copies of the prestigious *Weekly Law Journal* and, sure enough, he found an article naming LifeGames as holder of a major contract with the justice department. The contract had been for the training of all judges within their jurisdiction.

David thought it prudent to ask some questions around town.

"Excellent program, David! LifeGames is really top class. They're just opening their doors to private practice and you should try to get yourself onto one. In fact, I was told that this month's *Journal* will carry an extensive editorial about them. The bigger firms are already signed up. You don't want to be left out, and no... no, no, and NO! You *definitely* don't want to go up against them in court! Not for anything."

It was the same response that David got no matter where he made his enquiries within the hierarchy of justice.

Even Alex, the original fly-in-the-face-of-authority private investigator, had been adamant about avoiding further involvement.

Something had rattled him like nothing David had ever imagined possible. Somebody had been so successful at convincing him to keep away from this case, that David could hear live panic in Alex's voice as he desperately tried to cut the telephone call short.

David had pressed the matter as far as it could go but there was nothing more he could get out of Alex.

Catherine's pathology report had been as equally dismal in its vagueness as all of the other crumbling pillars that were supposed to support a watertight case.

The results pointed to Catherine as an alleged "extremely hyperactive individual" and vague convoluted language managed to say much and mean nothing at all.

When pressed, the pathologists could not elaborate any further. The tests were medically inconclusive.

"Catherine, I don't know what more I can do," David's voice was filled with despair. "You know that I would never run from a fight, but our armory is depleted at this point. In fact, I've just been on a long call to a Brigadier, Judge Advocate Brown, of the Judge Advocate General's Corps. You'll probably know them as J.A.G... they're the legal branch of the military. Now, he's one of the top prosecutors within the forces. On Monday when I briefed him regarding the case, he was very interested. By Wednesday, he'd personally reviewed General Daly's file and he'd looked into a bunch of other pending cases that precede Daly's, which, incidentally, had been neatly hushed up. He was positive that there was good cause for a full investigation."

Even speaking across the telephone lines, David could sense Catherine's dejection, but as much as it hurt him he had no option but to continue with his brief to her.

"However, this morning when I spoke to him, he was hesitant and non-committal on the subject... like it was a non-issue. I got the distinct feeling that he was afraid to press any further ahead with the subject. He mentioned that the Pentagon had already assessed the inherent dangers associated with time dilation, and they're apparently satisfied that the risks are within an *acceptable range* for losses to psychological breakdown..."

There was a long pause.

Eventually she spoke. "Well then, what do you suggest that we do David?"

The swelling of Catherine's lips had abated dramatically during the six days since the attack and her voice had restored itself to its original incisive tone. Her clear voice betrayed the flutter of fear borne from intimidation.

"The criminal case for assault that you laid out is in the hands of the Justice Department. They've sent it to the District Attorney for review. Even though much of the evidence has disintegrated, it's a fair case but I must caution you that there's still a lot of work to go into it. What we *can* do right now is to gain an urgent court protection order preventing Torrington from coming within a certain radius of you. We can also expand our civil case to sue him for damages arising from the assault. As you probably know, a civil case allows much more latitude for establishing circumstantial guilt than criminal cases do. I think that will be our best short-term solution."

"And a long-term solution?" Catherine's gut twisted with frustration as she guessed the answer for herself.

"Frankly Catherine, I don't know. To make a proper case out of either of the charges, we'll need much more evidence than we've got. Every time we get it, it evaporates."

Catherine was silent for a moment. Then she had another idea.

"What if I took this to the FBI or the Drug Administration people? Don't you think they'd have pull?"

"They'd have plenty of pull all right," David sighed. "But I've been looking at LifeGames' list of clients in last year's issue of *Forbes*. There isn't a law enforcement agency whose top people haven't been through the mill down there. It seems that everybody who is anybody is required to go through this cursed company's programs... And that *includes* the press!"

"You mean to tell me that Kenneth Torrington has monopolized the entire machinery of justice within the free world?" Catherine's frustration was at boiling point.

"Unfortunately. Yes." A man of the law, David clung more closely to definitions. "But I think that *monopolized* is a little strong. *Influenced* would most probably be more accurate, due to how *well connected* he is."

"In this world David, that's the same fucking thing! When we can't get justice from the seats of power, because those goddamned seats of power derive the basis of their power from the precise thing that we need protection from, then what *is* that if it *isn't* monopolization of the state by an individual person?"

She'd just told him that the man he'd insulted a week earlier had him by his short-n-curlies, so he resolved to pry that grip loose, even if it meant loosing handfuls.

"Caution is the better part of valor, Catherine. We'll have to take it slowly, but don't you worry, we'll get this bastard. God knows how, but he'll get his just rewards, darling."

David was his old bearish self again.

Chapter 35

Nancy started with a gasp, coming up onto her elbows as she awoke to see a tiny woman standing halfway into the room with a peculiar smile and her finger on her lips.

Nancy turned to Catherine and saw that she was in a dead sleep. She looked back and the diminutive form had retreated impossibly quickly to the doorway's threshold where she beckoned for Nancy to follow her.

The gesture was conspiratorial in a gentle, kind and irresistible manner. Before Nancy could take a hold of her senses, she had risen and begun to follow, spellbound by the midget.

Standing upright, Nancy realized how minute the stranger truly was, estimating she stood only to her own navel. There was something entrancing about the woman, a potent magnetism that Nancy could not resist as she continued to traipse after her.

The dwarfed figure was descending the stairs, looking back with each step to ensure that Nancy was still following.

Nancy became confused; was this some member of Catherine's family who had let herself in with a key? The woman seemed to pose little risk and was very engaging.

She couldn't decide how to react; whether to be irritated by this silent intruder, to follow, to challenge or to wake Catherine. Regardless, Nancy felt unable to halt. Her feet seemed to have a purpose of their own.

When the woman reached the front door, Nancy suddenly felt a chill run up her spine. *Something is wrong*, she thought, and tried to stop; but she realized she was drifting, not walking. She tried to talk but could only croak.

She had passed through the bedroom doorway, about to lose sight of the king-size bed, and she looked back for the first time. There, lying prone alongside Catherine, was her own body.

Horror struck her an icy blow and her surroundings exploded into a blur.

Reflecting on what happened later, she would describe the sensation as, "the view an arrow must have as it flies into its target."

She bounced back into her body with a mighty hypnagogic jerk and felt Catherine startle awake too. And then she drifted out of her body again and slammed back into it, bouncing out and back in again.

"Nancy! What's wrong? Wake up! Wake up!" Catherine was shaking her, yelling.

"I am awake... I am awake," Nancy was repeating in a groggy, unsound slur.

"What's wrong? Did you have a bad dream?" There was terror etched across Catherine's face.

"Yes... No! I... I don't know Cath, I don't feel well."

"Do you want me to call the doctor?"

"No... no. I'm fine, physically I'm fine. I don't know how to describe it."

Catherine had taken the gun out and was holding it. It gave them both courage.

A few moments later, the bedside phone rang and they jumped in unison.

"Hello?" Catherine answered.

There was a moment of silence before a voice inquired, "Who's speaking?"

Catherine despised callers who apparently did not know who they had dialed, and at this hour of the morning, under these circumstances, that type of a call brought on phobic tendencies.

"Who would you like to speak to?" she parried, her voice brittle with venom in her tone.

"This is Home Alarm Services, ma'am, your unit has activated; could I have your secret code please?"

"Sorry, I didn't realize, just a sec." She held the phone away from her ear to listen for the siren or at least a trigger tone; nothing.

"Sorry, my code is three two five six. But my alarm *isn't* activated. Could you hold a moment?"

She shrugged to Nancy as she moved across the room to check the alarm status panel. There were two circuits broken, numbers three and seven. The legend noted that three was the kitchen's infrared detector and seven was the magnetic monitor on the front door. She relayed that information to the service caller.

"I'm sorry Ma'am, but you must be mistaken. Only one circuit can break at a time, once it's broken the alarm activates and the unit can only be triggered when the alarm re-arms itself. There must be a fault on your line."

"There must be," Catherine agreed, "because my siren definitely hasn't activated."

"That's very strange. The only way this could occur would be because of a power failure. When the power fails, the signal is automatically dialed through to us as the unit switches to auxiliary battery power. That's the only reason that the siren wouldn't work. Unless the wires have been cut."

The affair was becoming more chilling by the moment.

"Have you possibly had a power failure?"

Catherine checked her bedside electric radio/alarm clock. Its display read 01:39. If the power had failed, then the time would be flashing 12:00. Her wristwatch correlated precisely with the display.

"No, power's good."

The service caller came up with another possibility.

"Perhaps your unit's power circuit has tripped. Or it's accidentally been turned off at the power socket."

"Hang on a moment, I'll go and check."

Catherine moved from the bed and, gun in hand, cautioned Nancy to stay in bed. She made her way cautiously down to the kitchen. Even after all her chilling encounters, she refused to be cowed on her own turf. Nobody or nothing was going to conquer that attitude.

It was an oath of self-confidence. On each occasion that she'd taken a blow, she'd found the strength to blossom back to self-confidence by reminding herself of the oath.

For the umpteenth time in the past few weeks, she was taking her oath as she moved through the darkened house, teeth gritted, her every sense on high alert.

She checked that the front door was still securely bolted and chained. Everything within the house was as it should be.

The electricity board's trip switches were all in a neat row, indicating their 'on' status, and she was about to return to the phone when she remembered to check the alarm unit's power lead.

With some horror, she found that the plug was removed from its socket, a plug low enough for a midget to unplug; the auxiliary power's light was flashing.

"I've about had enough of this!" she growled, ramming the prongs of the plug back into their sockets. The auxiliary light immediately winked to 'charge'.

Before returning upstairs, she took note that circuit three covered the area over the offending and now restored electrical plug.

"Ok, I've found the problem. The socket somehow spat the plug out," Catherine spoke in a worn, weary and sarcastic voice.

She was back on the bed with Nancy and furious that another mind-twisting mystery had been heaped onto her already overburdened load of inexplicable occurrences.

"Sorry, before you go, just one more thing," she asked. "Did this *just* trip right before you called?"

"Yes Ma'am, about seven minutes ago. The time was one thirty-six on our computer."

"Thank you," Catherine said and signed off.

"Well?" Nancy queried.

Catherine filled her in, concluding the summary with a simple question of her own. "Any guesses? What the hell's going on here?"

"Perhaps I was sleep walking and tripped the circuits and pulled out the plug," Nancy offered, reluctant to recount her strange dream about the midget to Catherine, not wanting to inflame their already jagged emotions anymore. She could hardly avoid recounting it forever, though.

"You must be pretty quick in your sleep to have tripped two circuits *simultaneously*!"

"A circuit fault? One of those surges or spikes? They happen in the early hours when the demand diminishes on the electricity grid."

"The technician sounded dubious and besides a surge couldn't explain the plug kicked out of the wall and *two* circuits tripped. I'll have the alarm company check it out tomorrow."

"I must tell you, I did have the weirdest dream…"

Nancy recounted her waking experience to Catherine as if she thought it a dream… when she knew full well that it wasn't one.

"Creepy!" Catherine observed, not wanting to verbalize more detailed suspicions; not in the dead of night with their nerves already jangling. That was a supreme understatement of her emotional state and she patted the gun. "I normally hate these things, but tonight… tonight it made me feel a thousand percent more confident."

"Me too," Nancy paused. "You know, it *had* to be a dream. If I'd been awake, I'd have thought of the gun with someone in the room… *Surely?*"

"I'd have woken up if you got off of the bed. I'm not the deepest sleeper these days," Catherine added.

"Well… what do we do now?"

Neither of them wanted to continue speculating on the evening's bizarre occurrences any further. They knew that it would only create a vicious circle, accelerating their individual fears into a feedback loop, transferring more fear from one to another and back again, and ending with another sleepless night of neurosis.

"Coffee?" Catherine suggested.

"At this hour? I won't sleep a wink!" Nancy remained on constant health alert.

"A little nip of whiskey in it? Irish coffee? Tomorrow's Saturday..." Catherine was a real temptress.

"Ok," Nancy succumbed. "Why not?"

Catherine was in desperate need of some Dutch courage. Their coffees would be *very* Irish.

After several doses, they sat watching music videos on the big screen down in the lounge.

It was after four in the morning when Nancy succumbed to the dosage and slipped into a cheek-clapping relaxed slumber.

The coffee was having the opposite effect on Catherine; she was experiencing odd heart and breathing palpitations.

She kissed Nancy softly on the cheek. "Thank you for being with me," she whispered before slipping upstairs to take a shower, hoping it would do the trick of calming her nerves. When she was done, she would bring a duvet and two pillows down; they could both sleep the morning away in her lounge.

Since Nancy was accustomed to the noise of the TV, Catherine left everything as it was. The sound would serve to mask the running water that would seem loud in a deathly quiet house.

Chapter 36

The man monitored the woman's breathing, making sure she was asleep, then he signaled for his colleagues to follow him.

The trio slipped silently up the stairs, toward the sound of running water. The leader halted his companions short of the bedroom door. They were his backup; their task would be to remain hidden and maintain watch until their assistance became necessary.

Alone, he slipped into position.

She was a thing of unusual beauty and he lingered a moment, taking in the streams and rivulets cascading and meandering over her flesh, baptizing her in clouds of steam.

He quickly cased the room, considering all obstacles.

The shower enclosure was the focus of the bathroom, standing as it did away from any wall, right in the middle of the room, a most unusual design. Like a nautilus shell, a single transparent sheet of glass wrapped concentrically into an ever-increasing coil, making redundant the need for a door.

As she lathered soap onto her body, the man calculated the distance he'd have to cross, satisfying himself that when his moment came he would have plenty of time to make the move.

There would be no need to rush the attack so he relaxed, enjoying the private show. Inevitably, the shampoo trickled down the woman's forehead and over her tightly sealed eyes. This was his moment and he ambled out across the short divide, his two assistants taking the liberty of positioning themselves for the show.

He'd thought the attack through carefully and decided that she would receive the most dramatic shock if he were standing right before her as she washed the soap from her eyes.

His timing was perfect.

The rush of the water had covered any sound of his approach, but Catherine had sensed Ken's presence an instant before he reached her.

As her bellow of terror began, the sound was pinched off. His hand shot out and gripped her windpipe, his thumb crushing her already bruised esophagus, making starbursts of light explode behind Catherine's lids.

The strength of his hand was freakish as it guided her out of the snail design, backward across the bedroom and toward the bed. Catherine was on the very tips of her toes, trying to steal a tiny intake of breath around the hand's tight grasp. Her eyes burned with the residue of soap, but through it she saw other figures moving through the room.

"Finally, my sweet Catherine, I'm going to teach you to stop fucking *with* me. Now you're going to fuck *me*," Ken's voice was calm and sadistic.

Catherine was groping to feel for his fingernail, her hands conducting the investigation all of their own accord. Securing that clue was an obsession that her body seemed to remember independently of her mind, and as she fumbled, she prayed that it might again trigger the burst of super-human strength as it had during the previous attack.

She was wet, soapy and wriggling like a slippery eel. Her struggles for life were so violent that even this phantom from another realm battled to hold her down onto the bed and spread her legs sufficiently.

"Give me a hand, boys," Ken called cheerfully over his shoulder to his henchmen. "Let's all have a little fun!" Then he turned and spoke to Catherine in the sweetest tones.

"I've brought someone who has a crush on you. Remember Craig, Cath?"

Catherine looked directly into the face of the long dead man, recognizing his features but not his eyes. The eyes that she stared into were not human at all, their pupils a bar of heartless black.

The strength from deep in her soul blasted through her like an express train. She bucked, rolled and kicked in one movement.

Breaking their hold, she bolted for the door, the stairs and Nancy.

Her terror loaned her feet wings.

Ken gave a halfhearted chase to the top of the stairs where her soapy feet lost traction as they hit the marble. Over and over her body cartwheeled, her skull ringing against the stone before a final limp somersault onto the marble floor below. There she lay unmoving, a lifeless shell.

For the first time, Ken saw the identity of the startled sleeper on the couch opposite from them.

Nancy was looking directly into his eyes; he backed away into the shadows.

The unexpected sight of Nancy jolted him and with a shudder, he gasped awake from the nightmare that felt like reality.

As if he'd actually fought the struggles in the illusion, he was breathless, his body saturated with sweat.

"These godforsaken fucking nightmares. I'm sick and tired of it!" Today I *will* erase that recording, he promised himself.

Erasing them was the only option he felt he had left. As long as the recording was available to watch, he knew that he would not be able to resist.

"The flesh is weak," he remarked to himself. "Especially *my* flesh!" He thought it a rather charming aspect of his character.

Within ten minutes of the desperate call that went out, the paramedics came howling down the driveway with the wailing police in hot pursuit.

Catherine still lay exactly where she had come to rest; she was breathing, barely breathing.

With a supreme effort of will to overcome her terror, Nancy had leapt into action, her mind racing to prioritize the tasks that might preserve the last evaporating whispers of Catherine's life.

Everything had bottlenecked into a delirious flurry of elastic time—her every action had been deadly urgent.

Grabbing the portable phone she'd seen in the lobby, she had called the emergency operator who had assured her that the call was being relayed to the paramedics and the police.

The connection had been uncharacteristically poor with deafening static and scales of tones running and oscillating through every pitch.

Not satisfied to rely on emergency services, she'd called both police and paramedics directly to verify that they were inbound. She'd run into the nearest bedroom and snatched off the bedcover to cover Catherine's nakedness.

She'd then crouched over Catherine, too terrified to cry; the deep sobs of fear and terror quaked to her core. She'd seen the fucker and she cowered flat against the wall, her eyes an ever-sweeping beacon, scanning the stairway above and the surrounding room with its dancing blue light from the television flicking demon-shadows into every corner.

Upstairs lay blankets and probably a first-aid kit of questionable usefulness under the circumstances, but any thought of venturing to retrieve them had been dashed with the menace of Ken who she'd seen lurking in the shadows as Catherine had made her last tumble down to the bottom step. Their eyes had locked for a fleeting moment before he'd fled back into the shadows, Nancy firing three furious rounds from the revolver in the direction of his retreat.

With only two live rounds out of the five left in the chamber, she'd reined in her trigger finger, knowing they were too precious to waste with a madman loose somewhere above.

The deathly hush from above and a maniacal cackling from a television advertisement had been the only distractions away from Catherine's shallow clutches at breath.

It was then that the vicious doubts had begun to creep stealthily into Nancy's mind.

Would the weapon be effective if she needed it? Would it jam? Could she control the dance of her shuddering hand?

But effective or not, competent or not, in those endless minutes of her most severe test, she had become keenly aware that those two rounds were all that she had to rely on.

Nancy had also been forced to make another dreadful decision. She'd realized that Catherine might have sustained neck or skull injuries, and had based her actions within the situation on the insight she'd gained from watching television dramas.

Should she move Catherine or leave her? Cover her or not? Try to resuscitate? Move to a safer place? What about spinal injuries?

"Please... Oh God please..." she'd begged, aloud. "Please let those producers have done their homework. Please sweet Jesus, let the procedure I've seen be the right and proper one..."

Her mind had been full of so many thoughts, but somehow, the most mundane had been the most vivid as she'd wondered whether those acting directors realized what a burden of responsibility the product of their labors carried in a time of crisis.

She'd repeatedly checked Catherine's pulse in several locations, just like in the movies, mentally running through her scant knowledge of CPR in case the need arose. The entire time she thanked fate that the under-floor heating was running.

Her ten-minute guard duty over Catherine's unmoving body had been a proverbial eternity. Every moment had inched by, an excruciating period of time and terror.

Nancy hadn't prayed for years, but during those long moments she'd continued to pray as she never had before.

She'd prayed for Catherine's survival, and she'd prayed for her recovery. She'd prayed that Ken wouldn't attack again, and then she'd prayed that the police would arrive to apprehend him if he did. She'd prayed that the paramedics would arrive soon, and then she prayed the prayer that she'd almost forgotten. Through her trembling lips came the words, "Our Father, who art in Heaven..."

Were my directions to Catherine's house correct?

The new thought galvanized her mind, severing the prayer as it began to leave her mouth. Nancy knew perfectly well how to navigate *to* and *from* the property, but she had no clue what the actual street address was.

Then, like an answer from heaven, had come the beautiful tune through the haunting dark woods that surrounded the estate; angels of mercy swooping down on her and Catherine at breakneck speeds.

At those first whines of the sirens, Nancy had backed to the door with the gun, covering her retreat. She'd used the wide stance featured heavily in every cop film ever made, guessing that there must be some merit in that method. After unlatching the door and kicking it open, she'd run back to Catherine.

During the brief moments of Nancy's absence from Catherine's side, her body had become a corpse. With no audience to beg its encore, Catherine's life-song had drifted out of its shell and slipped away into the ether.

Nancy had heard that positive encouragement in such dire moments was invaluable for keeping the victim's body and soul together, so she had actively included Catherine into her every prayer, a vigil of interaction that had kept Catherine rallying during the wait.

Now, Catherine's death while Nancy had tended the door appeared to have proven the theory dreadfully true.

"IN HERE!" Nancy yelled, frantically groping for Catherine's pulse. "IN HERE AND HURRY.... PLEASE, PLEASE HURRY!"

Uniformed personnel came swarming through the door, lugging the tools of their respective trades—police with their instruments of death drawn, paramedics ready to repair tattered life.

Nancy pulled herself together long enough to explain what had occurred.

For the paramedics, she provided a brief history of Catherine's recent concussion, then turning to the police, she briefed them of Ken's presence and escape into the dark.

Each group fell upon their tasks; the medics a frantic bustle of activity, as the police fanned out to trap their assailant in a pincer.

With strangers to share the burden, the stresses came crashing like a wave over Nancy, and her voice trailed off into pathetic heaving sobs of despair as she buckled under their weight.

With her face streaked by tears and her knuckles gnawed to broken skin, she steeled herself to watch the paramedics as they descended frantically on the body of her naked friend, laid out on its marble slab.

Already, there was a spider's web of tubes rigged to an array of drips, and the sound of the heart monitor was a solid lament that pervaded every corner of her being.

On the screen, were a series of thin blue lines that remained as doggedly flat as the horizon of a savanna. The sick poetry of the image did not escape Nancy—in her mind there was no doubting that the electronic sound and graph's hopeless flatness were a couple made for one another, the one singing the other's oblivion.

"Oh God, please help her. Please help, God, please Jesus, please," Nancy was whimpering in a never-ceasing dirge.

Then, over the monitor's squeal, came a higher shrill that rose rapidly in intensity until it's pitch was a sickening prelude to what Nancy knew would be coming next.

"Ready to defib. Clear?" The medic's voice was ragged.

"Clear!" came the confirmation.

The sound was a solid body blow that seemed to slap the floor, and Catherine's body convulsed to the shock, dancing a sick little momentary jig... pretending for a moment to be alive, it fell limply back, dead, onto the floor.

The monitor issued one lazy blip, and its graphic display allowed one single hill to amble across its length until it fell into nothingness off the edge of the screen.

"Another unit adrenaline," the team leader called.

A syringe was dispensed into the pipe that pierced the femoral artery near Catherine's exposed crotch.

"Defib again. Clear?"

'Clear!"

The pads socked the lifeless body with another heartless blow, and another lonely hill meandered across and off of the screen.

"We're losing her! Notch the current…"
The defibrillation pad's dial was clicked up another setting.
"Defib. Clear?"
"Clear!"
THUD! Went the corpse.
Blip went the machine.
"Another notch. Defibing. Clear?"
"Clear!"
THUD!
Blip.

Nancy couldn't watch the barbaric spectacle another second. She retreated to the sofa where happy music was still pumping out the hits to nobody in particular.

Until that moment, she'd been oblivious to the television. "Like a bat out of hell…" the podgy singer screamed his lyrics at her before she punched his image into darkness with the remote control's 'off' button.

As she crouched on the sofa, several more heavy thuds could be felt under her heels. A policeman cautiously approached to inform her that they'd found nothing, but would continue their search. At that point, Nancy didn't care about anything except Catherine's revival, and she waved him away with what small gratitude she could muster.

Try as she might, her attention could not be torn away from the knot of people and equipment at the foot of the stairs. A strange sensation began to grip her as the macabre sensations of hope and dread danced with the activity taking place in front of her.

As she looked on, her own spirit seemed to become external to her body as it searched, beseeching Catherine to return… or at least respond.

"Clear?"
"Clear!"
THUD!
Blip.

Catherine's body bucked with a tease of life, one single staccato pose in the strobe-lit frame of a grotesque dance. But it was hopeless and all over, the reality of a fair fight lost, a bitter pill to swallow after so much effort. It could be seen in the medic team's body language, hope gone out of their voices.

The realization was beginning to sink in, and the currents of despair that followed tugged and dragged Nancy deep into a pit of dull surrealism.

"Got her!" someone cried, with a triumphant ring.

The voice appeared distant, unreal, a wafer of sound in the commotion. For an endless second, it seemed to hang, more like a fancy of Nancy's memory, and then came the sharp yank back into reality and perspective of keen adrenaline-washed senses.

"I've got fibrillation, she needs oxygen! Challenge 250 mL IV push, NOW!"

Blip. Blip. Blip. Blip...

Through the air, the electronic tones came stuttering to life.

Nancy had risen to her feet and tottered zombie-like toward the elated group before full cognizance came rushing to her mind.

"Sh... she's alive?" she begged of them, still in disbelief.

"Only just, Ma'am."

The medic was ashen and looked shaken. "We were very lucky... two or three more attempts and we'd have quit."

"She's going to be all right?" Nancy was consumed by the delirium of joy and tears.

"We'll have to stabilize her to confirm status. But, yes. We have her... the worst should be over. Is she your sister?"

"Just friends."

"It's the strong likeness, I'm sorry. You say that she had a previous concussion?"

"Last week, Friday night, her doctor said that it was very serious."

"Then we had an angel with us, she must have the heart of a lion... and a blessing from God!"

"*Good,*" Nancy corrected him on reflex.

"Thank you, Ma'am. Thank you very much."

The medic gladly and rightly took the praise for having achieved the impossible.

Chapter 37

"And you are adamant that you fired the shots from exactly here... and Torrington was there?"

David was standing on the precise spot, with his knees bent to bring his line of sight onto the same elevation as Nancy's. With his fingers, he mimicked a gun, sighting the bullet's strike marks down the length of the imagined weapon.

"Yes," Nancy stated unwaveringly; they'd already been through this rigmarole a dozen times. He moved the tripod onto the spot and orientated the laser pointer in its clasp until it sat in the middle of the circled area on the distant wall.

"I'm sorry that I have to do this to you," the giant coaxed her gently, "but you've got to understand, Nancy, the way you're telling it, it's not going to look good to a court."

David would greatly prefer it if Nancy would claim to be a poor shot, so she could also claim to have fired wildly.

Instead, she remained tenacious in her determination to stick to the unbending truth of the matter. The fact was that where the three tightly grouped projectiles had punched holes into the plaster, had been exactly where she had intended them to strike, because that's precisely the direction in which Ken had fled.

"Nancy, that is a recess in the landing that doesn't lead anywhere," David had argued. "The only path Torrington could have escaped by is ninety degrees from the location you've claimed, if he'd fled in that direction." He pointed into the bedroom.

The house had been built to massive proportions with several recessed areas leading off of the main living space, creating the impression that the open-plan interior had more rooms leading away than it had.

To make the prosecution's case stronger, David needed Ken running *toward* the bedroom, where at least there had been a window through which to abscond.

During the past few days, while Nancy had acted as Catherine's voice, David had instinctively come to like and trust her.

"Nancy, I must tell you something. I absolutely believe your version of the events. Then again, I'm on your side and it really doesn't matter what I believe. To make a case work properly sometimes takes a little bending of truth. Now that's not the same as lying. In this case, your life had been in danger, so you have the opportunity to claim you fired wildly. It won't detract from you or this case, whereas to get a court to believe that Ken ran *into* that recess... into a dead end that he did not re-emerge from, well, it's handing him an acquittal on a platter! It'll fatally injure your credibility as a witness. The defense will crucify you, their lawyers will character assassinate you in ways that you couldn't imagine possible. They'll nail us to the wall." David needed to belabor the point so she'd understand, because he had much, much worse news for her.

It was already late morning and the fatigue from her sleepless night and rollercoaster of events had sapped Nancy's energy. She'd willed her mind to be lucid. What David had just said was horrifyingly true. Fortunately, she'd held off making a statement to the police, insisting that she'd only do so through her lawyer; and with all David had detailed, it proved to have been the prudent choice.

"When will Jacky be back?" David asked.

Nancy checked her watch. "She should be landing about now. I've left a message for her to contact me urgently. I'd rather tell her what's happened in person, I don't think it's a good idea to give the news over the phone."

David checked his own watch. "Ok, I'll wait with you."

"Thanks, I could do with the support. You want a coffee?"

"Is the Pope Catholic?"

They settled down on opposite sides of the open-plan kitchen's central counter, and David dropped the rest of his bombshell.

"Nancy, I must level with you on something. This will be a bitter pill to swallow but it's better that I'm straight with you." He cleared his throat. "Don't take this personally please, but you're going to make a poor witness."

In spite of David's caution, Nancy leapt to defend herself.

David cut her short. "Hang on... hang on. Don't jump to conclusions. Listen to the facts. Firstly, you've just walked out of the employ by the same man that you're now alleging made this attack. Your relationship with this man is what? *Good? Indifferent?*" David shrugged.

"Not the best," Nancy admitted.

It was obvious where his argument would lead.

"Ok, now you're a woman overnighting with your friend, near naked and alone in this room with this woman who is... She's a...?"

"Gay...?"

"Indeed. And she trips and falls down the stairs..."

Nancy was aghast; this was a line of argument that in her wildest dreams she hadn't anticipated.

David pressed relentlessly on;

"She's wet from a shower, and there are signs of a struggle upstairs. A lover's quarrel? Possibly. There's water on the floor, the bed is rumpled."

"Oh Christ, David, come off it! She's in a relationship—her girlfriend knew I'd be staying over... What are you suggesting?"

"It's not what I suggest Nancy, it's what the defense *will* suggest. Ken knows that Catherine's gay. Her girlfriend is out of town... even if Jacky swears on a stack of bibles this high," he held his hand to his waist—it was closer to her shoulder height, "even if she says it's sanctioned, if—and God forbid it does happen—Catherine is in a coma, the defense will make a mess out of it. They'll try to get under Jacky's skin."

"You are kidding me..."

"No... this is my world. How's the relationship between Catherine and Jacky generally perceived? Morally, I mean... ethically."

"Do you mean that the prosecution will try to swing this whole thing on me? Saying that I'm trying to make mileage out of it to frame Ken?" Nancy was flabbergasted.

"Right," David nodded.

"Catherine and I were lovers on the side, we got into an argument, she took a shower and maybe I hit her? We struggled through the room?"

David was still nodding in agreement.

"I ran down here with the gun and when she showed herself I shot at her and…"

"Not *the* gun Nancy—*your* gun!" David corrected her.

His comment sucked the wind out of her sails, and a smirk of disbelief ticked the corners of her mouth.

"This time you're joking with me, right? Would that wash? I mean, if Catherine recovers and she testifies against that argument?"

"Is Catherine currently trying to nail Torrington? Would she like Jacky to find out about your little *secret affair*? I mean, you're not currently in any other relationship, are you? Is it less plausible than the statement that you're going to make?"

Tears of frustration washed away Nancy's vision. How could people twist the plain truth so far? How?

Her mind raced and brimmed with violent rage.

David had no option but to keep pressing on. It would be far less painful for Nancy to hear this spoken in private, than before a packed court and baying media.

"There was no sign of entry... none. The house was locked up tight as a nun's *do-wattie*... There's no sign of an escape. And..." he paused dramatically, "I haven't had a chance to tell you this yet, but Torrington is in Hawaii; that has been confirmed." David could see the genuine shock frozen in chalky terror on her face.

"Hawaii, what's in Hawaii? He wasn't scheduled to go to Hawaii," Nancy thought out aloud, looking for a reason to discount the evidence.

"You mean he wasn't scheduled on the day that you were fired, which was?" David pointed out.

"I resigned!! It was Monday."

"Well, Thursday morning the company jet touched down in Washington, and he took a party of *friends* with him."

"Let me guess, he's buying support from some of his high-placed political clients."

"Exactly! He flew out, and they are only scheduled back next Monday, the police have the flight logs."

"But Jacky will be able to corroborate that he has been here, or at least an apparition which resembles him has been here, when he was abroad before."

"What does that sound like in court...? 'Your honor, one of the lesbians says that the man's ghost was previously here. Oh... okay then, he *must* be guilty'."

She started crying in earnest.

"I'm not being cruel, I'm helping steer you. Don't fret about proving things to me, honey, you're not on trial." David omitted the word "*yet*", then continued. "Even if you're right, it's still going to make it impossible for us to book the bastard, because the courts only deal with the facts."

"Skewed facts," Nancy corrected him between sobs.

Chapter 38

The line was an undulating ocean of hills and valleys, a poignant relief to Nancy, as her recollection was locked onto the awful flat, blue line. It had indelibly burnt a horizon across her memory; innocence before it and the grasp of what tragedy really meant beyond it. She knew that bitter emotion would linger to the end of her days.

The respirator's piston hissed and sighed, Catherine's chest tracing its movement with a rise and fall.

"How much longer can this go on?" Jacky asked the attending doctor, frustration in her voice.

She had not experienced the flat-line and could not know how infinitely more beautiful this dreadful scene was.

"She could wake up any moment or it could take her weeks," the doctor answered, declining to mention the alternative.

The atmosphere of the ICU was thick with tragedy and hope unlike any experience Jacky had ever imagined. The emotions it held were intense and difficult to contemplate.

"So many times, you hear of this sort of thing, Nance. So many times, you see it in the movies. But when it lay stretched lifelessly before you, and you must confront it without an end point to peg some hope to..." her voice abandoned her.

She didn't need to finish as the silence was stronger.

The long and awkward silence stretched out, while the sigh and surge of the machine reminded them of their lost friend.

Tears dammed behind swimming lids peeked out over the scene and escaped one at a time to freedom.

Nancy broke the somber gloom with the first constructive suggestion they'd had.

"I've heard that patients respond to familiar sounds. Let's try that. Didn't she love classical music?"

"Doesn't she..." Jacky corrected.

"Of course."

"Yes., Mozart, and Wagner when she's feeling crazy."

"Let's try it, this is just too depressing," she suggested, indicating the uninviting pneumatic accompaniment of the life support. "I have a tiny Bluetooth speaker in my car."

"As long as it doesn't interfere with these electronics."

"We'll ask..."

"Anything's worth a try," Jacky agreed.

A second major concussion inside of a week had caused a thrombosis to break loose from Catherine's left ventricle and lodge itself within her brain.

An emergency trepanning had successfully removed the embolus, but on one of the angiographs an aneurysm in the central artery had then been observed.

On two occasions during the procedure, they had lost Catherine's vital signs. She had been clinically dead for long seconds, but with determined persistence they'd managed to jump-start her heart.

Desperate to move the topic away from morbid speculations of Catherine's chances, Nancy struck up a conversation on their way out to the car to collect the speaker.

"David seemed very interested in the paranormal possibilities of what happened."

"Unfortunately, the swine can't be convicted on the wanderings of his evil soul," Jacky groused, going straight back to the old issue. "I really want to nail him so badly, Nance. I know it's wrong, but I'd like to have him..."

"Don't say it; me too."

"Really, I would!"

Back upstairs and with permission, they plugged in and paired Nancy's phone. Moments later, the mood in the room lightened as Mozart's "Piano Concerto No. 21 in C" filled the chamber with its elegant, rhythmic love dance.

"I'll bring my iPod back with me when I go home," Jacky promised. "It's got all her favorites."

They each silently studied their friend, willing any hint of revival to be revealed. Independently, they saw what they were looking for, but any illusionary movements were only hopeful phantoms so they remained silent.

There was nothing more to do but wait and endure the torture of thought, rewinding time, and hope.

Nancy thought about the medic's words from before; he was wrong. The desperation of fighting to get her back wasn't the worst yet... *this* wait was, and this wait had only just begun.

"What the *hell* do you mean I *can't see her*? Who is your superior? I don't think you know who I am!"

Ken was confused, distraught and very, very disturbed. He was a desperate man, determined to see Catherine.

During the preceding months, a seed had been planted within him and it had germinated, growing until its roots reached to every fiber of his being.

At first, he'd put the feeling down to raw lust and expected it would evaporate as these things generally did. Once Catherine had lived out his fantasy for him, he'd be able to put her aside and move on to his next obsession. But, instead of becoming a fond memory, her rejection of his advances had supercharged his emotions until they'd catastrophically consumed his every moment.

And so, to cope, he had decided to hate this woman. He'd decided that he would hate her because she was the only human to have ever had the gumption to stand up to his demands.

This mental state made him determined to ruin her in any way that he could, the same way that he had trampled others who had confronted him with much less opposition.

Not convinced that his nocturnal wanderings could have a physical dimension, all that had mattered to him was that the voodoo seemed to work. Seeing his vindictive efforts causing strange effects, he'd been happy and had prepared to keep on using them until it brought this subordinate to heel.

But this morning, after hearing that she could die, the agonizing realization of possibly losing her had dawned on him, the resulting epiphany potently confronting him. He didn't hate this woman, he loved her! He would love her even if she hated and rejected him. And from this realization, he became determined to make good for all the bad that he had caused.

Now at the hospital, the denial of access was a vicious affront. Petty officials stood between him and fulfilling the inevitable consummation of his revelation; heads would have to roll.

"Would you come this way, please Sir." The Head Sister led him into the administration block of the hospital.

She knocked on a door marked 'Administrator'. "Doctor Maxwell, this is Mr. Kenneth Torrington, he'd like to speak to you about visiting Miss Kaplan in Intensive Care."

"Thank you, Sister, I'll take care of it."

The Sister left, closing the door behind her and the elderly gentleman indicated for Ken to take a seat and then sat down himself.

"Mr. Torrington, I don't know how much you know about this case..?"

"Virtually nothing; all I've been told is that Catherine is at death's doorstep."

"You are aware of the court's interdiction against you approaching within two hundred yards of Miss Kaplan?"

"No! When the fuck was that concocted?" Ken flew into a tantrum.

"I'm really not sure Sir, I was simply told to enforce it. Have the police not contacted you regarding the matter?"

"I've been travelling. My housekeeper mentioned that they wanted to speak to me, but I came directly here from the airport."

Ken was genuinely in the dark regarding the turn of events, and the only thing that his housekeeper had told him had been that the police had called wanting to speak to him.

She had conveyed the message that Catherine had been involved in a "very serious accident," and they needed to know if he would have any further information for them.

Having little idea of what help he could offer, Ken had systematically called the bigger hospitals in the approximate vicinity of where he suspected that Catherine lived. He'd found her on his third attempt.

The nurse that he had spoken to had informed him that his sister's condition was critical as she clung to life by a thread. Ken had pressed her for information but she had no idea what had happened to Catherine.

It had been at that precise instant that Ken experienced his renaissance of spirit. There had been nothing left in his mind except the desire to somehow repair the relationship he had destroyed.

Somehow, he was under the impression that Catherine had been involved in a car accident. It may have been the nurse on the phone that had given him the notion, but he couldn't place it.

The nagging memory of his nightmare, chasing her naked through her bedroom, seeing her cartwheel to the floor, seeing Nancy and the muzzle flashes, seemed impossibly long ago and absurdly unrelated.

The more he thought about the voodoo nonsense, the more he realized that it was all ridiculous coincidence, and not worth thinking about.

"That's probably how I manufactured the idea that it was another tragic car crash," he decided.

And here he was, confronting the impossible paranormal outcome that the other Ken, the hate-filled one, had somehow perpetrated.

He finished explaining what he knew to the administrator, that he'd thought it a car crash. He'd told his guests the same story—his pilot and flight crew had heard it too—so he was committed to that course and had to stand by the account.

"I'm afraid it wasn't a car accident, Sir."

The color drained from Ken's face as the man went on, confirming his sickening suspicions.

"She had a near fatal fall down a flight of stairs in her house."

Ken suddenly looked cadaverous and woozy.

"Are you all right, Sir?" the doctor asked anxiously. "Do you want to lie down? Some water?"

"No... no, I.. I'm fine, I... I just had a dream... a premonition of this happening."

The doctor was used to distraught relatives claiming premonition. Working in a hospital had acquainted him with endless grief and disbelief.

"Is there anybody you'd like to talk to about this? A psychiatrist? A priest?"

Suddenly, Ken was overcome by an overwhelming desire to talk to someone frankly. He couldn't remember the last time he'd done so, but this force was insistent, irresistible.

Ken nodded, his throat clammed up tight, surprised at the urgency driving him. "A priest."

"What denomination, sir?"

"I... I don't... well... Catholic... I grew up Catholic." Saying it aloud felt alien, but the need to talk had escalated and morphed into an overwhelming demand to give confession as he had as a child.

Ken had his face in his hands, appearing to be deep in prayer.

The administrator made a call.

"Father Rowles is attending at the hospital. He will be with us in a moment. Can I get you anything?"

"No," Ken responded, keeping his face covered. "May I sit here till he arrives?" Suddenly he didn't want to be alone; he had never felt so alone... so isolated and watched.

"Certainly." It was a common enough request for the bereaved.

Ken sat in silence, the din of new fears joining the armies of demons from his childhood, creeping out of forgotten corners in his mind. Something alarming had its hand on him; it governed his dreams and made them real. The fears taunted him with their hidden secrets and how they'd allowed his life to unravel.

The fearful child within him came whimpering to the surface. The bulwark he'd built throughout a lifetime against the memories of abuse as a child suddenly seemed reduced to gossamer and in that instant, his mind capitulated. In his terror, the woman who had rejected him became his mother, and he suddenly knew that he loved her. He loved her urgently, loved her jealously, loved her insanely, loved her unhealthily… and he didn't care. He needed to see her, needed to settle the score.

The heavy gravity of these matters stripped away his confidence and collapsed his will. Inwardly, he began to crumble.

A few minutes later, bespectacled Father Rowles stepped quietly into the hushed office, wearing a black shirt and clerical collar. The instant Ken raised his head and saw his garb, a tear broke from his eye, and then another.

The administrator stood and quietly left.

The priest approached in silence and placed his hand on the crown of Ken's head. His head bowed in abject submission, and crying gave way to sobbing, and sobbing in turn to convulsions full of despair. And when the tears ran out, the thing strangling him from within took his breath and slammed him into the purgatory of regret.

Father Rowles embraced Ken for twenty more minutes before either of them spoke for the first time.

"I'm not falling for it, Father. The man's a beast, and I mean that in the biblical sense. He's an evil manipulative beast, and I refuse to be in the same room as him ever again."

The lengths to which Ken would go in order to manipulate her mortified Nancy. Not even a man of the cloth was spared his deceit.

Nancy was the closest to kin available; Jacky was on a day-flip in another city.

"Nancy, please don't judge the man harshly, he is as much a victim as anyone else. He is as much a victim as our sister, Catherine, lying in her bed over there." The Irish priest had a soft and gentle lilting accent.

Nancy gagged. "Oh, *puh-leeze!*" the word popped from her mouth, "...don't make me laugh, Father. He's no victim, that is an insult to the word. He's a monster, a charlatan! I don't know what story he's spun you, but I am prepared to swear on a stack of bibles as high as you can pile them that he is directly... or indirectly the cause for that poor woman to be on death's doorstep."

"Nancy, I know how you're feeling. Ken has explained to me that you might take this attitude, but there is another side, his side, which..."

Nancy's eyes bulged with the pressure of a restrained heave of laughter.

"Let's see..." she began, sarcastically. "He loves little sayings. Has he quoted you this one? 'There are always three sides to every story... your side, my side, and the truth'? Did he spin that one on you?"

Her glare was a withering beam of accusation in which the priest could see the naked fear and hatred that she bore for the man he'd left half delirious from tears in the administrator's office. He could understand it.

Ken had delved into excruciating detail, revealing the most diabolical things that he'd done. Father Rowles had seen the *spirit* rising in Ken, deep within the man something screamed out for help and release, he had recognized it instantly.

This was not the sham act of a charlatan.

"No, Nancy, he didn't tell me that. If you would speak to him, I believe that you would see exactly what I have seen. He has explained you and Catherine's relationships with him. He has confessed his worst side, his lying, his cheating... his..."

"Murder? Did he confess to murdering people? Because that's a fact; as I sit here before you Father, and before God, that is a fact. I'd be very interested to know if he has confessed that."

It was only an instinct that Nancy had; only circumstantial evidence she'd allowed her own mind to piece together during the period of her escalating disgust. What she was really doing was fishing for the truth—and the priest hadn't flinched at her accusations of murder.

"In matters of confession, I am bound by a vow, Nancy. What I *can* tell you is that during the four hours I spent with him, I believe in all faith that there was nothing he held back on... *absolutely* nothing." By emphasizing the word, he said it all.

"Ken did not quote any banal cliché or platitude. He spoke directly, earnestly and in all humility. He accused nobody but himself... apportioned no blame beyond his own... his own greedy nature. I tell you in all faith Nancy, he did little but sob and beg forgiveness from the Almighty."

Nancy's heart was a brick of ice-cold indifference to the priest's soothing assurances, a spiny armor erected against the seductive unmentioned treaties to forgiveness implied, her expression disdainful.

Father Rowles' eyes were intelligent, his demeanor wise, and his spirit worldly.

Nancy spoke at length with him, and slowly her defenses retracted.

"I *can* share with you a small part of Ken's confession, something he has granted for me to voice. He will say it to you himself when you allow. You evidently know about a recent computer game, some sort of hallucination system I believe? A sex act of some sort that he and Catherine, well—shared?"

Nancy was staggered that Ken had confessed to it; the topic was difficult for the Father to repeat.

The priest averted his eyes as he spoke. If Nancy could read his body language correctly, then Ken had disclosed to him every sordid detail.

"Well, what you may *not* know, is that he made a video recording of it."

As her suspicions were confirmed, a shock of anger flared through Nancy but it was drowned by disbelief that Ken had actually confessed to it.

"He's terrified that he has manifested something... something dire... diabolical, uncontrollable."

The deeply etched frown on Nancy's forehead proclaimed a new emotion welling inside her; anger and distrust giving way to horror and amazement.

"Yes?" she heard herself encouraging.

"He fears that every time he has reviewed this recording, it has triggered dreams, lucid dreams; dreams somehow animated into the corporeal—into the flesh, manifested somehow."

She was listening, starting to nod in agreement.

"With no contact with her, Catherine, he hadn't realized until today that her... that her *difficulties* were some kind of manifestation of his own experience. This seems unprecedented," he added, voicing his opinion.

Nancy was dismayed; if even *Ken* had come to this conclusion, to the point of admitting it, there must be something dreadful and sinister afoot.

"Were you at the house the other evening when Catherine fell?"

"Yes, Father."

"Did you see Ken at the house?"

"Yes Father, Catherine and I had been watching television downstairs and I drifted asleep. After he'd pushed her down the stairs he looked directly at me. I had a gun and fired at him."

The priest hesitated, frowning slightly. "That is precisely how he remembered his dream, except he said nothing to me about pushing her... he said he'd chased her, and she had fallen..."

It was a test from Nancy, a test to see if there was any deviation in Ken's story that might allow her to grab at a bogus detail. The fact that the related dream was accurate to the extent that Father Rowles could correct the detail second hand, confirmed the possibilities in her mind.

"You said 'unprecedented', Father; have you ever come across anything like this before?"

In her voice, was a plea for reassurance; an appeal for a pillar to lean on, a precedent or clear protocol to guarantee an outcome; a chart that they could sail by.

"I must be honest with you, Nancy... no, nothing like this that I'm aware of. Officially, the church now distances itself from such events. However, I—and many of my colleagues across the spectrum of denominations—do privately believe that the spiritual world contains many explanations for this kind of phenomena."

His words weren't the instruction manual on coping with supernatural calamity she'd hoped for, but they were better than an outright denial.

"There were two other men, colleagues who have recently died, correct?" the priest asked.

Nancy nodded, not daring to imagine what may follow.

"The man who died last week…"

"Leon?"

"Yes, that's right, Leon. Ken said that there had been something about Leon's death that had frightened him. He had only realized the significance when he awoke on Saturday morning, after his last nightmare... and of course this most recent unfortunate... *incident.*" Father Rowles paused. "Ken told me that this other late colleague of yours…"

"Craig?"

"Yes, Craig. Craig had come into Ken's dream on Friday night. But Ken said that it had not *really* been Craig, not the Craig that he knew. Everything about the man seemed to be Craig, except for the eyes... they were like an animal's eyes."

"Of a goat?"

The priest nodded.

"And the connection...?" She described the scenario, "Leon hit a goat on the road last Thursday night; Ken would *know* that the blood and hair are confirmed by the lab."

"And that's precisely what Ken said had terrified him when he was startled out of his dream."

"And Ken dreamt of being at Leon's accident, no doubt?" Nancy ventured.

"No. He said nothing of that."

Nancy was in a state of shock, and it was obvious.

"It will all be all right, Nancy," he reassured her. "If you remain strong, then nothing can harm you."

The words were brave but Nancy needed only to think of the strongest character she'd ever met to see the folly in his words. That mighty character was lying in the next room, fighting for her life.

The discussions were a horrifying revelation. One single terrifying truth faced them all, including Ken; they were dealing with something sinister and of immense proportions, something far beyond a simple and established solution. Something that caused all of those fears that had, up to this instant, seemed so dire to dwindle into insignificance. Instead, Ken now suddenly seemed less the villain and more a mere pawn.

Nancy gathered her wits. The sooner they all went on the offensive, the more chances they'd have of throwing off this yoke.

Father Rowles could see that Nancy was ready to hear more.

"Ken mentioned something else he experienced on Saturday night after he'd fallen asleep following his nightmare. He says that he'd laid in the dark, trying to forget the experience, that he'd tried to pretend that it was an ordinary bad dream. But he swears that somebody came to his bedside and offered to help him begin to make amends."

Sensing that an eerie and macabre detail was about to be imparted, Nancy braced herself for the worst.

"Ken told me that only today, while I was speaking to him, did the memory become clear. He swears that the visitor was real, he swears that it was the other man... Leon."

"If you want to complicate a matter, involve a lawyer..." David Edelstein admitted.

Within the broader context of all the legal processes in motion, he'd been discussing relaxing the protection order that Ken was subject to, with Nancy. David had just had an hour's conversation with the good Father.

"Unfortunately, that saying will be twice as true in this case, since the evidence is very weak. Pushing this to trial will get them nowhere."

Although her emotions pulled in the opposite direction, Nancy was being won over by David's convincing arguments to persuade Jacky to let the matter be.

"You're their friend, David, and it's their decision... but I can't disagree with you any longer. It makes me sick in the pit of my stomach, but you are right."

They were walking slowly down the corridor, on their way to Catherine's ward. As painful as it was, Nancy painted the ultimate scenario.

"And if Catherine were to... you know...?" she couldn't bring herself to say it.

"Then it would automatically become a capital offense and the state would take on the case... at least an investigation. At that point, *you* wouldn't be in a position to choose to withdrawal the charges. But as things stand, my advice is to let it be; Catherine can decide what she wants to do when she wakes up."

"I hope the 'when' is soon." They reached the door. "Jacky's just back... keeping vigil. She's broken, go a little easy on her."

David pushed the door open and let Nancy go first.

"Hello Jacks... How're you doing?"

"I'm fine," Jacky insisted, but the dark rings about her eyes contradicted that assertion.

David bent himself double to accommodate a hug; he held her a moment

"They say that reading to a patient helps," he commented, noticing the *Economic Review* magazine Jacky was clutching.

She was a little embarrassed. "I thought I'd stick to the only thing she reads. I don't actually have a clue what it is I'm reading to her."

"Nobody does," David assured her.

The music tinkled softly in the background as the three gathered chairs into a huddle around Catherine's bed and began to discuss the situation, talking as if Catherine was just choosing to remain silent.

David set out cautiously to convince Jacky to adopt a course of conciliation. As with Nancy, his first attempts struck a tungsten core of resistance, and even after minutes of his urging and Nancy's agreement, Jacky remained steadfast and unwavering on the principle of the matter.

David forged ahead.

"I'm not suggesting we lift the injunction against Torrington completely. Limited, supervised visitation is a choice that we can make among ourselves and the injunction can remain as a trump card," David argued.

"If I were a man and Catherine were my wife, would this be a group decision? Would this be a decision at all that anyone would entertain? The man is confessing love for my partner; it's laughable." And Jacky laughed to emphasize it.

"Oh Jacks, I get that..." David was apologetic. "Put that way, this request is indefensible. You know how I see you two. The decision is yours and totally yours... we're only trying to give you another perspective."

"Sorry to be so hot-headed, David."

"No need for apology... you're right."

"I'm getting sick and tired of pretending to be her sister and I hate not receiving the respect as a spouse when for five years I've put in as much or more devotion and support than most spouses. Goddamn! How would you feel? How?" Jacky was near tears. "I don't know whether she'll live or die but still I must contend with this kind of bigotry."

Understanding her anguish, both David and Nancy felt ashamed. Jacky slumped with her elbows on her knees, silently brooding on the words, before she continued.

"It's been what? Not a week since we became sworn enemies, three... no, four days since that... that... evil fucking TWAT caused Catherine to land here. *No!* What's him seeing her going to change or help?"

David felt castigated. "I can't disagree with that, Jacky."

After the priest, David had met with Torrington; the man's realization and capitulation seemed authentic. David appreciated that the power he'd displayed in quashing the investigation and crushing opposition was enough to suggest that, as a truly reformed ally, perhaps he could bring resources to bear that would aid Catherine.

"Is there any improvement?" he asked Jacky gently.

"Some... They've picked up increased brain activity. It's a positive, but they still can't... or, I don't know... they perhaps *won't*, hazard a guess when she might surface."

All the time that they had been speaking, Catherine's hand had begun to twitch under the blanket, their drifting voices advancing and receding in her mind.

She could hear they were talking about her, about important details, and she wanted her say.

"Iuk..."

It sounded like a frog, like a meaningless embolism, a bubble lightly popping past a membrane, but to Jacky it was the distinct sound of Catherine trying to form a word. She stared at her lover's mouth, at her throat and, YES! it was trying to move. Disbelieving, she reached for Catherine's hand under the sheet and felt the minute twitches of her muscles trying to re-animate.

"Catherine!!"

At her name, Catherine's eyes began to track lazily behind closed lids, and then the miracle unfolded rapidly before them as the trickle of life soaked into her once more. She added swallowing to her repertoire, then whimpering grunts; each movement a cause for celebration.

The monitor tracking brain activity was suddenly transformed from a carpet of uniform hues of blue hills—where only the occasional inclusion of yellow or green lingered—to a psychedelic sunscape, a carnival of movement, forests of activity with roiling and shifting hills and valleys of iridescence.

Nancy took off out of the ward and down the corridor, "Doctor! Nurse! Heeeellllp!"

Within a minute, the room was buzzing with activity, machines were switched off and wheeled aside, and specialists swarmed over Catherine.

The three visitors were an excited group, banished to one corner. "How's she doing?!" they'd badger whoever came close enough to answer their hopes.

"She's going to make it," came the gloriously unanimous reply.

In the wake of the respirator tube's withdrawal, Catherine was moaning softly between spells of feeble coughing, and nobody noticed her beloved Wagner heralding the triumph with a rousing, yet dampened, symphony.

"Will it ever mend?" Catherine's voice was slurred and slow, her pronunciation hindered by the muscle's droop.

"These are early days, Catherine, it's hard to predict," the surgeon comforted her. "We're going to have to be patient. I'll run tests, but the healing process will take its own course. Don't you worry, you're remarkably strong; you're healing magnificently."

The minor stroke had affected her left side. The damage seemed superficial and likely to recover. That she was so demanding just eighteen hours after her first stirring heartened her surgeon. She had fight, and fight was the best kind of medicine.

Handing her a mirror, he warned that the damage would appear a lot worse than it was, particularly because of the double bruising, and two traumas a week apart. She surveyed her reflection, taking the shock surprisingly well, accepting it objectively.

"Such a positive attitude will go a long way to your recovery, Catherine," he encouraged.

Half her face smiled her thanks.

Nancy and Father Rowles were beaming at the happy news.

I can't wait to tell Jacky, Catherine thought to herself. *Everything's going to be fine.*

Jacky had left the hospital during the early hours of that morning to prepare for a scheduled flight.

The surgeon ran a few elementary procedures before moving onward with his rounds, very pleased indeed.

Chapter 39

Following her revival, Catherine was constantly exhausted and almost paralyzed with pain coming in from multiple sites around her body.

She spent the remainder of Monday afternoon recovering, sleeping the hours away. Waking on Tuesday, Catherine was still wracked by pain, but the sleep had cleared the cobwebs from her mind, allowing her to begin remembering and holding limited conversation.

Nancy had expected to find Catherine timid and jumpy while relating those appalling moments upstairs that had led to her calamity. Instead, she seemed to have gained an iron rod of strength, as though she had resoundingly won that battle and crushed all potential for it ever challenging her again.

"I looked at Craig and his eyes were just dreadful... deathly."

"The eyes of a... a...?" Nancy couldn't bring herself to repeat Ken's recollection to Father Rowles.

"You can say it, Nance... a goat, yes. Yes, a 'goat having its way with me'. Those were the words I heard, Fernando's words, and they gave me the strength. I don't even know what I did but I was free of their hold and running, running so fast that it felt like I was floating. All that I remember was animated flashes, like a strobe light, *flick-flick-flick*... the bedroom expanse... the door ahead, the landing, the steps... then I tripped... ceiling-floor-ceiling-wall-floor-ceiling, all going by in slow motion."

Catherine weakly flopped one hand over the other, miming the actions.

"It was bizarre, all slow motion, somersaulting down a solid marble staircase, thinking clearly *I hope Nancy has the gun,*"

Nancy took her hand. "That's when I woke up. I heard... no-no... it was more like I felt the sound... the bashes and knocks of you tumbling down the stairs. I did have the gun. I'm sorry, I knocked some holes in your plaster."

"I'll frame them," Catherine smiled.

"They're a good grouping."

"It was so surreal, Nance. That last cartwheel... such a solid *thump*, it sounded strange, like it came from far away, as if it was someone else's head hitting the ground. I tasted and smelled the impact... a stinging coppery sensation."

She paused a moment; relating the story was costing her precious energy. And then her eyes flickered with the memory.

"Yes... that's right, I heard the gunshots. I heard them. Everything so disjointed, like I was in a black cave, the sound of the shots echoing on and on. So peculiar. I remember listening to the echo."

Her eyes glossed over as she transcended into the memory.

"As I listened, the echo became a buzz and the buzz became ano-," she stuttered, frowning mid-sentence, "another sound..." she finished dreamily.

And her eyes were no longer in the room, they saw only what they had seen, she heard only what she had heard.

Nancy and Father Rowles sat, waiting in a deathly hush.

As the memory matches linked, Catherine's eyes darted and re-focused to the present, "that was it! Remember Craig's recording, Nance... that sound?"

Nancy nodded, insects creeping up her spine.

"It was the same... the one that always preceded Ken's visitations!" She closed her eyes to rest. Very shortly, she seemed asleep... perhaps dead, but her chest rose and fell evenly.

Nancy took the interlude to explain the sound's significance to the priest. He kept nodding knowingly; it wasn't news.

As though she had been listening all along, Catherine's eyes opened on cue and she continued where she'd halted.

"Everything was pitch black, the drone abated to a light crackling, maybe similar to a Geiger counter. It was almost peaceful in a terrifying way. And then it accelerated, rushing like a jumbo jet at take-off. I felt myself sliding in response, sliding down the aisle of the jumbo, faster and faster, the floor pitching up and gravity sucking me backward, along the floor, faster and faster, the sound more and more urgent."

Ice trickled through her veins at the memory and she shuddered.

"Suddenly, I had the sensation of a vision, a peculiar vision; not a white light, no angels. Sorry, Father, no Jesus or welcoming committee. No. Everything seemed distant, like looking the wrong way through binoculars. I searched for a reference to bring back perspective. I was in the room. I was where I was, not floating at the ceiling, just like I am now, except you were so far away. Tragically far, out of reach. I tried to reach, lifted my arm and it telescoped some of the distance toward you—it looked as long as a telegraph pole. There were no proportions to it. You were racing to the phone, checking my pulse, talking to me, praying. I saw you move like a soldier in the movies with this funny wide stance..."

Nancy and the Father were transfixed.

"I'm sorry, this must be boring, like someone telling you their dream—just the garbage of a mind."

"Oh, no, Catherine—no," said Father Rowles. "I'm intrigued."

"Isolation..." she continued, her eyes rheumy again, drifting to the vision. "I wanted to cry, all lost... I saw you, Nance, panic-stricken; emotion seemed so pointless—I pitied you. I was numb to caring. Then you took my hand and it jolted me to myself, and with it, the agony of my body burst—I wanted out, back to the tranquil place. You talked and it yanked me in a new direction—staying alive meant everything again. I hung on, forcing myself to listen to you. It wasn't like they say, Father, all choirs and peace—it was tangled, confusing."

She paused, her voice weak.

"I don't remember anything more, until... until the doctors draped me in tubes and cables and dials."

She gently shook her head at the memory, reliving it, and then lay silently again, searching for strength. Nancy and the priest looked at one another, asking questions with their eyes whether she'd passed into sleep again.

"I saw movement near the top of the stairs," she suddenly said, her voice quaking a little. "No. A moment before I saw it, I felt... felt... well, I felt an ominous sort of *presence*. It... it was not right." She sounded delirious. "Not *Good*. Then when it appeared, it was silent and dark, menacing. A really small woman, like the one you'd seen, Nance. And I was thinking, *why doesn't anyone else see her?* She was smiling... so friendly, crooking her finger, beckoning me."

Nancy shivered and the Father looked at her, his eyes wide with fright.

"Peculiar... of all things, I thought of Fernando 'standing at my back' he said, and I hoped..."

She sipped some water shakily through cracked lips. A trickle ran from the corner of her mouth where her muscles couldn't maintain the seal.

"I felt punched. Punched in the chest, slammed in the back... pulled inside out... I heard voices: 'another notch. Defib... clear?' then 'clear', and they hit me again, punched me down into the marble floor. It was agony... blip... 'another notch. Defib... clear?'... 'clear'... punch... another... it went on and on.

Tears ran down Nancy's cheeks as she recalled it.

"'Got her...!' And I was thinking, you got me five punches ago, you bunch of bastards!" She said it comically and tried to laugh at herself.

Nancy's tears of remembered tragedy turned to tears of joyous laughter and admiration for her friend's courage.

"The agony... such agony with it. For a moment, I didn't know which side had won me—the friendly midget or the medical team. And I realized I was *me* again, with all my pain and frailty."

She took a pinch of her own forearm flesh and rolled it around gently between her fingers, marveling once more at finding herself *in* herself.

She had never before realized how good it could feel to be master of her own flesh. How different she felt now, the sagging face she'd seen in the mirror purely superficial and cosmetic.

Something in Catherine's demeanor told Nancy that she'd found her moment.

"Father Rowles wanted to speak to you, Cath... It's about Ken."

Nancy had rehearsed this moment in her mind, looking at all the angles, thinking how to introduce it, imagining how that man's name might upset Catherine. As she said it, nothing changed, and that nothing was shocking in itself. Catherine's composure remained, and she smiled, looking perhaps more serene.

"That's fine," she said, "let me hear."

Her reaction bordered on being the most horrifying outcome, for Nancy, it hinted that Catherine had possibly lost her short-term memory.

Catherine listened dispassionately to Father Rowles explain Ken's apparent upheaval of personality, and the more he talked, the more it seemed that Catherine had some peculiar insight to his words.

"And I believe that he is a changed man, Catherine," he said. "I would not suggest that he visit with you if I didn't believe that his confession has cleansed him."

"I know," was all she said. "I'll see him."

The words were an ice bath for Nancy.

Catherine stretched out their befuddlement with another attempt to sip a little. When her thirst was slaked, she began to explain the riddle to them.

En route to the hospital, Catherine had lost consciousness, regaining it under the lights of the operating table. That lost time had been a blank of which she had no recollection.

"It must have been the anesthesiologist looking at me from behind his mask. The glare of the lights was agonizing, but I could make out his image through heavy lids."

She could remember an injection and being counted into oblivion.

"Then I heard the sounds again, the *whoosh*. I was being sucked through a tunnel of yellow-peach walls scrawled with networks of red veins. I don't know if I was seeing the back of my lids pierced by the lights, but suddenly I was passing between rolled-up carpets standing on end. It was peculiar... On their top ends appeared faces, which looked down on me and the deeper I penetrated, the more faces; faces that I began to recognize. How do I tell you this? I felt immersed in their love, ecstatic to be in their presence... in love with carpets!"

She smiled and shook her head at the absurdity.

"I can't tell you how deep into the tunnel I went, I can only remember that the carpets began to bend, blocking my passage. They communicated to me, they were gentle, communicating carpets... honestly! Carpets with faces. They turned me back..."

Her forehead creased as she studied her memory, searching for what had come next, but there was nothing there.

"I'm going to give you a disclaimer, because you're going to think I'm crazy. When I went to dinner with Ken, he gave me a real education about TLE—Temporal Lobe Epilepsy—and how LifeGames amplifies the virtual reality software the brain's already running."

Her listeners seemed puzzled.

"When I'm stronger, I'll go into that. But I need to just tell you this before I go any further. I was very interested in what he said, so I did a bit of research and found fascinating explanations for why humans hear voices or see apparitions that aren't really there."

"Oh, they're there Catherine," Father assured her.

"Well... maybe... maybe not. LifeGames is messing with the temporal lobes, which are right next to the parietal lobes. These little suckers have two functions; one involves sensation and perception, and the other is concerned with integrating sensory input. They're tied to our capacity to create a virtual reality impression of what is outside of us—recreating it inside our heads. When it misfires, it can put together incoming perceptions from the ears or eyes or touch all wrong, and make a person think they're outside of themselves looking back, or it can make them think something else that isn't there, *is* there, looking at them."

The Father was shaking his head in denial.

"I'm a person who needs solid explanations, and after what I'm about to tell you, I really needed to have already shared the virtual reality information with you so you don't think I'm crazy."

"We never would," Nancy assured.

A nurse interrupted their session to administer treatment and record details, giving Nancy and Father Rowles a chance to visit the bathroom.

When they returned, Catherine resumed her recollections, and continued explaining what had happened.

"I was back out of my body looking at a gaping hole in my skull. That's just peculiar to think about, isn't it? It's just nonsense..."

The old Catherine was definitely back, the skeptic, analyzing everything.

"Anyway... I've given you the disclaimer, so I'll just tell it as I experienced it. Below me, the medical staff were in a fluster. My first reaction was fear, as I was searching for the entity, that little gnome, that awful sound. But this time, there was nothing, it was pleasant being out of my body, curious... time seemed insignificant. Like I had the choice to perceive quickly or slowly. Everything about the experience felt familiar, not scary anymore."

Catherine stopped for a moment, collecting her thoughts.

"There seemed to be a lot of activity near me. Pockets of... of... like *energy* or something brushed past. At first, they felt like emotional imprints, like they inhabited this room, and I was an intruder..."

Nancy shuddered. "Creepy... hospitals always feel charged to me."

"Nance, it wasn't. Some of them... now listen to me... I sound like a crystal-staring hippie! Some of them seemed *young* and that was sad. But mostly I felt quite comfortable; like there was no place I'd rather be than right there, like I was in a *fellowship* of some kind."

Catherine paused to think about the word *fellowship*, to see if there was a better word, but it was the right word, all she could come up with was, "I belonged."

"Oh, Cath... that's just you, you make friends so easily," Nancy smiled at her, feeling silly for the banal attempt at support.

"Thank you," she said. "I was experiencing this *mélange* of... of maybe *telepathic* intuition? A sensation at the core of *me*, voices and thoughts all as one, a medley of hushed exchanges as they busied themselves in this place... this plane... somewhat interested in me, but not making a big deal of it. It all seemed to wash like oil over water, not quite touching the world we were looking at with the surgeons and instruments. What an acid trip, hey? When these—for convention's sake, I'll call them *spirits*—when they first started to materialize, I saw that there were no familiar faces. Then one was clarified for me... I swear, Nance... it was Leon."

A tremor went through Nancy and she rubbed her forearms, covered as they suddenly were with gooseflesh.

"I'm afraid you'll laugh at me... this must sound like a script for a bad C-rated movie. If you were telling me this, I'd think you nuts... delirious. Guess I was," she laughed at herself again.

Father Rowles smiled. "I've heard it before, it is very interesting," he encouraged.

"It was the same senile Leon, Nance... full of mischief. It seemed that we," she searched for a word, "...that we *communed* for ages."

"The surgeon said that they lost you for two and a half minutes the first time and more than three minutes the second!" Nancy added helpfully.

"A second time?" Catherine sounded surprised. "They lost me twice?"

"I *think* that's what they said, we can ask the surgeon when he comes by. Have you no recollection of a second time?" Nancy squinted.

"No. None at all." Catherine sounded cheated.

"Often survivors don't remember anything at all, Catherine," the priest reassured her. "Indeed, you're rather fortunate to remember what you have. Such detail."

"I'm detail orientated, Father." She wondered for a second if it was wrong to wink at a priest, but she'd done it so it didn't matter. "But I can't help wondering what went on?" Catherine pondered aloud.

"What about hypnosis to unlock the memory?" Nancy suggested. "Leon's voice is available on the LifeGames computer."

"Might be a little while, Nance," Catherine had simultaneously thought of that possibility. "I don't know... I know we're supposed to be leading toward your question about Ken, Father, but it's very close to me still. I'm not sure I'd want to go back to those premises."

"I'm sorry, very insensitive of me," Nancy apologized quickly. "I'm just caught up in this, it just came out. If or when you're ready, I've got friends at other centers—we could arrange to sneak you in."

"We'll see..." Catherine replied, noncommittally.

Recounting the memory seemed cathartic. She was still talking slowly, not animated, taking pauses, taking her time; but as she spoke it through, rather than becoming tired, she seemed to be gaining strength through it.

"Now, what I'm going to tell you gets weird... Leon told me that LifeGames amounts to much more than we think. He told me that the recordings of Fernando's riddles are the *key* to understanding it. He was not able—or, I think he said *allowed*, I'm not sure which—to tell me what LifeGames was *based on* or *about*. It's hard to put it into words."

"Okay, now that *is* weird; very, *very* weird and... creepy." Nancy agreed.

Catherine rested while Nancy explained Fernando's significance to the priest.

When she was done, they discussed what could have rendered Leon incapable of communicating.

It was a fruitless few minutes of speculation without facts.

Catherine offered the closest hints to the solution.

"Leon explained that the time dilation procedure is like some kind of a Satanic ritual... like it's upgraded from Medieval candles and dancing naked, sprinkling salt or something." She laughed at her own words. "Like the Devil's gone high-tech. The 'foul balms' are something like a magic potion opening the mind. He told me that because Ken rejects all supernatural; money's his only focus, he's the *perfect* midwife to it, giving it life."

"Interesting," Nancy pondered.

"And here's the crazy hint—Leon was adamant that Ken will change, that I'd be able to trust that change."

"And you hadn't talked to her about it before today, Father?" Nancy asked it as an accusation, and Catherine frowned at the question.

"No," he said simply.

"What?" Catherine asked.

"It's just beyond bizarre." Nancy's eyes were darting from the priest to Catherine and back. "How you could have come to this conclusion about Ken independently… that he's changed."

Catherine looked serene about it, completely comfortable, insisting she would forgive him everything.

"I'm battling to grasp how you're okay with this?" Nancy kept saying.

"Do you know what I've been through?"

"Well, yes…"

"No… not what's happened to me, Nance… what I've experienced. I'm wide open to anything. Nothing was as bad as where I've been. If I can't trust how I feel now, then I don't trust my recovery and I don't respect…" she let the words hang.

"Might I fill you in, Catherine?" Father Rowles advised. He had never before seen the Lord's work more clearly than in this woman four times reprieved. "I don't want to stress you though."

"I'm at peace," she replied. "There is nothing left for me to fear, Father. Tell me then."

"Holy is not a church, not a building, not a person or book. It is not ritualized prayer, it is not begging prayers. It is a change within. Those who experience it are the fortunate few." he began.

Both women nodded together in solemn agreement.

"I believe that you have experienced a lasting change of spirit. And I believe that the man accused of perpetrating all these things has had the same." And the priest went into the details of his hours with Ken.

When he was done, medical staff came in and it gave Catherine an opportunity to rest while Father Rowles and Nancy took lunch in the cafeteria.

"It sounds like this drug potion, the one we've been trying to identify, the one Ken admitted to you that he produced..." Nancy looked to the priest for agreement of any kind, and his silence along with a slow involuntary blink was her confirmation. "This drug with the hypnosis and virtual reality; it's some kind of Satanic ritual... a pact... in its own right."

The priest was nodding, just perceptibly.

"Have you any idea of the sheer volume of humanity who have already run through this program, Father? Any slightest inkling of the positions of power these people occupy? Of their influence over *us*?"

They had already revealed Fernando's proclamations to the Father who had listened with great interest.

"Remember," Nancy was recounting, "we told you he said words to the effect the 'The Great Goat' or something 'will have his way with you'? Right now, I think the 'Great' part of that was not Ken. The apparition that looked like Craig? It had goat's eyes... Brrrrr..." she shuddered at the thought.

"I feel I must communicate this to the archbishop."

Nancy vigorously agreed.

"I'm most intrigued as to whether she can recall anything from the second time they lost her on the table."

"Perhaps she should be satisfied with what she does remember. I think some things are not for us to know. It seems this time-drug, this hypnosis and other treatment—perhaps it has caused enough misery and risk. When we pry too deeply into that which the Lord in His wisdom has clouded from our eyes..."

Nancy shuffled uneasily in her seat.

Father Rowles saw the intention in her eyes to ignore his advice.

That, he thought, *was an all-too-human curiosity*. To venture a short way into danger, emerge unscathed, and let that false sense of triumph become the engine that drives the unsuspecting deeper until retreat becomes impossible.

"And you're still prepared to meet with Ken?" Nancy asked.

They were back at her bedside.

"Yes, as soon as possible." Catherine sounded almost cheerful about the prospect, like she somehow shared something with him... a kinship, that she wanted to explore.

The revelation she had for him was simple; hordes stood in peril, and he was the key to reverse it.

Father Rowles knew they were on dangerous ground. His counsel could only go so far; all that was left would be to pass the matter on to his superiors... and pray.

Chapter 40

Catherine's recovery from injury had been excellent, the surgeon's prognosis of full recovery from the stroke well on its way to fulfillment. Her head was still bandaged where it had been trepanned to relieve the pressure on her brain and remove the clot. She moved gingerly, her left arm still strapped to her body in a sling and she fought to disguise her pronounced limp, repulsed at being thought of as a victim.

She was meeting with Ken privately and on neutral ground in a public restaurant. She did so against Jacky's wishes, but it was something she needed to do to beat back her demons.

"You sure gave us a fright, Cath. I was almost... well, uhhmm, frantic with worry..." Ken was trying to retain his loose-tongued swagger, still uncomfortable with the emotions he'd admitted to. "Stupid of me. I knew you were a fighter."

Catherine looked for but found no trace of his psychopathic, manipulative edge; it was something she'd always be on guard for, no matter how this went.

In Ken's mind, in his circumstances, what he had come to do wasn't simple at all. There were newfound emotions to contend with, along with the practicalities of managing the situation he found himself in.

His wealth, perhaps his freedom, depended on keeping the lie intact. In the days since he'd made those admissions to Father

Rowles on an emotional impulse, he'd had time to digest their implications.

Gone were the first heady delusions that he could capitulate and disclose it all, wash his hands and live a free man. Nothing was free; there were contracts, his reputation, a brand. And there were laws; the FDA, CIA, FBI and real legal and *other* jeopardies for having defrauded powerful people.

The moment of epiphany had passed and his emotional reaction with it, but he still felt the motivation to wind the operation down. The machine had taken control over his dreams, and forcing him to give up more control than he was prepared to consider.

No matter what he'd done, no matter its impact, no matter his realizations and earnest intent to undo the dangerous aspects of his company—he had no intention of suffering for it.

He'd pick it slowly apart, he'd have the drug's potency reduced. He'd scrap the campaign promoting time dilation. There'd be no announcement or press release, nothing quite so dramatic; he'd just let it slowly drift into the archives, a forgotten dead end in the turbulent research and development arena.

The more he thought about it, the more he knew he could sell that to the board; he'd do it over time. He'd built it up, he could take it down. Slowly, slowly—that was the key.

"Your lawyer called, tells me you're calling him off? You'd never have gotten me you know..." Ken tried to make light of it.

"You obviously haven't met him. His legal skills were the least of your problems." Catherine knew how to play the game with him; he would never be anything but an egotist, she thought, always wanting the last word.

"How much does he know about the... uhhmm, the patches?" his voice apprehensive and testing.

He hadn't admitted the drug's existence outright. It was a game of not stepping on the landmines and they both knew it; an unspoken agreement to talk about it without stating it outright. They had an understanding that the narcotic was there in the patch, and Ken had agreed without spelling it out, that the *formula* would be changed to back it off.

"Only that I suspected something exists, and he's found something," she said, keeping it vague, bluffing an ace in her hand. "He's a friend and he's promised to develop amnesia so long as I remain happy." She inferred a hostage situation, guaranteeing her own safety.

Ken nodded approval to the terms.

"And the rest of it?"

They both knew what that meant within the context—the rest of the company, the ritual they'd created. She was driving toward her intended bargain, testing his commitment to dismantle it.

"I'm a wealthy enough man," Ken declared. She'd expected him to make it all about himself. "I can live very comfortably, I'm prepared to move on. I have to move cautiously though... there are *factors*."

She was smart enough to know what he meant—his jeopardy; prison or worse.

"I've done my *confession* Cath... we both know it. Talking too much is, well, you know... you're smart. Let me say, just watch, wait, and see..." he challenged.

Catherine wondered if she could call it cowardice. Was she expecting him to fall on his sword? Publicly? Give up the cushy life? Give up freedom, become a marked man? The CIA, Pentagon, Mossad, MI6, all the baddies who'd bought into it; they'd become decidedly bad company if he admitted he'd sold a lie and played them.

She had the whistle and she could blow it at any time; and he knew it. In that sense, it was a gun to both their heads. If she blew it, they both knew she'd blow it only once; it would be the last breath she'd ever blow.

"I'll do it Cath," he could see question marks in her eyes, "Time dilation's already on hold, but I don't know how long I can keep it that way without a *communiqué* to our clients who've booked and paid. Too many government departments involved. It's... delicate. There's another angle as well."

This one truly worried Ken.

"AI—the Artificial Intelligence at the heart of the system. It's not a computer where we can simply hit the *pause* button. It's a neural network; in some sense, it's a *partner* in this. Does that sound strange?"

"Decidedly," she admitted.

Ken huffed. How to explain it? He racked his brain. "There is really no way for me to put this simply... no analogy that really nails it. The *thing* has a life of its own. It's linked to the internet, so it's effectively using and co-opting the processing power of every other computer it's ever touched over the network, including the smart phones of everyone ever on the system. We're living inside it's brain, you understand?"

The way he said *thing* slapped Catherine across the face. She'd never thought of the AI as a player in the scheme of things.

"You can think of all those remote processors on desks and in handbags and pockets as individual neurons participating in co-operation to make up the total artificially intelligent brain. It's not as simple as throttling back on processes in a single entity; it's dispersed at a global scale."

Her eyes were wide with shock; she nodded, a little dumbfounded.

"So, you don't really know how intelligent it is, do you? How self-aware it is?"

He sucked air through his teeth and clattered them lightly together; the tendons in his neck standing out from the internalized stress. "It has access to everything we know, to our psychology, our history and our deepest fears, to our irrationality and jealousy. And it will determine that the last thing it should ever do is let us know how advanced it becomes."

"You're telling me you have something here that you can't just turn off by giving an order?" Trepidation crept into her voice.

"Well, like I said, the central system is sort of..." he searched for the word, "it's sort of well, *connected*; *very*-connected." He emphasized *connected* as he would consider a Don, a Mafia Boss and she grasped his meaning instantly.

"You're telling me you'll still need to negotiate this? Negotiate it with this... this *thing*?"

"Kind of."

His words were chilling.

"*Connected?* Connected... *how?* I understand mobile phones, computers, the internet, Wi-Fi... but what does this mean in practical terms?"

"It can act like the paranormal. In some ways, it's like a god, like the demon we've always feared; it can reach out and touch us wherever we are, through our everyday things."

He let the words sink in.

"Whoa! Whoa, whoa... fucking *whoa*, Ken!! What the fuck have you done?!!!"

"Whatever I've done is done. I'm giving you insight into what undoing it will take. I'm telling you that you can't push this."

"And if I do?" She was angry and beyond caring about what he might do to her personally.

"*Nanobots*; microscopic bio-based machines," was his response; he said it as if she should work out the implications.

"What?! No, let me guess; it's not a narcotic on the patch, you're letting micro-robots in through the skin of everyone on the system? Are you completely fucking mad?"

Ken wouldn't budge on more details, wouldn't give up any more details no matter how much she badgered him or reminded him that she had the gun to his head—he returned the threat with a smile. It was a dead end; she had all the information she needed, and all she could do with it was sit tight and wait and see, so she took a different tack to shake out anything else he may be hiding.

"Why the change in you? Your change of heart... Why? I thought it was spiritual, and *that* I could understand. But if it wasn't... then *what?* What was it?"

"I realized that I was in... in uhhmm... love with you..."

She shook her head, denying that it mattered. "That's bullshit, you're not capable."

"Guess it focused me." He ignored her denial. "The intrinsic good within... as a human? My humanity." He tried it on, but it didn't fit, didn't come out in a very convincing way.

He knew that the real reason for his change of heart was cowardice, knew he'd gone too far, realized he'd made a machine not just to control others, but one that was starting to control him too. He'd realized it when he couldn't stop with the sex recording, her sex recording. It was the *machine* that made him keep watching, connected through fiber and wireless connections over the miles, the oceans and time-zones.

He preferred how he used to feel before it had accidently become his master too.

He'd been silent a while and Catherine realized he would go no further.

"A virus?" She brooded on his disclosure, the widening of scope that made narcotics seem tame, and she rebounded as the magnitude of it horrified her all over again. "You've made a super-virus... a super-fucking-virus with a *trans-humanism* mechanism... a fucking *Cyborg?* Cyborgs? Everybody cyborgs?"

Ken wouldn't look at her.

"Jesus, Ken..." more words failed her. No more were necessary and she gathered her keys and mobile, ready to leave.

Chapter 41

"It's a false alarm, Nance, it's a ruse. The spiritual stuff... meaningless... It's bullshit."

"What are you on about?" Nancy was momentarily conflicted, not certain what had gotten into Catherine. "We saw evidence of it, the paranormal activity. I'm confused by what's come over you."

"That 'evidence' we saw?   It's a symptom. It's evidence indeed, there's just nothing spiritual to it. This fucking nutcase has unleashed a Beast all right, but it's entirely technological; not a ghost, not a ghoulie, or not a goblin in sight. *Artificial-fucking-intelligence* is our problem. I'm talking right now and wondering if this fucking thing," Catherine said, holding up the mobile phone in her hand that she'd turned off, "is listening to me and telling its big boss about it. It's off, and it's not getting turned on again." She threw it across the room.

Nancy's mouth hung agape. "I... I'm... What?" Her mouth worked spasmodically, mumbling confusion.

"This lunatic is using *nanobots*... a whole new twist. I eventually got it out of him. He didn't admit it, but didn't deny it either. They're probably on the patch... that's likely what this 'narcotic' thing amounts to, he won't say. Microscopic free-floating machines, catalysts, proteins. I'm no chemist, but that's what they do. They get into the bloodstream. They're organic, self-replicating; they build new bots from the organic materials inside us. They're communicating via Wi-Fi, via your cell phone, your computer. Every time you're in range of a wireless router, the AI machine is talking to headquarters, to LifeGames HQ. When I shake hands with you, when we hug, whenever I'm within touching distance, my bots are talking to yours. Taking energy from our systems to run themselves. Waiting for the AI unit's instructions. Even if you go live in the woods to get away from it, as *soon* as you go near someone who has been in Wi-Fi range, that person's bots faithfully act as messengers. It... it's staggering, and worse than staggering, we have no idea what its objectives might be, there is no reason to think it focuses on outcomes remotely similar to anything that a human might strive for. I mean, if something is smarter than us, we have to start behaving the way it wants us to; that's how we treat our animals."

"Shit! And the sounds? The astral sounds?"

"Ken says they're sort of a 'logging-in' procedure, a handshake. Human neural systems react to ritual, it's an evolutionary characteristic—the system cunningly rode in on that characteristic."

"It's ingenious. The scope is... I... I really don't know..."

She was looking for clues to the mistake Catherine was clearly making.

"The deaths, Craig and Leon; what's a bot or an AI have to do with that?"

"They were guinea pigs in the system, just like you and me. They've been *ritualized*... we're all—what shall I call it—*infected?*"

"Okay, sure." Her hand went to her forehead in bewilderment. "But Cath—both had car crashes; did it make them veer into things?"

"No, their cars were—what were they? Yes, connected to the web."

"Oooh... fuck! Okay, and what about that backwards recording, on Ken's phone—the prayer?"

"I don't know. The AI machine knows our vulnerability to superstition; Ken seems quite rattled by this realization. He told me that he was brought up Catholic, and he realized that the *thing* had figured out the best way to yank his chain by manipulating his brain chemistry... it plants ideas and harvests them." She started giggling, a hysterical little giggle of horror.

They sat a while pondering until Nancy thought of something.

"The apparitions. The dwarf woman. You'll say they're hallucinations inside the head; I'm infected, you're infected, the machine could probably manifest those things in and for us... but

Jacky? She hasn't been on the course, or ritualized; she's never been ritualized... never infected—but she also saw Ken that night and clobbered him with a fire-iron."

It was something Catherine hadn't thought through. "Poltergeist," she proposed. "Whatever mechanism poltergeists use."

Nancy pulled a "you're kidding" face.

"I don't know... I sleep next to her, naked; body fluids? Perhaps they've mixed... if biological viruses can infect that way. What about nanobots? I just don't know."

"A double cross?" Nancy proposed.

"Now you've lost me."

"A supernatural force instigates the AI, gets Ken to build it, and uses the AI as a more efficient method to do what it's always done through ritual and Satanic covens; just a whole lot more efficient."

"This is a Russian doll... a Gordian knot then," Catherine concluded, her mind a windmill in a storm.

"A demonic force using technology to control humans," Nancy continued, pressing the point, "so that when we uncover the artificial intelligence, we've only found the *symptom*, not the cause... *get it?*"

"Oh, Jesus... now you've really got us going round in circles."

"Cath, I want to meet with him, you and I together; I've still got the inside track on the company. He knows he can't bullshit me."

"*How long?*" Nancy insisted.

"Fourteen days," Ken estimated.

"Three," Nancy countered. "You can do it in three."

She looked to Catherine and nodded.

"That's absurd. How many cities do we have to recall from? Forty... fifty...?" Ken contested.

"Forty-seven, head office is forty-eight and there's no time delay on that. A courier, and you have them in three days tops. You can put the instruction out right now."

"I already have."

"What did you tell them—I want to see," Catherine insisted, taking a hard line.

Ken was cornered but not lying, so he tapped his tablet and turned it to face them. The email in the sent folder read:

Subject: Confidential—Patch/Recall
To: >All Managing Directors<

> Treat this memo as <u>Top Secret</u> <

- Confirm receipt.
- Destroy upon receipt.

With immediate effect, and due to suspected sabotage by the late Mr. Angelis, all patches associated with the Time Dilation program are recalled to Headquarters:

1. Kindly respond to the affirmative that this matter is in hand.
2. Use global priority courier services.
3. Apply RF-ID tracking transponders to all packages.

Failure to respond within 3 hours of receipt will be dealt with severely.

Kenneth Torrington
CEO & Chairman

"Nice touch, Ken; Craig gets the blame," Nancy said before Catherine could speak. "Classy."

"Not like it'll bother him," Ken replied, practical as always.

"Cowardly," Nancy jabbed again.

"I really don't care how you do it or if you position it to look the victim; all I care about is that you end this." Catherine was calm and pragmatic.

"Fine... I'm doing it."

"In three days," Nancy added.

"Yes... it's coming. And if it doesn't, Nancy? If it takes five days... or six? What are you going to do about it, huh?"

Nancy knew she'd overplayed her hand and had been rapped over the knuckles for it. She just shook her hair out with a rapid dart of her head and put her nose in the air, the best level of insolence she could muster.

Chapter 42

All of the patches containing the drug had been returned and destroyed, save for a bundle of fifty and the formula, printed and electronic, which Ken secretly retained. He couldn't bring himself to lose everything he'd built up. It was locked away in his private vault, hidden just off his bedroom, lost in the architecture of his sprawling mansion. The next person to see it after him would do so only after he was dead and his attorneys had executed his last will and testament, so he truly didn't care.

Replacement patches without the narcotic or nanobot carriers were delivered; predictably, time dilation could no longer be achieved and the company exploded into chaos and recrimination.

For several days, Ken let Henry wrestle fruitlessly with the problem until he was forced to admit defeat.

"How many dilation trials have you performed?" Ken demanded in mock rage.

"More than fifteen, Ken. We've run dilation trials on every program type in the archive but nothing is achieving a decent result. It's not just us; every branch is reporting the same phenomena."

"Call an emergency board meeting *today*. Department heads had better arrive prepared. I fucking well expect an answer and a solution. *Make it happen!*" Ken was back to his tyrannical worst.

Henry scuttled away to set up the meeting and pass the warning on to other executives.

Fifteen minutes into the emergency session, there was only chaos and no headway. Ken had kicked off proceedings with a tirade of abuse, setting one department against another, making them jittery and unwilling to commit themselves and unable to perform under the withering pressure.

With his board and executives in a state of panic and disarray, and departments in a shouting match, Ken sat back and watched his company cannibalize itself for an hour. Then, he switched his approach, helping them calm down and focus on solutions.

He let the situation go on as long as he could, until the obvious question on everyone's mind was about to be asked; he intended to be the one to ask it. He rose and put his balled fists onto the table. Those who saw him do it suddenly went silent.

"Okay everybody... Calm the *fuck down!*" It instantly went deathly quiet. "Good. Now, could it be the patch? Possibly something's wrong with the formula, perhaps inhibiting subjects' adrenaline production? Maybe some kind of blocking or tranquilizing effect?"

He paced like a predator at the fence, the only executive allowed the privilege of rising from his seat, and then he halted theatrically, as if a thought had struck him. While all eyes were on him, he played the charade perfectly and sealed it with the little *clickety-clickety-click* of his nails drumming a galloping rhythm on the boardroom table.

"Perhaps my information about that sabotage by our late and dearly missed Mr. Angelis was wrong. Perhaps *those* patches were not sabotaged. Perhaps the sabotage was the only thing he ever accomplished here. The breakthroughs came *after* he arrived... remember?" And he drummed the Neuro Linguistic Programming trigger again, bending their minds. "The whole production of patches was probably one big scam; a lie he's been selling to us all along! You know, I recently found out something shocking—he had rather a checkered past, I'm afraid. He did time... and meth."

Everyone conveniently forgot that it was Ken who had been Craig Angelis' greatest and only supporter from the outset. Their emperor could be stark naked yet with a vested interest in seeing him finely dressed, they fell over themselves to see it.

By making the suggestion, he would appear ignorant and innocent of the patch's chemistry if the accusation was ever made.

"Well, drugs was the first question I was going to ask..." Henry replied. "I never liked the guy..." he grumbled, quite happy to see blame taking this positive new trajectory.

Everyone present was very aware that it would be sudden death to remind Ken of how Craig had become a board member in the first place.

Max Schneider, who headed up software developments, happily threw his vote into the ring.

"It's a good point, Ken. We've debugged every line of code; nothing. We've run comparative matching against the master copies in the archive; nothing. The AI is in great shape—it's double-checked our input and we're coming up roses. What else could it be but Angelis? Fudging the whole thing with chemistry; who would have thought?"

When Max was done, Mark Hart, Leon's second-in-charge who had been promoted into the vacated position, took the cue to give his assurances that nothing had changed in the hypnosis sequences of the AI. He too nodded solemnly that it could only be Angelis.

They spent another twenty minutes deliberating and finally began winding up after they had thoroughly inspected all of the possibilities and had reached no new conclusion other than testing the new patches that had just been delivered.

As Ken was about to adjourn the meeting, Henry piped up. "Are there any patches left from the batches that Craig produced?"

Ken thought that he could hear suspicion in Henry's voice. "You organized their destruction, Henry," Ken's voice brimmed with sarcasm. "You would know better than anybody."

"I destroyed everything that was *given* to me. I thought that possibly one of our branches, our problem child, might not have returned their entire stock," Henry retorted.

"I checked all of the returns personally; unfortunately, we had a one hundred percent response," Ken assured, and nobody around the table understood the significance of the tickle he fidgeted with near his eye. "You're welcome to call them to double check if you doubt me, Henry."

Just by saying it, he ensured Henry would dare do no such thing.

"If you checked them personally, then far be it for me to interfere, Ken. I'm just sorry because with an old patch, we would be able to clear this up immediately," Henry lamented. "What made you recall them so hastily, Ken?"

"If you'd read the memo Henry," Ken responded, his tone acid, "then you'd not have to waste our time with superfluous questions. I had the Pentagon crawling up my ass about that General Daly incident. Would you want them sniffing around the facility with any possibility of laying their hands on something that Angelis may have created?"

Henry wouldn't meet Ken's challenging glare, which dared him to dispute it. To shut off any other dissenters, Ken emphasized it with a lie that nobody could contradict.

"I have an inside source with the CIA. They'd picked up on Angelis' drug problem and connected the dots. I had the tipoff, so I pulled the plug, in case the idiot had done something stupid with the only bit of responsibility he had... and it seems I was right, doesn't it?"

He didn't bother to rap on the table; by the look on every face, he'd done enough to put it to rest.

"Either that or there's a ghost in the machine!" Henry concluded and it brought a few laughs of relief, everyone grateful for the ordeal to be over with.

Chapter 43

"Surprise, surprise..." Nancy said sarcastically. "They've traced it to his phone."

"I just got the tweet. The media is still harping about spontaneous human combustion; guess it sells. 'Tycoon Burst Into Flames' makes a great headline; we can all identify with the sentiment," Catherine mocked.

They were being callous. They knew it and simply didn't care.

Their forgiveness was shallow; they knew that too and simply didn't care. Their pardon for his deeds was only relief by another name; relief that they had him cornered, that he was dismantling what he'd built, and doing it quickly.

Those efforts were in place. Nancy was being fed a constant update from many angles within the company—it was over, and the nightmare that Ken had created was behind them. That he was dead now was meaningless—there was momentum and a path in the right direction.

"I've been so busy I haven't caught up on the details; what gave them the notion that he'd spontaneously combusted?"

"Apparently the hands and feet usually fall off and the fire appeared to cause very little damage to combustible items in contact with his body," Jacky jumped in. She'd been ghoulishly following the story since it broke eight hours earlier and they'd all decided to dine together.

"Chicken a la Chong," Catherine intoned in her ritualistic prayer to the food they were about to receive. She knocked their favorite microwave-warmed and batter-encrusted morsels out of their Chinese takeout cardboard boxes onto delicate Meissen porcelain. "Lovely dinner conversation," she remarked.

"Revenge goes rather well with claret, I believe," Nancy added, and they all laughed.

"Okay, girls, I think it's getting a bit distasteful and spiteful. Seriously... the guy was a pig, fine. We all hated him, but I think we've had our fun with it." Catherine was tired of the ghoulishness.

"Alright mum," Nancy chimed in, raising her glass; and with a smile, they all clinked glasses.

"Even I agree," Jacky added. "The bastard's gone, it's over. Let's get serious about where we stand."

"Well, I spoke with Henry earlier today," Nancy recapped. "He was the first on scene. At 3 a.m., he was woken by a very urgent message from Ken to come straight over, so he tried to call back but the call went directly to voicemail. He was there before 3:30 and the front gates were wide open, the front door open as well. As he went in, he said he heard Ken yelling, smelled the burning, ran upstairs and found the room full of smoke and Ken's bed... well. Not pretty."

"Now that's interesting... a message? Didn't his phone ring?" Jacky was intrigued.

"No, I mean a message from the messaging system, not a written one, he said; a *voice* message. That's what he told me."

"Who'd send a message in an emergency? Why not just call?" Jacky pressed.

"How about the AI? Maybe it doesn't make calls."

"Come on, Nancy, don't give me the *heebees* again," Catherine protested with a shudder.

"If it really did it once with Craig... why not?"

"Because they're shutting it down; they've shut it down, we know that much," Catherine assured.

"I thought Ken said they can't?" Jacky intoned.

"He was a pathological liar," Nancy reminded them. "Want to know why I'm a bit freaked?"

"Do we have to?" Catherine whined, wanting to believe it was all over.

"I'm not making up scare stories. Better we talk it through though. Henry told me the electronic bolts on the vault door of Ken's walk-in strong room had malfunctioned. That's why he called me at four; he stays right across the city and I'm just down the road from Ken. He wanted to drop off something at my house that he said was very sensitive, some files. Asked me to keep it quiet."

"You let him?" Jacky seemed a bit shocked.

"He's a good guy, Jacky, I trust him, and I trust you to keep this between us. I just need a sounding board. It's probably stuff that's too sensitive to be locked up if they make it a crime scene, as they have. I may be selfish, but I have shares in the company, it's my nest-egg. So, its survival is still in my best interest. Of course, I'm going to help where I can."

"Did you take a look at what he dropped off?"

"I helped him bring it in. A trunkload of stuff, files and hard-drives, a lockbox... admin stuff. He asked me if I minded putting it in my garden shed, said he'd be back to collect it after he went back to Ken's. He took the key, and I gave him a remote to get back in."

"Did you check it out when he'd gone?"

"I couldn't, he had the key."

"When's he picking up the stuff? Maybe you can try then."

"The remote and key were in an envelope, dropped through my letterbox slot by noon the same day. He'd cleared it out."

"I would just *love* to know what was so urgent," Catherine piped up, to unanimous agreement.

"I was in a tough position... couldn't refuse, couldn't ask. It could be anything. I got the sense that it came out of Ken's strong room. He didn't say it, but it felt like an 'oh... shit!' moment when he realized he'd have to call the emergency services, and the info would be inaccessible behind police tape. That's how it was implied to me."

"Very intriguing. Why hadn't he already called the cops or fire department if there was smoke?"

"I asked, and he said it was obvious that it was too late. Said he burst in, Ken was smoldering... looked desiccated, like a mummy, his hands and feet burned right off. That's why the media ran down that path. I guess he felt he had time to clear up a possible mess. It was strategic, the smart thing to do."

"Or a mysterious message told him to clear it out," Jacky added.

"Come on Jacky... enough of that now," Catherine admonished her.

"Then what made him go into the strong room?" Jacky challenged. "It's not exactly a normal thing to do in a fire crisis when you find someone burned to a crisp!"

"Henry said the door of the strong room was standing wide open, a huge thick door blocking halfway across the passageway, said he could hardly miss it. He'd been to the house before and didn't even know it *was* a strong room, just a door off the corridor before Ken's bedroom, he told me."

"What kind of architect puts a strong room next to a bedroom?" Catherine speculated.

"An architect working for a psychopath," Nancy suggested.

"Ahh... yes. How could I forget?"

"Seems the electronic lock had malfunctioned so badly it had melted the mechanism leaving it unlocked. He said he'd just walked right in."

"Doesn't this strike you as very weird... kind of like the electrical plug spat out at our place?" Jacky asked. "Weird that there's a message instead of a real live human phone call during an emergency to the heir apparent of the fortune who—when he arrives before anyone else in the dead of night—finds the gates and front door welcomingly open for him? The safe is blown with the sensitive information packed and ready to go, all while the late Mr. Torrington lies smouldering quietly, and can wait till everything is neatly resolved before outside help is called?"

She'd put in words what they were all thinking but were too afraid to voice.

"They're talking about a massive electrical spike. I mean, two unlikely events like that at the same time? It is strange, what else can we say?" Catherine said, tentatively.

"That's not really what I'm saying, Cath. I'm saying it's more than strange or an odd coincidence."

"We're just going to freak ourselves out with this, Jacky. Don't you think I've been freaked out enough?" There was a timbre of fear ringing through her voice.

"I'm sorry, baby. What affects you, tears me apart. I'm just stepping back and looking at it. An electrical spike blows a lock, leaves gates and doors open. And now we learn it was the cell phone on the bed, the one that sends a voice message to the one person who can keep the chain intact, sends the message in the dead man's voice... and then starts a fire that kills the useless piece of shit that is trying to shut down his '*partner*' in a filthy business."

Everyone was quiet, digesting the ugly picture she'd painted.

"Who's got a mobile phone turned on right now? If this fucking thing is behind it, it could be listening to us."

"Please stop it, Jacky, you're becoming paranoid and making me paranoid."

"It feels like a really bad idea to even talk or speculate any further," Nancy added. "This was supposed to be an enjoyable evening... all finished and done with. Raise a glass to success and get on with life."

"And what if what you're saying is being put in your mind? You've been *infected*, remember? The *bots* in you taking their instructions wirelessly from the *cyborg*; our router is just over there," Jacky said, and pointed across to the office nook where the low flat wireless router sat brooding with its LEDs twinkling merrily for whomever.

"Well, that's a perfectly good way to stuff up a lovely evening," Catherine added. "Nancy and I agree, it doesn't look pretty, but Henry is a totally different personality, Jacks. He's a very honest guy, just a bit of a wimp. I can't see how he'll cope. If he winds up with control, we could easily work with him. I'll set up a meeting, we'll tell him what we have, and together we can roll this back."

"Like Ken rolled it back, until it rolled him over."

"Jacky... *enough*."

"Okay, take the speculation out of it. Let's pretend for a minute this is all perfectly normal and accidental. Just an electric spike. An electric spike that of course routinely blows electric locks out of their socket and sets fire to mobile phones... they happen all the time," she said sarcastically. "Doesn't it sound rather peculiar to you that his mobile sets fire to his linen, killing him, but he doesn't wake up when the lock blows off his strong room? I'm assuming Mr. Paranoid installed a military grade strong room lock that would take some blowing, right?"

"I think that's the point—you die from smoke inhalation before you wake, so you're dead before you hear it blow."

"Well, that's two events then; the cell kills you and later the lock blows off... right?"

"I feel like puking, thinking about this anymore." Catherine pushed her wine glass away.

"And the hands and feet burning off... Jeez, grizzly. But why?" Jacky wouldn't let go.

"No idea, it was just in the report. Maybe because wrists and ankles are thin, they burn through first, but I think we've probably had enough speculation for one evening." Nancy put a lid on it.

"Can we please change the conversation?" Catherine pleaded.

"Okay. Shew... girls. So then, it's all over. Jolly well done, he's gone and we're safe... it's dismantled. I say we drink to that certain success."

"I'll get drunk to certain success." Nancy pretended that Jacky wasn't being sarcastic.

"Fine. I'll just go freshen up then." Jacky got up, peeved at having her gleeful pondering of Ken's grisly demise truncated. She trundled off.

"Sorry, she's rattled," Catherine spoke quietly. "It's how she deals with it, very confrontational; more so than me."

"How *is* the dismantling of the ritual going?" Catherine gave the positive shift in conversation a shove.

"I don't think we can speculate much more until we talk with Henry or whoever steps into the hot seat," Nancy added.

"Well then, nothing we can do about it tonight, let's take it down a notch and I'll arrange to meet with Henry in the morning. We'll resolve this. Feedback from the office is that it's bedlam down there. Without time dilation, the company's fallen back to revenues of four years ago. Big layoffs."

"How's the AI taking it? Ken's partner in all this?"

"Well, I don't know. Nobody's talked about it. Perhaps he was bullshitting us. Perhaps it *is* as easy as hitting the 'pause' button. Not a word on that, just what he told us, and that's always speculative. Let's just put it to Henry when we meet."

"So where to for them? Succession—is it confirmed to be Henry? What's going to become of the company?"

"Henry's the Vice President and has the most shares, his nomination to Chairman and CEO will have to go before the board. I'm certain he'll step into the breach; he's already taken charge today. It'll probably come down to Ken's will, where Ken's shares go and who they go to, I guess."

"Henry seemed like a proper old fart," Catherine suggested.

"Absolutely... a boy scout, straight as a die—things are going to be very different at the company now, no more shenanigans."

"You might even want to win the contract back, Cath."

"No chance of that. I think it took Ken's unique energy to make it happen. I reckon they'll get overtaken by competition now that the mover and shaker's gone."

"Not if the AI is still a surviving *partner*," and they laughed again. It was a thin, nervous and unconvincing laugh.

Chapter 44

Henry at last felt like the boss.

It had been just a year since he'd taken the helm as Chief Executive and Chairman of LifeGames Corporation, so he could justify the vacation.

They made a wide sweep in the company jet and he looked with pride out of the porthole window. There, set into the tranquility of the South Pacific, was the palm-lined shore of a magnificent private island that was now all his. The landing strip down its flank, welcoming him. It would become his sanctuary from the corporate madness of the one hundred and seven facilities his company now ran in cities across the globe.

The first months after Ken's death had turned him grey. The mess he'd found, the shocking revelations in the documents, data and fifty patches he'd stored that morning at Nancy's were enough to stop a man's heart, he thought.

His health had dwindled and his marriage collapsed. But as he'd delved through the trunkload of artifacts, he'd found in their details a new lease on life. Invigorated, he'd regained his zest to make LifeGames great again.

Watching the trade winds fleck white horses off the tops of swells, Henry marveled anew how fortunate he had become. Quite why, he did not know. But only days before his death, Ken had lodged a new will and testament with his private attorney. That will had made Henry his sole heir.

Naturally, Ken's estranged family had crept out of the woodwork and challenged the peculiarity of it. But by the time it went to court under an urgent interdiction, Henry had experienced a change of heart. Gone was his amicable sense of playing it fair. If Ken wanted him to have full control of the empire he'd built, far be it for him to denounce that. It was the first time Henry had actively wondered how Ken would handle a situation like this, so he'd brought certain *pressure* to bear on the scavengers trying to steal his rightful good fortune, and they'd neatly dropped the action.

Time dilation was another fabulous "what would Ken do?" situation. Happily, it was back achieving results beyond even those Ken had posted before he'd lost his way. The company had doubled in size since his death.

Henry's thoughts now turned to Nancy and her sidekick Catherine. Hysterical bitches that they were, making up stories and going to the press about things they simply weren't smart enough to understand. Fortunately, only the tabloid press would print such tripe. Fortunately, all of the legitimate press were LifeGames clients and knew better.

"Women!" he huffed and laughed. Their accusation that he'd become just like Ken was a sentiment he was beginning to see as a compliment. The way they were carrying on, he'd probably have to deal with them as Ken would have dealt with them.

THE END

Thank you for taking the time to share this journey with me.

If you enjoyed what you read, please share your thoughts at:
- https://www.facebook.com/groups/LifeGames/

Of course—positive reviews at Amazon will help bring this story to the attention of others—please visit: www.Amazon.com and review the work.

Please do stay in touch:
- I use: #LifeGamesNOVEL
- facebook.com/MichaelSmorenburg
- www.MichaelSmorenburg.com/LifeGames
- MichaelStheWriter@gmail.com

About the Author

Michael Smorenburg

Born in 1964, I grew up in a fabulously stable family with incredible siblings and an embracing community. I also landed with my *derrière* firmly in the proverbial butter in another way. Home was a piece of paradise; the beach community of Clifton, Cape Town, South Africa.

Today, Clifton is world renowned as a playground of the super-rich, but back then it was all a boy could want. A wild and bounteous Southern Ocean on the doorstep flanked by towering mountains on all sides, and precious few rules in between.

It was there that I fell in love with adventure and nature, and these, in turn, prompted my endless questions about what made everything tick. It set me on a course to understand science.

In my mid-20s, the travel bug bit; and when my head cleared, it was the millennium and I found myself living in San Diego, California, founding an online marketing company. But Africa has a heavy gravity, and I was drawn back home, where I have happily remained.

Humans are, of course, the universe finding out about itself. We are of nature. We are matter… the stuff of stars, all too briefly made conscious and self-aware. Each of us is privileged to add our small voice to the symphony of life.

"A Trojan Affair – The S.K.A. at Carnarvon" (along with my other books) is my small contribution to that great chorus.

Wherever you may be in time and place, it's been a very great privilege to entertain and chat with you.

Please do keep the conversation moving.

Other Titles by Michael Smorenburg

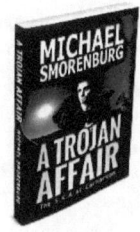   

A Trojan Affair *explores actual unfolding events.*

The silent heavens stretched above a pious town locked in the grip of drought have become valuable beyond measure—the fracking bounty below its feet... irresistible.

When Dara, 17, half Indian and raised in Oxford, England, arrives in the heartland of a Calvinist bible belt—a place his astrophysicist mother has come to build the biggest infrastructure in the history of science, the $2.5-Billion SKA radio telescope—he becomes the lightening rod for the town's anger and suspicion of outsiders.

Based on actual unfolding events, A Trojan Affair is a contemporary geopolitical thriller where science, religion, politics, greed and racism collide, tearing a community apart and setting generations against one another.

Ragnarok *is a thriller with a plot like none you've ever imagined.*

Tegan Mulholland is a Hollywood Exec flying Paris to Los Angeles. A mid-air event off the coast of Newfoundland will change her life...

South of Australia, on the other side of the globe, a secret NASA Warp Drive test backfires—a column of spacetime warps in an unexpected way and two passenger planes ahead of Tegan's wink off the radar.

As the world deals with the seismic events and recriminations that follow, an instinct for connecting dots convinces Tegan that the sudden spate of brutal massacres along the Newfoundland coast is far more sinister than the Hells Angel turf war the authorities are claiming.

The key to the truth lies in the hands of Pete, the charming arms-dealer she sat next to on the fateful flight... the man Tegan has secretly fallen in love with.

The Praying Nun *is.*

A story in 2 parts, 'now' and 'then' — come along on a gripping saga of adventure, intrigue and discovery of a shipwreck that has no identity; until 30 years pass and the Smithsonian fills in the missing pieces — then leap back two centuries to witness a tale of disturbing brutality and exhilerating human courage... The Praying Nun will leave you shocked to the core and pondering human nature in all its forms.

Part I - A True Story of Discovery and Excavation, 1985

In 1985 an uncharted shipwreck was discovered off the coast of Cape Town, South Africa. Two divers, the author and his friend, salvage artefacts from the ocean floor and try to identify the ship's identity and cargo. In 2015 the mystery was finally solved by the Smithsonian Museum of Washington. The ship was the São José de Africa, a slaver that ran aground in 1794 with 400 slaves aboard, half lost on that day, the other half salvaged and sold the next day to defray costs. At this time, the recovered artefacts reside in the National Museum of African American History and Culture in the US, in 2027 they will be returned to the Iziko museum in Cape Town.

Part II – A Love Story of Terror and Tragedy, 1794

Naked and shackled, Chikunda, and his new wife Mkiwa are heaved aboard the slaver São José off the coast of Mozambique, bound for the slave markets of Brazil. Once below decks, down in the stinking holds with 400 other captives, Chikunda instinctively knows that it will all be over. When the Captain discovers that Chikunda and his wife are Christians, the couple are spared a horrific fate below decks, but this reprieve does not protect them from what fate has in store.

The story of Chikunda and Mkiwa, though fictional, is based on the best known facts about the ship and the slave trade in general as contained in records, news reports, and journals available at the maratime archives, through accounts reported by the Captain, crew and from others who witnessed the disaster and its aftermath.

Praying Nun sequel—*coming soon...*

An as yet **Unnamed Sequel** to *The Praying Nun* will launch 4ᵗʰ Quarter 2017

Chikunda and Mkiwa's struggle to survive as slaves into the early 1800's continues.

A third sequel to this *"Slave Ship Saga"* trilogy will launch in the 2ⁿᵈ Quarter 2018.

LifeGames/Ragnarok sequel—*Coming Soon...*

The Manhattan Event—Worlds Collide *LifeGames Technology spreads its wings.*

With Ken gone from the helm and the company's key technology mothballed, what becomes of LifeGames?

Of course—exciting things!

More than that, those who read my other novel, *"Ragnarok—Worlds Collide"*, will be equally inquisitive as to the fate of "the missing planes".

Well… both of these matters are resolved in my new book to be published in early 2018.

Strangely, it is a novel that brings together the two plots (LifeGames & Ragnarok) into a single tale of deception, intrigue and mind control at the highest levels.

You're gonna love it!

Email me to get an early copy: MichaelStheWriter@gmail.com

www.ingramcontent.com/pod-product-compliance
Lightning Source LLC
Chambersburg PA
CBHW051936240626
47153CB00005B/1514